THE

Physick Book

OF

Deliverance Dane

Mandragora fœmina.   Chelidonium minus.

THE
Physick Book
OF
Deliverance Dane

A Novel by

KATHERINE HOWE

voice

Hyperion

NEW YORK

Copyright © 2009 Katherine Howe

Frontispiece © The Granger Collection

The Library of Congress has catalogued the hardcover edition of this book as follows:

Howe, Katherine.
    The physick book of deliverance dane : a novel / by Katherine Howe.
        p. cm.
    ISBN 978-1-4013-4090-2
    1. Witchcraft—Massachusetts—Fiction.   2. Marblehead (Mass.)—Fiction.
3. Salem (Mass.)—History—Colonial period, ca. 1600–1775—Fiction.   4. Trials
(Witchcraft)—Massachusetts—Salem—History—17th century—Fiction.
I. Title.

    PS3608.O947P47 2009
    813'.6—dc22   2008051627

Paperback ISBN 978-1-4013-4133-6

Hyperion books are available for special promotions and premiums.
For details contact the HarperCollins Special Markets Department in the New York office
at 212-207-7528, fax 212-207-7222, or email spsales@harpercollins.com.

Designed by Jessica Shatan Heslin / Studio Shatan, Inc.

FIRST PAPERBACK EDITION

10   9   8   7   6   5   4   3   2   1

For my family

I watch'd today, as Giles Corey was press't to death between the stones. He had lain so for two dayes mute. With each stone they tolde him he must plead, lest more rocks be added. But he only whisperd, More weight. Standing in the crowde I found Goodwyfe Dane, who, as the last stone lower'd, went white, grippt my hand, and wept.

—Letter fragment dated "Salem Towne, September 16, 1692"
Division of Rare Manuscripts, Boston Athenaeum

Part I

THE

Key AND Bible

Prologue

Marblehead, Massachusetts

Late December

1681

*P*eter Petford slipped a long wooden spoon into the simmering iron pot of lentils hanging over the fire and tried to push the worry from his stomach. He edged his low stool nearer to the hearth and leaned forward, one elbow propped on his knee, breathing in the aroma of stewed split peas mixed with burning apple wood. The smell comforted him a little, persuading him that this night was a normal night, and his belly released an impatient gurgle as he withdrew the spoon to see if the peas were soft enough to eat. Not a reflective man, Peter assured himself that nothing was amiss with his stomach that a bowlful of peas would not cure. *Yon woman comes enow, too*, he thought, face grim. He had never had use for cunning folk, but Goody Oliver had insisted. Said this woman's tinctures cured most anything. Heard she'd conjured to find a lost child once. Peter grunted to himself. He would try her. Just the once.

From the corner of the narrow, dark room issued a tiny whimper, and

Peter looked up from the steaming pot, furrows of anxiety deepening between his eyes. He nudged one of the fire logs with a poker, loosing a crackling flutter of sparks and a gray column of fresh smoke, then drew himself up from the stool.

"Martha?" he whispered. "Ye awake?"

No further sound issued from the shadows, and Peter moved softly toward the bed where his daughter had lain for the better part of a week. He pulled aside the heavy woolen curtain that hung from the bedposts, and lowered himself onto the edge of the lumpy feather mattress, careful not to jostle it. The lapping light of the fire brushed over the woolen blankets, illuminating a wan little face framed by tangles of flax-colored hair. The eyes in the face were half open, but glassy and unseeing. Peter smoothed the hair where it lay scattered across the hard bolster. The tiny girl exhaled a faint sigh.

"Stew's nearly done," he said. "I'll fetch ye some."

As he ladled the hot food into a shallow earthenware trencher, Peter felt a flame of impotent anger rise in his chest. He gritted his teeth against the feeling, but it lingered behind his breastbone, making his breathing fast and shallow. *What knew he of ministering to the girl*, he thought. *Every tincture he tried only made her poorly.* The last word she had spoken was some three days earlier, when she had cried out in the night for Sarah.

He settled again on the side of the bed and spooned a little of the warm beans into the child's mouth. She slurped it weakly, a thin brown stream slipping down the corner of her mouth to her chin. Peter wiped it away with his thumb, still blackened from the soot of the kitchen fire. Thinking about Sarah always made his chest tight in this way.

He gazed down at the little girl in his bed, watching closely as her eyelids closed. Since she fell ill, he had been sleeping on the wide-planked pine floor, on mildewed straw pallets. The bed was warmer, nearer the hearth, and draped in woolen hangings that had been carried all the way over from East Anglia by his father. A dark frown crossed Peter's face. Illness, he knew, was a sign of the Lord's ill favor. *Whatsoever happen to the girl is God's will*, he reasoned. So to be angry at her suffering must be sinful, for that is to be angry at God. Sarah would have urged him to pray for the salvation of Martha's soul, that she might be redeemed. But Peter was more accustomed to putting his mind to farming problems than godly ones. Perhaps he was not as good as Sarah had been. He could not fathom what sin Martha could have committed in her five years to bring this fit upon her, and in his prayers he caught himself demanding an explanation. He did not ask for his daughter's redemption. He just begged for her to be well.

Confronting this spectacle of his own selfishness filled Peter with anger and shame.

He worked his fingers together, watching her sleeping face.

"There are certain sins that make us devils," the minister had said at meeting that week. Peter pinched the bridge of his nose, squinting his eyes together as he tried to remember what they were.

To be a liar or murderer, that was one. Martha had once been caught hiding a filthy kitten in the family's cupboard, and when questioned by Sarah had claimed no knowledge of any kittens. But that could hardly be a lie the way the minister meant it.

To be a slanderer or accuser of the godly was another. To be a tempter to sin. To be an opposer of godliness. To feel envy. To be a drunkard. To be proud.

Peter gazed down on the fragile, almost transparent skin of his daughter's cheeks. He clenched one of his hands into a tight fist, pressing its knuckles into the palm of his other hand. How could God visit such torments upon an innocent? Why had He turned away His face from him?

Perhaps it was not Martha's soul that was in danger. Perhaps the child was being punished for Peter's own prideful lack of faith.

As this unwelcome fear bloomed in his chest, Peter heard muddy hoofbeats approach down the lane and come to a stop outside his house. Muffled voices, a man's and a young woman's, exchanged words, saddle leather creaked, and then a dull splash. *That'll be Jonas Oliver with yon woman*, thought Peter. He rose from the bedside just as a light knuckle rapped on his door.

On his stoop, draped in a hooded woolen cloak glistening from the evening's fog, stood a young woman with a soft, open face. She carried a small leather bag in her hands, and her face was framed by a crisp white coif that belied the miles-long journey she had had. Behind her in the shadows stood the familiar bulk of Jonas Oliver, fellow yeoman and Peter's neighbor.

"Goodman Petford?" announced the young woman, looking quickly up into Peter's face. He nodded. She flashed him an encouraging smile as she briskly flapped the water droplets off her cloak and pulled it over her head. She hung the cloak on a peg by the door hinge, smoothed her rumpled skirts with both hands, then hurried across the stark little room and knelt by the girl in the bed. Peter watched her for a moment, then turned to Jonas, who stood in the doorway similarly wet, blowing his nose vigorously into a handkerchief.

"Dismal night," said Peter by way of welcome. Jonas grunted in reply. He tucked the handkerchief back up his sleeve and stamped his feet to loosen the mud from his boots, but he did not venture into the house.

"Some victual before ye go?" Peter offered, rubbing a hand absentmindedly across the back of his head. He was not sure if he wanted Jonas to accept his offer. The company would distract him, but his neighbor was even less inclined to idle chatter than he was. Sarah had always allowed that a wagon could crush Jonas Oliver's foot and he would not so much as grimace.

"Goody Oliver'll be waiting." Jonas declined with a shrug. He glanced across the room to where the young woman perched, whispering to the girl in the bed. At her knees sat an attentive, disheveled-looking little dog, some dingy color between brown and tan, surrounded by muddy paw marks on the floor planking. Vaguely Jonas wondered where she might have carried the animal on their long ride; he had not noticed it, and her leather bag seemed hardly big enough. *Mangy cur*, he thought. *It must belong to little Marther.*

"Come by upon the morn, then," said Peter. Jonas nodded, touched the brim of his heavy felt hat, and withdrew into the night.

Peter settled again on the low stool near the dying hearth fire, the cooling trencher of stew on the table at his elbow. Propping his chin on his fist, he watched the strange young woman stroke his daughter's forehead with a white hand and heard the soft, indistinct murmur of her voice. He knew that he should feel relieved that she was there. She was widely spoken of in the village. He grasped at these thoughts, wringing what little assurance he could from them. Still, as his eyes started to blur with fatigue and worry, and his head grew heavy on his arm, the vision of his tiny daughter huddled in the bed, darkness pressing in around her, filled him with dread.

CHAPTER ONE

Cambridge, Massachusetts
Late April
1991

"IT WOULD APPEAR THAT WE ARE NEARLY OUT OF TIME," ANNOUNCED Manning Chilton, one glittering eye fixed on the thin pocket watch chained to his vest. He surveyed the other four faces that ringed the conference table. "But we are not quite done with you yet, Miss Goodwin."

Whenever Chilton felt especially pleased with himself his voice became ironic, bantering: an incongruous affectation that grated on his graduate students. Connie picked up on the shift in his voice immediately, and she knew then that her qualifying examination was finally drawing to a close. A sour hint of nausea bubbled up in the back of her throat, and she swallowed. The other professors on the panel smiled back at Chilton.

Through her anxiety, Connie Goodwin felt a flutter of satisfaction tingle somewhere in her chest, and she permitted herself to bask in the sensation for a moment. If she had to guess, she would have said that the exam was going adequately. But only just. A nervous smile fought to break across her face, but she quickly smothered it under the smooth, neutral expression of detached competence that she knew was more appropriate for a young woman in her position. This expression did not come naturally to her, and the resulting effort rather comically resembled someone who had just bitten into a persimmon.

There was still one more question coming. One more chance to be ruined. Connie shifted in her seat. In the months leading up to the qualifying exam, her weight had dropped, slowly at first, and then precipitously. Now her bones lacked cushioning against the chair, and her Fair Isle sweater hung loosely on her shoulders. Her cheeks, usually flush and pink, formed hollows under her sloping cheekbones, making her pale blue eyes appear larger in her face, framed by soft, short brown lashes. Dark brown brows swept down over her eyes, screwed together in thought. The smooth planes of her cheeks and high forehead were an icy white, dotted by the shadowy hint of freckles, and offset by a sharp chin and well-made, if rather prominent, nose. Her lips, thin and pale pink, grew paler as she pressed them together. One hand crept up to finger the tail end of a long, bark-colored braid that draped over her shoulder, but she caught herself and returned the hand to her lap.

"I can't believe how *calm* you are," her thesis student, a lanky young undergraduate whose junior paper Connie was advising, had exclaimed over lunch earlier that afternoon. "How can you even eat! If I were about to sit for my orals I would probably be nauseous."

"Thomas, you get nauseous over our tutorial meetings," Connie had reminded him gently, though it was true that her appetite had almost vanished. If pressed, she would have admitted that she enjoyed intimidating Thomas a little. Connie justified this minor cruelty on the grounds that an intimidated thesis student would be more likely to meet the deadlines that she set for him, might put more effort into his work. But if she were honest, she might acknowledge a less honorable motive. His eyes shone upon her in trepidation, and she felt bolstered by his regard.

"Besides, it's not as big a deal as people make it out to be. You just have to be prepared to answer any question on any of the four hundred books you've read so far in graduate school. And if you get it wrong, they kick you out," she said. He fixed her with a look of barely contained awe while she stirred the salad around her plate with the tines of her fork. She smiled at him. Part of learning to be a professor was learning to behave in a professorial way. Thomas could not be permitted to see how afraid she was.

The oral qualifying exam is usually a turning point—a moment when the professoriate welcomes you as a colleague rather than as an apprentice. More infamously, the exam can also be the scene of spectacular intellectual carnage, as the unprepared student—conscious but powerless—witnesses her own professional vivisection. Either way, she will be forced to face her inadequacies. Connie was a careful, precise young woman, not given to leaving anything to chance. As she pushed the half-eaten salad across the table away from the worshipful Thomas, she told herself that she was as prepared as it was possible to be. In her mind ranged whole shelvesful of books, annotated and bookmarked, and as she set aside her luncheon fork she roamed through the shelves of her acquired knowledge, quizzing herself. Where are the economics books? Here. And the books on costume and material culture? One shelf over, on the left.

A shadow of doubt crossed her face. But what if she was not prepared enough? The first wave of nausea contorted her stomach, and her face grew paler. Every year, it happened to someone. For years she had heard the whispers about students who had cracked, run sobbing from the examination room, their academic careers over before they had even begun. There were really only two ways that this could go. Her performance today could, in theory, raise her significantly in departmental regard. Today, if she handled herself correctly, she would be one step closer to becoming a professor.

Or she would look in the shelves in her mind and find them empty. All the history books would be gone, replaced only with a lone binder full of the plots of late-1970s television programs and rock lyrics. She would open her mouth, and nothing would come out. And then she would pack her bags to go home.

Now, four hours after her lunch with Thomas, she sat on one side of a polished mahogany conference table in a dark, intimate corner of the Harvard University history building, having already endured three solid hours of questioning from a panel of four professors. She was tired but had a heightened awareness from adrenaline. Connie recalled feeling the same strange blending of exhaustion and intellectual intensity when she pulled an all-nighter to polish off the last chapter of her senior thesis in college. All her sensations felt ratcheted up, intrusive, and distracting—the scratch of the masking tape with which she had provisionally hemmed her wool skirt, the gummy taste in her mouth of sugared coffee. Her attention took in all of these details, and then set them aside. Only the fear remained, unwilling to be put away. She settled her eyes on Chilton, waiting.

The modest room in which she sat featured little more than the pitted conference table and chairs facing a blackboard stained pale gray with the ghostly scrawls of decades of chalk. Behind her hung a forgotten portrait of a white-whiskered old man, blackened by time and inattention. At the end of the room a grimy window stood shuttered against the late afternoon sunlight. Motes of dust hung almost motionless in the lone sunbeam that lighted the room, illuminating the committee's faces from nose to chin. Outside she heard young voices, undergraduates, hail one another and disappear, laughing.

"Miss Goodwin," Chilton said, "we have one final question for you this afternoon." Her advisor leaned into the empty center of the table, sunlight moving over his silver hair, stirring the dust into a glittering corona around his head. On the table before him, his fingers sat knotted as carefully as the club tie at his throat. "Would you please provide the committee with a succinct and considered history of witchcraft in North America?"

THE HISTORIAN OF AMERICAN COLONIAL LIFE, AS CONNIE WAS, MUST BE able to illustrate long-dead social, religious, and economic systems down to the slightest detail. In preparation for this exam, she had memorized, among other things, methods for preparing salt pork, the fertilizer uses of bat guano, and the trade relationship between molasses and rum. Her roommate, Liz Dowers, a tall, bespectacled student of medieval Latin, blond and slender, one evening had come upon her studying the Bible verses that commonly appeared in eighteenth-century needlepoint samplers. "We have finally specialized beyond our ability to understand each other," Liz had remarked, shaking her head.

For a last question, Connie knew Chilton had really given her a gift. Some of the earlier ones were considerably more arcane, even beyond what she had been led to expect. Describe the production, if she would, of the different major exports of the British colonies in the 1840s, from the Caribbean to Ireland. Did she think that history was more a story of great men acting in extraordinary circumstances, or of large populations of people constrained by economic systems? What role, would she say, did codfish play in the growth of New England trade and society? As her gaze roamed around the conference table to each professor's face in turn, she saw mirrored in their watching eyes the special area of expertise in which each had made his or her name.

Connie's advisor, Professor Manning Chilton, looked at her across the table, a small smile flickering at the edge of his mouth. His face, framed with a fringe of brushed cotton hair, was seamed at the forehead, creased by folds from the corners of his nose to his jaw, which the low sunlight in the conference room cast in deep shadow. He carried himself with the easy assurance of the vanishing breed of academic who has spent his entire career under Harvard's crimson umbrella, and whose specialization in the history of science in the colonial period was fueled by a childhood spent shooed away from the drawing room of a stately Back Bay town house. He bore the distinguished smell of old leather and pipe tobacco, masculine but not yet grandfatherly.

Chilton was flanked around the conference table by three other respected American historians. To his left perched Professor Larry Smith, a tight-lipped, tweedy junior faculty economist, who asked knotty questions designed to indicate to the senior professors his authority and expertise. Connie glowered at him; twice already in the exam he had asked questions probing where he knew her knowledge was scanty. She supposed that that was his job, but he was the only committee member likely to recall his own qualifying exams. Perhaps she had been naïve to expect solidarity from him; oftentimes professors of his rank were the hardest on grad students, as if to make up for the indignities they felt themselves to have suffered. He smiled back at her primly.

To Chilton's right, her chin on one jeweled hand, sat Professor Janine Silva, a blowsy, recently tenured gender studies specialist who favored topics in feminist theory. Her hair was wilder and wavier today than usual, with a burgundy sheen that was patently false. Connie enjoyed Janine's willful denial of the Harvard aesthetic; long floral scarves were her trademark. One of Janine's favorite rants concerned Harvard's relative hostility to women academics; her interest in Connie's career sometimes bordered on the motherly, and as a result Connie consciously had to work to control the pseudo-parental transference that many students develop toward their mentors. While Chilton held more power over her career, Connie dreaded disappointing Janine the most. As if sensing this momentary flicker of anxiety, Janine sent Connie a thumbs-up, partly concealed behind one of her arms.

Finally, to Janine's right hunched Professor Harold Beaumont, Civil War historian and staunch conservative, known for his occasional grumpy forays onto the Op-Ed page of the *New York Times*. Connie had never worked closely with him and had placed him on her committee only because she suspected that he would have very little personally invested in her performance. Between Janine and Chilton she thought she had enough expectations to manage. As these thoughts traveled through her mind, she felt Beaumont's dark eyes burning a tight round hole in the shoulder of her sweater.

Connie gazed down at the surface of the table and traced the outline of the initials that had been carved there, darkened by decades of waxy polish. She roamed through the file cabinets in her brain, looking for the answer that they wanted. Where was it? She knew it was there somewhere. Was it under *W*, for "Witchcraft"? No. Or was it listed under *G*, for "Gender Issues"? She opened each mental drawer in turn, pulling out index cards by the handful, shuffling through them, and then tossing them aside. The bubble of nausea rose again in her throat. The card was gone. She could not find it. Those whispered stories about students failing, they were going to be about *her*. She had been given the simplest question possible, and she could not produce an answer.

She was going to fail.

A haze of panic began to cloud her vision, and Connie fought to keep her breath steady. The facts were there, she must just focus enough to see them. Facts would never abandon her. She repeated the word to herself— *facts*. But wait—she had not looked under *F*, for "Folk Religion, Colonial Era." She pulled the mental drawer open, and there it was! The haze cleared. Connie straightened herself against the hard chair and smiled.

"Of course," Connie began, shoving her anxiety aside. "The temptation is to begin a discussion of witchcraft in New England with the Salem panic of 1692, in which nineteen townspeople were executed by hanging. But the careful historian will recognize that panic as an anomaly, and will instead want to consider the relatively mainstream position of witchcraft in colonial society at the beginning of the seventeenth century." Connie watched the four faces nodding around the table, planning the structure of her answer according to their responses.

"Most cases of witchcraft occurred sporadically," she continued. "The average witch was a middle-aged woman who was isolated in the community, either economically or through lack of family, and so was lacking in social and political power. Interestingly, research into the kinds of *maleficium*"— her tongue tangled on the Latin word, sending it out with one or two extra syllables, and she cursed inwardly for giving in to pretension—"which witches were usually accused of reveals how narrow the colonial world really was for average people. Whereas the modern person might assume that someone who could control nature, or stop time, or tell the future, would naturally use those powers for large-scale, dramatic change, colonial witches were usually blamed for more mundane catastrophes, like making cows sick, or milk go sour, or for the loss of personal property. This microcosmic sphere of influence makes more sense in the context of early colonial religion, in which individuals were held to be completely powerless in the face of God's omnipotence." Connie paused for breath. She yearned to stretch but restrained herself. Not yet.

"Further," she continued, "the Puritans held that nothing could reliably indicate whether or not one's soul was saved—doing good works wouldn't cut it. So negative occurrences, like a serious illness or economic reversal, were often interpreted as signs of God's disapproval. For most people, it was preferable to blame witchcraft, an explanation out of one's own control, and embodied in a woman on the margins of society, than to consider the possibility of one's own spiritual risk. In effect, witchcraft played an important role in the New England colonies—as both an explanation for things not yet elucidated by science, and as a scapegoat."

"And the Salem panic?" prodded Professor Silva.

"The Salem witch trials have been explained in numerous ways," Connie said. "Some historians have argued that the trials were caused by tension between competing religious populations in Salem, the more urban port city on the one hand and the rural farm region on the other. Some have pointed to long-standing envy between family groups, with particular attention paid to the monetary demands made by an unpopular minister, Reverend Samuel Parris. And some historians have even claimed that the possessed girls were hallucinating after having eaten moldy bread, which can cause effects similar to those of LSD. But I see it as the last gasp of Calvinist religiosity. By the early eighteenth century, Salem had moved from being a predominantly religious community to being more diverse, more dependent on shipbuilding, fishing, and trade. The Protestant zealots who had originally settled the region were being supplanted by recent immigrants from England who were more interested in the business opportunities in the new colonies than in religion. I think that the trials were a symptom of this dynamic shift. They were also the last major outbreak of witchcraft hysteria in all of North America. In effect, the Salem panic signaled the end of an era that had had its roots in the Middle Ages."

"A very insightful analysis," commented Professor Chilton, still in his bemused, bantering tone. "But haven't you overlooked one other significant interpretation?"

Connie smiled at him, the nervous grimace of an animal fending off an attacker. "I am not sure, Professor Chilton," she answered. He was toying with her now. Connie silently begged for time to accelerate past Chilton's teasing, to catapult her instantly to Abner's Pub, where Liz and Thomas would be waiting, and where she could finally stop talking for the day. When she was tired, Connie's words sometimes ran together, tumbling out in an order not fully under her control. As she watched Chilton's crafty smile she worried that she was reaching that level of fatigue. Her stupid blunder over *maleficium* was a hint. If only he would just let her pass . . .

Chilton leaned forward. "Have you not considered the distinct possibility that the accused were simply *guilty* of witchcraft?" he asked. He arched his eyebrows at her, fingers pointed in a small temple on the tabletop.

She watched him for a moment. A rush of irritation, even anger, sped through her. What a preposterous question! Certainly the participants in colonial witch trials believed that witches were real. But no contemporary scholars had ever entertained that possibility. Connie could not understand why Chilton would tease her like this. Was this just his way of reinforcing how lowly she ranked in the hierarchy of academia? No matter how ludicrous it was, she had to answer, because it was Chilton doing the asking. Clearly he was too far away from his own graduate student experience to remember how dreadful this exam is. If he could remember, he would never joke with her today.

Would he?

She cleared her throat, tamping down her aggravation. Connie did not yet rank high enough in the scholarly universe to be permitted to voice her exasperation. She read not only sympathy and commiseration in Janine's narrowed eyes, but also registered her almost imperceptible nod that Connie should continue. *Jump through the hoop*, the nod said. *You and I both know that's what it is, but you have to do it anyway.*

"Well, Professor Chilton," she began, "none of the recent secondary source literature that I have read considered that to be a real possibility. The only exception that I can think of is Cotton Mather. In 1705 he wrote a famous defense of the judgments and executions at Salem, firmly believing that the courts had acted rightly to rid the town of actual, practicing witches. This was about the time that one of the judges, Samuel Sewall, published a public apology for his part in the trials. Of course, Cotton Mather, a renowned theologian, had himself officiated at the trials. Against the wishes of his equally famous theologian father, Increase Mather, I might add, who publicly condemned the Salem trials as being based on unreliable evidence. So Cotton Mather may have argued that the witchcraft at Salem was real, and that the killing of twenty people was completely justified, but he had rather a lot invested in not being wrong. Sir."

As Connie concluded her treatise she observed Chilton grinning mischievously at her across the table. In that moment she knew that the exam was over. Through the hoop she had gone, and now it was behind her. Of course she would have to go outside to await their official verdict. But at least she had come up with an answer. Now there was nothing more that she could do. She felt helpless, exhausted. What little color remained in her face ebbed, her lips fading to white.

The four professors exchanged looks in a rapid volley around their side of the table before turning their attention back to Connie.

"Very well," said Professor Chilton. "If you would just step outside for a moment, please, Miss Goodwin, we will discuss your performance. Don't go far."

Withdrawing from the examination room, Connie moved through the history building shadows, her footfalls echoing off the marble floor. She settled onto an institutional lavender sofa in the central reception area, enjoying the blissful sound of quiet. She let herself sink into the cushions, twiddling the tail end of her braid under her nose like a mustache.

From inside the conference room several doors away, she heard murmured comments, too muffled for her to distinguish who was saying what. She clicked her thumbnails together, waiting.

The early evening sun slanted across the floor, splashing warmth onto her lap. Across the room she glimpsed a flash of movement as a tiny mouse disappeared into the darkness behind a drowsy potted plant. Connie smiled wanly, thinking about the unseen generations of warm life living somewhere in the history department walls, worried about nothing more momentous than leftover water crackers and careless feet. She could almost envy a life that simple and straightforward. Silence descended over the waiting area, and Connie heard only her shallow breath.

At length she heard the door open.

"Connie? We are ready for you." It was Professor Silva. Connie sat up. For a split second she faced the certainty that the exam had gone horribly, she had failed, she would have to leave school. But then Connie saw Janine's kind face, framed with ruddy tangles of hair, break into a delighted grin. She threaded an arm around Connie's waist and whispered, "We're celebrating at Abner's after this!" And she knew that it was really about to be over.

Connie resumed her seat in the examination room. The single sunbeam was lower now, barely gracing the four pairs of folded hands that now ringed the table.

She arranged her features into a close approximation of professional coolness and detachment. *No one likes a woman academic who is emotional*, she reminded herself.

"After much discussion and debate," began Professor Chilton, face serious, "we would like to congratulate you on the strongest doctoral qualifying examination that we have seen in recent memory. Your responses were complete, thorough, and articulate, and we feel that you are eminently qualified to be advanced to candidacy for the PhD. You are more than ready to write your dissertation."

He paused for a beat while Connie processed what he had just said, the verdict working its way down through all her layers of worry.

All at once she felt the breath rush out of her in an excited hiss, and she clenched her fingers around the chair seat in an effort to channel her palpable glee into something safe, something that would not give her away. "Really?" she said aloud, looking around the table before she could stop herself.

"Of course!" piped Professor Silva, interrupting Professor Smith, who had started to say "Really excellent work, Connie."

"Most competent," concurred Professor Beaumont, and Connie smiled privately to herself. Thomas would doubt he had even said that much. Already Connie's mind was skipping ahead to the evening, when her thesis student would interrogate her about the questions that each of the professors had asked.

As the committee continued to praise her performance, Connie felt a sweet mixture of relief and fatigue rush through her arms and legs. The voices of her mentors muffled and drifted farther away as a fog of sleepiness rolled across her mind. She was about to crash. She found herself struggling to get to her feet, to spirit herself away to the safety of her friends.

"Well," she said, standing, "I can't thank you all enough. Really. This is a great way to end the semester." They all stood with her, each shaking her hand in turn and gathering up their things to leave. She nodded automatic thanks, and her hands began to scrabble for her coat. Professors Smith and Beaumont scuttled out together.

Professor Silva hoisted her satchel over her head. "C'mon, kiddo," she said, knocking Connie on the shoulder. "You need a drink."

Connie laughed, doubting that she would be able to withstand more than one of Abner's notorious old-fashioneds. "I should call Thomas and Liz. They demanded an immediate report," she said. "I'll meet you there?"

Professor Silva—Janine, now, for she insisted that her graduate students call her by her first name once they had advanced to candidacy—nodded appreciatively. "I'll bet they did," she said. "Manning, we'll talk next week." Then with a wave she was gone, the heavy paneled door closing in her wake.

Connie began to wind her scarf around her neck.

"Connie, wait a moment," said Chilton. It was more a command than a suggestion, Connie noticed with some surprise. She stopped, lowering herself back to the table.

Chilton dropped into the armchair across from Connie, beaming at her. He did not speak. Connie, unsure what he was up to, hazarded a glance as far as the polished leather elbow patch that rested in the last shard of sunlight on the table.

"I have to say that this was an incredible performance, even for you," began Chilton. As always Connie was momentarily distracted by Chilton's clipped Brahmin accent, in which the *r* wanders in and out of words unpredictably. *Pehfohmance*. It was an accent that one barely heard anymore, almost unrelated to the Boston accent that was caricatured on television. *Bahston* versus *Behstun*. Chilton himself often struck her as a sort of relic, a scarab beetle preserved in amber, not knowing that it is frozen and that time has left it behind.

"Thank you, Professor Chilton," she said.

"I knew when we admitted you to this program that you would excel. Your undergraduate work at Mount Holyoke was exemplary, of course. Your coursework and teaching have both been well remarked upon." *Rehmahked* thought Connie, then immediately chastised herself. *Pay attention! This is important!*

He paused, gazing at her, index fingers pressed over his lips. "I wonder if you have started putting any thought to your dissertation topic," he said. She hesitated, caught off guard. Of course she had expected to bring him a proposal shortly after her exam, assuming she passed, but she had counted on having weeks ahead of her to think things over. However, his attention signaled to Connie that her performance had guaranteed her new status within the department. Connie's ears buzzed, like antennae that have picked up a vital piece of information written in a code that has been only half-transcribed.

Academia, in many respects, forms the last bastion of medieval apprenticeship. She and Liz had discussed this idea before. The master takes the student in, educates her in his craft, shares with her the esoteric secrets of his field. The apprentice is a kind of initiate, admitted by gradual degrees into ever higher levels of mysticism. Not that most academic subjects were very mystical anymore, of course. But, by extension, the apprentice's skill reflects on the master's own ability. Connie realized that Chilton now viewed her as a particular asset to him, and that this new level of regard came with heavier responsibility. Chilton had plans for her.

"I have a few ideas percolating, of course," she began, "but nothing set in stone. Did you have something in mind?"

He regarded her for a moment, and she could see something indistinct, almost serpentine, glimmering behind his careful, veiled eyes. Then just as suddenly the glimmer disappeared, replaced with the bemused detachment that he habitually wore in place of an expression. He sat back in his chair, propping the top of a bony knee on the edge of the table, and waved one wrinkled hand dismissively. "Nothing as such. Only I urge you to look vigorously for new source bases. We need to think strategically about your career, my girl, and we can't do that if you are just revisiting the same old archives. A really marvelous, newly uncovered primary source can make you in this field, Connie," he said, looking sharply at her. "*New. New* shall be your watchword."

Watchwuhd, thought Connie. *If I don't get out of here this instant I am going to say something that will truly embarrass me.* Though why he would bother to tell her to look for new source bases she could not fully understand. Perhaps later he would tell her what exactly he had in mind. "I understand, Professor Chilton. I will give this some serious thought. Thank you."

Connie stood, easing her arms into her peacoat, pulling the scarf over her nose, and tucking her braid up under a knitted pom-pom hat. Chilton nodded appreciatively. "So you're off to celebrate, then," he said, and Connie fixed him with a thin smile.

"Abner's," she confirmed, silently begging him not to come along.

"You deserve it. Enjoy yourself," he said. "We shall continue this discussion more concretely at our next meeting." He made no move to rise and follow her, instead watching as she assembled herself to reenter the crisp spring world outside. As the door closed behind her, the last narrow stripe of sunlight vanished from the window, and the conference room went dark.

CHAPTER TWO

S INCE ARRIVING AT HARVARD, THREE YEARS AGO, CONNIE HAD SHARED
three dark, wood-paneled rooms in a building that had, a century before, been a private dormitory for clubbable young Harvard men. It now
held desultory pairs of grad students who shuttled, heads down, between library and home. Over the decades, Saltonstall Court's Gilded Age splendor
had faded behind successive layers of tobacco smoke, city grime, and plaster
Spackle.

Sometimes Connie thought she could feel the building's palpable dis-
dain for its sliding fortunes. Dark oak shelves now crowded with Connie's
history books and Liz's Latin classics had held generation after generation of
uncracked Greek textbooks and Gibbon's *Decline and Fall of the Roman Empire*. Even the brick fireplace evinced its contempt, belching forth smoke and
ash on the rare occasions when the women attempted to kindle a fire. Connie
tried to picture the anonymous, long-dead boys who had once lived in their

rooms, buttoned into woolen suits, experimenting with pipes as an affectation, shuffling cards for bridge. Some of these boys had brought valets with them to college, and Connie wondered which room had been the servants' room: hers or Liz's.

As she wove her way alone down Mount Auburn Street, after a blurry evening spent celebrating at Abner's, she reflected: probably hers. It had the smaller window.

The campus clock tower bonged once in the distance, and Connie's tired hand fell on the dormitory apartment's brass doorknob. The whiteboard nailed to her front door bore a scrawled note from the two chemistry students down the hall, wishing her luck on her qualifying exam, along with a cartoon version of her with a giant lightbulb illuminated over her head. Connie sighed and smiled.

She could not remember the last time she felt unambiguously pleased with herself. Maybe when she had graduated from Mount Holyoke—that was a pretty satisfying day. She had not even known she was getting magna cum laude until she read her name in the class day program. Perhaps once more, when she was accepted to Harvard for graduate school a year after that. But nothing since then. For the first time, really, since beginning her PhD program, Connie felt secure. Validated.

She slid her key into the lock and turned it silently, not wanting to disturb the sleeping Liz, who had stumbled home alone an hour earlier. As she slipped through the door and into the paneled hallway, two excited paws appeared, scrabbling at her feet.

"Hi, Arlo," she whispered, crouching down to enfold the wiggling animal in her arms. Something warm and damp lapped at her cheek. "Aren't you a grody little guy," she murmured. Connie scratched him behind the ears, and then she hoisted him up to her hip. She tiptoed with him into the galley kitchen off the study, groping for the light switch.

The kitchen flickered, filling with buzzing fluorescent light, and Connie squinted her eyes miserably. She placed the dog on the floor and leaned on the counter by the sink, gazing down at the small animal. As usual she could not decide what precise variety of dog he was; on some days he looked more houndlike, with droopy ears and dark, wet eyes, but on other days she would resolve that he was definitely a terrier, the kind that can fit down a badger hole. His fur was an indistinct, dingy color, something between mud and leaves, which changed and shifted depending on the sunlight and the season.

"So what did you do today?" she asked him, folding her arms.

He wagged twice.

"Yeah?" Connie said. "And then what?"

The dog sat down.

"That sounds like fun." She sighed, turning to fill the teakettle at the sink.

Connie had never had much interest in animals before Arlo; she had always found them worrisome and dependent, and the idea of keeping a pet touched a deep reservoir of anxiety within her. When she was troubled about her work back in college, as she often was, her dreams had grown populated by identical, replicating animals, snakes and mice or birds, all of them clamoring for food and care that she felt unable to provide. She had long regarded these dreams as an allegory for her worry about research, deadlines, and responsibility but nevertheless decided to take their lesson to heart. While the other women in her college cooperative dorm had brought home cat after cat, Connie held herself aloof.

A few weeks into her first semester at Harvard, however, Connie emerged from an evening class in the philosophy building to discover the little creature sitting camouflaged under a rhododendron hedge, nearly invisible in the shadows among the leaves. He materialized from under the shrubbery and fell in step with her as she crossed Harvard Yard. At first she tried to shoo him away with one foot as he dodged and weaved in her wake. Stopping in front of the library, she told him to buzz off, pointing with her finger back toward the philosophy building. He just wagged his tail, pink tongue flopping. Halfway across the Yard, she stopped again, telling him to go find his owner. But instead he followed her all the way back to Saltonstall Court, prancing through the door after her.

For the first few weeks, she had posted flyers around Harvard Square advertising FOUND DOG, to no avail. Then she tried posting a few DOG FREE TO GOOD HOME flyers, until Liz made her take them down. "He *chose* you!" Liz insisted, and Connie smiled at her roommate's unabashed sentiment. Liz was the sort of woman who studied medieval Latin because, secretly, she passed her hours imagining the days of knights battling mythical dragons, of ladies in wimples, and of courtly love. Connie appreciated Liz's fervor in part because Connie was herself a sentimental person, the kind often masked in a defensive layer of irony and cynicism. Without admitting to herself what she was doing, Connie gradually stopped looking for someone else to take the dog.

She never noticed that after Arlo entered her life, her nightmares about replicating vermin disappeared.

Now she turned from the simmering kettle and found a note taped to the refrigerator, in Liz's tidy printing. *Grace called 6:00* P.M., read the note. *Said call back ASAP. Late OK.*

"Look at this, Arlo," said Connie, gesturing to the note. "Your real owner called."

He tipped his head sideways.

"Aw, how could I say such things?" She chided herself for him, stooping to rub his cheek. "No, of course not really. It's just my mother." She checked her watch—1:20 A.M. That would make it . . . 11:20 in New Mexico. Connie smiled, pleased that her mother had remembered that today was her exam day. Of course Connie had taken the trouble to remind her a few times, in her otherwise sterile, if dutiful, letters and on her mother's answering machine. But for once the reminders had worked.

Connie poured the steaming water into a chipped mug, dropped a peppermint tea bag into the cup, and moved into the darkened study. She pulled the chain on the lamp that stood arced over her reading chair, a chintz behemoth that she had found yardsaleing in Cambridge.

The study was simultaneously spare and cluttered, fitting for two studious women. One wall housed the fireplace, framed by oak bookshelves overflowing with paperbacks and textbooks. Near the fireplace sagged a futon, a remnant of Liz's college life, facing a table positioned to support resting feet. Two institutional desks stood pressed to the walls on either side of the bookshelf, Connie's a picture of order, Liz's a riot of papers shuffled into heaps. The fourth wall consisted of tall leaded windows sheltering a small forest of potted plants and herbs for cooking—Connie's garden. By the plants sat her lamp and reading chair, under which she just glimpsed the disappearing rump of Arlo.

Connie pulled her knees up to her chest and balanced the hot mug under her nose. She rarely bothered to notice this room, as she spent so much of her time in it. Before too long, the day would come when she and Liz no longer shared this warren. The thought tugged at her excitedly, but under the excitement Connie felt distant, even sad. Of course, that day was still far off. Connie sipped at her tea, allowing its astringent taste to draw her back into the present.

Even for her mother, 11:20 seemed a little late. But the note had said to call as soon as she could. In truth Connie was so pleased that Grace had remembered her exam that she wanted to call now, even if it meant waking her mother up. In fact, she was not sure when she had last spoken with her mother. Had it been around Christmas? Connie had stayed in Cambridge to read for her exam, and they chatted on Christmas Day. But they must have caught each other on the phone since then. Connie knew she left messages, but she could not quite recall when she had actually reached her. Was it . . .

Connie placed two fingers on her forehead with a soft groan. It was when Grace had called to wish her a happy vernal equinox, the moment in spring when daylight and nighttime are exactly the same length. Of course. That was typical of Grace Goodwin.

In her more petulant moments, when she was younger and angry, Connie used the epithet "a victim of the 1960s" for her mother. As she grew older, however, she began to regard her mother with a detached, almost anthropological interest. Now the phrase that Connie produced when pressed to describe Grace was "a free spirit." It was hard to know where to start, when talking about Grace.

Perhaps Connie preferred to avoid discussing her mother because her own origin characterized Grace's fundamental lack of planning. Connie had been the unanticipated result of a love affair that Grace had had her senior year at Radcliffe, in 1966. An affair that Grace had had with her graduate teaching assistant in Eastern religion, it should be said, a fact that Connie regarded with unconcealed disapproval, particularly now that she herself was in graduate school. Leonard Jacobs, called "Leo" by Grace and her friends. Connie's eye drifted to the top shelf of her desk, where a black-and-white photograph rested, showing a sensitive, moist-eyed young man in a turtleneck, cheekbones high like Connie's own, with long sideburns and tousled hair. He gazed directly into the camera, unsmiling, a young woman with her straight hair parted down the middle leaning against his shoulder and gazing dreamily off to the side. Grace—her mother.

Leo's thoughts about Connie's imminent arrival had not been recorded for posterity, though Grace always intimated that they had made great, romantic plans. Unfortunately those plans were abbreviated by the machinations of foreign policy. Despite having drawn his research out for as long as he could, Leo finished his degree in 1966. He lost his academic draft deferment and was shipped to Southeast Asia three months before Connie's birth.

And while there, he disappeared.

Connie's sadness, yellowed with equal parts discomfort and distaste, was so great that she had never discussed it with anyone—not even Liz. When the subject of fathers came up in conversation with friends or colleagues, Connie skated quickly over the topic. Even reflecting on it now in the privacy of her study, her dog snoring under her reading chair, Connie frowned over her tea.

Grace, meanwhile, had finished school, barely, and then established herself and her small daughter in Concord, not far from Walden Pond. An undistinguished farmhouse with a pronounced list, the collective—for that is really what it was—had stood hidden behind a few acres of woods, with two knotty apple trees tinting the air in autumn with the pungent smell of cider. Connie suspected that Grace had filled the house with people in part to push away the void that Leo's loss had left. Whole coteries of warm, earnest young people traipsed through their house: musicians mostly, but also students, poets, women serious about pottery.

Connie's first conscious memory was a morning image of the kitchen of this farmhouse, warmed by a woodstove and furnished with a naked picnic table and potsful of thyme and rosemary. She was a toddler, roughly the same height as the table, and she was crying. She remembered Grace bending down until her open, young face was level with Connie's, long straw-colored hair falling from her shoulders, and saying, "Connie, you need to try to *center* yourself."

Grace's means of support during Connie's childhood had been varied and obscure, including at one point a macrobiotic bakery, which failed to appeal to the staid New England matrons of Concord. Once Connie reached adolescence, however, Grace's interests coalesced around something that she called "energetic healing." Clients would seek her out, complaining of ailments both physical and spiritual, and Grace would effect a change in them by moving her hands through their biologic energy fields. Connie wrinkled her nose still whenever she thought about it.

As a teenager, Connie rebelled by building around herself a predictability and order in direct contrast to her mother's flexibility and freedom. Now that she was an adult herself, Connie viewed Grace with more sympathy. From the comfortable distance that stretched between her haphazard childhood and the chintz reading chair where she now sat, Connie could regard Grace's eccentricities as being sweet, or naïve, rather than irresponsible and dissolute.

When Connie left for Mount Holyoke, Grace sold off what remained of the disintegrating farmhouse and moved to Santa Fe. Grace claimed at the time that she was ready to live somewhere "full of healing energy." Connie scoffed whenever she thought of this phrase but then stopped herself. Her mother, after all, had a right to be happy. Connie could admit that her own life choices might seem incomprehensible to an outside observer, and doubly so to one as critical of established institutions as Grace was. Grace must have wondered how she ended up with such an alien offspring, and yet she had always supported Connie's choices in her own unorthodox way.

Grace probably tried terribly hard to remember that today was her exam day. She had never tried to insist that Connie not study history, not be bookish, not be serious and orderly. Grace occasionally wished that Connie would "investigate her soul truth," but Connie always interpreted that as a hippie way of saying that Connie should just do what seemed right for her.

Connie placed her empty mug on the floor and reached for the telephone.

It rang four times, and as Connie was about to hang up, the receiver rose with a clatter and a breathless voice said, "Hello?"

"Mom?" said Connie. "Hi! Liz left a note that you had called. I hope it's not too late." Her eyes lit up with a rising warmth of affection for this odd woman with whom life had yoked her together. Over the past year or so, Connie had invented more reasons to telephone, leaving messages peppered with questions; the ostensible need for answers carried a built-in need to call back. Her garden usually provided a good excuse.

"Oh, Connie!" Grace cried with relief. "Yes! Yes, I did call. No, this is perfect. Good. How are you, my darling?"

"Great!" she said, bursting. "I'm great, I guess. Kind of drained, obviously. I mean, today was a pretty big day."

"Was it?" Grace said, the sound of her rummaging through a box of something noisy chinking down the telephone line.

"Well, yeah," Connie said, her smile slipping a little. "My qualifying exam?" she prodded. The rummaging sound continued. "I left you messages about it. That huge exam that I had to take to be advanced to candidacy?" Still Grace said nothing, the air coming in short bursts through her nostrils as she toted the unseen box across the kitchen of her adobe house.

"The thing I have been preparing for an *entire year* to take?" Connie said, anger and hurt pinching her face. Her brows crumpled together over her nose. Without realizing it she got to her feet, as if standing would bring the point home to Grace more clearly. "It was today, Grace," she said, her voice devolving into the same stern, disappointed chill that it used to have when Connie was a teenager. She pressed her lips together, suppressing the urge to cry, to yell, or do anything else that would suggest that she needed to *center* herself.

"Indeed," said Grace indifferently, shuffling the phone from one ear to the other. "Now listen, my darling. I have a very important favor to ask you."

CHAPTER THREE

Marblehead, Massachusetts

Early June

1991

"I STILL CAN'T BELIEVE SHE DID IT," SPAT CONNIE. SHE ROLLED THE window down on her side of the car and chucked out a withered apple core that had been sitting on the dashboard.

"I still can't believe you're letting it get to you this much," said Liz mildly, peering at the map accordioned across her lap. "You should veer right up here."

"How could I have let her talk me into this?" Connie growled, the right front wheel well of her rust-speckled Volvo sedan quaking in protest as she turned.

Liz inhaled an exasperated sniff of air through her nose before saying, "You know, you didn't have to agree to it. You're trying to put all this on Grace, but I don't see her twisting your arm—"

"*Always*," continued Connie before Liz was finished. "It's always like this! She has some disaster, and no matter what I happen to be doing, I have to drop everything and pick up the pieces. You'd think after twenty-five years of self-actualization she'd be able to manage her own *mess*." Connie downshifted as the Volvo hurtled into a laneless rotary, Nahant peninsula spiraling out into the sea on their right as they trundled northward, the car swaying slightly under the weight of Connie's plants and belongings. In the backseat, wedged between two jars overflowing with rosemary and mint, Arlo sat, swaying with the motion of the car. A thick rope of drool swung from his mouth.

"So I suppose it's Grace's fault that you said yes," said Liz, voice pointed. "Really, Connie, this is your doing as well."

"How exactly is this my doing?" Connie demanded, brushing a loose floss of hair off her brow with the back of one wrist. "I was perfectly happy! I was just *doing* my *work*. Look at Arlo. I think he's going to be sick."

"Then why did you let her talk you into it?" Liz pointed out.

Connie sighed. Liz was right, of course. In fact she had been right for the past six weeks, which made it all the more difficult for Connie to maintain her self-righteous anger.

"Just because you're right doesn't mean I have to be happy about it," Connie grumbled.

"Well, if I were you, I'd take a more pragmatic approach," Liz said. "You've agreed to do it, so the only thing you can do at this point is adjust your attitude. Watch out for this guy—I don't think he's yielding." A pickup truck peeled out of a side street, screeching onto the seawall drive just in front of them. The car rocked as Connie stamped on the brake.

They drove on for a moment in silence. The white-gray sea rolled away to the horizon, dotted in the distance by six or eight tiny sails. Liz cranked her window down a crack and turned her face into the breeze. The briny smell of seawater crept into the car, freshening and cooling the air. They passed a boatyard crowded with masts and boat hulls propped up by rusted scaffolds. Next to the boatyard, at the base of a rotting wooden dock, stood a heap of wire mesh lobster traps clotted with seaweed. As she watched, a fat seagull flapped leisurely down to perch atop the stacked traps, folding his wings along his back and gazing out across the shimmering water.

"You could be looking at this a whole other way," Liz ventured, turning the map over in her lap.

"Oh?" asked Connie. "And what way is that?"

Liz leaned her head back against the headrest and smiled.

"It's pretty here," she said.

AFTER A HALF HOUR OF GOOD-NATURED SQUABBLING ABOUT THE PROPER orientation of the map and the incomprehensible layouts of New England towns, which follow no sort of logic, they drove the Volvo around a curve and down a narrow lane shaded with weeping willows. The lane was lined with small, boxy houses, their windows punched at uneven intervals, their wooden cladding bleached pale gray by decades of sun and salt water. Connie squinted to see the numbers nailed to each slowly passing door.

"What number are we looking for again?" she asked.

"Milk Street. Number three," said Liz, peering through the passenger window. Next to one of the houses leaned a shed festooned with stained lobster trap buoys hung up to dry. Another was almost completely obscured by a sailboat parked on wooden pilings in a driveway choked with weeds. Liz could just make out the lettering on the stern of the forgotten sailboat: *Wonderment, Marblehead, Mass.*

"Wonderment," whispered Liz.

"These houses are ancient," remarked Connie. "Pre-Revolution, maybe."

Liz spread the map across the Volvo dashboard and inspected it. "The map does say this is 'Old Town.' "

"I believe it," said Connie dryly. "There's seventeen. So it must be on this side of the street."

Connie slowed the car down, gradually rolling to a halt near the dead end of the street. The lane petered out a few yards away, disappearing into a graveled trail that wound into a sparse wood.

"It should be right here," she said, looking out the window at a thicket abutting the stand of trees, obscured by a dense wall of brambles.

In the backseat, Arlo started wiggling and released an excited bark.

"What's his deal?" asked Liz, turning back to the little animal and scratching his neck. He lapped at her wrist.

"Maybe he's just excited that the car has finally stopped. At least he didn't get sick." Connie paused. "I don't know, Liz. I don't think there's anything here. Are you sure this is Milk Street?"

"You have to go to the bathroom, little guy?" Liz cooed to the dog, whose entire hind section was vibrating with excitement. "I think he needs to be let out. Let's take him over to those trees to do his thing and then we'll take another look at the map."

The air smelled moist and fresh, like new earth, but with a hint of brine—nothing at all like Cambridge. Connie stretched her arms overhead, feeling her spine pop in two places, and then rubbed her neck with one hand while opening the back door for the dog.

"C'mon out, mutt," she said, but before the words were completely out of her mouth the animal had vanished, reappearing an instant later directly in front of the bramble thicket. He barked, tail cutting half-moons in the air behind him.

The two women started toward the wood at the end of the lane, expecting the dog to follow them when he lost interest in whatever vermin he had spotted in the thicket.

"So whose house is this supposed to be again?" asked Liz, picking idly at a hangnail.

"Granna's," said Connie. "My mother's mother."

"But you said you'd never been here before," Liz said.

Connie shrugged. "I haven't. My mom and Granna—Sophia was her name—didn't get along, as you can imagine. All Grace's hippie stuff. And

Granna was apparently very old-style New England. Stiff, restrained. So they were only sporadically in touch, I guess. And then she died when I was really little."

"Sophia," Liz mused. "That's a Greek root, you know. It means 'wisdom.' Did you ever meet her?"

"Mom says that I did. She came to our house in Concord pretty often, but it always drove Mom crazy. Apparently Granna didn't approve of Mom's raising me in 'such an environment.'" Connie waved her fingers in mock quotes on either side of her head.

"Sounds like you would have gotten along with her pretty well, actually. At least you and she would have agreed about Grace. Do you remember any of this?" Liz asked.

"Not really," said Connie. "I think I maybe remember when she died. Mom being sad. Her holding me and saying something about 'universal life energy,' and me asking if that meant 'heaven,' and her saying 'yes.' I must have been about three or four."

"But if she died over twenty years ago, what's been happening with the house this whole time?"

Connie rolled her eyes before she could stop herself. "Well, apparently it has just been *sitting* here. How typical is that? Mom never even told me." She shook her head.

"So why would she ask you to deal with the house now?" asked Liz. "And, more importantly," she said, joking, "why have we been paying to live in the dorm all this time if there was an empty house less than an hour away that might as well belong to you?"

Connie laughed. "I think the answer to that question will be apparent when we find the house. Mom says it's a total dump. And as for why she's asked me to deal with it now, it would seem that my very responsible and attentive mother has neglected to pay the property taxes on the house since Granna died." Liz gasped in disbelief. "Oh, yes," Connie continued before she could say anything. "It's been adding up, but until recently the rate was so low that the town didn't really care. Then last year they changed the law.

And this spring the town sent her notice that the house will be seized in six months if she doesn't make restitution."

"Wow," said Liz. "How much?"

"I don't know the exact figure," Connie said, tugging on the end of her braid. "Grace was being pretty coy. I'm supposed to sort through all the junk that's in there, throw everything out, and arrange to have the house sold, if anyone cares to buy it. And whatever proceeds it can get will be used to pay off the town."

Liz whistled. "At least it's just for the summer. Then you can come back to Cambridge and have all this out of the way."

By this time they had reached the wood, and the women stopped at the base of the trail where the gravel thinned to beaten earth. Connie gazed down at the wild angelica plant bursting forth in the clearing between trees. The fragile white flower clusters nodded in the early summer air, weedy and lush, and insects hummed unseen in the hollows under the trees. Connie stared at the flowers dappled by the sunlight, her eyes widening. As she watched the flashes of light play upon the surface of the petals, her mind loosened, grew soft, moving into a daydream, and she thought that she perceived the image of an older man, dressed in muddy work clothes, stooped under the weight of a canvas bag stuffed with firewood and kindling, trudging through the shadows. *Lemuel?* a voice called out, audible only in Connie's mind. *Comin', Sophier!* The image called back before it pulled apart, the details of the daydream dissolving out of her reach. She was brought back to herself by the sound of Liz asking a question.

The image had felt startlingly immediate, tangible. She reached a hand up to massage her temple, which ached gently where it had been fine a moment ago. Liz was watching her, waiting for her to respond to something she had just said, but Connie had no idea what it was. "I'm sorry," she said, confused. "I zoned out for a second."

"I said, where's Arlo?" repeated Liz.

The pain in Connie's head had begun to clear. She looked around, but the dog had not followed them. "That's odd," Connie said.

She started back down the gravel path to the lane. When she emerged from the wood she discovered the dog sitting at attention, still facing the dense thicket across from the car.

"Hey, mutt," she said, squatting next to the animal. "What are you watching?" He gazed up at her, wagging, and then looked back into the thicket. "Is it a squirrel?" Connie turned her face toward the spot in the dense thornbushes where the dog was gazing and gasped. To her astonishment, under the tightly wound bramble branches was the outline of a rotted iron gate.

ॐ

BY THE TIME THAT LIZ ARRIVED, CONNIE HAD ALREADY PULLED ASIDE A significant heap of dead vines and weeds. As soon as a gap opened between two of the gate's rusted bars, Arlo wriggled his way through and disappeared into the shadows. Liz jogged to a stop behind her friend, out of breath with what she had seen.

"Connie!" Liz puffed. "I think that we might have found the house!"

"Yeah! Arlo spotted the gate," she grunted, hauling aside another armload of undergrowth.

"No, look," Liz said, tapping Connie on the shoulder. Connie stood, wiping her dirty hands on the seat of her jeans. Liz pointed up.

Connie stepped back into the lane, tightening the flannel shirt that was knotted around her waist, and craned her neck. Following Liz's extended finger, she traced a towering elder tree draped with vines upward, upward, upward, and then at the very top of the thicket, Connie made out the unmistakable outline of a cedar-shingled rooftop emerging from underneath the leaves and branches. In the center of the outline she could just glimpse the hulking rubble of a brick chimney. She caught her breath.

"I can't believe it," she whispered.

"I told you this was Milk Street," said Liz, poking her. Connie arched one eyebrow at Liz.

"There is almost no way to tell that there is a house in there," Connie remarked, running a soiled hand through her hair as she surveyed the thicket. Now that she knew what to look for, she imagined that she could make out the faint tracery of the iron fence underlying the dense shrubbery. Rising farther from the riot of leaves, she thought she might also see the blurred shape of windowsills.

"Well, you said that no one has been here since Sophia died," Liz said.

"Yeah, but this looks like it has been abandoned a lot longer than twenty years," said Connie.

The two friends stood in silence, arms folded, gazing at the house clad in its layers of vegetation and neglect. Finally Liz broke the quiet.

"Here," she said, "let me help you clear off the gate."

The vines and ivy gave way easily, and within half an hour they had made a soft pile of branches and roots to one side of the gate. As they worked, they heard periodic rustling and barking from inside the garden.

"At least Arlo's having a good time," Connie muttered, brushing her hair aside and leaving a streak of mud on her forehead.

"I think we almost have it," said Liz.

After a few more minutes spent yanking on the last stubborn vines, Connie sat back on her heels and regarded the revealed gate. Its iron was so pitted with rust and age that she feared it might dissolve at her touch. Gently she reached forward and lifted the latch that held the gate to the fence. It whined with the sound of metal long frozen in place, but yielded. Slowly, carefully, she pushed the gate in until it was open about two feet wide, creating a doorway in the dense hedge. "Well?" she said, turning back to Liz. Liz shrugged.

Connie got to her feet and edged through the gate.

The garden was not nearly as dense as the hedge implied. She stood on the outline of a flagstone path leading up to the moldering front door of the house, the entire surface of which was overgrown with several different varieties of vine. Over the front door draped a blooming purple-green wisteria, its thick syrupy smell puddling in the air. Several tall, slender trees—the elder that she had seen from the street, as well as an alder and a

hawthorn—dotted the garden, forming pillars that supported the tented su-
perstructure of vines stretching from the hedge to the house. Under the trees
and vines, the garden was shady without being dark. It felt private—secret.

Connie became aware of a displaced, intrusive ache in her stomach, a
creeping sorrow that she had never seen this hidden realm. Sophia, her grandmother, had made this garden. But she would never know her. The finality of
this realization felt leaden and inescapable. Connie superimposed her long-
stored mental image of Sophia over the garden scene before her, seeing her
grandmother kneeling by the corner of the house with a trowel. Connie relaxed, allowing herself to move deeper into the fantasy, and to her surprise
the stooped man from her daydream in the woods—she now recognized
him from old photographs as Lemuel, her grandfather, who died while Grace
was in college—appeared from around the corner of the house, still carrying his load of kindling. *That'll do*, her imagined form of Granna said to the
man. *Just put it in the hall.*

Connie pressed her fingertips to her eyelids, splotches of blue and inky
black spreading behind her eyes. When she dropped her hands and opened
her eyes again the scene had melted into the ground, vanished. Of course,
her sleep had been erratic in the days leading up to the move—even more so
than was usual for her. Last night she barely slept at all, instead lying awake
with Arlo in her arms, staring into the darkness. She must be overtired.

Instead of a lawn, riots of wild herbs and plants overran one another in
an incoherent mass. Connie recognized most of the herbs standard to a
home kitchen garden: thyme, rosemary, sage, parsley, a few different mints,
fat turnip greens, dandelion leaves, dense soft dill blossoms, short tufts of
chives that had not been harvested for years. Connie's eyes moved over the
plants along the far side of the garden, alighting on some obscure flowers
that she knew only from horticulture books: monkshood, henbane, fox-
glove, moonwort. A thick, ropey belladonna clung to the left corner of the
house, sinking its roots deep into the wooden framework. Connie frowned.
Hadn't Granna known that a lot of those flowers are poisonous? She would
have to be careful with Arlo.

Beyond the herbs and flowers, the garden on the near side of the house seemed overrun with vegetables. Fuzzy green leaves as wide as dinner plates shaded the nascent blobs of summer squash, muskmelon, and pumpkin. To the right, under a wide gap in the vine growth overhead, a tangle of plants clung to the opposite corner of the house, heavy fruits as big as Connie's fist dangling under the leaves. Connie looked closer, and to her surprise saw that they were tomatoes. But not grocery store tomatoes—these were queerly multicolored, deep purple-reds, striped green, glowing yellow, and their shapes were globular and alien. The base of the tomato plants was as dense and wide as a small tree trunk, as if this tomato plant alone in the world did not die at the end of every summer. Arlo was digging in the shade under one of its leaves.

Liz appeared next to Connie, her footsteps silent on the mossy stone pathway. "This garden is crazy. Look at those tomatoes!" she exclaimed. "They're enormous." Liz paused, sensing Connie's quiet, and glanced side-long at her, touching Connie's shoulder. "Are you okay?"

Connie turned to Liz, still feeling off-kilter and fogged from her vivid daydream. Her friend's face shone with excitement at their discovery, and Connie hesitated to share her own strangely reflective mood. "I'm fine," she said, producing a smile for Liz's benefit. "Just a little tired. You see that endive? We can have salad for dinner!"

Grace had mentioned that the house was old, but she had never suggested *how* old: it was practically antediluvian, handmade by a craftsman using the same techniques carried over from late medieval England. Its windows were small, with lozenge-shaped panes held together with lead. Her eyes widened in wonder as she gazed upward at the facade, never so much as glimpsed by a preservationist. The silent house stared back at her, wizened and aloof.

She brushed aside the curtain of wisteria flowers and traced her fingertips over the door. The wood had probably once been painted white, but now it carried a dark greenish tint from mildew and time. Connie tried to imagine her mother as a small child living here, and the image jarred, incongruous. Grace and Sophia and Lemuel, her grandfather, a taciturn Marbleheader whom Grace never mentioned, all of them moving around one another in little bubbles of subjectivity, intersecting in this house. Grace was too lively, too active, to belong here.

Perhaps that was why she had left.

The garden and the house seemed to belong to their own abandoned world so completely that the presence of any person, lively or otherwise, felt like a grave mistake. Connie dug in her blue jean pocket for the key that her mother had mailed and brushed aside the crust of dirt in the keyhole with one thumb. The key slid in, and after some resistance turned, emitting the grinding squeak of long-locked metal. With one gentle press of her shoulder, Connie nudged the door open.

The jamb reluctantly released its hold, billowing forth a cloud of dust. Connie coughed and gagged, waving the dingy haze away from her face. As the door wrenched open, she heard a metallic *ker-chunk* from just overhead, and something small and fragile clattered to the stones at her feet.

Nailed to the threshold overhead, almost completely obscured by the wisteria, Connie discovered a dented horseshoe rusted almost to a shadow. One of the square nails holding it to the suppurating wood had come loose, leaving the shoe dangling at a dangerous angle. Connie pocketed the tiny handmade nail and stepped into the waiting house.

THE HOUSE CONTAINED EXACTLY THE KIND OF AIR THAT CONNIE WOULD have expected to find in a sealed sea chest retrieved from the bottom of the ocean: woody, salty, and stale. Most of the afternoon light was screened out by the dense layers of leaves twined across the windows. Connie paused, letting her eyes adjust to the darkness. The interior assembled around her out of the gloom, a perfect simulacrum of a first-period, pre-1700 house, with furnishings of subsequent generations added gradually over the centuries. Except that the house was not a simulacrum.

"My God," she breathed, disbelieving. "How long has this been here?"

The silent interior felt so timeless, so untouched by the outside world as to seem unreal.

The front door opened into a tiny entrance hall across from a spiral wooden staircase so narrow and steep as almost to qualify as a ladder. In its original orientation, in the seventeenth century, the household would have done most of its living—eating, cooking, sleeping, sewing, praying—on the first floor, using the attic loft overhead for extra sleeping space and storage. Each slat in the stair was of polished Ipswich pine, with deep depressions worn away by generations of passing feet. The remainder of the entryway consisted of a rickety Queen Anne table weighted down with several months' worth of unopened mail, yellowed and brittle. Over the table hung a simple Greek Revival mirror, its glass misted with clinging dust and cobwebs, the gilding peeling and faded. A gnarled, long-dead plant sat in the corner under the stair, in a China-export porcelain pot split down the middle by a dry brown crack. The floor of the hallway bore a rotted soft spot, and Connie cringed to see a thick mushroom pushing up from between the boards. Her eye detected a flash of movement on the periphery of her vision, and she jumped, glimpsing the vanishing tail of a garden snake slipping into the shadows behind the potted plant.

To the left of the front hallway was what looked like a little sitting room; Connie could just make out shelves stuffed with leather-bound books and a couple of mismatched armchairs grouped around a shallow fireplace. The threadbare needlepoint upholstery promised dampness, mildew, and mice, filling the air with a faint, humid miasma. The obstinate bulk of a Chippendale writing desk crouched in the corner, its carved paw-feet gripping the floor. More skeletal plant remnants hung motionless in the windows. The floorboards were of the same heavy yellow pine as the staircase, some of the boards almost two feet wide, stretching along the entire length of the house and studded with square-headed nails.

To the right of the entryway Connie found an austere dining room, furnished with another Queen Anne table surrounded by shield-back side chairs—mid-eighteenth century, she marveled, and judging from their silhouettes, carved in Salem. The room had clearly not been used for dining, even when Granna was alive; in every available corner stood stacks of newspapers, a chest or two, some blackened sealed jars. The dining room also held a fireplace, but this one was older; it was wide and deep, bristling with iron hooks and pots of varying size, and had a beehive-shaped brick cavern for baking bread. Connie suspected that the dining room had originally been the hall, which was the early term for the main living room and workroom, the functional heart of the house. To the left of the fireplace stood built-in shelves crowded with plates, mugs, and bottles so encased with filth that she could not tell what color they were. A few framed paintings dotted the walls, but the shadows kept their images veiled. To the right of the fireplace, a narrow door leaned, closed with an iron latch.

Connie reached one arm into the dining room, groping for a light switch near the doorjamb, but finding nothing. The air was silent and still, implicitly unwelcoming, as if the house had settled into its own decay and did not wish to be disturbed. She started to tiptoe across the dining room, each footfall leaving a dark circle in the coating of dust on the floor.

"I don't know why I should be tiptoeing," she said aloud, irritated at her own trepidation. For the rest of the summer, this was *her* house. She lowered her heel onto the floor, striding with purpose over to the latched doorway. It yielded to her touch after slight persuasion, and opened with a creak.

Behind the door, instead of the closet that she was expecting, Connie found a cramped kitchen, unceremoniously tacked onto the house sometime within the last hundred years. On the right side of the kitchen stood a deep porcelain sink watched over by another window, clogged with leaves and overgrowth. The room featured an iron woodstove, a low icebox, a floor covered in curling linoleum, and a cheap wooden door leading into the garden behind the house.

What Connie noticed in the room, however, were not these archaic appliances, but the shelves upon shelves of glass bottles and jars ranging over the walls, all of them containing unidentifiable powders, leaves, and syrups. Some of the jars bore illegible labels stained with dried paste. In the corner stood propped an old-fashioned broom made of bunches of dried twigs fastened with twine to a long ash branch. The broom seemed roped in place by skeins of spiderweb.

Connie stood in the kitchen gaping at the bizarre assortment lining the shelves. Grace had always insisted that Granna was not one for cooking, and so Connie could not account for the bottles and jars. Maybe she had a canning phase at the end of her life, and they were all dried out and blackened because they were not sealed properly. Like Grace, Granna had been prone to phases, in her own way. The only Christmas with Granna that Connie could remember, Granna had appeared, just before she died, at the Concord farmhouse with hand-knitted sweaters for her and Grace, the same fisherman's pattern in three different colors. Unfortunately Sophia's command of shoulder-to-arm proportion had been idiosyncratic, the sleeves stopping halfway down the arm on the left and well over the knuckles on the right. Connie chuckled with affection at the memory.

The air in the kitchen was close and dry, with a palpable scent of decay, and the jars were all coated in a thick drapery of grime. As Connie stood, hands on her hips, her excitement at the undiscovered house tempered by vague disquiet, soft footsteps approached behind her, and she glanced over her shoulder, startled. She was met with the beaming face of Liz carrying a sweatshirt fashioned into a makeshift sack bulging with tomatoes and endives. At her feet sat Arlo, smug, a root protruding from his mouth. His tail brushed aside thick layers of dust on the floor behind him.

"We've been scavenging for dinner," Liz announced. "Is this the kitchen?" She pushed around Connie, dumping the vegetables in the sink. She twisted the brass faucet handle, and the pipes released an echoing groan, shuddering and coughing dryly before spewing forth a brownish trickle of water. "I'm glad you packed Palmolive. Grace was right—this house is a pit."

Liz rinsed the dust out of the kitchen sink and scrubbed the vegetables she had taken from the garden. "So I was thinking we start the cleaning in the kitchen, since that's where you'll have to eat, and then we do the bedrooms after dinner, so we have a clean place to sleep. Also, how long do you think it'll take us to reach the train station tomorrow? Twenty minutes? I just want to know when we need to get up in the morning. I think we can make some real headway tonight so you're at least kind of sane for the coming week."

Liz's bright, efficient chatter shook Connie out of her reverie, reminding her that Granna's house might feel like a gap, a stitch dropped in the fabric of time, but it was really just a house like any other—older, perhaps, in much worse shape, but still just a house. Connie rubbed her hands along her upper arms, turning over in her mind the embodiments of normalcy that she had brought with her, like talismans: Liz, her plants, her books, her dog. This would be an unusual summer, to be sure, but really not that different from any other. A lot more cleaning than she was used to, that's all. Reassured by these thoughts, Connie squatted down next to Arlo to disengage the root from his mouth.

"What's this, little man?" she asked, reaching gingerly between his teeth. "Did you find a wild carrot?" The animal obediently dropped the root into her hand, then looked up at her, waiting for praise.

When Connie saw what she was holding she let out a scream, recoiling in horror and dropping the root on the floor. Without thinking, she immediately wiped her hand across the seat of her jeans, rubbing away any residue that it might have left on her skin.

"What's the matter?" asked Liz. "Does it have bugs?"

"Oh, my God," Connie panted. The pulse at her throat beat heavy and fast, and she forced herself to inhale slowly to calm her breathing. "No, it's not that. Don't touch it!" She knelt on the kitchen floor, peering at the inert vegetable where it lay in a spatter of mud.

"Why?" asked Liz, looking over Connie's shoulder. She wrinkled her nose at its malformed hideousness. "Ew. What *is* that?"

Connie shoved away the dog, who was starting to realize that the burst of praise that he had expected was not forthcoming. She swallowed, eyes searching the kitchen for a tool that she could use to pick up the root.

"I am reasonably certain that our friend here has brought us a mandrake," she said. Using two fingers and a dense wad of paper towel, she picked up the plant by one leaf and held it at arm's length for Liz to see. "I've only ever seen drawings of them in gardening books, but their roots are supposed to be shaped kind of like a person. See?" She indicated the leglike shape of the bifurcated root, with two fat protuberances where arms might go.

"So?" asked Liz.

"So, they're among the most poisonous plants known to man," said Connie. "So poisonous, in fact, that legend had it that anyone who tried to dig one up himself would die on the spot. As a result, anyone who wanted one needed a dog to dig it up for him." She glanced down at Arlo. Surely, she told herself, that legend spoke more to the fact that dogs will dig up anything, poisonous or not, than that men could not collect mandrakes safely. The creature wagged at her. "Also," she added, "some early modern horticulture books claimed that when the mandrake is uprooted, it screams."

"Freaky," whispered Liz, peering at the plant. "What would your grandmother be doing with something so dangerous growing in her yard?"

"Beats me. She has some other crazy stuff outside, too," Connie said. "Did you see the belladonna vine?" She shook her head, still holding up the homunculus root. "Maybe it's a volunteer plant that just showed up on its own. Like a weed. I can't imagine that anyone in her right mind would want something like this hanging around the house."

"What are you going to do with it?" Liz asked, voice worried.

Connie sighed, suddenly overwhelmed by the prospect of the tasks that lay ahead of her. She did not want to have to worry about poisonous plants in the kitchen, garden snakes in the living room, tax liens on the house. All she really wanted to do was eat some dinner and pretend as if the summer were not about to happen.

"We'll just put this up here for now, where no dogs can eat it," she said, tucking the root onto a shelf between two blackened jars.

CONNIE JERKED AWAKE, HER HEART LURCHING IN HER CHEST. FOR A long minute she could not identify where she was, and she was not sure if she was awake or still asleep. Gradually the shapes in the room swam into focus: the needlepoint armchair across from her, the Chippendale desk lurking in the shadows behind it. She wiped a hand over her face, crisscrossed by pale red marks where it had been pressed against the back of the chair. The details of the dream receded, leaving their emotional content but not their substance. Vague, terrifying shapes bending over her, long ropes reaching down, chasing after her . . . or perhaps they had been snakes? She peered around the small sitting room, its benign forms seeming like skins draped over something else, something menacing. As her mind struggled for focus, the borderland between dream and reality felt slippery and imprecise. She must have dozed off in the chair in the sitting room.

Before retiring to one of the four-poster beds discovered upstairs, Liz had managed to crank open one of the windows in the sitting room, so the room's overpowering mustiness was now tempered somewhat by the soft breath of summer. Outside Connie heard only the occasional sawing of crickets. After her years in Harvard Square, she found the quiet strangely foreboding. It roared in her ears, demanding her attention, where sirens would have passed by unheeded. She was accustomed to being kept awake by the whispering of her anxieties, but here the whispers sounded even louder in the pervasive, disquieting silence.

Now completely awake, she shifted her weight in the chair, toying with the oil lamp that glowed on the table at her elbow. Connie could not fathom why her grandmother had never had the house wired for electricity. It seemed impossible that there could be a house in America at the end of the twentieth century that did not have electric light, but a concerted search had revealed no switches, no lamps, no power cords of any kind. And no telephone! God knew how her mother expected to sell it this way. *I'll be going to bed pretty early this summer, looks like*, Connie reflected, sullen. At least someone had thought to add running water somewhere along the line. The makeshift kitchen was echoed on the second floor by a simple lavatory, accessible through another modified closet in one of the two attic bedrooms. It contained a deep claw-footed bathtub with no shower, a pull-chain toilet with a wooden seat, and a tiny sink. Liz, as was her wont, had remarked as they brushed their teeth that the tub held out the possibility of long, romantic baths by lamplight. When Liz had said this, Connie had blushed, embarrassed. Connie was uneasy around men; she disliked this aspect of herself, for it seemed materially different from Liz's sweet, self-conscious silliness. So yes, the tub would be great, if there were anyone to share it with. Which, of course, there was not.

She frowned, feeling the possibility of sleep grow increasingly remote. Liz had collapsed over an hour ago. Connie told herself that she was probably anxious about tomorrow, when Liz would take the train back to Cambridge. Liz was scheduled to start teaching in Harvard's summer school on Monday—Latin declensions for overachieving teenagers. Soon the house would have her all to itself. Connie felt like she was being abandoned on a high plank, extended out over a dark lake that she could not see. Liz was right. She should never have agreed to this.

Connie rose from her seat by the empty fireplace, carrying the little brass lamp with her toward the bookshelf, craving distraction. Maybe an old temperance novel, or a book of bridge strategy. She smiled at herself. Just thinking about reading those things would send her to sleep.

Her fingers ran gently over the cracked spines of the books, fine brown powder lifting off the untreated leather and staining her fingertips. None of the spines were legible in the dim, flickering light. She pulled a slim volume from the shelf, dirt and bits of binding raining onto the floor in its wake. She flipped to the frontispiece: *Uncle Tom's Cabin*. Typical. Every old New England house was guaranteed to have a copy of *Uncle Tom's Cabin*. It was like a calling card, announcing that *this* family was on the right side of the Civil

War. She sighed and slid the book back into place on the shelf. Sometimes New Englanders could be so self-righteous.

She drew the light along the spines of the books, its yellow orb illuminating three spines at a time together with her chin and knuckles, leaving the rest of the room swathed in black. Connie moved the lamp to the bottom shelf, where the thickest, heaviest books were kept. These would be Bibles, or possibly Psalters. Puritan doctrine held that literacy was necessary—even vital—to receiving divine grace. As such, every proper New England home must have its own copy of the revealed word of God. Placing the lamp on the floor, she wrestled the largest volume out of the shelf, supporting it with one slender arm while she thumbed it open. Yes, a Bible—an old one, judging from the idiosyncratic spelling and the fragility of the paper. Seventeenth century, she thought, pleased with her training. For a fleeting moment she caught herself weighing what a Bible like this might be worth. But no; Bibles were the most common printed texts, so not all that rare, even when they were this old. And this one was rotted with mildew and water damage. The pages felt pulpy and begrimed under her hands.

As she thumbed a page midway through Exodus, Connie wondered to herself what she might hope to find as she sifted through this house. Liz had said that Connie and Sophia sounded as if they would have gotten along, but she had never really known Sophia. Who was this odd, stubborn woman? Whose story was hidden here?

At the moment that these idle thoughts wandered through her mind, the hand that was holding the Bible vibrated with a hot, crawling, pricking sensation—something between a limb falling asleep and the painful shock that comes from unplugging a frayed lamp wire. Connie screamed in pain and surprise, dropping the heavy book with a thud.

She rubbed her hand, the strange sensation so fleeting that after a moment she doubted she had ever really felt it. Connie knelt to see if she had damaged the antique book.

The Bible lay open on the floor, raked by the glowing light from the oil lamp, surrounded by a rising cloud of dust stirred by its fall to the carpet.

Kneeling on the floor, Connie reached forward to gather up the Bible when she noticed something small and bright protruding from between its leaves. Nudging the lamp nearer, Connie traced her fingertip down the edge of the pages until she found the little glimmering object, then slowly withdrew it from its hiding place.

It was a key. Antique, about three inches long, with an ornate handle and hollow shaft, probably designed for a door or a substantial chest. She turned the key over in the soft light from the lamp, wondering why it had been hidden in the Bible. It seemed too bulky for a bookmark. As she warmed the small metal object in her hands, puzzling about what it could mean, she noticed the tiniest shred of paper protruding from the end of the hollow shaft. She knitted her brows together in concentration.

Carefully, delicately, she caught the end of the paper with her thumbnail and withdrew it slowly from the shaft. It looked like a miniature parchment, tightly rolled into a tube. She laid the key in her lap and held the parchment up to the lamp, unrolling the crisp, brittle slip one millimeter at a time. It was brown and stained, barely as long as her thumb.

On it, in a watery ink barely legible in the flickering light, were written the words *Deliverance Dane*.

Interlude

Salem Town, Massachusetts

Mid-June

1682

Major Samuell Appleton, Esquire, flexed his toes inside his boot and frowned. His big toe had carried a dull ache for weeks now, and he could not stop himself from worrying it. He could feel it, swollen and hot, chafing egregiously inside the stiff leather of his shoe. His thick woolen stockings only made the boiling in his toe worse. He sighed. Perhaps his wife could fix another poultice for it, when the day's work was done. He shifted uncomfortably in his seat and dabbed at his moist forehead with a handkerchief. The afternoon yawned before him, and he sent a private request to God to make it pass quickly.

The day outside was dusty and warm, and yellow sunbeams spilled through the meetinghouse windows, casting bright puddles of light on the wood-planked floor. Appleton sat in a majestic tapestried armchair behind the broad library table at the front of the room, elbows propped on the table, arms folded. The room in front of him hummed with low conversation as the men and women crowded onto benches and side chairs awaited the beginning of the court session. White coifs bent over knitting and needlework; men leaned sunburned heads together, nodding. Those being brought to the bar for their offenses sat sullen-faced near the front, some of them wringing their hands. Appleton grunted to himself. Court days always made for good spectacle. For a godly people, he reflected, his neighbors surely took their interest in one another's sins. *Whores and blackguards all of them*, he thought.

Appleton glanced off to his left at the smug knot of jury men seated in a row of straight-backed chairs, waiting to pass judgment on their peers. He knew most of them by sight: Lieutenant Davenport, the jury foreman, was a decent man with a frightening countenance. He bore a deep pink scar across his face from the Indian wars at the Eastward that made him look ferocious and angry, but it masked a forthright soul. Next to him sat William Thorne, a genial fellow who ran a tavern out on Ipswich road, and Goodman Palfrey, a cordwainer who was forever volunteering for town committees. Appleton snorted with distaste. Palfrey had sat on almost every jury this year, on top of being elected town fence viewer. There were rumors he was putting himself forward for full church membership as well. Appleton detested a man who did not know his place. The other three men were unknown to him— local artisans most likely, propertied enough to serve, but still of a largely middling sort.

Appleton waved over the clerk, a slight, nervous young man named Elias Alder. The little clerk leapt to his feet in a tangle of limbs, slid a heavy sheet of paper across the library table toward the judge, and withdrew off to the side, holding the tip of his quill anxiously to his mouth. By the end of the session his lower lip would be black with ink, Appleton reflected. Appleton held the paper at arm's length, squinting to make out Elias's unfortunate penmanship. Four suits scheduled this afternoon. He sighed again, returned the paper to the clerk, and nodded. The throb in his toe was no better.

The clerk cleared his throat, Adam's apple bobbing visibly in his neck, and the murmuring meetinghouse grew quiet.

"Deliverance Dane versus Peter Petford for slander!" he announced, and the assembled populace burst into a rising twitter of commentary that continued for a full five minutes.

"Enough!" bellowed Appleton, and the roar quieted down without fully disappearing. The judge surveyed the meetinghouse with a withering eye, casting his magisterial gaze over each watching face. When he felt the attention of the room settling on him once again, he continued. "Goodwife Dane, you shall render your deposition."

A young woman rose from the front row of deponents, smoothing her skirts as she did so. Her dress was of a neat dove gray, and her collar and modest head covering were improbably fresh and white for a woman of her station. A heavy knot of tree-bark hair rested on the nape of her neck, just visible beneath her coif, and her soft cheeks shone with warmth and health. Appleton knew that this woman was spoken of in the village, but he had never seen her before. She wore a placid expression like a veil overlying the unmistakable confidence that radiated forth from her face. Appleton reflected that in some women such confidence might be mistaken for pride.

She lifted her eyes to his, and for a moment he was bathed in their coolness. As the young woman held his gaze he felt the bustling room recede around him, and an unfamiliar tingling sensation, like a beam of sunlight entering his forehead. Appleton felt his putrefying toe submerge as though into a cold, babbling stream, and the numbness of it carried away the dull, burning ache. Unaware that he was doing so, Appleton let out a soft sigh of relief. All at once the moment passed, and the judge shook himself, blinking, the sound of the meetinghouse pressing in around him once more. He flexed his foot inside his shoe, and the toe did not protest. He looked sharply at her. The Dane woman wore a small, knowing smile.

She reached into the pocket that was tied to her belt to withdraw a folded sheet of paper. She spread the paper out in her hands and began to read aloud in a softly modulated tone.

"I testify and saith that on the eve of the new year the said Petford bade me come see to his child that was sick and that he had a good mind it was afflicted by some mischief. I hastened to the said Petford's house whereupon I found Martha, Petford's daughter, aged about five years, suffering a pain in her head and near dead with fever. I brewed a tincture of physick for the said Martha who drank it down and grew quieter and slept. As she slept the said Petford did rail and moan that surely some evil sorcery had been worked upon the child, for she had thrived yet one week previous.

"I made to sleep upon the floor nearby the child's bed. Some hours hence I awoke to Martha's awful cries as she clutched herself and saith, O, I am pinched, and now, O, I am burnt, and she tore at her clothes. I took her into my arms and held her as she pitched to and fro in her fits, and then loosed one final breath and died.

"The said Petford, being much aggrieved for the death of his only child, cried what witch hath murdered Martha, and looked upon me strangely. I saith that none ha' killed his child but it was God's will, and then I hastened back to Salem.

"Some weeks hence Susanna Cory saith to Nathaniel, my husband, that she had heard the said Petford tell Goody Oliver that I must surely have written my name in the Devil's book. He ha' spake sundry unfair cruelties by me though I only crafted physick for his daughter, thereby murdering my good name, and since then I ha' felt angry carriages in the town."

As she read her account the townsfolk gathered in the meetinghouse listened rapt, gasping aloud at the drama of her recitation. When she finished, the room vibrated with controversy as the onlookers weighed her statement, dying down to a subdued hush when the clerk stood up from his desk.

Goodwife Dane passed her deposition to the clerk, lowered her gaze to the floor, and resumed her seat on the bench. Whispers eddied around her, but she gave no sign of hearing them.

"If Goodwife Cory be here she shall render her deposition," demanded Appleton, reasserting his control over the room. How he hated these old gossips with their wagging fingers.

A frank-looking woman of about fifty years stood from her place next to Goody Dane. She held her head stiffly, her hands planted on her hips, unashamed of the darning and patches that spotted her dress. She pulled a paper from her own pocket, held it up close to her good eye, and read aloud in a rasping monotone.

"I testify and saith that as I passed the said Petfahd's house one fawnoon I huhd the said Petfahd tell Goody Olivah that that Deliverance Dane of Salem is a common rogue and witch that she ha' murdered his darter as part of her pledge to do the Devil's work. I tarried and saith to that Petfahd that she seemed none a witch to me but only a wise woman. I saith also that I ha' known the said Deliverance's mother and that she were cunning also. The Olivah then countehed that Deliverance once bought several bottles of her and that when she asked Goody Dane whehfoah she wanted bottles she said to read the watah with. Goody Olivah and Goodman Petfahd then told diverse other tales of felonious sawceries which I could scarce believe. I ventured to the afawsaid Dane's house to tell them what were being said."

After surrendering her testimony to the clerk, Goody Cory cast a glower toward the man whom Appleton assumed to be Petford, a roguish-looking sort sitting on the opposite bench with his head cupped in his hands. She sat and folded her arms, sniffing her disapproval of the proceedings.

"Very well," said Appleton. "If Nathaniel Dane be present, he shall deliver his deposition."

A tall young man seated on Goody Dane's other side rose. He was simply and neatly dressed, and looked like he might smell pleasantly of burning leaves. There was an out-of-doors quality to his countenance that made Appleton muse that this Goodman Dane would be a top fowler.

The man uncrumpled a little slip of paper, glanced down at his wife, and then paused a moment to draw breath. Appleton noted that the young man's eyes had dark circles under them, and that his face was whitish yellow under his sunburn. The room waited.

"I testify and saith," he read, pronouncing each word with deliberation, "that my wife be no kind of witch, but that the said Petah Petfahd ha' hardened his heaht for sadness at the loss of his child Mahther, and only sought to blame where naught could be helped."

He started to recrumple the paper before Elias plucked it out of his hands and then settled himself again next to his wife. Appleton just glimpsed Goodman Dane brush his fingertips over his wife's knee, and in that tender gesture the true depth of Dane's fear unfurled before him. To have one's wife talked about as a sorcerer was a worrisome thing indeed. If she did not prevail in this slander case, the rumors would only grow worse; a reputation for demoniac doings might never be undone. *Heaven help them if Petford not be found guilty,* he reflected. To think that a weak man's grief could undo a young family such as this. Appleton, embarrassed by this limpid feeling of pity and sorrow for the couple seated before him, looked for help back at the clerk. Elias prompted him by mouthing the name of the next witness.

"If Goodwife Mary Oliver be here she shall present her deposition," Appleton barked.

A woman of indistinct middle years arose on the other side of the meetinghouse aisle, her puckered face bristling with a tobacco-stained mustache. Just looking at her made Appleton think of tart pickled plums, and he pursed his lips with displeasure. She unfolded her own sheet of paper, raised her nose an inch or so, and spoke.

"I testify and saith that the said Deliverance Dane was a known healah and like a witch also, sost say so could be no defamement. One John Godfrey did tell me at this instant month that he hud a calf which were wasted and afflicted and asked the said Goody Dane whehfoah the animal was sick. She took watah of the calf into a bottle and boilt it in a kittle upon the fyah, whereupon she told the said Godfrey that his calf would be well though it was bewitched. And thus the calf was wal."

At this the assembly gasped aloud, and a fresh swell of murmurs swept through the meetinghouse.

"Silence!" bellowed Appleton. "You shall continue, woman."

Goody Oliver seemed to enjoy the effect of her testimony, surveying her audience with a proud smirk. "Anothah time," she began again, "I ha' sought physick from heh for a pained foot. She bade me entah heh house and did apply some liniment to my foot which she made by mashing hairbs and readin' in some book. I asked her what book war this and she said nowt but placed the book on a high shelf and asked me if my foot weh feeling bettah, which it was."

The townsfolk gathered in the meetinghouse burst forth in a fresh torrent of commentary as Goody Oliver pressed her lips together in satisfaction. She surrendered her deposition to Elias with great ceremony, remained standing a moment longer than was strictly necessary, and then resumed her seat. Appleton gazed on her with distaste. He could already imagine her recounting this minor testimony to her neighbor over a fence post with all the authority attendant on a capital trial. *Telt 'em, I did*, he imagined her saying. *That Dane shan't think to chahge so much of me next time my foot be pained!* Scurrilous hag.

"Mr. Saltonstall," Appleton intoned, casting an impatient eye on the muttering audience, "you shall examine the defendant."

In the far rear corner of the meetinghouse a pair of boots adorned with overlarge, well-buffed buckles dropped down from where they had been resting, crossed, on the seat of an empty chair. Their owner, dressed in overcoat and breeches of fitted richness, fashionably snug about the elbows, topped by an ostentatious lace collar stretching almost to his shoulders, pulled himself up to his full six feet and ambled to the front of the room. *Someone ought to have a word with young Richard Saltonstall*, Appleton reflected. *I'd slice those curls off myself given half a chance.* Richard's father had never carried himself so. No sooner does God grant favor on your ships than you forget to pay obeisance to God.

"Thank you, sir," said the lawyer, his voice polished and confident. "'T'would be my pleasure." He turned to face the crowded benches and announced "Goodman Peter Petford, defendant, shall submit to examination!"

The roguish man whom Appleton had noticed rocking and holding his head during the depositions looked around himself and rose, uncertain. Saltonstall gestured him toward a chair at the side of the library table, and Petford seated himself uneasily. In the corner Elias hovered, quill poised to jot down his every utterance. Saltonstall looked to Appleton for approval, and Appleton nodded.

"Goodman Petford, yeoman," Saltonstall began, "you stand accused of sundry acts of slander for telling lies most grievous and spreading ill will of Goodwife Dane in the town. You are now before authority. I expect the truth of you."

"I am a gospel man," said Petford, his voice wavering. He hung his head down near his shoulders, gaze averted. Appleton noticed that Petford's cheeks appeared hollow and dark, the skin of his head clinging to his skull. He looked dreadful, broken.

"How came you to ask Goodwife Dane to call upon your ailing daughter?" asked Saltonstall, addressing his question boldly to the assembled populace. He stood with his hands clasped behind his back, voice booming into every corner of the meetinghouse.

"I ha' heard tell that she were able with physick for those ill," muttered Petford.

"Who spoke thusly?" demanded the lawyer.

"Them as took notice of it," said Petford, unsure. "Goody Dane be known in the town."

"And Martha your daughter was some poorly."

"Of a Monday she were at her labors in the gahden, only to take to her bed Tuesday eve. One week hence she were dead."

"Dead how?" asked Saltonstall.

"I know not," whispered Petford. "She cried out in toahments and said she was pricked. Her clothes seemed to trouble her, as though she were boilt up." His voice caught for an instant, and he paused to clear his throat. "She was in her fits," he finished.

"Did Goodwife Dane come direct you called her?" prodded Saltonstall.

"She did, and expressed no surprise that I would ask her," Petford nodded.

"She came to your house to see the child," Saltonstall confirmed.

"She did."

"How did the aforesaid Dane minister to the child?"

Petford scowled, thinking. "It seemed she held her head and whispered to her, then fed her something from within her pocket."

"What sort of physick did she give the child?" asked Saltonstall.

"A tincture of some kind, I dasn't know what."

Saltsonstall paced thoughtfully across the room, nodding. "And how smelt it?" he asked, cocking one eyebrow at the defendant.

"Most foul," said Petford.

"And the child did drink the physick?" Saltonstall continued, this time looking directly at the men of the jury. They sat in a body, frowning, Palfrey nodding his head.

"She did," said Petford, "and on a sudden she war sorely molested by invisible hands, as if she were beaten about the head and shouldeahs." At this revelation the crowd gasped, and many eyes turned in their corners toward where Deliverance Dane was sitting.

"Did you see her beaten?" asked Saltonstall.

"I sar not the hands, but I sar her body twitch, and heard her cries."

"Then what did you?"

Petford paused a moment, looking down at his hands. He pressed his lips together and lifted his face for the first time to the waiting meetinghouse. The townsfolk watched, waiting. Knitting needles stopped. "I war so affrighted that I couldnae move, and begged Goody Dane to make her torments stop. But she looked steadfast upon me, and held her arms above her heid, and saith some mumblings that had no sense, and her eyes glowed like burning coals. My limbs were frozen to the spot, as though unseen bands had tied me. Marther's cries grew quiet and she fell back amongst the bedding,

and she did not move again. Then I knew this must be witchcraft that ha'
killed my Marther, that this Deliverance Dane must be a wicked sorcerah!"

A commotion broke out as the young woman leapt to her feet and cried,
"You dare thus to lie in all this assembly! I am wronged! She was bewitched,
but *not by me*!"

The audience exploded in a flurry of shouts and scraping chair legs,
women wailing and clutching their hands together. Appleton stood from his
armchair and commanded, "You shall sit quiet, Goodwife Dane!" He saw
Goody Dane's husband grab her by the hand and pull her back into her seat.
Her cheeks burned scarlet, and her white-blue eyes grew paler.

Saltonstall waved his hands in a gesture of calm, meeting the eyes of the
meetinghouse with a knowing gaze. The shouts died gradually into a low
rumble, and Saltonstall nodded with authority.

"If," he resumed, "the child were bewitched, how came Goodwife Dane
to know it?"

"I know nowt," said Petford, "but that she bewitched her."

Saltonstall strode to the center of the room, standing arms folded with
his back to the witness. "Have you heard tell of others so troubled?" he
boomed to the back of the room.

"These several months since Marther died I ha' heard tell sundry other
tales of Deliverance's wickedness. There are them as feel afeart when she
cast her eye on them," claimed Petford, his voice growing stronger.

Saltonstall moved to stand directly in front of the jury, hands clasped
behind his back. "Are you a liar, Goodman Petford?" he asked, eyes locked
on Lieutenant Davenport, the jury foreman.

"I am not," affirmed Petford.

"Do you swear so to this jury and these standers-by?" Saltonstall asked,
still standing before the jury.

"I do," said Petford.

"Very well," said Saltonstall. "You may step down."

Petford made his way shakily to the bench where he had been seated
while the assembly resumed its debate over the merits of the case. Goody

Dane sat immobile, back straight, her hands clasped in her husband's, pretending to ignore the vast tide of ill feeling that was lapping at her feet.

Appleton turned to instruct the jury in their deliberations but paused, taken aback. The hatred toward Goody Dane that Appleton saw twisting Goodman Palfrey's face told him already what the verdict would be.

CHAPTER FOUR

Cambridge, Massachusetts

Mid-June

1991

"THERE IS THE DISTINCT POSSIBILITY THAT IT COULD BE A NAME," remarked Manning Chilton, turning the little slip of parchment over in his hands.

"You think?" Connie asked. She shifted in the stiff wooden chair opposite her advisor's desk, peeling the backs of her knees one after the other off of the seat. This was the first real summer day of the season, and a trickle of sweat was working its way from under her armpit down her rib cage. Connie always faintly worried that her disheveled appearance would reveal the disordered state within herself. She marveled that Professor Chilton seemed impervious to the elements—she had never seen his shoes caked with winter salt or his palms touched with sweat. He sat today behind his broad leather-topped desk, crisp Oxford cloth shirt matched with a tidy bow tie. He laid the parchment on his desk and settled back in his armchair, looking at her.

"But of course. The Puritans, as you know, were rather partial to names drawn from the cardinal virtues."

"Well, sure," Connie agreed. "But I thought they generally favored biblical names. Sarah, Rebecca, Mary . . ."

The dryness and warmth in the room drained her concentration. *You'd think with all their money Harvard could install some central air*, she thought. A fan perched atop Chilton's bookcase oscillated in the afternoon sun, stirring the heavy air near the ceiling of the office without managing to cool it.

"That they did," said Chilton. "But they had a distinct fondness for the virtues as well. Quite common, really. Chastity, Mercy, what have you."

"But Deliverance?" she pressed. "I hadn't encountered that one before."

"Not as common as Mercy, perhaps, but not unheard of," he replied, bringing his fingertips into a little temple shape before him, elbows on the armrests of his chair. "You found this where, again?"

"My grandmother's house. Marblehead," said Connie, pulling the slip back across Chilton's desk.

"A puzzle," said Chilton. Behind his fingertips his eyes glimmered with interest, as if a delicious shape had crossed before him that Connie could not see. "Perhaps you could stop by their historical society to ask. Or check in the local church records to see if there is a birth or marriage entry. Just to satisfy your curiosity, of course."

Connie nodded. "I think I might," she said, cradling the slip in her palm. She had not told Chilton about the key, largely because she could not explain its being where she found it. Why would anyone have hidden a key inside a Bible? The discovery had puzzled her since she'd found the key with its curious parchment. She carried it in her pocket, fingering it every so often, as if meaning could be leached out of the metal.

"But, Connie," said Chilton, gazing at her over his folded hands, "where do we stand with the dissertation proposal? I had expected to see something by now."

"I know, Professor Chilton," said Connie, shrinking inwardly. She had hesitated at first to take her find to him, for fear that the full weight of his expectations would descend upon her. Now she saw them massing over his head like a great cloud, or a tarpaulin filling with rainwater, about to spill over. "I'm sorry. I've been so absorbed by having to sort everything out with this house." Even as she said the words, the excuse sounded feeble.

"Your responsibility is to your research," he began, pushing back his chair. The ringing of the telephone on his desk interrupted him midword. Irritated, he looked down at the telephone, over at Connie, and then back at the telephone. "Blast," he said, "would you excuse me a moment?" and picked up the receiver.

Connie accepted the momentary reprieve gratefully and turned toward the books lining Chilton's office, letting her gaze roam over the spines. Connie and Liz had often joked that grad students make terrible dinner party guests, because they cannot be gotten away from reading the spines of the books.

The shelves within closest reach of the desk all held essential texts of American colonial history—narratives of the settlement of English colonists, of the early Indian wars, of the collapse of the Puritan theocracy. She owned most of them herself. The higher shelves held books that she had never heard of: *Alchemical Symbolism in Jungian Psychoanalysis. Alchemy and the Formation of the Collective Unconscious. History of Medieval Chemistry.*

"I am aware of that," Chilton said quietly into the receiver. "But I can assure you, the paper will be ready. Yes." Connie kept her gaze steady on the bookshelves. Behind her, she heard Chilton clear his throat. Glancing over her shoulder, Connie's eyes met Chilton's and saw that he was waiting, his hand over the telephone receiver.

"Oh!" Connie exclaimed, sensing his meaning. "I'm sorry." She stood, excusing herself from the room.

Connie idled in the vestibule before Chilton's office, looking with disinterest at the ceiling. For a few minutes she heard murmurs from behind the door, broken suddenly by the sound of Chilton raising his voice, muffled but clearly audible.

"My God, how many times must I say it! September, at the Colonial Association conference!" he bellowed. Connie frowned. Chilton never raised his voice. She edged farther away from his office door, staring hard at a painting hanging on the far wall of the vestibule. It was a sickly green landscape, with a blasted half tree trunk in the foreground. The sky was blackened with storm clouds, obscuring a heavy yellow moon on the left side of the canvas and a bloody sun on the right. Eerie. Who would want to have to look at that every day?

"You have my word," Chilton said behind the office door. "Yes. Before you make the decision, I would ask you to wait until you have seen what I have to offer." His voice dropped again, and though she told herself that she was focusing only on the painting, her curious ears strained to hear what else Chilton said. The words were too muffled to make out. *Substance*, she thought he said, *rather than stone*. Then she could not hear any more. Several minutes passed in silence, Connie's gaze traveling along the winding river in the landscape painting until it curved, vanishing into a forbidding wilderness. The painting was so detailed that she could almost recognize the many different species of herb and vine, grouped incongruously together, as if night plants and day plants could all simultaneously exist, flowering all at once.

"I do not want you to be sidetracked by trifles," Chilton snapped, causing Connie to jump where she stood. The painting had so absorbed her attention that she had not heard the door open between his office and the vestibule. Stepping back into the office after him, Connie blinked, trying to shake the disquieting image of the landscape from her mind. She settled into the seat across from Chilton's desk, baffled by what she had overheard.

"Well?" Chilton said, leaning forward. Connie wrestled her attention away from the image with its half-formed associations and forced herself to attend to what he had asked her. What had it been? Something about wasting her time with trifles. What was he talking about?

"I'm sorry, Professor Chilton. I . . . it's just so warm today. What did you just say?" Connie asked, loathing the words as they came out. She always felt her tokenism in the department keenly and took pains to appear focused whenever she met with Chilton. Her ears burned as Chilton's mouth drew into a withering smile.

"Trifles. We don't want you to be distracted from your work," he reiterated.

"No, of course not," she stammered.

"It's all well and good to have these other interests, spending the summer cleaning and whatnot," he continued. "But we cannot regard the summer as if we were mindless little undergraduates, can we?" Chilton lapsed into the royal "we" only in the deepest throes of aggravation. She found the degree of his displeasure unnerving. "My girl, you simply have to focus. In the academy, the summer is when we are fortunate enough to be free to give uninterrupted attention to our work. I would hate to see you fritter away the opportunities that lie before you."

Connie paused, unsure if she was reading his tone correctly. *My girl*, she thought. Janine Silva would lose her mind if she found out that Chilton referred to Connie in these demeaning ways. If challenged, she knew that Chilton would think he was being encouraging, even affectionate. That he did not apply such nicknames to his male graduate students Chilton would explain as a sign of his special regard for her. His smile broadened, condescension glinting in its corners. Without thinking, she rubbed the key inside her pocket for reassurance.

"I have no intention of wasting my time this summer, Professor Chilton," Connie said coldly.

"Of course you don't, my dear. I just have no wish to see distractions get the better of you. All we need is a remarkable, unusual primary source. When you follow up on your little mystery, don't lose sight of your real goal. In fact . . ." He paused, leaning back in his chair and reaching his long fingers toward the pipe that rested in a brass ashtray on his desk. As a match flamed behind Chilton's cupped hand, Connie felt the meeting drawing to a close. He shook the match out, finishing his thought. "This find of yours could be serendipitous. Your source awaits you. All you need to do is look."

She rose, nodding, and slid her bag over her shoulder. With one hand resting on the knob of his office door, Connie turned back to him. "Out of curiosity, Professor Chilton," she ventured, treading lightly, "will you be speaking at the Colonial Association conference this year? I was trying to decide if I should go." She eyed him, wondering if he could tell that she was prodding at the substance of his telephone call.

For a long minute he watched her under his lids, as though balancing a mental equation. At length he puffed on his pipe with two thin lips, releasing a haze of smoke through his nose, and chuckled. "Ah," he said. "So you heard me." He puffed again. "I have been working on a particular project for some time. I suspect it will be ready for the Colonial Association, yes."

"What sort of project?" she asked, eyes sliding a degree down his face. Chilton's skin looked sallow. The folds around his eyes and mouth seemed deeper than she remembered.

"Ach—plenty of time for all that later," Chilton said, his voice glossed with a casualness that failed to conceal its evasion. "I know that you are anxious to get under way with your own research."

"I am," Connie said, watching him. He smiled at her, but it was a smile drained of warmth or mirth. Connie struggled to find a word to describe his smile to herself, but the closest that she could come was *hungry*.

THE FOLLOWING DAY, THE SUMMER AIR GREW DENSE WITH MOISTURE, and a heavy layer of damp descended onto Connie's skin. The atmosphere in Granna's house grew leaden and thick with the heat, and so Connie fled to the main street in what passed for Marblehead's downtown. She stood in the lone telephone booth, one sandal propping the door open, receiver wedged between her shoulder and her ear.

"Thank you, I'll wait," she said to the sleepy-sounding person on the other end of the telephone. The receiver clicked and went blank as she was placed on hold. Across the street, teenagers in bathing suits clustered in an ice cream shop, flipping through months-old copies of *People* and elbowing one another. She wiped her forearm across her upper lip and caught herself staring at the chattering kids with a feeling akin to envy. Or perhaps nostalgia. Connie had nearly forgotten that there had been a time in her life when summer was for loafing, for filling long, bored hours.

The receiver clicked again. "Nothing?" Connie replied to the crackling voice. "Are you sure?" The telephone chirped and squawked.

"What about alternative spellings? Like *D-e-i-g-n*?" The phone squabbled again. She scribbled notes on the pad that she held open over the phone bookshelf.

"Okay," she said, sighing in frustration. "Thank you." She replaced the telephone in its cradle, resting with her hand on the hot plastic receiver. Connie contemplated calling Grace. She had not spoken with her mother at length since arriving at Granna's house, and now she idly wondered what Grace would have to say about the peculiar, vivid daydreams that had been intruding into her consciousness over the past couple of weeks. Connie pressed her lips together, scowling. Either Grace would worry that Connie was not sleeping enough, and so launch into a long discourse on what herbal teas would help; or, she would believe that Connie was "tapping into her second sight" and would want to talk about aura healing. Only Grace, of all the people Connie knew, would consider hallucinating to be a good thing. On an impulse Connie dialed the number for the Santa Fe house, allowed it to ring four or five times, and hung up just as Grace's machine started to say *Blessed be this day, dear caller!*

Connie blew an exasperated breath through her nose and stepped with relief out of the booth. The scorching afternoon felt almost cool after the greenhouselike glass box. She felt the top layer of sweat lift off of her skin. That took care of the historical society, then. No records of any kind that mentioned a Deliverance Dane. Or a Deliverance Deign. Or any other kind of Deliverance, for that matter. She pulled the key out of the pocket of her cutoffs and turned it over in the white afternoon. It glinted.

Chilton had also suggested that she try local church records. That morning she stopped by the Marblehead meetinghouse, and a friendly matron in bright Lilly Pulitzer Bermuda shorts informed her that First Church by the Sea, Congregational was affiliated with First Church in Salem until around 1720, and that their early membership records were stored in Salem. The afternoon felt so dense and slow that Connie almost welcomed the excuse to travel to the neighboring town. When that search turned up empty, as she expected it probably would, she would adjourn to the beach in defeat. A striped umbrella and towel waited in the trunk of her Volvo, along with a bathing suit and a horror novel bought at the church thrift shop. Chilton's disapproving face hovered before her momentarily, and Connie glowered. *No one can work in this heat*, she insisted to herself, and the thought of Chilton dissipated. She wondered if Liz would want to come up for a swim. Then Connie remembered that it was a Wednesday—Liz would be teaching.

"Small rocky road, please," she said to the teenage girl behind the ice cream counter as she pulled a crumpled dollar bill out of her pocket.

The girl looked at her, then turned back to the television sitting on the counter behind her. *Days of Our Lives*, from the look of it.

"Be right with ya," said the girl. On any other day Connie would have been impatient with the girl, but it was too hot even for that. She hooked her thumbs in her cutoff pockets and leaned against the counter to wait. She ought to be grateful that she, at least, did not have to wear a pink-and-white-striped hat while working. But Connie knew that she could not in good conscience laze at the beach that afternoon. If she was putting off pawing through Granna's house, she must at least make progress on her research. She dangled her flip-flop on the end of a toe, turning over in her mind the lack of Deliverances in the town records.

Perhaps this means that Chilton is wrong. Maybe it isn't a name. Maybe it's something else. But what?

When the show cut to commercial, the girl unfolded herself from her chair and sashayed up to the register. "What size'd ya want again?" she asked.

"Small," said Connie. Then adding, "In a waffle cone." *Life is short*, she thought. Get it in a waffle cone.

"Shah," said the girl, making clear to Connie that she was doing her a favor. Connie watched her carve round balls of ice cream out of the vats in the cooler below, suntanned arms sinewy from the effort. Under her striped hat, the girl radiated the casual indifference of the townie. In another year or two, her prettiness would start to look a little tough, and the lines around her mouth would harden.

"You all set?" she asked, passing Connie the cone.

"Actually," Connie said, sliding her dollar across the countertop, "I wonder if you could give me directions to the First Church in Salem."

The girl regarded Connie impassively, rolling her gum to the other side of her mouth. She chewed once. Twice.

"'S Wensdee," said the girl.

"Yeah," said Connie.

The girl stared at her a moment more, then shrugged. "One fawteen," she said, jerking her thumb, "then ya left on Practah."

"Thanks," said Connie. The girl arched her eyebrows, nodding toward the coffee can on the counter marked TIPS. Connie stuffed a quarter into the can and moved back into the glaring day.

AN HOUR OR SO LATER CONNIE STOOD IN THE DOORWAY OF THE MEETING-house, unable to discern any shapes more precise than the shadowy rows of pews marching forward into the dark. The door swung shut behind her, blocking out the summer day and encasing her in cool air, scented with wood and furniture polish. She had knocked at the door to the office across the street but found it locked. A peek through the mail slot had revealed a tidy gray office with all papers put away, and empty chairs. She waited, her eyes straining to adjust. The outlines of tall, arched windows began to resolve themselves along the walls, and the room's contours gradually emerged from within the dimness. Occasional rustlings and creakings circulated around the periphery, but the stark, echoing interior made Connie unsure where they were coming from.

"Hello?" she called, and her voice sounded hollow in the cavernous room.

"Yeah?" someone replied, and again the sound was placeless. Connie peered left and right but saw no one.

"I'm sorry to bother you," she began, "but I am looking for the minister?" She felt irritated with herself for turning the statement into a question.

"He's on the Vineyard," called the muffled, disembodied voice. "Not back 'til August."

An unexpected development. Connie paused. This would be the perfect opportunity to go recuperate on the beach. But she felt the key's weight in her pocket, its outline pressed into her thigh.

"Well I don't really need to see him, exactly," Connie demurred. "I just wanted to check something in the church archives."

"Hold on," said the voice, which now sounded as if it were coming from above. Connie heard more rustlings, followed by a shrill whine like a fishing reel being cast, and a dark shape thunked down about three feet in front of her, right in the center aisle of the church. She stepped back in surprise. Presently the shape unfolded into the form of a rangy young man, dressed in paint-dappled coveralls, with a tool belt slung around his slim hips. He unhooked his rappelling harness from the ropes that Connie now perceived to be hanging from a scaffold near the ceiling, and strode forward to take her hand.

"Hello," he said, grinning crookedly at her surprise.

"Oh!" she gasped. Her mouth opened and, when no further sound came out, closed again, and her hand snaked up to grasp hold of the end of her braid where it dangled over her shoulder, as it often did when she was nervous or excited. His smile widened.

"Hello," Connie said finally, releasing the braid and returning his hand-shake. His palm was dry and firm, and Connie suddenly was aware of how sweaty and rumpled she felt.

"I don't think Bob would mind if I showed you the archives," said the man, pulling her back into the conversation. "Hardly anyone ever wants to look in there." Under his nose Connie just glimpsed a septum ring, and she smiled, amused. He probably had a grunge band. Connie pictured him explaining sincerely to some hapless girl that he really needed to get serious about his *music*. She smothered a giggle.

"Bob?" she asked, holding her laughter under her tongue.

"The minister. I thought you knew him?" The man looked at her curiously.

"Oh, no," she said. "I don't, no. I'm a graduate student. Starting research on my dissertation."

"Yeah?" said the young man, leading Connie down the side aisle toward a stairwell. "Where? I went to BU for my master's. Preservation studies."

Connie was surprised, and just as quickly ashamed of herself. She had taken him for a handyman. "Harvard," she said, sheepish. "I do American colonial history. My name's Connie."

"I knew some people in that program. Few years ago, now. But if you're a colonialist, then you are in the right place." He smiled. If he had sensed her error, he did not let on.

The young man ushered Connie toward a doorway hidden under the staircase that led, Connie presumed, to a choir loft, and pulled a large ring of keys off of his tool belt. He located a small, ornate one and fit it into the door, pushed the door open, and gestured for her to enter. Connie felt his eyes on her as she edged past him through the doorway, close enough that her T-shirt brushed against his coveralls.

The room was windowless, illuminated by a single overhead fluorescent light that hissed and snapped as it was turned on. On each wall towered row upon row of almost identical leather-bound reference books, ranging in appearance from tattered to almost new. To the immediate right, tucked under the curve of the stairwell, stood wooden card catalogue files, and in the center of the tiny room rested a plain card table flanked by folding chairs.

"Christenings," said the man, pointing to each of the bookcases in turn, "Marriages, Deaths, and—my favorite—Annals of Membership. That's where you will find who was permitted to officially join the church." He paused. "And who was required to leave it."

"This is incredible," Connie exclaimed, surveying the room. "I'm amazed that you all have so much material. And intact!" She placed her hand atop the card catalogue. "Indexed, even!"

"Mostly, yes. A few gaps here and there." The man folded his arms, smiling. "It's not 'me all,' however. I'm just working on the restoration of the cupola. Should be done by July, August sometime. Then I'll do the steeple, and then it's off to another job up in Topsfield." He produced a business card from a pocket in his coverall and handed it to Connie. SAMUEL HARTLEY, it read. STEEPLEJACK. "I'm Sam," he clarified.

Connie broke out in laughter before she could check herself. "*Steeplejack?* Are you serious?"

The man—Sam—looked at her with mock wounded pride. "But of course!" he replied. "I'll admit there aren't that many of us around. After grad school I worked for a while at the Society for the Advancement of New England Antiquarianism."

"They have an awesome preservation program," Connie interjected, recognizing the name. "Some of those properties would just be knocked down if it weren't for them."

"That's true," Sam agreed. "They do great things. But I hated sitting at a desk all day. I mean, I went into preservation so that I could touch cool old stuff that no one else is allowed to. So"—he gestured to his tool belt—"I moved into restoration work. New England is just about the only place with enough antique steeples to go around."

Connie grinned at him. "Plus you get to wear your rappelling gear," she said.

"That, too," said Sam, smiling back at her. "So. What are we research-ing?"

Connie was tempted to show him the key. She found his warmth and enthusiasm infectious—so different from the detached chill of the career academic. She tried to picture Manning Chilton radiating fervor for his ob-scure histories of alchemy, but the image fell flat. Even her thesis student, Thomas, who Connie felt certain was destined for the academic life, ap-proached his passion in a methodical manner that seemed already purged of wonder. Talking to Sam reminded her of a time when she still found history exciting, tantalizing. He leaned in the doorway, one boot crossed over the other, arms folded. His forearms, under the rolled sleeves of his work clothes, were tanned and lined with muscle. She realized that she was staring and pulled her gaze away.

"I was going through some old papers in my grandmother's house in Marblehead," she said, hedging somewhat in her description, leaving out men-tion of the key. "And I found something. I think it's a name, but I'm not cer-tain." She pulled the tiny parchment from her pocket and handed it to him.

Sam rubbed his thumb over the paper, gazing at it. "Could be." He nod-ded. "And you've tried the historical society out there, I take it."

"Nothing. No Deliverances of any kind. Then I tried the church, and they told me that their records are all here."

"And you're thinking it dates from the first period of colonial settle-ment?" he asked. "Why?"

"Well, the age of the paper and the handwriting, for one," said Connie. "And if it is a name, it seems too old-fashioned to be Revolutionary. And if it were nineteenth century, wouldn't it more likely be 'Temperance' than 'De-liverance'? But really I'm just working on a guess. It might not even be a name at all."

Sam scratched the stubble under his chin. "All your reasoning seems to make sense. The handwriting certainly resembles some early examples I've seen." He caught her looking at him, eyebrows raised. "I spend a lot of time at the landmarks commission office," he explained.

Connie paused, surveying the rows of undisturbed records books. "I guess this could take a while," she said.

"I needed a break from painting anyway," Sam said with a laugh.

THREE HOURS LATER, SAM AND CONNIE SAT BACK TO BACK AT THE CARD table, hands grimy with book spine fragments, resting. They had checked the card catalogue for the name in a myriad of different spellings, and when that proved futile, they started pulling ledgers off the shelves two and three at a time, beginning with the oldest. Their search had been fruitless so far—no Deliverance Dane in any of the christening records from 1629 all the way through 1720.

"'Course, if Dane was her married name, she wouldn't be in the christening records," Sam pointed out.

"True enough," said Connie. "But I had to start somewhere. That's one reason researching women can be so much trickier than researching men. Their names can change several times, depending on how many times they marry." She paused. "It's like they become different people."

Next they found only scattered marriage records for people with the last name Dane, including a Marcy Dane who married someone named Lamson in 1713. Neither of the married Danes were named Deliverance, and they did not appear to be related. They could not be completely sure, as some pages seemed to be missing from the marriage records for the 1670s, but after a few hours' unproductive research both were starting to suspect that the phrase might not be a name after all.

Then they plunged into the death records, skimming rapidly.

"Aw, here's poor Marcy Lamson again," murmured Connie, turning a brittle page in the deaths ledger dated *1750–1770*. "She died in 1763." She felt a strange tugging in her chest, unfamiliar and solemn. Connie propped her chin on one dirty hand and gazed into the middle distance.

"Something the matter?" asked Sam, looking up from the *1730–1750* deaths volume open across his knee.

"Oh, not really." Connie sighed. "Just thinking."

"It's weird, isn't it?" asked Sam, leaning closer to her over the card table and dropping his voice.

"What's weird?" she said, turning to him.

"That you can have this whole entire life, with all your opinions, your loves, your fears. Eventually those parts of you disappear. And then the people who could remember those parts of you disappear, and before long all that's left is your name in some ledger. This Marcy person—she had a favorite food. She had friends and people she disliked. We don't even know how she died." Sam smiled sadly. "I guess that's why I like preservation better than history. In preservation I feel like I can keep some of it from slipping away."

As he spoke Connie noticed that his face was attractive in a wonderfully flawed sort of way; it held a sharp, straight nose peeling with sunburn, and mischievous green eyes bracketed by deep smile lines. His hair was pulled back in a ponytail, a brown color bleached by the sun. Connie smiled at him.

"I can see that. But history's not as different as you might think." She brushed her fingers over Marcy Lamson's name scrawled on the page. "Don't you think Marcy would be surprised if she knew that some random people in 1991 were reading her name and thinking about her? She probably never even imagined 1991. In a way"—Connie hesitated—"it offers her a kind of immortality. At least this way she gets to be remembered. Or thought about. Noticed."

As her fingertip touched the surface of the page, Connie saw with stunning clarity the image of a smiling woman's face, freckled, shaded by a broad straw hat. She was old, her blue eyes lidded and soft, and she was laughing at something. Then just as instantly the impression vanished, and Connie felt like the breath had been squeezed out of her chest. The intensity of the effect was staggering. Connie no longer felt like she could explain it to herself as a daydream; the sensation was utterly different, like having the real world replaced with a bright cellophane film still, overlying her field of vision.

"True," Sam was saying, closing the book on his lap and folding his hands behind his head. He leaned back in his chair, exhaling, not noticing anything amiss.

"Well," she said, smoothing her voice and massaging her temple. She must discuss this with someone—Grace. Or maybe a doctor. "Looks like this was a waste of time. Thank you, Sam, for helping me out so much. I didn't mean to take over your whole afternoon."

"Are you kidding?" he said. "The cupola'll be there. I love an excuse to mess around in these archives. But," he said, "there's one place left for us to look. Annals of Membership."

Connie groaned. "Come on. If she was a person, which we don't know, then she wasn't born here, she wasn't married here, and she didn't die here. What would she be doing in Annals of Membership?"

Sam made a *pshaw*ing sound. "Look at this. And I thought Harvard was supposed to be a good school." He rose, pulled three volumes from the bottom bookshelf by the door, and dropped them unceremoniously on the card table. "Don't they teach you how to do thorough research at your big fancy university? This is a very second-tier-school attitude I am sensing. Let's go, Cornell. One more hour and we'll be done."

Connie reached for the volume nearest her, laughing in spite of herself. Liz had gone to Cornell and was forever reminding people, bristling, that it was in the Ivy League. Sam's teasing warmth pushed aside the spreading ache in Connie's head, bringing her back to the real pleasures of her work. She cast an appreciative glance over this strange young man, who made her feel disarrayed and yet was somehow making her better at her work. He grinned back.

They worked for a further hour in silence, paging through lists of townspeople proposed for full church membership, some names appearing repeatedly over decades before their membership was confirmed. Connie marveled at the reserve, the closed-ness implied in these pages, and felt a sour bloom of distaste for this culture that she had given her life to studying. On most days she enjoyed the opacity of this kind of archive. It was a puzzle waiting to be solved, disparate isolated facts that, if properly assembled, could create a picture of a world that had long since ceased to exist, but that had left residues of itself almost everywhere that she looked. But sometimes the completed picture that the facts implied was startling in its cruelty. For all their idealization by the fantasists of history, the New England colonists could be as harsh and abrasive as any other real, flawed, people: petty, deceitful, manipulative. She reached for the final ledger, riffling through the blank first pages until she found the title page. Her eyebrows pulled up in surprise. EX-COMMUNICATIONS, it read.

The book appeared still technically to be in use, as there were several unfilled pages toward the back. The last recorded excommunication dated from the mid-nineteenth century, after which the First Church of Salem must have turned its attention toward less doctrinaire problems. Many New England congregations had been intensely active in emancipation work in the years leading up to the Civil War, and Connie imagined that congregational infighting must have seemed a petty concern when compared with human slavery. Slowly she paged her way back to the beginning.

The first excommunication dated from 1627, but a portion of the page was damaged by a water stain, and Connie could not make it out. Isolated cases turned up every few years after settlement, never with any explanation attached. A small cluster of cases all within a few years of one another seemed to correspond with the Antinomian crisis, when a religious schism over whether good behavior was sufficient to attain God's grace rocked the Puritan world. After the crisis subsided, the excommunications resumed their sporadic pattern until Connie turned one final page.

"My God!" Connie cried, unable to keep the excitement from her voice. "I know why Deliverance Dane isn't in any of the records!"

"What?" Sam asked, looking up from his ledger.

Connie hoisted her own book up to face him on the table and drew his attention to a line on the page. There, near the bottom of a lengthy list of hastily scrawled names, was written *Delliveranse Dane*, the spelling presumably mangled by a semiliterate clerk.

"Look at the year," said Connie.

Sam looked, and his eyes narrowed with confusion. He looked up at her, head cocked, waiting for her to elaborate.

The date read *1692*.

"Sam," Connie said, reaching across the table to grasp his arm, "Deliverance Dane was a witch!"

CHAPTER FIVE

===

"EXPLAIN THIS TO ME AGAIN," SAID SAM, SLIDING A HEAVY PINT OF beer toward Connie. She sat with her elbows on the bar, drumming her fingertips excitedly on the top of her head. Sam settled on the stool next to her and slurped the foam off of his own beer. At the opposite end of the bar, a small group of middle-aged men in orange foul-weather gear and Top-Siders joked and guffawed, clinking their Cape Codders together. The bar where they sat was dimly lit, hung with regatta pennants and sepia photographs of men in horn-rimmed glasses, grinning into a sun of forty years ago.

"This is one of the ten great sailing bars in the world," said Connie, re-calling one of the asides in the letter that her mother had sent her, together with the house key. In suggesting that Connie visit this bar while she was living in Granna's house, Grace recalled her teenager-hood spent loitering in this repurposed sail loft, watching local boys get tossed out on their ears and hustled home by the constable. Some of the raucousness seemed to have aged out of the loft since then, though the sailors at the end of the bar tried gamely to make up for it.

Connie had driven Sam with her back to Marblehead, an impulsive move. She had offered to buy him a round to thank him for helping her all afternoon, and he had come along naturally. No phone calls to make first, no clothes to change. Glancing sidelong at his profile next to her at the bar, Connie watched the texture of Sam's skin as he licked the foam from his upper lip. It was rich and satiny, the smile brackets around his eyes burned into place by the sun.

"Uh-huh," said Sam, scratching his stubble and eyeing the sailors more warily. "But the date," he prompted her. "I'm rusty on the seventeenth century. Tell me again."

"Mmmmm." Connie sighed, sipping her own beer. "I was so hot all day today." She draped her arms across the bar in front of her, feeling the afternoon's exhilaration ebb as she started to relax. "I usually don't like beer, but this is just perfect."

"*Connie*," he prodded, nudging her elbow with his knuckles. She paused, beer glass suspended halfway in the air, mouth still open. His eyes met hers, warm and eager.

"Right," she said after a minute, smiling. "The date." She swiveled on her stool to face him. "So it all started in January of 1692, when the daughter of Salem Village's minister, Samuel Parris, fell ill. Betty was her name. Pretty young, too—she was nine, and her father couldn't figure out what was the matter with her. He was kind of a divisive guy, this minister. Some people in the Village were totally behind him, but others thought he had demanded too much money. Over his years in the Village he made all sorts of unconventional demands, including free firewood, title to his parsonage—"

"Title to his parsonage! The nerve of him," Sam interrupted, voice tinged with sarcasm, holding a hand to his chest in false shock.

"Yeah, right?" Connie said, laughing, placing a hand on Sam's arm.

"Who does he think he is? So by the time Betty fell ill, Parris had already made a few firm enemies. The Villagers were pretty bristly people by all accounts, anyway."

Connie paused to sip her beer. "Rather like today, actually," she mused, and Sam smiled out of one side of his mouth. "Anyway," she continued, "Reverend Parris called a doctor, but the doctor couldn't figure out what was wrong."

"Not that a doctor would have been able to do much back then, anyway, right?" he asked.

"That's true," Connie agreed. "One of the weirdest things about this time period is that it's *before* the Scientific Revolution. They didn't have the scientific method, and so they couldn't tell the difference between correlation and causation. The world would have seemed like a big, incomprehensible progression of random occurrences and acts of God."

"That's why whenever I catch myself getting nostalgic about any period of history, I just think about *antibiotics*," Sam said, archly. "Do go on."

Connie grinned. "Anyway. The doctor—his name was Griggs, I think—probably would have just bled her, which would have made her even worse. This is right about when doctors are starting to first appear as a respected profession, expected to have a formal education. So maybe the doctor was just passing the buck, trying to save his reputation. Who knows? At any rate, he tells Reverend Parris that Betty isn't sick, she has been bewitched. And so the minister starts claiming in his sermons that evil has come to Salem Village. He thinks that his daughter is being punished because the town has grown sinful, and he tells everybody that the evil must be drummed out of town.

"Of course, it could be that Parris is passing the buck, too. Some historians think that the minister fueled the accusations to hide how unpopular he had become. Regardless, soon everybody is talking witchcraft, and other young girls in town start falling into fits just like Betty. Abigail Williams, Parris's niece, who lived as a servant in the minister's house, is one of the most famous ones. Arthur Miller used her as the protagonist of *The Crucible*."

"And so began the Salem witch panic," finished Sam. "Damn!" He wove his fingers together and cracked his knuckles.

"Right," said Connie. "And we all know what happened next. Reverend Parris's slave, Tituba, is accused of bewitching the girls. Historians argue about Tituba; no one has ever been able to decide for sure if she was black, or if she was Native American. Anyway, the important thing is that Tituba *confesses*! She says that the Devil came to her, wearing a long black coat, and promised her she could fly home to Barbados if she agreed to work for him." Connie sipped her beer again and smiled. "A few historians have pointed out how closely Tituba's description of the Devil resembles Reverend Parris himself. No small wonder. There was no other way for her to say what she really thought about the man."

Sam smiled.

"Anyway," Connie continued, "the minister tells her that she can have forgiveness from Jesus if she will only tell him who else in the town has pledged to work for the Devil. She names a couple of women, local beggars, who of course say that they are innocent. But the afflicted girls all support Tituba's accusations. Soon enough things spiral completely out of control. Over the next several months, hundreds of people from all over Essex County are accused, and almost twenty are hanged. One man, Giles Corey, was even pressed to death between stones as the court tried to force him to enter a plea." Connie shuddered.

"That," said Sam, "would be a hideous way to die."

"The story goes that his last words were *More weight*," Connie remarked contemplatively. She took another sip from her beer, gazing into the middle distance for a moment before continuing. "Which is pretty hard-core, if you ask me. And that as he died someone used the tip of a cane to stuff his protruding tongue back into his mouth."

She paused, then seemed to shake off the unpleasant image. "But apart from that," Connie continued, "there have been a lot of competing explanations for why the panic spread the way that it did. Isolated cases of witchcraft popped up all over New England in the seventeenth century, but this was by far the most lethal. No one fully understands why it got so out of hand—whether the girls were just enjoying wielding power over mostly middle-aged women and educated men, which totally flipped the Puritan hierarchy, or whether there were other factors in play. But here's the thing. Before any of the accused witches were put to death, they were *excommunicated from the church.*"

She sipped at her beer again. "So anyone listed in that church record book as being excommunicated in 1692 was almost definitely caught up in the trials in some way. Probably because they were going to be hanged within the week."

"But why would they be kicked out of the church first?" Sam asked.

"Because witchcraft was a kind of heresy." Connie shrugged.

"Really?" asked Sam. "I thought it was more of an alternative religion. Like its own separate thing." One of the sailors at the end of the bar loudly recited an off-color joke that involved a blonde, a fish, and a bartender. His compatriots' shoulders rocked with laughter, and the bartender—herself a blonde—rolled her eyes and reached for another pint glass to polish.

"Actually, no," said Connie. "I mean, everything I have read implies that first of all, witchcraft was more of an imaginary threat than a real activity in the seventeenth century, and second of all, the ministers made a big deal of it because it was a profanation of Christian practice, borrowing all these prayers and devotional systems from pre-Reformation Catholicism. More than anything it represented people, and especially women, trying to take too much power into their own hands; power that Puritan theologians thought should belong only to God."

"So you're saying that witchcraft was just a projection of social anxieties, and nothing more," said Sam, folding his arms.

"Yeah." Connie sipped her beer again. "Pretty tough, being put to death because of a social anxiety."

"You almost finished with that beer?" Sam asked, watching her.

"Pretty much. Why?"

"Because I have something to show you. Come on."

They stepped out into the night, shadows falling between the saltbox houses forming navy blue pools on the gravel. Connie tucked her sweater more tightly around her shoulders and wished that she had thought to change into jeans. In Cambridge the night sky in summer was obscured by a hazy chemical orange glow, and the asphalt radiated heat that it absorbed during the day. Marblehead at night entered a cool, dark plane: the houses encased in shadow, the chill of the sea washing over the land, the stars like little points of ice. As Connie walked alongside Sam, matching his stride, she found that she could sense him there, in the dark next to her, unseen but present. The tips of her fingers and thumb on her right hand brushed themselves together, yearning to reach out for Sam's hand. Instead Connie thrust her fists deep into the pockets of her cutoffs, keeping her eyes on her feet.

"Before I was hired to do the cupola job, I had a few restoration projects going in Old Town," whispered Sam. Connie appreciated his whisper—it showed that he, too, was touched by the quiet of the town.

"What sort of restoration jobs?" she asked.

"Strip-outs, mostly," he said. "A lot of Boston people are buying up the old fishermen's houses and redoing them. A couple of times I've been brought in to rip out all the modifications that have built up in the houses over the years. Especially the houses that were divided into apartments in the fifties and sixties. New buyers come in and want to get rid of the acoustical tile ceilings, expose the original beams, add fancy new kitchens. I've been asked to consult on a few of these when the buyers actually care about preserving the historical character of the house."

"That's good, isn't it?" asked Connie.

"Good for me, 'cause I need the work, and good for them, 'cause they get a well-done house. Not so good if you are a fisherman, or if it's your apartment being bought out from under you for some banker's weekend retreat." He glowered. Connie smiled at him. "Sorry," he said. "That's one of my rants."

"Don't worry," Connie said. "I'm full of rants."

"But that's not why I brought it up. On one of those Old Town redos I found something pretty interesting. I want to show it to you."

"You mean we're going to someone's house?" Connie asked, alarmed.

"Don't worry," he reassured her.

He turned abruptly down a nameless side street, so narrow that a car could only just pass without taking a few front doors along with it. The houses along this street were short and packed tightly together, leading Connie to suspect that this had at one time been a mews, or a row of carriage houses and little barns to serve the grander houses one block away. Some of them were painted in cheerful, ridiculous colors—ochre, vermillion, puce. Tiny windows held planters overflowing with pansies and wilted tulips. "It's not far from here," said Sam, urging her to hurry.

They rounded another corner, to the street of houses that would have been served by the mews. These houses had twin chimney stacks and tidy wooden shingles, and a few of them were surrounded by modest but luscious green lawns dotted with dandelions. The houses were separated here and there by wooden fencing, or by a crumbling stone wall layered with moss, screened from one another by whispering oak trees. Connie estimated the houses' ages as ranging from the early eighteenth to the mid-nineteenth centuries—ship captains' houses, if not quite merchantmen's houses. The moonlight cast a gray-white sheen across the surface of the leaves and the grass, making the shadows blacker. Connie could smell burning apple wood from an unseen fireplace; the sensation reminded her of sitting in the kitchen of the Concord commune with Grace. Her heart swelled a little at the memory, and Connie resolved to reach Grace by telephone tomorrow. She could tell her that she had finally visited the sail loft; Grace would probably enjoy that. And she could tell her about the daydreams. Maybe.

Sam caught up Connie's hand to pull her after him as he moved toward the stone wall, but Connie balked. "Sam!" she whispered. "What are you doing? We can't just go sneaking into someone's yard!"

"Shhhhhhhh!" Sam shushed her, smiling. "There's no way they're home. And just in case, we'll tiptoe."

"Sam!" she hissed, her fear heightened by excitement and pleasure.

"C'mon!" He tightened his grip on her hand, and Connie thrilled at the warm feel of his skin, smooth but callused, allowing herself to be pulled along the stone wall deep into a little copse of woods between two of the houses. Sam touched his way along the wall, finally stopping by a block of granite, about two feet high, standing out at an angle from the stone wall. The wall and surrounding trees cast the block in thick shadow, and Connie looked nervously back at the nearer of the two houses, certain that she would catch a face behind a curtain, or the sudden snapping on of a porch light to show that they were about to be caught. "Hold on a sec," Sam muttered, rummaging in a pocket of his coveralls. Connie heard a snap and a hiss, and the whiff of phosphorous reached her just as the match flamed to life. "Okay," he said, crouching down to hold the flame near the granite block. "Now look at this."

Connie knelt next to him and gazed at the granite block, now illuminated in a bright yellow circle that collapsed the surface of the stone into a flat plane. On the block, Connie saw carved a simple stick figure of a man, about one foot tall, wearing a hat or headdress, hands and feet held out straight. Next to the left hand was carved a five-pointed star, next to the right a crescent moon, by the left foot a sun, and by the right foot a serpent or lizard. The carving was untutored and imprecise, errant chisel marks still visible in the old stone. It had clearly not been wrought by a headstone carver or other person trained for such work. Above the rough picture was carved a single word, in all capital letters: TETRAGRAMMATON.

Connie's eyes opened wide, unsure what she was seeing. "What is this?" she whispered. "I don't understand what I am looking at."

"This, my rationalist friend, is a boundary marker," replied Sam, shaking out the match and casting it aside into the grass. He lit another before continuing. "In the early days of settlement, one way to demark the boundary of your land before going to the trouble of building a fence was to place a big, visible stone block in each corner of your lot. If you look around Old Town you'll see these all over the place, sometimes right next to the front door of a house if the lot is very small."

"Right," said Connie. "I think I've noticed some of those. But the carving!"

"That's why I wanted you to see this. I found it under what used to be a compost heap when I was checking the structural safety of the wall for the new owners. Since finding this one I've come across a few others with carving marks, but most of the chiseling has been worn away by the weather. The carving isn't very deep, I'm guessing because whoever did it didn't really know what they were doing. This is the clearest one I've found so far."

"But 'Tetragrammaton'?" asked Connie. "What does that mean? Why would someone carve on a boundary marker like this, instead of just writing 'This pasture belongs to so-and-so'?"

Sam shrugged, shaking out the second match. "I don't know what the symbolism means, but as far as I can tell, it's meant to be a charm. To ward off evil."

"Evil, huh," Connie said.

"I'm just saying. It's totally possible that someone was practicing magic then. If the idea of witchcraft existed, someone was bound to give it a try. People are people, after all, even Puritans. This carving clearly meant something, to someone. There was something in this town to be afraid of." He looked closely at her. "This was not just academic to them; it was real life. And real life had real terrors."

Connie brushed her fingertips against the shallow nicks on the granite marker, entranced by what Sam was saying. Of course his argument made sense. But everything that she had read insisted that witchcraft was just a stand-in for other things: the irrational social tool of a pre-Enlightenment world, used to displace fear of the unknown onto vulnerable members of society. A thrill rushed through her as her hand lingered on the face of the stone. Magic was not just a stand-in, not just some psychoanalytic category to explain away a world without apparent cause and effect. To some of the colonists, magic was real. The idea made her catch her breath. Here was tangible, touchable proof, buried in a compost heap for over two hundred years.

She was about to reply, when a distant voice called out "Is someone there?" from the back door of the house. Connie and Sam looked at each other, mouths open in surprise. "I told you!" she whispered, smacking him on the chest. He spread his hands out in a gesture of innocence, shrugging, as if to say *What can I say?* Then he caught her by the hand, and gasping and laughing, they started to run.

CHAPTER SIX

Salem, Massachusetts
Mid-June
1991

ONNIE STOOD, ARMS FOLDED, BEFORE THE IMPOSING GREEK RE-
vival edifice of the Salem city courthouse, wondering what she was
doing. The blazing heat of the previous week had continued unabated, and
the entire town was shuttered against the summer world outside. Boutiques
stood vacant. A lone school bus spilled day campers out into the street, the
image of them running hand in hand down a cobbled alleyway obscured by
the heat waves shimmering up from the asphalt. Connie stepped through the
iron-grilled doors of the courthouse, which were propped open with a metal
folding chair to capture any passing breeze.

The marble entrance hall felt dim and cool after the glare of the street,
and Connie paused to let her eyes adjust. The security desk sat empty, and
Connie slid her Harvard identification card back into her cutoff pocket, reflecting that summer breeds a special kind of indifference in the normally
overly ordered New England consciousness. She passed through a second

set of oak doors, also propped open, and turned down a musty hallway, following the printed placard that read WILL AND PROBATE DEPARTMENT, indicated with an arrow.

A week had passed since she and Sam had been chased out of a stranger's backyard, and in that time the pleasurable confusion that she felt in Sam's presence had lingered even in his absence. Chatting with Liz that morning on the pay phone downtown, she had blamed the heat, which always seemed to smear her thinking, like a wet fingertip wiping an ink stain.

"I don't think it's the heat," Liz said.

"Oh, you have no idea," Connie moaned. "Granna's house is stifling. And I can't even plug in a fan. Last night I just filled the tub with cold water and sat in it for half an hour. It's turned Arlo into a glob instead of a dog."

"Whatever. You've been hot before," Liz said, dismissive. "I think that meeting this guy has thrown you off your game. But in a good way."

She was taken aback; Liz, as always, had a way of clearing aside her obfuscations to articulate what Connie herself was not able to say.

It was true that she responded differently to Sam. The boys she had dated in college had all been pleasant enough—indifferent, genial guys who were happy to stand next to her at a fraternity party and supply her with beer, but nothing more. Connie had been unable to make many personal inroads with the men at Harvard; she claimed that they were too absorbed in the rigors of grad school to spend time socializing, but Liz insisted that they found Connie intimidating. Sam, on the other hand, was neither indifferent nor intimidated. Her lips twisted into a crooked smile as she thought about him. She felt paradoxically at ease with Sam and disordered; when she was with Sam, she was able to surprise herself.

At the end of their day together, Sam had extracted from her a begrudging promise to keep him apprised if she learned anything more about her mysterious witch, and she nodded, avoiding looking at him. The late-night service bus arrived to carry him back to Salem, and she watched him climb on board, his departure slowed as he walked to the back of the bus, the vehicle advancing around him while his movement seemed, momentarily, to hold him in place. He waved at her, and then the bus pulled him away, and Connie had felt solitude descend again around her like a curtain.

If she discovered something about Deliverance Dane that afternoon, she would have an excuse to stop back by the meetinghouse where Sam was working, to tell him what she had found. The thought of finding something to show him caused a rill of excitement to rush through her arms and legs. She had studied the Salem witch trials as part of her qualifying exam, but she did not remember seeing anything about someone named Deliverance Dane in the secondary source literature. If Deliverance had been one of the accused witches, she must have been almost completely purged from the historical record. Connie had not yet formed a hypothesis about why that would have happened. An undiscovered Salem witch! She quickened her pace down the hall, eager to begin.

A TALL DESK DOMINATED THE WILL AND PROBATE DEPARTMENT, STAFFED only by an oscillating fan and a small metal bell. Connie dinged the bell and leaned over the desk, about to call out when a curt voice behind her hissed, "Yesss?"

Startled, Connie turned to find a tiny, withered woman in a tight bun and spectacles, dressed in an A-line skirt and Keds. Her arms were folded, and her mouth was pressed into a narrow, bitter line.

"Good afternoon," said Connie, collecting herself. "I am here to re-search a probate record."

"Do you have an appointment?" the woman snapped, casting her eye over Connie's cutoffs and flip-flops with disapproval.

Connie surveyed the silent archive, devoid of either staff or researchers, and planted her hands on her hips. "No, I'm afraid I don't," she said firmly. "But it will only take a minute. I can see that you are busy."

The woman scowled at her. "Indeed," she spat. "We usually only take folks who make an appointment."

"In that case I very much appreciate your making an exception for me," said Connie, congratulating herself on her diplomacy. "I am looking for a will that would have been probated in the 1690s."

"They're by name, not by date!" the woman barked.

"I see," said Connie, the muscles in her jaw tightening, like a rope wrapping around a cleat. "And the files have not been cross-referenced by date?"

"No call for it," said the woman. *No call for it.* The New England character as a matter of course privileged sameness above all else, including efficiency. *Because it's always been that way* was an explanation that Connie had encountered before in her research; it stood like a breastworks, keeping the non–New England world at bay. She felt a passing wave of sympathy for Grace's teenage will to rebel. Granna's household must have been ordered according to a similar system of consistency at the expense of progress and change.

"In that case, would you kindly point me to the section of names that begin with *D*?" Connie said with a tight smile.

"Card catalogue theah," said the woman, pointing in a direction that indicated the overall left half of the archive. Then without further comment she turned on her Keds and disappeared through a little door marked STAFF ONLY.

"Thanks," Connie said to the empty room, dropping her shoulder bag on a long reading table and turning to the card catalogue.

Connie knew that if Deliverance had died before her husband (assuming she had a husband), all her property would have been turned over to him automatically. If she had outlived him, then at least one-third of his property would have been given to her by law, with the remainder being given over to any children. Things grew trickier if she had never married, but that was highly unusual in the colonial period. Connie reflected that she had no evidence for how old Deliverance would have been during the witch trials. Statistically, most accused witches were middle-aged, from their forties through their sixties—the age when colonial women were at the height of their social power. Accused witches usually were anomalous in some conspicuous way: they had fewer than average children, or they were economically marginal. If Deliverance was a statistical witch, there was a good chance that she was an older woman, possibly a widow, and possibly with no children.

Because the will and probate records were active legal documents, despite their age they were kept in the same filing system as more current records, with no special archival steps taken to preserve them. Connie roamed the rows of metal filing cabinets, finally alighting upon a numbered drawer marked PROBATE: DAM–DANFORTH. She heaved the drawer open and was met with a billow of dust followed by hundreds of file folders. Each file represented an entire life. Within each folder lay clues to personalities long dead and family dynamics long forgotten. Farms carved into smaller and smaller parcels. Marriage prospects made or ruined. Connie always found herself moved by the narrative drama that sometimes lay hidden in such dry-seeming archives. But it was Sam's enthusiasm that had reawakened this taste for investigation in her. *I wonder if Marcy Lamson is in here somewhere,* she thought as she began to root through the files. The memory of the smiling older woman's face lingered in the back of Connie's awareness as she walked her fingers through the grimy folders.

Finally, squashed between DANEFIELD, HARVEY, DECEMBER 12, 1934 and DANEFIELD, JANICE, FEBRUARY 23, 1888 appeared a thin, dirty file folder of crumbling cardboard marked only D. DANE. Connie pulled the file out from its hiding place, excitement at the discovery displacing her initial irritation at its incorrect location, and settled at the table to read.

The twentieth-century probate files consisted of an official-looking typed cover sheet bearing the date on which the will was probated and the signatures of the executors and the state clerk, followed by many fat pages of legalese and bequests. A cursory look proved that these cover sheets were fairly standard—they appeared, written in longhand, in the nineteenth-century files as well.

When Connie opened the Dane file, however, the cover sheet was missing. Without the cover sheet, Connie would have no way of confirming the date of Deliverance's death. She presumed that Deliverance would have

been put to death after her excommunication in 1692, but without the dated
probate sheet she could not be absolutely certain. The file folder, which appeared to have been created some time in the nineteenth century, contained
only one lone sheet of paper. Connie rose and strode over to the door behind
which the archivist was hiding, opened it, and thrust her head into the staff
office. The archivist, seated at a desk with a romance novel open in her lap,
was raising a coffee mug to her lips when the sound of Connie's voice caused
her to start in her seat.

"Excuse me," said Connie from the doorway. "The file I am researching seems to be missing its cover sheet. Can you tell me if it might be filed
elsewhere? Or if there is a ledger that records the dates of probated
wills?"

The small woman glowered at her. "*No*," she said, her voice clipped. "All
sorts of nonsense happens in three hundred years." She replaced her coffee
mug to signal to Connie that that was all she had to say on the subject.

Connie sighed and shut the door again. She returned to the table, fingering the probate list on the table before her. She cast her eyes over the list: the
sum total of Deliverance Dane's life and fortune. She pulled her notebook
out of her shoulder bag and copied the handwritten list verbatim, knowing
that the archivist was unlikely to grant her permission to photocopy such a
fragile document.

Deliveranse Dane

farmhouse and 2 acres arable land Mhd £63. [water stain]
divers linnens and cloathing   £13.-12s*
furnishings: bedstead, table, 6 chairs, cupboard   £12.25s
sundry pieces iron cookware   90 shillings*
earthen crockerie   67 shill.*
sundrie household wares   54s.*

glass bottels	30 shil.
wooden chest	22 sh.
Bible, receipt booke	15 sh
other bookes	12 sh.
1 hog	£1.5
1 milk cow	£2.5
7 chickins	34 shillings
taxes ow'd	£12.10 s
to only issue Mercy	

Connie stared at the document for a few minutes, thoughts simmering. She closed her eyes and began to construct a picture of the stark rooms that would have been the scene of Deliverance's life. She began with an imprecise, standard pattern of the interior of a late-seventeenth-century house, wooden-floored, large hearth, empty. Slowly, the paper revealed clues that Connie painted into her mind's picture, building layers of detail, as an artist shades in blocks of color.

Deliverance must have been a widow, as the probate list did not mention a husband. Connie mentally placed a woman of indeterminate age standing by the imaginary hearth, alone. She was of low to middling economic position; she owned some land, but not a whole farm, and basic household fixtures, though nothing of particular value. No silverware, for example, and no pewter. The furniture was valued almost as much as the linens, which indicated that the furniture must have been decent, but not remarkable. No details about the chairs, so they were probably not upholstered or armchairs. No rug was listed for the tabletop, and no turkey work. From these conclusions Connie sketched in furniture around the imaginary woman, adding a plain wooden table with turned legs, topped with simple dishes, an iron cauldron simmering over the hearth fire, stiff wooden chairs drawn up to the table, but only one or two places set. No rug on the table. Across the room, or perhaps one room over, in the keeping room, a bedstead heaped with linens and feather mattresses, the most valuable items in her house. For fun, Connie added some herbs and flowers drying overhead. The imaginary woman folded her arms.

Connie's mind's eye pulled out from the interior scene, filling in a vegetable garden around the house—greens and peas, probably, together with roots that could be stored in winter, and possibly a fruit tree or two. Next to the house sprouted a heap of firewood that Deliverance either chopped herself or traded for with another family. Connie drew in a rough wooden enclosure for the hog—she gave the hog black and white patches, and floppy ears—and added a simple shed at the rear of the yard for the cow. Connie completed the picture by scattering some chickens pecking in the dirt by the front door of the imaginary house. She pulled still farther away and surveyed her mental construction of Deliverance's life.

From this vantage point, Deliverance appeared solitary but capable. She could provide much of her own food, and could trade simple things— eggs and cheese, maybe even laundry or mending—with her neighbors. But a few details were difficult to explain. Without any specific birth or death dates, for example, Deliverance's age was a mystery. The probate listed a single child, a daughter named Mercy. Deliverance could have been a young widow, Connie reflected—perhaps she had not had time to have any more children or remarry before she was put to death. But if that were the case, the estate would likely have been turned over to her father or other surviving male relative, rather than a young child. That Mercy Dane inherited from her mother suggested that Mercy had reached adulthood but had not yet married. In that instance, Deliverance's house would have been unusually empty of people for her time period. It held no passel of young children, no indentured servants, no elderly relatives. Connie frowned, unsure what to do with the suggestion of two adult women, a mother and daughter, living alone.

The glass bottles also posed a problem. To be mentioned specifically rather than obscured under "sundrie household wares" implied that there were rather a lot of them, or that they were worth mentioning for another reason. Connie tried to superimpose a vast assortment of glass bottles of varying shapes and sizes into her image of Deliverance's living space, but they did not fit in a way that made sense. Connie mentally scattered some bottles across the table and arranged more in the cupboard. Why would Deliverance have had so many? Connie leaned her weight into the table, elbows planted on either side of the probate list, chin in hands. The imaginary woman in her mind smiled at her.

"Misssss?" slithered a voice by her ear.

"Yes?" she said, irritated. The dessicated archivist stood over Connie, arms crossed, attempting to loom but failing in her slightness.

"We close in half an hour." She gestured with her sharp nose to a schoolhouse-style clock hanging over the card catalogue.

"Thank you. I won't be much longer." Connie watched as the archivist withdrew behind the filing cabinets, then turned back to stare again at the sheet of paper.

Something else was bothering her about this probate list. Something was off, and Connie drew her lower lip gently under her teeth as she tried to puzzle out what it was. The tax rate seemed about right—the estate was not over- or undervalued. The assortment of animals was about what she would have expected. Books? But most Puritan households would have had some books—no novels yet, but published sermons sold in Boston, tracts disseminated for moral uplift, certainly a Bible.

"Bible, receipt booke," Connie read aloud.

Receipt book?

Connie peered more closely at the paper before her, as if squinting to see the exact quill scratches on the page would clarify the meaning behind the words. Receipt book? Like a ledger? Did Deliverance run a business of some sort? What would she want with receipts? Connie stared, thinking, eyes wide, eyebrows crawling up her forehead, and the imaginary woman still standing in the room in her mind placed her hands on her hips, impatient. Connie rolled the words around in her mouth, feeling the imprecision of language that sometimes results when nonstandard spelling and pronunciation collide. An idea swam though Connie's thoughts, but she could not quite grasp at it, could not yet make out its form.

Receipt.

Recipt.

Recipe.

In an instant the idea dropped, crisp and perfect, squarely into the forefront of her mind. Connie gasped, her head bolting upright just as the archivist snapped out the lights.

Interlude

Salem Town, Massachusetts
Mid-July
1682

This tree is exceeding comfortable today, the little girl reflected. She settled herself against its bark, wedging more firmly into the groove between the fat branch where she was sitting and the knobby trunk against which her back was pressed. She dangled her feet idly off one side of the branch, enjoying the sensation of her ankles flopping loose in the breeze. It was cooler up in the tree, and the summer air gathered and dispersed around the girl, lifting loose wisps of hair off her forehead and sneaking up her sleeves and under her coif. She giggled, but then quieted herself.

The ground slanted away several feet below her, and within the sheltering grasp of leaves and twigs, the girl enjoyed sitting hidden and safe. Her high vantage point gave her the delicious feeling of being able to spy on others without their knowing that she could see them—afar down the lane already she could see Goody James in a straw hat, bending in her garden, and well beyond, at the bend in the road, Goodman James driving his mule in the direction of the wharves. Goody James leaned up from her work and pressed her hands into her back, and the little girl smiled.

In the yard below her, the girl could hear the rhythmic whistle and thunk of her father chopping firewood. *Thud, whistle, thunk!* And then the dull clatter of a freshly split log thrown onto the growing heap behind him. *Thud, whistle, thunk!* She knew the leaves screened her from his sight, and she tried to hold very still lest she be discovered. Since the minister had said those things about idle children in meeting that week, the townsfolk had turned a sharper eye to their offspring. The little girl knocked her head against the tree trunk behind her, wrinkling her nose.

Her stomach gurgled, and she pressed her hands to her belly to silence it. Twisting a length of her hair around one finger, the girl peered at the eye-level branches, thinking about food. Though most of the flowers had fallen weeks ago, the apples in the tree were still just tight little buds. She pulled a leafy bud-cluster toward her and cupped it in her hands. Already some of her mother's friends had spoken with approval of her "way" with plants, and the girl thought shamefacedly about these words of praise as she narrowed her gaze on the little apple-knots just forming on the branch. *'Tis a sin to be so proud*, she scolded herself. But her stomach rumbled again, and she stared hard at the leaf cluster, feeling her will seep through her hands and drain into the tree branch. Under her eyes the biggest apple bud seemed to stir and bubble, distending like a blister, straining against its own skin and gradually darkening from pale green to a deep russeted red. It pressed and swelled in her hands, burbling until it was the size of the girl's fist, then her two fists together, then all of a sudden it had twisted off of its stem and dropped in a sickening moment through the air, only to burst open in a pulpy mess on the ground.

"Mahcy!" she heard her father call out, the swinging of the ax suddenly suspended. The girl's lower lip extended, and she knew she was caught.

"Mahcy Dane, you come down now," he said, nearer the base of the tree. The little girl, Mercy, pouted for a moment until her father's sunburned face finally appeared through the leaves directly below her. Mercy looked worriedly down, expecting to find him wrathful. But the face was smiling, deep creases forming on either side of his eyes. She smiled back. He beckoned to her, and Mercy obeyed, grasping the branch with two hands and swinging down in a tangle of skirts and apron, finally dropping to the ground not far from the dissolving remains of the fallen apple.

"Peas want shelling, an' you loafing in the tree all day," he said, shaking his head, arms folded. She hung her head, saying nothing, hands hidden under her apron. "What if I should be sogerin', and us not having any wood to cook with? What then?"

She shrugged, drawing a little circle in the dust with one toe.

"Mahcy?" he prodded.

"I'm sorry, Papa," she whispered.

"Well, then," he said, resting a rough hand on her shoulder. "Get you to it." He indicated the woven rush basket that she had abandoned at the foot of the tree some hours earlier and turned back to the chopping block, hoisting the ax out of the wood. Presently he was back at work, *thud, whistle, thunk!* Mercy slunk back to the base of the tree, retrieved the basket, and made her way to the vegetable garden at the rear of the house.

The day was warm, and her dress felt uncomfortably heavy and hot under the pressure of the sun. She pulled green pea pods off the vine one after the other, dropping them into her basket on the ground, humming a tuneless hymn under her breath. As she neared the end of the garden row, she happened upon a dappled, dirt-colored tail lying in the dust, which proved to be attached to a small dog dozing on his back in the shade under the vine leaves. "Hullo, Dog." She knelt to greet him, and he responded with a tremendous yawn, stretching his short legs out like a cat. Mercy reflected that she had much rather trade places with Dog; she would sleep naked in the shade while he shelled peas in the hot kitchen with her mother.

"Meeeercy!" a woman's voice called from within the house.

"In the gahden, Livvy!" her father responded from the woodpile. Mercy hurried to her feet, wiped her nose on her sleeve, collected the unwieldy basket, and loped to the back door of the house.

She edged her way into the hall, heaving the basket of peas up onto the long board in the center of the room. The cooking fire had been going in the big hearth all morning, and the room felt considerably warmer than the summer day outside. The three windows were open, but they were so small that little air made its way in. Mercy blinked her eyes against the smoky, close atmosphere, and climbed into a chair by the board on trestles that served as a table to begin shelling.

"There you be!" said a woman's exasperated voice at the door, and her mother entered the room, wiping her hands on her apron. Her usually warm, open face had grown thinner over the past weeks, but Mercy did not know why. Her mouth, normally prone to smiling, now looked sort of pinched, and she was more likely to snap. As a result Mercy had taken to spending more time hidden, up trees and behind cupboards, or in the Jameses' cornfields with Dog.

"I'm shelling, Mama!" said the little girl quickly, ripping through a pod with her thumbnail and popping the fresh new peas out with her fingers.

Her mother watched her for a moment. "So you are." She sighed, then turned her attention to the bread loaf that was baking in the hive-shaped hollow in the hearth bricks. They worked for a time in silence, broken only by the *thud, whistle, thunk* of Nathaniel Dane's chopping in the yard, and by the leisurely appearance of Dog through the back door, who then settled in a heap under the table.

At length the front door opened, and a broad expanse of woman flowed through the door frame and into the hall where they were working.

"Aftahnoon to you, Livvy Dane!" boomed the woman, who wore a wide straw hat over her knotted coif. She moved smoothly over to the table and deposited a fabric-wrapped parcel next to Mercy's basket of pea shells. Deliverance turned around from the hearth and smiled at the woman.

"And to you, Sarah." Mercy felt her mother's sharp index finger dig into the space between her shoulder blades.

"Good noon, Goody Bartlett," squeaked the little girl. Mercy had always been a little uneasy around Sarah Bartlett, though she knew her to be a kind woman. Her prodigious largeness made Mercy feel very small. The woman smiled down at her, and patted her on the hand.

"Take some cider?" asked Deliverance, proffering an earthenware mug to the woman, who was settling her bulk on a narrow bench at the wide board worktable. "Frightful hot this day."

Sarah waved her off. "Het's no bother," she said, unpinning her hat. "But I thank you."

"How fares your calf withal?" Deliverance asked. "Brought you his water?"

"Ach," said Sarah, reaching into the pocket that was tied around her waist. "I did. He won't take the teat. Stubborn rogue. Goodman Bahtlett fers we shall lose him. But his strength is good." She pulled a small, stoppered glass bottle full of yellow liquid from within her pocket and placed it on the table. Deliverance picked up the bottle and held it in the narrow sunbeam leaking through one of the windows. She turned it left and right, brows knitted. The bottle glinted in the sunlight.

"Look you, Mahcy," said Sarah while Deliverance was at the window. "What do you think I ha' brought your mother?"

The little girl shrugged her shoulders. Sarah untied the parcel on the table and lifted a corner for her to peek under.

"Blueberries!" cried Mercy, clapping her hands together and wiggling in her chair. Sometimes she found blueberry shrubs on her rambles with Dog, but usually the crows had stripped them clean. Now she regretted her initial wariness, deciding that Sarah Bartlett must rather be one of the nicest women in the town, even if she was louder than most.

Deliverance placed the bottle of calf urine back on the table and smiled at her daughter. "Ah, Sarah. Blueberries are a great favorite of hers. Thank you kindly. And for your calf," she continued, "let us try some other physick."

She pulled a large, heavy book from the bottom shelf of the cupboard and opened it before her on the table. She leaned over on one slender arm and paged through the tome, running her finger down each page and reading silently.

"My son gathered 'em," Sarah said. "Sends greetins for you, and for Nathaniel." The room fell quiet again while Deliverance hunted through the book. Mercy kicked her heels against the legs of her chair and shelled another few peas. Sarah cast her gaze around the hall, groping for conversation.

"Nasty, all this Petfahd business," ventured Sarah. Mercy saw a wave of tension run up her mother's spine, and when she turned again to the table a black cloud had collected in her mother's blue eyes. "Goodman Bahtlett never ha' no use for half them jurymen. Mary *Oliver*, well," she snorted in a manner indicating that one always knew what one was likely to get from the Mary Olivers of the world. "And that Peter Petfahd, he is shah desput and distracted." Sarah waved a thick finger in the air to show her seriousness.

Deliverance stood and folded her arms. "He hath lost his only daughter," she said quietly. "We are all bewildered by God's providences." She dropped a few metal pins into the glass bottle, restoppered it, and tossed it into the hearth fire. Then she hunted in the dried herbs that hung overhead, plucked down the bunch she was looking for, and cast it into the fire as well. It exploded in a smoking, crackling flame, filling the room with a sour, pungent odor, like the underside of a rotted log. As she did this, she murmured some inaudible words under her breath. Mercy felt a charge of excitement surge through her stomach, the same charge that she always felt when she watched her mother do her work. She did not yet know what herb her mother had chosen, but she would ask when Goody Bartlett had left.

"You knew not that poor Mahther Petfahd, did you, Mahcy?" Sarah started to ask before Deliverance shot her a look and shook her head once.

"Ah," Sarah stammered. "Indeed, that physick smells most foul, Livvy. Then 'tis shah to work, ain't it?" She laughed weakly.

Deliverance smiled a tight smile and wrapped more of the same dried herb in the cloth that Sarah had brought to cover the blueberries. "Grind this to powder with a raw egg and some water and boil it over the fire 'til it forms a paste. Spread the liniment on the cow's teat, and the calf should take it well."

Sarah's round face filled with relief as she took the package from Deliverance and stuffed it into her pocket. "Indeed," she said, "I knew you'd ha' the solution. I said to Goodman Bahtlett, I did, of all cunning folk in the county that Livvy Dane knows her way wi' the physick above all." She chuckled uncomfortably again, and stopped when she saw the anxiety on Deliverance's face.

Sarah reached again for her hat and started moving toward the door. "Why, all folks know it. They do."

She paused, then placed an uncertain hand on Deliverance's shoulder. "Look you, Livvy, don't you harrer up your feelins. None can believe you'd hahm a child. All this evil talk, 'tis bound to settle soon enow." Sarah squeezed Deliverance's shoulder with her big reassuring fingers, nodded at Mercy, and withdrew into the day.

In her place in the doorway appeared Nathaniel Dane, linen shirt soaked through with sweat, arms and face streaked with dirt and splinters of wood. He carried a heap of freshly split logs and moved around the table to deposit them near the fire. Mercy felt a wave of nervousness that he would tell her mother that she had been shirking her work. She could see by the lines in her mother's face and the whiteness between her knuckles that a misbehaving girl might get the worst of it. She hastily shelled another few peas, making a great show of her industry and diligence.

"War that Goody Bahtlett I sar waddlin' down the lane?" he asked his wife, dropping the wood with a clatter and mess and wiping his hands on the seat of his breeches.

"'Twas," said Deliverance. "Oh, Nathaniel." Her voice caught in her throat, and she stifled a sob with the corner of her apron. He wrapped his arms around her and she hid her face in his neck, shoulders trembling. He stroked the back of her coiffed head with one smudged hand.

"Shhhhhhh, shhhhhh," the girl's father soothed, and Mercy looked up at her parents and reflected that she had never before seen her mother cry.

CHAPTER SEVEN

Marblehead, Massachusetts
Mid-June
1991

THE SHOULDER BAG SLIPPED TO THE FLOOR WITH A DULL THUD AS Connie surveyed the first floor of Granna's house from where she stood in the doorway. Late afternoon sun crept through chinks in the dense ivy overgrowth on the windows, speckling the broad pine floorboards with flecks of light. The house had soaked up the summer heat while she was away at the archive, filtering it through the layers of wood and plaster and horsehair insulation until warmth filled each corner of every room. It seemed especially thick in the entry near the stairs, like a wall; crossing the threshold into the house always gave Connie a measure of pause. But now her hypothesis buzzed in her head, and the tingling heat of the house on her skin melded with the energy in her nerves until her whole being felt alert, watchful. The natural place to begin was with the books in the sitting room. As Connie passed the ladderlike staircase she kicked over the mushroom, enjoying the wet thump of its flesh falling onto the rotted patch on the floor.

According to Grace's sporadic accounts, Lemuel Goodwin had been a plain man, unschooled past high school, not given to books. He spent his entire life in Marblehead, the son of shoe factory workers, and his chief pleasure had been lobstering on the weekend in the pots he kept off Cat Island, near the mouth of the harbor. A picture rested on the mantel over the sitting room fireplace, bleached almost white by the passage of time: Lemuel, squinting into the camera, his arm wrapped proudly around Grace's shoulders under an ornate archway leading into Radcliffe. The white gloves and tidy little hat that Grace wore dated the picture to 1962, the year that she left home. Connie rubbed her thumb against the photograph frame, wondering why Grace had always said so little about her father. Connie did not even know exactly how he had died, beyond that it had been sudden, accidental. She often wondered if the ignominious end of Grace's college career was related to Lemuel's abrupt disappearance from her and Granna's life. The buffer between them had been drawn away.

If her understanding of Lemuel was correct, then most of the books on the shelves would have belonged to Granna. Up until this point Connie had given scant consideration to why Deliverance Dane's name would have appeared in this house; Yankee thrift demands that nothing still remotely usable be discarded, and so detritus accumulates from families of surprising distance and remove. But now Connie entertained the thought—the hope— that if Deliverance's name could have lodged deep in Granna's old family Bible, then perhaps some other residue of Deliverance's life might persist here as well. Perhaps Granna's Bible was the very one mentioned in Deliverance's probate record! Connie stood, hands on hips, dragging her gaze over the spines of the books. Arlo appeared at her feet, pawing her leg. She reached down to rub one of his mud-colored ears.

"Did you ever catch that garden snake like we talked about?" she asked the animal. "It's disgusting, having reptiles running around all over the house. You really need to start pulling your weight." He did not respond, instead leaping onto one of the needlepoint armchairs. Connie sighed, exasperated, and decided to begin with the largest books first.

If the receipt book had been listed together with a Bible, possibly even the very Bible she had already happened upon, then she might conclude that it was roughly the same dimensions as a Bible. The books on the bottom shelf were each tall, dense slabs of text, substantial in their heft, and Connie pulled them out one at a time. The first was the Bible in which she had found the key; it seemed to have been printed in England in 1619, and the edges of some of its pages had been glued together by water damage. In addition, the shelf held two other Bibles, one from 1752 and one from 1866. The inside cover of the nineteenth-century one held a fragmentary map of Lemuel's ancestors—Marbleheaders all of them. A needlepoint bookmark in a church steeple pattern was wedged into the book of Matthew, its threads eaten away by silverfish.

Two Psalters followed, and then what looked like a ship's log, a cursory glance at which suggested that it had been kept by the captain of a clipper trading guano fertilizer and molasses out of the Salem port. Connie next pulled down a hymnal from the First Church by the Sea, Congregational—had Granna just walked off with it?—published in the 1940s. Connie blew an exasperated breath through her nose and slid the hymnal back into the shelf, where it met with some resistance and a gentle crunching sound. Gingerly Connie threaded a finger behind the book, bracing herself for something unsavory—a mouse skeleton, a beetle shell. Instead she pulled forth a tiny corn husk doll, dressed in a scrap of dimity with a faded yarn bow around its neck. On the husk knot that was its head, someone had crayoned a wide orange smile.

"Weird," Connie murmured, turning the little effigy over in her hands. As she did so she felt a sharp nip, and pulled her thumb away to observe a round, crimson bubble of blood rising from the grooves of her thumbprint.

"Ow!" she said aloud. Looking closer, Connie withdrew a slender needle, still entangled with thread, from where it had been stored in the folds of the doll's dress. She stood, settling the little doll next to the picture of Grace and Lemuel on the mantel as she soothed her injured thumb with her lips. She gazed at the doll, frowning. Its orange grin smiled back at her. The little doll seemed too old to have been a toy of Grace's, and yet it was hidden

behind a book of relatively recent vintage. She supposed it could have been
Granna's when she was a girl. Grace could have played with it, hidden it
away, and forgotten. Connie would ask her when she called tonight. Assuming Grace was there to answer the telephone.

A further hour spent perusing the books on Granna's shelf revealed only
the standard tomes of the New England middle class: hardbound selections
from the Book-of-the-Month Club, worn from rereading and without dust
jackets. Several nineteenth-century books of history, three or four volumes of
math puzzles, a guide to strategies in duplicate bridge. *The Yachtsman's Omni-*
bus. A handful of texts on horticulture and garden cultivation. And, yes, *De-*
cline and Fall of the Roman Empire. Nothing that spoke to her hypothesis, and
nothing—other than the first Bible—from the seventeenth century.

Connie shifted her eyes around the sitting room, alighting first on the
desiccated plants dangling in the windows, then roving over to the Chippendale desk. Her eyes lit up. Connie hurried to the desk, running her hands
over its dense, polished cherrywood, feeling for she knew not what. Perhaps
a drawer that the antique key would unlock? She had tried it in the front
door and a few of the chests in the dining room, to no avail. Oftentimes
these desks included a removable panel in the center front between the cub-
byholes, masking a secret repository for important papers. Her fingers lit
upon a little ledge underneath the writing surface, and her pulse quickened.
A concealed drawer? She got to her hands and knees to look under the desk.
No drawer—just a strut, awkwardly nailed in place by someone who did not
know how to repair colonial furniture. Connie laughed at herself. Ridiculous. There would be no hidden book in this desk. It held only old receipts
from the greengrocer, crumbling pencil erasers, a few jotted reminders that
Granna had left behind when she died.

The sunlight was beginning to drain away from the windows, retreating
behind the advancing dusk. In the half-light of early evening, Connie always thought she detected movement in the corners of the house, just beyond the reach of her peripheral vision. Whenever she turned to face the
flickering, it disappeared. Mice, she suspected, through she had not caught

any in the traps she had scattered along the yawning seams between the walls and the floorboards. Soon it would be too dark for her to look. She almost felt as if the house were hastening the coming dark, to push her away from prodding through its secrets.

Connie struck a match from the box on the old kitchen mantel in the dining room and lit the oil lamp, rolling down the wick until the tongue of flame settled into a round glow. The dining room held several closed sea chests and a built-in wall of dishes and crockery, which Connie had not yet been able to bring herself to clean. She carried the lamp over to the mantel, gazing down at the assortment of iron bars and hooks that bristled from the wide, empty hearth. When the house had first been built, this hearth had been its epicenter. A few ashes still sat collected at the bottom of it, cold and abandoned. She placed the lamp on the mantelpiece, resting her elbow next to it and gnawing on a knuckle.

Connie ran a finger through the layer of dirt along the crockery shelf, leaving a naked trail along the wood in its wake. She would have to wash off all of these dishes eventually. Box them up. Sell them. The enormity of the unpleasant task made Connie feel tired, overwhelmed. She pulled one of the shield-back chairs out from the table and sat, resting her chin on her hand as darkness gathered in the silent house. Across the room, between two more deceased hanging plants, a three-quarter portrait of a brunette woman with pale blue eyes smiled primly down at her, dressed in the narrow waist and sloping shoulders of the 1830s.

"What are you looking so smug about?" Connie asked her. The portrait, unsurprisingly, said nothing. Instead, two small dog feet planted themselves in her lap, and Arlo's nose worked its way under her arm.

She looked down into the animal's eyes and smiled. "I think that's a great idea, Arlo," she said, getting to her feet.

THE DAY'S HEAT HAD APPARENTLY BEEN PRESSING INTO OTHER HOUSES in Old Town, Marblehead, as well, and so the small downtown block was almost crowded by the time Connie rounded the corner on her way to the telephone booth. The windows of the ice cream shop were jammed with teenagers, all elbows and legs, reveling in the air-conditioning. Down the street, noise poured from the open front door of an Italian restaurant as the teenagers' parents clustered at the bar. Cheers erupted in response to a baseball game on the bar television. A coterie of boys rolled by on skateboards, and Arlo took cover behind Connie's legs as they passed.

"Wimp," Connie said to him. She pulled open the phone booth door, draped her towel over her shoulder, and dialed New Mexico.

She was completely unprepared when Grace answered on the first ring. "Mom?" she said, unable to conceal her surprise.

"Connie! I'm so glad I caught you," said Grace Goodwin, her voice cheerful.

"I called *you*," said Connie before she could stop herself.

"Oh, my darling. Always so literal. But how are things? How are you finding the house? Have you settled in?" Grace always sounded so positive. This trait used to irritate Connie no end when she was a teenager. Now she found herself appreciating it; she discovered that she was smiling.

"Yes, thanks, but you were right—the house is a disaster. I'm amazed it's still standing, quite frankly. The garden's gone positively feral."

"Yes, well, your grandmother always said that the old ways of doing things were better." Grace chuckled. "I presume she would have put house construction in that category as well. But tell me—how are *you* liking being there?"

"It's . . . different," Connie admitted. "It's not Cambridge, to say the least."

"Indeed not," Grace agreed. Connie wondered what Grace had been doing, that she was so near the telephone. She closed her eyes, groping her imagination forward as she tried to picture the raftered living room of her mother's adobe house. She pictured Grace sitting in her deep Mission armchair, jeans rolled up, feet sunk in a wide metal bowl full of something aromatic. Connie worked her own feet unconsciously, and felt her arches ache.

"What were you doing today?" she asked, pulling on the telephone cord.

Her mother sighed. "Oh, you know. Not much. I went on a desert hike with my women's group. Four hours, up and down these rocks and things. And I wore espadrilles, if you can believe it," Grace said, laughing at herself. "Talk about poor planning."

Connie smiled, privately amused that she had surmised correctly. "Mom," she said, venturing a guess. "Do you know anything about someone named Deliverance Dane?"

"Who?" Grace asked, incurious. Connie imagined her leaning her head back against the deep armchair, eyes closed. It would just be sunset in Santa Fe. In the street outside the telephone booth where Connie stood, a boy pedaled by on a bicycle, causing a pickup truck to screech to a halt. The driver's arm extended from the window of the truck, and he hurled epithets that Connie could not hear. Arlo scratched at the glass door, and Connie held up a finger to indicate that he should wait.

"I found that name on a slip of paper hidden in a key inside one of Granna's Bibles," Connie said. "I think she might have been caught up in the Salem witch trials. I was looking through the house tonight to see if I could find anything else, but so far there's been nothing. I wondered if you knew anything."

Connie heard her mother laugh softly. The sound went on for a while. "Oh, my darling," she said. "You and your history. Now, don't get angry," Grace began, and as she said it Connie steeled herself to do exactly that. "But have you ever considered that you might prefer to spend time thinking about people who are long gone because you are a tad overwhelmed by knowing people fully in the present? Let's focus on the now. Tell me about how *you* are doing."

A red burst of anger exploded across Connie's eyes, and she fought the urge to hang up. "Mom, it's my work. My research *is* how I'm doing."

"Nonsense," Grace said smoothly. "I can tell by your color that there's something else going on." This was Grace's way of saying that Connie's aura had changed, and Connie had to struggle to contain her irritation. She pinched the bridge of her nose, squinted her eyes closed and counted silently to ten. "Is it a boy?" Grace asked coyly before Connie could speak again.

"Actually, I have been having much more vivid daydreams since moving up here," Connie said, divulging this detail as a sort of peace offering. "They appear, and then my head hurts afterward. I've been thinking maybe I should see a doctor."

"Oh, you don't need a doctor," Grace said, sounding unsurprised. "What are the dreams about?"

"Granna mostly," Connie said. "And of Lemuel, which is weird, since I never met him."

Grace was silent for a moment, and Connie felt remorse. She worried that the mention of Lemuel would sadden her mother. Grace sighed again.

"Ah, you would have loved Dad," her mother said, her voice a little wistful. "He wouldn't have understood you, any more than he understood me, but he would've been crazy about you. I'm glad you've been thinking about him."

Connie swallowed, suddenly sorry for her irritation. Grace just had an idiosyncratic way of expressing things. Connie reminded herself that she had pledged to try to listen to the substance of what Grace had to say, rather than her language or her idiom. "That's not all, Mom—" she started to say.

"The thing about auras, Connie," Grace said, interrupting her, "is that they have a way of lingering on things. Perceptive people can often pick up on these little remnants that get left behind. They can be surprisingly specific, you know. And I've always thought you were a very perceptive girl."

Connie felt an odd mixture of pleasure at her mother's praise and aggravation at the subject matter. Auras, indeed. Connie was willing to believe that she had an active imagination, and willing to believe that she was lonely, and so inclined to look for things that might not be there. But that was as far as she was willing to go.

"Mom, I've got to go," she said. "There's a heat wave over here, and this phone booth is killing me."

"Are you sure there isn't a boy?" Grace asked, voice wary. "If there is, you should really tell me, my darling."

"*Mom*," Connie said, exasperated. "I've got to go. I'll call you again soon, I promise. And you had better pick up."

Grace began to laugh, and Connie smiled. She started to hang up the phone, thought better of it, said, "I love you, Mom," and waited.

"I love you, too, my darling. Call me on Sunday if you like," said Grace.

"I will," said Connie, cheeks flushed as she hung up the phone.

WITH ARLO SNUFFLING IN HER WAKE, CONNIE TIPTOED DOWN THE wooden gangplank that led from the public park on the western shore of Marblehead harbor to the swimming raft that was anchored off the granite cliff face. The humid evening air had grown thicker and heavier since she left the house, and where it met the cool harbor water it congealed into a fog so dense that Connie could almost mold it into shapes, like clay. When she reached the raft, the fog closed off the gangplank behind her, and she found herself alone. She dropped the towel that she was carrying, and Arlo settled on it, stretching out his legs with a sigh. In the diffuse moonlight his fur looked mottled gray-black, almost invisible against the wood of the raft. Connie paused, inhaling the briny smell of the sea, and listened.

Only the muffled clanking of sailboat rigging through the mist told her that boats were moored sixty feet away from where she stood. The water slopped against the side of the raft, calm and waveless. She sighed with relief, pulling off her sweat-stained T-shirt and stepping out of her cutoffs until she stood in her underwear, invisible in the dark. The fog felt cool and comfortable against her skin, and she slid noiselessly into the harbor, feeling the heat from her suffering body pulled away by the delightful embrace of the salt water. Connie dropped beneath the surface, swimming sightless through the black night water, the silence closing in around her, conjuring nights stealing naked into Walden Pond when she was a child.

Her face broke through the membrane of the harbor surface some distance away, and she found that the fog curtain had obscured the image of the raft. Stretching out on her back, she floated, a pale island in the night. She was glad that she had reached Grace. Though their conversation had been vexing at times, she nevertheless felt reassured. And she hadn't even told Grace that she had been to the sail loft! Connie grinned, a little salt water leaking into the corners of her mouth. She would tell her on Sunday. She reached one hand up to touch the fog, trailing her fingers in the mist.

A bark rang out, dampered by the moisture in the air, and Connie raised her head, treading water. "Arlo?" she called out. Happy whimpering answered her call, and then she heard a splash. She started to swim back in the direction of the raft.

The fog trailed apart as she advanced, and she could tell by the shift in vibration that there was something in the water with her. "Arlo?" she called again, casting her arms before her for the paddling shape of her dog. Her hand struck something, and a voice said, "Watch it!"

Connie cried out in surprise, and the voice said, "Connie?"

She looked closer, and saw that the lumpen shape emerging through the mist in front of her belonged to a young man, who seemed to be hanging on to the raft with one arm. Above him the silhouette of her dog stood, tail vibrating. "Sam?" she asked, unbelieving.

"Hi!" he said, letting go of the raft and sidestroking over to her.

She laughed once, utterly surprised. "What are you doing here?"

"*Swimming*," he said, with authority. "Ask me another one."

She batted some water at him impatiently. "I mean, what are you doing swimming *here*? You live one town over!"

"And have you ever seen Salem harbor? It could spontaneously ignite, it's so polluted. I swim here all the time." He ducked his head under the water, rising again with his head tipped back to smooth the hair out of his eyes. The moonlight shone on his skin as the water ran down his face in rivulets, glinting on the small ring under his nose. Connie wondered how long he had

had that. She usually detested jewelry on men, but Sam's nose ring looked unconventional. Dangerous.

"So, I met Arlo," Sam remarked, breaking into her thoughts. "He's pretty cool. Didn't bite me, anyway. Though I don't think he'd let me steal your towel without a fight."

"He wouldn't," she said, mouth twisting into a wicked smile. She paddled leisurely away from the raft, and he followed behind her.

"So," he ventured as they swam, "any developments on your favorite witch?"

Connie rolled her eyes and kicked out with one foot, directing a focused splash squarely into his face.

"Hey!" he sputtered, flailing. "What was that for?"

"For talking about work when it's too hot," she said. "And I'm not afraid to do it again."

"Fair enough," Sam said, chastened. "We will not discuss work." He paused, creeping closer in the water and shifting his eyes left and right. Connie watched him, treading water. Her pale shoulders just emerged from the black harbor surface, and her unbraided hair swirled around her in the water, dark brown brows swept together over her eyes. "You know, it might be dangerous for us to be out swimming here this late at night," he said, voice low.

"Why is that?" she said, dropping her voice as well.

"Well," he said, assuming a mock-serious tone, "because of the squid."

"The squid," she repeated, arching one eyebrow.

"Oh, yes. The rare North American poison-spitting squid. They only come out to hunt in the fog. If you feel something brush against your leg"— he moved still closer, dropping his voice to a whisper—"it's probably already too late."

Connie felt a set of toes grope across her knee under water, and she reached one hand down, grasping the ankle that belonged to the foot and hoisting it up out of the water. "Hey! I got one!" she exclaimed in triumph as Sam pitched backward, ducking his head below the surface in a froth of laughter. "Oh, wait—this one is covered in tattoos," she remarked, inspecting the leg as Sam's arms waved and splashed for the surface. He wrenched the leg away and, gasping, splashed after her as she paddled away, laughing.

From where he lay on Connie's towel, Arlo heard water splashing and great whoops of laughter, mingled with calls of "You are *so* dead, Cornell!" and "You've got to catch me first, Hartley!" He raised his head at one point, ears pricking forward, searching for sound, when the laughter died to quiet giggling. But then his questing ears found their voices whispering, and so he dropped his head back to his paws and waited, fading to the pale moonlit color of the fog.

CHAPTER EIGHT

Cambridge, Massachusetts

Late June

1991

CONNIE STOOD IN THE CRAMPED LADIES' ROOM ON THE FIRST FLOOR of the Harvard Faculty Club, weaving her hair into what she hoped was a tidy-looking braid. She paused to examine the results in the mirror and saw a bump of hair poking up from the top of her head.

"Dammit," she said, undoing her work. She ran the comb under water in the sink and then pulled it more tightly through her hair, digging its teeth into her scalp. She had never quite mastered the art of looking pulled together. On dressy occasions she always felt wracked with anxiety, mindful of falling into hidden sartorial traps. As she braided she muttered under her breath. Why had Professor Chilton insisted on lunch here, anyway? She could just as easily have met him in his office. He usually took graduate students here only to celebrate something. Or to intimidate them.

"Stupid," she said, wrapping an elastic around the end of the braid and tossing it over her shoulder. She gazed at her reflection in the mirror. Behind a waxy purple orchid, which filled the bulk of the visual field over the sink, the mirror reflected an image of a young, blue-eyed woman in a droopy floral dress, its basic conservatism making up, she hoped, for what it lacked in style and tailoring. Sensible Mary Janes replaced her habitual flip-flops. Her shoulder bag was just a shoulder bag. Connie sighed. She should have borrowed something from Liz.

"Ridiculous," she said aloud, not sure if she was commenting on the situation or on her outfit. Perhaps both. She looked at her watch, decided that she had hidden in the bathroom as long as she could justify, and opened the door.

Graduate students never ventured into the reading room of the Harvard Faculty Club, and as Connie edged her way inside, she wondered why. It was meant to be inviting. Deep, tufted sofas and polished leather armchairs sat grouped at either end around low coffee tables, and the rugs on the floor were bleached by decades of loafered feet and unfiltered sun. The room was watched over by the benevolent, painted eyes of clerical Harvardians, long dead. Its air smelled reassuring, a blend of polished wood, coffee, and "cake box" pipe tobacco. And still, grad students cringed away, as if something in its rarefied air might be toxic.

That afternoon, the sweet pipe tobacco smell was emanating from a white-haired gentleman settled on the divan under the grandfather clock, an open newspaper level with the gold spectacles on his nose. He rattled the newsprint and puffed without removing the pipe from his mouth. Connie moved to the opposite end of the reading room to wait.

She admitted to herself that she was excited to tell Professor Chilton what she had learned so far. Imagine how surprised he would be! She jiggled one foot in anticipation, a wry smile bending the corners of her mouth.

"Miss Goodwin?" a voice asked, and Connie started. She had not heard the waiter approach.

"Yes?" she asked, tugging at the hem of her dress with nervous fingers.

"Professor Chilton asks if you will join him in the dining room," said the waiter, smirking so slightly that only a practiced cynic such as Connie would be able to detect it. *Of course he can't come retrieve you himself,* said the smirk. Connie sighed.

"Guess I'll just go into the dining room, then," she said, rising.

"Very well, Miss Goodwin," said the waiter, bowing a fraction of an inch.

THE DINING ROOM WAS CURTAINED AGAINST THE AFTERNOON SUN, AND Connie had to hunt for a few minutes in the dark before she located Manning Chilton seated at a table in a plush alcove. He was reading a dense book—*Alchemical Practice as Moral Purity*—which he stashed in a satchel under the table at her approach.

"Connie, my girl," he said, rising in a dignified half-crouch. *There he goes with that "my girl" business,* Connie thought as she shook hands with her advisor. She plastered over her annoyance with a bright smile, and the waiter pulled out a chair for her.

"I am so pleased that you could join me today. Shall I ask James for a menu, or do you know what you would like?" Chilton asked. The waiter, James, hovered at Connie's elbow, one eyebrow peaked in the same ironic manner with which he had retrieved her from the reading room.

"Ah," Connie said, stalling. The dining room, with its crisp, ironed linens and silver butter knives, always made her ill at ease. Most grad students survived on a mishmash of foodstuffs culled from the ends of departmental meetings. For one whole week last semester she and Liz had subsisted on a cheese plate stolen from the classics department new-student reception. When free food was scarce they could resort to the dining hall, with its steady diet of spaghetti with plain tomato sauce and tuna casserole. *It's a wonder more of us don't come down with rickets,* she thought before realizing that she had not yet answered Professor Chilton. James cleared his throat delicately.

"May I see a menu, please?" she asked, aiming her question into the uncertain air between Chilton and the waiter. A tall leather folder appeared in her hands, the florid descriptions of the food on offer swimming before her like a foreign language. She looked closer and realized that it *was* in a foreign language: French.

"Just the chicken, I guess," she said, hoping that the menu actually included chicken as it was plucked from her grasp and James vanished into the dim recesses of the club.

"Now then," Chilton began, rubbing his hands together in anticipation, "tell me of your great discovery." Connie glanced at him to see if he was mocking her, but then decided that he was serious.

"I have found my unique, perfect primary source," Connie started to explain. "Actually, that is not accurate, strictly speaking. I have found evidence that my unique, perfect primary source *exists*."

Chilton leaned forward, elbows folded on the table. "Tell me," he commanded.

Connie began by describing her adventures looking for Deliverance Dane in the Salem meetinghouse archive, leaving a gaping Sam-shaped hole in her narrative. When she started her story by returning to the strange name that she had discovered, Chilton frowned but said nothing. Connie spoke quickly, squelching any opportunity for him to interrupt. She carried him up to her visit to the Salem Will and Probate department, and listed the inventory of Deliverance's belongings at her death.

"Connie, I am waiting to hear where this litany is going," Chilton interrupted. "So far I have only heard you spending a lot of time mucking about in archives with little result."

Connie pushed aside her aggravation at Chilton's comment, her own enthusiasm outweighing her desire for his approval. "But I was confused by the list," she continued, undaunted. "I couldn't figure out why the executors would have listed a receipt book on the same line as Deliverance's Bible, rather than treating it like any of the other books that she had in the house. Why would a ledger book have had the same value, financially speaking, as a big expensive family heirloom?" She paused to take a swallow of ice water.

At that moment James appeared again at her elbow, silently thrusting a steaming plate of chicken fricassee onto the table between her silverware, and a platter of grilled salmon before Chilton. "Will there be anything else, sir?" James asked. Chilton looked questioningly at Connie. She shrugged.

"Not at this time, thank you, James," Chilton said, dismissing him. She smiled apologetically at the waiter, who sent her the faintest hint of an eye roll in response before disappearing.

"Now, Deliverance left everything to her daughter, Mercy," Connie continued. "So I thought, if the book was that important, maybe it would be mentioned in *Mercy's* probate record, too." Connie gesticulated with her fork, and a shadow of disapproval traveled across Chilton's face.

"Indeed," he said, toying with his fish.

"But get this," said Connie. "I couldn't find Mercy anywhere. I know that records can sometimes be incomplete from this period, but it just seemed kind of strange to have her vanish with no trace whatsoever. But then I realized that I was just being too narrow."

"In what sense?" asked Chilton, watching her.

"Say 'Mercy,'" said Connie.

"I beg your pardon?" Chilton asked, taken aback.

"You have an old-style Brahmin accent, Professor Chilton," Connie said, wondering if she was stepping out of bounds. Do people with accents know that they have accents? *Let's hope that Chilton has a sense of humor*, Connie thought, knowing that there had been no prior evidence in her years as his student to support that hope. Ah, well. "Please just humor me."

"Mehcy," he said, straight-faced.

"Right," said Connie. "The dropped *r*, the flattened vowel. Now, say the name that is spelled '*M-a-r-c-y*.'"

"Mehcy," Chilton said again.

"Exactly!" Connie said, gesturing with her fork again. "In phonetic spelling, which is how they did things before dictionaries and printing standardized the language, the names 'Mercy' and 'Marcy' are the same name!" Connie forked an overlarge slice of chicken into her mouth and chewed with triumph. Chilton smiled at her enthusiasm. Connie felt pleased to see that she was beginning to win him over. "When I started looking for *Marcy Dane*," she added, "I found all kinds of stuff. In fact, it turns out I had even stumbled across a number of her records at the First Church already without knowing that she was important."

"Such as?" Chilton prodded.

"I couldn't figure out exactly when she was born, but she belonged to the First Church in Marblehead for her whole adult life and was in good standing the entire time. She married a guy named Lamson in Salem, but I haven't found his first name yet. She was involved in some kind of lawsuit in 1715. And she died in 1763. Leaving a probate record."

She paused for another drink of water and saw that Chilton was now fully absorbed, though she suspected that he could have no idea where she was really going.

"And . . . ?" he asked.

"And listed on her own probate record, along with the same house that Deliverance left her, was something described as 'book—receipts for physick.'"

"Another ledger?" Chilton asked.

"That's what I wondered at first," Connie said. "But in the course of poking around town I found some interesting material culture." She described the boundary marker with its strange charm and carvings. Again she left Sam out of her account. She was not sure if this omission was because she wanted to impress Chilton with her research acumen, or if it was because she wanted to keep the warm sensation that she felt whenever she thought about Sam a secret, for herself alone. Even now, perched across from Chilton at the table, zipped into awkward clothes, turning her thoughts to Sam made Connie feel taller, more alive. A pleasurable tingle traveled from the crown of her head down the back of her neck, and she smiled a tiny, private smile.

"Connie, I don't follow you," Chilton said. "What does this boundary marker have to do with a ledger book?"

"Wait," Connie said, polishing off her chicken. "The boundary marker is a vernacular example of magical thinking at work in the real world. Now, think back to what we know for sure about Deliverance Dane. She was *excommunicated* in 1692. In Salem."

"Excommunication was hardly uncommon in the Puritan religious structure," Chilton pointed out.

"But it was also the first thing that happened after someone was tried and convicted of witchcraft!" Connie struck her plate with her fork in her excitement. Chilton's mouth began to pull into a smile.

Connie pressed on. "I started to think that if Puritan culture could produce a would-be magical object like the boundary marker, then perhaps that culture would have left other evidence of magical thinking as well. What if a receipt book isn't a receipt book at all?" Connie paused.

Chilton waited, saying nothing

"*Receipt* is also a variant spelling of *recipe*," Connie clarified.

"Recipe?" Chilton repeated, brows knitted.

"When I found Mercy's probate record I was finally sure. What kind of book would be valuable enough to get its own listing in a probate record, would be handed down from mother to daughter, and would contain recipes for 'physick,' also known as 'medicine,' and would have been owned by a woman who was probably convicted of practicing witchcraft?"

Surprise and pleasure began to crawl up Chilton's face, and his lips slowly drew back into a wide grin. Connie reflected that she had never known her advisor to smile while showing his teeth before.

"A spell book!" Connie announced.

Chilton gazed across the table at Connie, his eyes gleaming with a hard, cold light.

CHAPTER NINE

Marblehead, Massachusetts

Late June

1991

"So where'd ya wannit?" asked the man, plopping his tool case onto the flagstones with a dull thump.

Connie smiled from where she stood in the front doorway. "Well, I don't know, really. What's usual?"

"Just the one?" he asked, lifting and then resettling his baseball cap on his head, affording Connie a fleet glimpse of shining scalp. "Front hall."

"Sounds good," she said, ushering him in. "You want some coffee or something?"

"I'd take a beah," said the man.

Connie hesitated for a moment, but then shrugged. *Why not*, she thought. *It's hot out, anyway.* "Just a sec," she said to the man.

"Be stahtin' outside," he replied.

In the kitchen, Connie lifted open the antique wooden icebox and reached down into the slush inside. She was going through ice at an amazing clip so far this summer. She paused, enjoying the cool breath of the melting ice on her moist face before closing the icebox again. *Ice'd last longer if you did that less often*, she told herself as she carried the beer out to the yard.

She found the man kneeling in the little vegetable patch near the front door, toolbox open. He had prised off a loose shingle and was uncoiling a length of wire.

"Ya had one heah before, turns out," he told Connie as she placed the beer on the ground next to him. Arlo had appeared from under the tomato plants and was now sniffing at the soles of the man's work boots. The dog quickly gathered all the information that he needed from this investigation and then returned to his spot in the shade, chin resting on his folded paws.

"Yeah?" she said, surprised. "What happened to it?"

"Got took out," he said, working away with a small pair of pliers.

"Oh," said Connie. She watched him work for a minute, thumbs hooked in her cutoff belt loops.

"Gonna be a while," said the man without looking around.

"Oh! Sure," said Connie, embarrassed. "Sorry."

She made her way back into the house, being careful to leave the door unlocked, and then settled at the Chippendale desk in the sitting room to wait. Now that she thought about it, she hardly ever bothered to lock the door anymore. Granna's house was so obscured by brush and overgrowth that she was even a little surprised the man had been able to find it. Connie smiled to herself. Wouldn't Grace be astonished when Connie called her from the *house*.

Connie had been feeling confident since her lunch with Chilton. He was even more delighted with her possible primary source than she had antici-pated.

"Of course, there are surviving examples of manuals for *finding* witches," Chilton had said. "The *Malleus Maleficarum* from fifteenth-century Germany, even Cotton Mather's 1692 treatise on the *Wonders of the Invisible World*."

"Right," Connie affirmed. "But so far my research indicates that there are no surviving colonial North American examples of any book or instructional text for *practicing* witchcraft. We usually interpret this to mean that nobody was actually practicing it, right? So if Deliverance's book is what I think it is, and if it has survived, it would be an amazing find. Its contents could change the way history looks at the development of medicine, of midwifery, of science. . . ." Connie trailed off.

"To say nothing of changing our interpretation of the Salem panic. Those are quite a lot of 'ifs,' I'm afraid," Chilton said. "But too tantalizing not to pursue."

Two dishes of warm bread pudding appeared at their table, and as Chilton chewed he watched Connie thoughtfully. "Tell me, my girl," he ventured. "You were planning to attend the Colonial Association conference this year, weren't you?"

Connie nodded. "I think so. I'm not on any of the panels or anything, but I was going to go, just to hear the papers." She dipped her fork into the soft pudding, prodding at a golden raisin with one of the tines.

"Always a good idea," Chilton said. "Ground yourself in the current work in the field." He paused, seeming to weigh something before continuing. "You know, I'm to give the keynote address this year," he said lightly.

"Really?" she asked, surprised.

"Indeed. Just a general talk on the development of my research on the history of alchemical thought. Presenting some exciting new conclusions." He paused, catching Connie's eye when she looked up. "I may wish to introduce you there," he finished, setting his fork aside with finality.

"But why?" she asked, puzzled.

Chilton chuckled. "We can discuss that in more detail later. Let us not get ahead of ourselves, my girl. Your only concern at this point is to find the book, and see if it is everything that you suspect. I trust you will keep me closely apprised of your progress." As he spoke, Chilton had folded his hands into the temple shape that always indicated he was deep in thought.

As she left the Faculty Club that afternoon, Connie's mind had been humming with excitement, veering between pleasure at Chilton's approval and plans for the next stage of her research. She was so submerged in her own thoughts that she collided with Thomas, her thesis student, as he approached her on the path by the undergraduate library.

"Ow! *Connie*," Thomas whined, rubbing the toe that she had trod upon. She laughed.

"I'm sorry, Thomas!" she cried, grabbing at his skinny elbow to keep him from toppling over. "I'm fresh from a dissertation meeting with Chilton. I was just thinking a little too hard."

They crossed Harvard Yard together, Thomas hopping at intervals to underscore to Connie the mortality of his injury as she chatted with him about his summer job reshelving books at the library.

"I can't believe you haven't called me," Thomas said, sulking. "How am I going to get my grad school applications done without your help? I'm already starting to outline my personal statement, and it's a total disaster."

She sighed. "Oh, Thomas. You don't want to go to grad school, do you? You could just graduate and get a nice job at a bank or something."

Thomas scowled. "That's what my mother said. Now you're sounding like my mother."

"Sorry. I guess I'm getting old. Anyway, I can't call you. Granna's house doesn't have a phone."

"It doesn't have a *phone?*" Thomas repeated, incredulous.

"No electricity, either," she affirmed. "What can I say? I'm being rustic this summer. And people will be lining up, I am sure, to buy a house with all those environmentally conscious, inconvenient, nonelectric appliances. You've probably never seen a nonelectric icebox, have you?"

"Why don't you just get one installed?" Thomas suggested. "Rotary phones don't take electricity."

Connie stopped, looked at her student, and grinned.

"ALL SET," THE MAN CALLED THROUGH THE OPEN FRONT DOOR. CONNIE was still sifting through her notes on the desk, and the sound of his voice made her notice the darkness beginning to puddle in the corners of the sitting room. She was always puzzled that people say that darkness falls. To her it seemed instead to rise, massing under trees and shrubs, pouring out from under furniture, only reaching the sky when the spaces near the ground were full. She rose, stretching and cracking her knuckles.

"This is great," Connie said, passing her hand over the black rotary phone that now squatted on the tiny side table in the front entry.

"Most folks like a cordless now, ya know," the man commented, lifting and settling his hat again.

"Yeah," said Connie. "No plug."

The man shrugged, betraying no apparent surprise that an inhabited house in a closely settled town at the end of the twentieth century could still be unelectrified.

"Bill'll come in the mail," he grunted, turning to make his way back down the flagstone path that led to the street.

"Thanks!" she called out after him.

"Need some lights out heah" was the vanishing response, and then Connie was alone.

❧

THE TELEPHONE RANG FOUR TIMES BEFORE IT WAS PICKED UP WITH GREAT commotion, and Grace's voice said, "Hello?"

"Mom?" said Connie. She leaned in the doorway between the entry and the dining room, watching the shadows of evening collect in the bowls of the dead potted plants that hung motionless, like dried spiders, in the windows. She should really throw those away. Why hadn't she gotten around to that yet?

"Connie, my darling! What a pleasure. I didn't think I'd hear from you again so soon," said Grace. For some reason, Connie imagined that Grace had been baking. She pictured her mother, hair still long, graying, standing with the telephone pressed to her cheek in the kitchen of her Santa Fe house. She imagined she saw Grace's hands caked with flour, a splotch of it now spread across her telephone receiver.

"Fine. What are you making?" Connie asked, hazarding a guess.

"Samosas. But I can't get the consistency right—the batter keeps pulling apart."

"You should add more ghee."

"I am, but that makes them so greasy!" Grace sighed, and Connie imagined her blowing aside a loose strand of hair. It would still be light outside in Santa Fe, and Connie pictured her mother's kitchen sink, its windowsill crowded with fat, bristling cacti and hybrids of thyme. When she moved west, Grace's plants had all taken on a prickly, dry quality. *Changing with the mandates of the earth,* Grace called it, whatever that was supposed to mean. Grace had complicated ideas about the relationship between weather and consciousness, for plants as well as for people. She liked to claim that electromagnetic fields caused by changing weather patterns could directly impact the auras of people, even changing their personalities or their abilities. Connie usually met this idea with patience, if not agreement. Grace had complicated ideas about most things, actually.

"I could do with a samosa right about now," said Connie. Grace chuckled.

"So tell me, darling," said her mother. "How is the house coming?"

"Slowly but surely," Connie replied, twisting the stretchy telephone cord around one thumb. The digit flushed red, and Connie freed it. "I've . . . started making a few changes, I guess."

"Putting in the telephone was an excellent idea," her mother said, her voice traveling together with the sound of a wooden spoon stirring wet batter.

"Mom! How did you know?" Connie laughed.

"Where else would you be calling from at dinnertime? Mother used to have one, you know. Took it out sometime in the sixties. Too much hassle, she said. Used to worry me sick, that something might happen and she wouldn't be able to reach anybody. There was no changing her mind, of course."

"She must have been very particular," said Connie.

"Oh, you have *no* idea," said Grace, and for an instant Connie heard in her voice an echo of her mother's teenage self. "How much longer before it's ready to sell?"

"Ah." Connie stalled. She had spent so much of her time on research that she had barely begun on the house. But if she was honest with herself, there was more to her reticence than that. Her eyes slid past the dead plant in its cracked porcelain China-export pot, traveling into the dim sitting room with its armchairs. The previous week she had scrubbed down their needle-point upholstery with gentle wool detergent, and they now glowed a warm reddish brown, comfortable and clean. After dinner Connie planned to kindle a small fire and read there until she grew sleepy. She felt oddly protective of the little room, unwilling to disturb it. "Awhile yet."

"*Connie,*" her mother began, voice once again that of a forty-seven-year-old woman.

"It was a real mess, Mom. It's going to take longer than I thought," Connie insisted.

Grace sighed. "Uh-huh. So tell me. If you haven't been working on the house as we discussed, what have you been doing? How are those headaches you mentioned?" Connie heard the sound of a spoon being laid to the side and batter being rolled out on a chopping block. A bleep sounded as Grace's chin dug into the keypad of her telephone.

"They're fine," Connie said, aware as she did so that while her daydreams had stayed vivid, she had not noticed the headaches afterward nearly as much. The shift had been gradual, almost imperceptible, but there it was.

"See? You didn't need a doctor," Grace interjected.

"Yeah," Connie said, dismissive. "As a matter of fact, I've been doing dissertation research." She attempted to imbue her voice with a mote of authority.

"Oh?" said Grace, losing interest.

"Remember that name I asked you about?" Connie said. "I did some background work on it, and I think it's led me to a possible primary source for my dissertation."

"A primary source? What sort of primary source?" asked Grace. Her voice carried a faint gloss of suspicion, but Connie pushed the thought away.

"It looks like Deliverance Dane might have actually owned some kind of instructional magic book! Isn't that incredible?"

"Incredible," Grace echoed, her voice flattening.

"It goes against everything historians have always said about the relationship between women and vernacular religion during the colonial period!" Connie exclaimed, voice rising.

"You were right," her mother said over the whisper and squish of dough under her fingers. "I did need to add more ghee."

"*Mom*," said Connie.

"I'm listening," said Grace.

"Now all I have to do is find the book. So far the probate records seem to be pretty much intact, so I have to follow the trail of the book as each owner dies. That assumes that each successive generation finds the book significant enough to mention in a will. But even if the book is probated together with several other books, I might still be able to trace its movement within the collection. Then, maybe, I'll get lucky."

"Oh, my darling, you don't need some dusty old book to be lucky." Grace sighed.

"Grace," said Connie, sliding into a seated position in the doorway of the dining room. "This is an important find for me. It could be a real research coup. It could make my reputation. Why is it so hard for you to understand that this is important to me?"

"I know that it's important to you, sweetheart," said Grace. "I'm not trying to dismiss what you do. I just worry that all this energy that you put into your *work*, as you call it, just takes you further away from really knowing yourself."

Connie inhaled deeply, wrestling her rage into a jagged ball under her diaphragm, and exhaled silently through her nose. Darkness had spread through the dining room, swallowing the shapes of the table and chairs, even rubbing away the hanging planters. Arlo wandered over from where he had been resting under the table and settled on the floor next to Connie, his furry chin in her lap.

"I know myself perfectly well," she said, trying to wring the sound of anger out of her voice.

"I don't mean to upset you, my darling," her mother soothed. "Hold on, let me just pop these into the oven."

Connie heard the clatter as the telephone was placed on a tile countertop two time zones away. A creak and scrape signaled the opening of Grace's oven and the sliding in of a cookie sheet heavy with samosas. Connie pictured her mother briskly wiping her floured palms on her apron—that one that Connie really hated, that said OM IS WHERE THE HEART IS. The receiver knocked against something, and then her mother's soft breath carried down the telephone wires and washed over her cheek. Connie felt her annoyance throb a little less.

"All I'm saying," Grace said, "is that it couldn't hurt to spend a little time looking into yourself and see what's going on in there. You are a special, remarkable person, Connie, whether you find the book or not. At this point, I just don't think you need it, that's all."

Connie felt her upper lip twitch and her nose and cheeks flush with salt water. She swallowed, reaching down to grab hold of one of Arlo's ears. She tugged on the dog's ear for a moment, saying nothing.

"Now," Grace said, pretending to ignore Connie's rising silence. "Are you ready to tell me about the boy yet?"

Connie breathed deeply, smiling in spite of herself through the tear that was snaking its way into the corner of her mouth.

"No," she managed to say.

"All right, I suppose it can wait." Grace sighed. "But we'll have to talk about it sooner or later."

Connie rolled her eyes. "Okay, Mom," she said. And then she hung up.

CHAPTER TEN

Marblehead, Massachusetts
Somewhere around the Summer Solstice
1991

"HEY, CORNELL!" A VOICE SAID, AND THE WORDS FLOATED IN SANS serif script across the plane of Connie's dreaming mind. They drifted over the image of Grace—or was it the woman in the portrait downstairs?—in a hospital gown, standing barefoot in the snow. The woman in the dream extended her arms, mouth open, screaming, but no sound came out. The sky overhead had a sun and moon in it together, and then the woman disappeared under a writhing coil of snakes, replicating and spreading out across the snow, coming toward her. Connie scowled in her sleep, limbs twitching.

"Hey! *Cornell!*" The words appeared again, the visual form of them breaking apart in little droplets of rainwater at the vibrating sound of something banging on the front door of the house. The dream dissolved into trailing skeins of thought as Connie was pulled upward toward consciousness. She became aware of the bed underneath her, of the pressure of dog feet against the back of her neck. She opened one eye.

The banging had followed her out of her dream and was now vibrating up through the floor, rattling the door latch. Connie sat up, hair askew, and wiped her eyes with one forearm. Arlo rolled onto his side with a yawn, legs stretching into the warm space in the bed that she had just vacated.

"What the *hell*," she muttered, shuffling across the slanted attic bedroom. She made her way down the stairs, toes hanging over each narrow step. Scratching her hair midyawn, she opened the front door.

"Hold this," said the voice, and a carryout cup of coffee was thrust into her hands. Behind the coffee cup Connie found Sam, in cargo shorts, Doc Martens, and a Black Flag T-shirt, holding a box of doughnuts. "Keeping grad school hours, huh?" He grinned, edging around her into the front hall. His arm brushed against her shoulder, leaving a tingling patch on the skin underneath her T-shirt.

Connie blinked.

"Ah, dining room!" said Sam, ambling into the old hall and setting the pastry box on the table. "You want a plate? Nah, you don't need a plate."

"Sam, what—" she started to ask.

"Eleven-thirty," he said, offering her a chocolate-covered Boston cream wrapped in a paper napkin.

"Wow. Really?" she said, accepting the pastry.

"Drink some of that coffee, you'll feel better," he assured her.

"But how did you find—" she started again.

"Easy. Looked for the only house *totally* obscured by vines," he said, settling in one of the shield-back chairs and propping one boot on the table-top with a smile. "It's a great one, by the way. Terrific shape."

"Are you kidding?" she asked. "It's a wreck. Every time I go upstairs I'm a little afraid it's going to fall over completely."

"No way," he said, shaking his head.

"Look." Connie dug a fingernail into one of the naked wooden beams crossing the threshold between the dining room and the entryway, and crumbled wooden dust spattered down from overhead. "Falling apart." She lowered herself into a chair at the dining table, glancing at him as she did so.

Sam looked up, then shrugged. "Powder post beetles. You expect that in a beam that old. Probably came in with the wood, back when it was built. About 1700, right? Then they've been gone for two hundred years, easy. It looks bad, but inside, that beam's like steel."

He bit into a jelly doughnut, leaving a white smear of powdered sugar around his lips.

"When they built it," he continued, "they used green wood for the pegs to hold the posts and beams together, so it would go in soft around the joint and then harden into place. The only thing that's going to take this house down is a bulldozer." Sam grinned, wiping slowly at the powdered sugar with the back of one wrist. "Nothing beats old hardwood," he said, watching her.

Connie swallowed, her ears blushing, and hastily pulled her gaze away. She bit into her own doughnut, not looking at him.

"There are women who would find this pretty weird, you know," she said presently, sucking crumbles of chocolate off her thumb.

"Yeah," he conceded. "I've gone out with a few of them." As Sam chewed, Arlo materialized under the table and sniffed at his leg. They ate for a moment in silence, Connie slurping her coffee. She became acutely conscious of the fact that she was sitting in front of Sam in faded plaid pajamas. Why that felt more intimate, more embarrassing, than swimming in her underwear with him in the dark she could not say. Their night swim, obscured as it was by darkness and fog, felt almost as if she had imagined it. They had passed several hours together, splashing and playing in the water. When they tired of swimming they had stretched out side by side on the raft, gazing up at the sky as the fog parted just enough to reveal a sprinkling of stars overhead. They lapsed into silence, not touching or speaking, Connie intensely aware of Sam's proximity, but frightened of letting her fingers take his hand, afraid that if she did so the unreality of the night would vanish. Now in the clarity of daylight she knew that it had been real. The warm blush on her ears started to creep down from her hairline onto her cheeks, and she crossed her legs without thinking.

"So," Sam said. Wagging, Arlo reared up and put a pair of happy front paws in his lap. Sam rubbed the animal's cheek and turned to Connie. "What are we doing today?"

"What?" Connie said through a mouthful of cream filling.

"I have the day off," Sam explained. "I've been thinking about your mystery witch. I figured you probably have a lot of research to do, and I'm kind of invested in your topic now. So . . ." He spread his hands out, shrugging. He waited for a beat, and when she did not respond immediately, said, "Of course, if you don't feel like working today, I could always just show you around a little. Whatever." He plucked another pastry out of the box, not looking at her.

Connie felt a shiver of pleased excitement vibrate in her middle and wander down her arms and legs, and she smiled. "Just give me a minute to get dressed," she said.

๛

A SMALL CHILD RAN UP ON QUICK FEET, AN OVERLARGE BLACK WITCH HAT covered in purple spangles balanced on its head. "Abracadabra!" she said, hands splayed for maximum effect, and then scampered to hide behind an ivy plant next to a woman seated at a café table who, Connie assumed from her beatific smile, could only be her mother. Sam, meanwhile, had tumbled to the brick walkway, arms and legs cartwheeled out at an angle.

"Ooof!" he cried. "She got me!"

The hat poked up from behind the ivy, shading a pair of anxious eyes.

"Get up!" Connie whispered to him. "You'll scare her!"

"You have to say the magic words!" moaned Sam, rolling his head back and forth in false pain and anguish.

" 'Please'?" guessed Connie.

"No, the other magic words!" He clutched at his imaginary wounds. "Quick!"

" 'Get up, doofus'?" Connie suggested.

Sam raised his head. "You're not very good at this, are you?" he asked.

Connie sighed. "Abracadabra?" she said.

Sam sprang to his feet in triumph. "Oh, thank goodness! I am saved," he whooped, and the hat shook with giggles. The woman smiled at them. Connie cast her eyes heavenward.

"That was a close one," said Sam as they moved into the shade of a nearby tree. "I thought she had me."

"It's based on a wimple, you know," Connie said, offhand. "Or a hennin."

"What is?" he asked.

"The witch hat that the little girl was wearing. The tall pointy part derives from a fifteenth-century headdress called a hennin, and the wide brim is a simplified form of an English wimple. Common middle-class women's headgear in the late Middle Ages, basically. Nothing inherently witchy about it."

Sam laughed, throwing his head back and wrapping his arms around his middle. "Hoo," he said, wiping his eyes. "You still haven't come back from orals-land, have you?"

The open-air passage where they were walking wound through the old city center of Salem, from the empty wharves, past the old hotel, around a small museum full of Chinese porcelain and model ships, all the way to the graffitied commuter train station, moving as it did so through each successive stage of Salem's community life. Knots of tourists strolled at a holiday pace among the vendor carts that dotted the walkway, perusing tie-dyed WITCH CITY T-shirts, "lucky crystals," iced lemonade, bonsai trees.

"And what about all the other stuff?" he asked.

"What other stuff?" she said, picking up a Witch City snow globe, examining it with a shake, and setting it back down on a nearby cart.

"Brooms? Black cats?" he teased. "You know. Witch stuff."

Connie snorted. "Well, the cat is just a stand-in for a familiar. But they weren't always only cats."

"Familiar?" he said, toying with a crystal on a long leather thong on the cart.

"A devil or spirit in the guise of an animal, that did the witch's bidding. In one of the Salem trial transcripts I've read they accuse some poor woman of having an invisible yellow bird perched on her shoulder. A little girl who was accused told the court her mother gave her a snake for a familiar, which she suckled from a wart between her fingers." Connie frowned. "I don't know why popular culture pairs witches exclusively with cats at this point. Maybe cats have their own folklore that just got mixed up with witches. And the broom I only know about because Liz showed me a woodcut in a book that she had to read for *her* orals."

"So tell me," he said

"The broom stuff is crazy," she said. "So a medieval witch on her way to a sabbath would strip off all her clothes." She laughed as Sam blanched. "Then smear her naked body with flying ointment, straddle her broom with the *straw end up*, which is important, because that's where the candle goes so that you can see when you're flying in the dark, then say a spell and be swept up the chimney. Isn't that nuts?"

"Mmmm. Flying ointment," Sam said, one eyebrow arched.

"Shut up," she teased, smacking him gently on the chest.

A group of middle-aged women with cameras shuffled by, clad in shorts and feathered witch hats. They clutched bulging plastic shopping bags advertising a witch trials–themed trolley tour. A teenage girl in heavy black eyeliner posed, lip curled, before a shop front wax museum that advertised DUNGEON AND BURNING-WITCH DIORAMAS.

"They really play up all this witch stuff, don't they?" Connie reflected.

"Summer solstice today," said Sam. "If you think this is bad, you should see it at Halloween."

"Yeah, but it speaks to how alienated we all are from history," Connie grumbled, blue eyes darkening. "For generations the witch trials were such an embarrassment that no one would discuss them. A proper history of them wasn't even written until the end of the nineteenth century. Now look at it—it's a carnival."

Connie looked around at the relaxed people milling about the esplanade, gazing into the windows of costume shops and card readers. She tried to imagine other violent, oppressive periods of history that had similarly been transformed into a source of amusement and tourism but could not think of any. Did Spain have Inquisition wax museums, showing effigies of people broken on the rack?

"There's something fascinating about violent death," Sam remarked, sensing her disaffection. "Especially if it happened to someone very distant from you. Look at the Tower of London. The tours there are all beheading, all the time. Generations of kings and queens in chains, getting their heads lopped off. And while you're there, be sure to admire the Crown Jewels! Their wealth and privilege is what makes them distant from us, in addition to their place in the past. And so we don't feel guilty reveling in their suffering."

"It's horrible," Connie said. "The people accused in Salem were just regular, everyday people."

"It's not all bad," said Sam, leading her away from the stoop of the wax museum. "One weird offshoot of all the witch stuff is that Salem has become a huge magnet for modern-day pagans. They come from all over the place." He gestured to a verdant shop front in a narrow alley off the main walk. Its hanging sign read *Lilith's Garden: Herbs and Magickal Treasures* in looping, hand-painted letters.

Connie sniffed with disapproval. "That's almost worse. Real pagans coming here to make a buck off of tourists with a morbid curiosity about people who were persecuted three hundred years ago. And the dead people weren't even pagans! They were Christians who just didn't fit in."

"Feeling cynical today, are we?" asked Sam. "You should have a little more faith in people, Cornell. C'mon." He took her by the elbow and pulled her, protesting, into the little shop.

As the door opened, a soothing gong sounded in place of the bell that usually rang over souvenir shop doors, and Connie was met with a waft of unplaceable scent—incense, but she could not tell what kind. Dark and spicy. Soft pan flute music played from a tape deck on the counter, its sound made slightly tinny by a dribble of hardened purple candle wax melted into the speaker mesh. Under the glass counter ranged crystals and jewelry of various kinds attached to black leather strings, and pewter figurines of wizards and fairies holding opalescent marbles aloft on their thin metal arms. A rack of wind chimes adorned one wall, and they released a torrent of clanking and tinkling as Sam's shoulder brushed against them.

"Merry meet!" piped a smiling woman, leaning on her elbows over an almanac open next to the cash register. "A joyous summer solstice to you both." Her hair was gathered in two lush pigtails over both of her shoulders, and half-moon earrings dangled from her ears. On her chest, peeking out between the ruffles of her blouse, lay a tattoo of a pentacle entwined with roses and lilies. Connie muffled a snicker between her lips, and Sam pinched her to keep her quiet.

"Hello," he replied to the smiling woman.

"Can I help you find anything?" she asked. "We have some special events today, just so you know. Tarot readings start in half an hour, and at five we'll have someone doing aura photography."

"We're just browsing," said Connie at the same moment that Sam said, "Can you tell us where the books are, please?"

The woman arched one penciled eyebrow and smiled wider. "Sure. They're right in the back, on the left."

"Thanks," said Sam, pulling Connie along in his wake.

"Blessed be," said the woman, nodding.

They made their way to the shelves in the back, which held racks of paperback books on Aleister Crowley, tarot reading, astrology, and something called "astral projection."

"Where are the magic eight balls?" asked Connie dryly, and Sam sighed.

"Don't you think it's interesting?" he said, prodding her. "I'm always intrigued by the different ways people decide what to believe. I mean, look at this—they're taken from all over the place. Celtic knots, Eastern philosophy, the New Age. Past and present collapsed into a buffet of equivalent options, all in pursuit of the divine. It's fascinating. This funky pagan element is one of the reasons that living in Salem is so interesting, even to a hardened old agnostic like me."

Connie perceived the real, guileless curiosity shining in Sam's eyes and immediately regretted her own curmudgeonliness.

"An agnostic steeplejack? There's a contradiction for you," she said, arms folded. Then she relented. "You're right, Sam. It *is* interesting. I'm sorry. I guess it just reminds me of some of the loopier aspects of my upbringing." Connie fingered a knitted prayer shawl hanging from a wire display rack and looked down at her feet.

Sam took her by the shoulders. "Hey," he said, stooping to look into her face. She glanced up at him, half-smiling. "Don't worry about it." His green eyes twinkling, he smiled down at her, holding her gaze. She swallowed.

"What do you think Deliverance Dane or Mercy Lamson would have to say about all this?" she joked, breaking the fleeting quiet that had gripped them. He laughed.

"God knows. I bet," he said, picking up a paperback collection of alien abduction narratives, "that *this* would have been Deliverance's favorite."

Connie laughed, turning away from the bookshelves. She stopped midchortle, stepping back in surprise. Opposite where she stood, stretching from the floor to near the ceiling, towered rack upon rack of powdered herbs and potions in little plastic envelopes with calligraphy labels.

"Wow," she said, moving in for a closer look. The selection ranged from common kitchen herbs, like oregano and savory, to inorganic substances, like ground yellow sulfur and vials of liquid mercury. She recognized most of the plant names, noting with some surprise that many of them seemed to grow wild in Granna's garden. She touched the little plastic packets, forehead crinkled in thought. The racks reminded her of something.

Of the jars and bottles in Granna's kitchen actually. The faded labels in the kitchen looked just like these, though largely illegible after so much elapsed time. "How odd," she whispered, pulling an envelope of henbane from one of the shelves and examining the label. GATHERED IN JUNE 1989 was typed in tiny script on the lower right-hand corner. Connie sniffed. Anyone with the most rudimentary knowledge of horticulture knew that herbs started to lose their efficacy almost the instant that they were gathered. Even cookbooks were explicit about this; the difference in flavor between dried herbs and fresh was an elementary fact of cooking.

"What a racket," she muttered, placing the packet back on its shelf. She caught up with Sam, who was perusing a selection of nose rings under the glass at the front of the shop.

"Do you think I should stick with the septum ring, or expand the options a little?" he asked as she approached, toying with the ring under his nose. "They've got little opal studs, cubic zirconia. . . ."

"Their herbs are all expired," Connie groused to him. "They're best if they're fresh, but you really have to use them within like two months of drying them. Otherwise they're no good. The ones they've got in the back are all, like, two years old. It's a total rip-off."

"Did you find everything you were looking for?" the pigtailed woman interrupted. She was affixing price tags to lavender Witch City coffee mugs. Her penciled brows were thrust together in a glower. Connie wondered if she had overheard their conversation.

"We're all set, thanks," said Connie, employing the universal New England expression that signals the end of a transaction. To be "all set" can mean that you are finished eating, that you do not need a fitting room, that you have the directions already, that the car has plenty of gas. It often means that you are not going to buy anything. A thundercloud gathered in the pigtailed woman's eyes, and she turned her shoulder toward them, half-moon earring swinging, and slapped a few more price tags on a few more mugs in chilly silence.

"Let's go," Connie whispered, taking Sam by the arm. An uneasy feeling suffused her, but as they passed under the gentle gong attached to the door, the feeling started to fall away.

THE SKY OVER SALEM HAD COOLED, AND A PALE PINK STAIN WAS SEEPING through the field of blue-gray stretching overhead. Connie inhaled, savoring the saline bite of the evening air, and let out a long, contented sigh.

"Are you going to finish this?" asked Sam, peering into her carryout box of pad thai. His chopsticks were poised expectantly. Connie laughed.

"What is it about boys?" she teased him. "Every boy I know can eat his own weight in food. You should see my thesis student. He looks like he weighs ninety pounds, but every time we have a lunch meeting he's always getting seconds and thirds."

Sam laughed through a mouthful of her noodles. "Just lucky, I guess," he said. "Mmmmmm. Yours is better than mine."

Connie dangled her bare feet over the end of the dock and surveyed the harbor stretching away below her. Several yachts were moored together, growing darker under the pinkening sky, and the soothing sound of halyards clanking against masts traveled across the surface of the water. She tried to picture what the wharves would have looked like when Salem was a bustling seaport, one of the great city centers of the colonies. Even for her practiced mind the distant picture was difficult to conjure. She tried to place a great wooden triple-masted sailing ship alongside the wharf where they sat, tried to see the piles of sea chests and the boxes of live chickens, sacks of grain and hardtack, oiled barrels of rum heaped together on the wharf. She filled in rickety warehouses and sail lofts lined up in tight rows along the edge of the long wharf, wooden signs swinging in the breeze. She strained to hear the sounds of the sailing master barking orders at the sailors working in the rigging overhead, but all she heard was the cry of a seagull seated atop a rotting piling twenty feet out in the water. Maybe Grace was right. Maybe she did spend too much of her time in the past and not enough noticing the present moment.

"We don't have much time," said Sam, edging nearer to her on the dock.

"Oh, we don't have to be anywhere." Connie smiled at him.

"Ah, but we do," said Sam, rising to his feet and offering her his hand.

She followed him down a darkening alleyway that ran through the neighborhood behind the old mercantile exchange building, and was surprised when they came to a stop outside of the First Church, where she had first met him. They had approached it from the opposite direction, and Connie experienced the odd vertigo that she always felt when coming upon a familiar place from an unfamiliar standpoint. He unlocked the meetinghouse door and held it open for her.

"Now that I've led you astray for a day," Sam said as he steered her to the staircase that she had noticed on their day in the church archives, "what's your next step? You've already seen Mercy Lamson's probate record, right?"

"Yes," said Connie, watching her footing as they climbed in the close confines of the circular stairwell. "Mercy left a book called 'receipts for physick' to her daughter Prudence."

"*Prudence,*" Sam repeated. "Whoa."

"Yeah," Connie acceded. "These names are pretty intense."

"So are you going back to the Will and Probate office after dear Prudence?" He paused to hum a bar or two and his voice echoed as it fell down the empty center of the stairwell. The stairs grew steeper and bore a musty smell, of rare use and dead wasps. Sam had not turned on any lights.

"Maybe," she said finally. "I mean, yes, definitely. But Mercy was involved in some kind of lawsuit in 1715, and I'd like to find out what it was about. So I guess that's what I'll be doing tomorrow. Going to the courthouse. Then I'll go back to Prudence's probate record after that." She was starting to grow short of breath from the climb. Presently Sam came to a halt in front of her, and she heard him fumbling at his key ring.

"Here we are," he said, fitting a key into the locked door ahead of him. With one shoulder he eased the heavy wooden door free from its frame, and turned to grasp Connie's hand. She hesitated for a moment, then fitted her hand into his palm. "Watch the doorjamb," he said before pulling her out into the evening sky. Connie caught her breath.

They stood behind a fragile brass railing that wrapped around the bell tower of the meetinghouse, and spread out below them Connie saw the city lights of Salem beginning to wink on in the advancing night. From this height they could see over the clustered brick houses and treetops and shop fronts down to the wharf where they had been sitting, to the harbor and beyond that to the little peninsula of Marblehead lying against the blackening sea. Overhead the sky turned from a frail pink into a deep blushing red-orange, spreading its color onto the rippling surface of the water.

"Oh," she breathed, eyes widening at the view of the city stretching away beneath her feet. He placed one hand over hers on the railing, and his skin felt warm and dry against her knuckles. His other hand traced her jaw, coming to a rest alongside her neck and ear, and as she turned to ask him a question, his lips met hers in a deep kiss that lasted until the orange curtain of the setting sun had been pulled completely away to reveal the stars glimmering overhead.

Interlude

Salem Town, Massachusetts
Late October

1715

*T*he thinning patch had been there for at least two winters, but of course it would be on this day that the cloak would rip. And she with no darning materials even to pass the time. Mercy Lamson scowled as she poked her thumb through the offending hole, feeling the harsh wool scraping against her skin. She was tempted to tear the hole wider and wider, to wreak on her tattered cloak the anger that she felt. But she thought better of it. *New cloak would be too dear*, she told herself, frowning. She scanned the townsfolk ranged on the benches around her, half-expecting them to have seen into her passing distemper. If they had, they gave no sign. Scattered women pulled crewel work needles through little scraps of cloth. Men murmured. Behind her, a man she did not recognize slept, head propped on the hard bench back, mouth stretched open in a soundless snore. She sighed and settled herself again in her seat, smoothing the frayed ends of the hole into some semblance of order. *Time enough for patching later*, she thought.

Mercy surveyed the room where she had passed the last several hours, her pale eyes traveling over every square inch of wainscoting in a meager effort to keep her mind occupied. Many years had lapsed since she made her home in Salem, and her confusion had been great when told the case would be heard in the new town hall rather than at the meetinghouse or in the magistrate's parlor. Right on the common it sat, like a proper English courthouse, or so she had heard. Two stories, good new brick, and not far from the wharves. *But in England the courthouse wood never smelled so polished and new*, she supposed. Mercy had never given much thought to England. Not until she married Jedediah.

The room where she sat, surrounded by fellow petitioners squirming on benches, bore a magisterial splendor that had been unknown in Mercy's youth. At the front of the room rested a raised bench, festooned with scrollwork, flanked on both sides by heavy wooden boxes for the jurymen. Below the bench stood two fine carved tables, for the lawyers and the clerk, and then, between the tables, in full sight of the jury, bench, and onlooking townsfolk, an empty space before the bar. Already this morning she had watched four piteous souls led to stand alone in this space, the keen focus of the entire room rendering them as if under heavy magnifying glass. A wave of nausea washed through Mercy's stomach, and she felt her forehead grow cold and moist. Her turn would come soon enough.

Behind the judge's bench hung a life-size portrait of a regal man in fine robes trimmed in fur, with long, curling hair and heavy rings. She returned her attention to this apparition; she had been contemplating it the better part of the morning. Never had she seen such a lavish likeness of a person. Even from her distant vantage point in the gallery, his eyes seemed warm and kind, and his skin flushed a healthy pink and white. Once she had caught herself wondering how that fine, curling hair would feel pulled through her fingers like a comb—soft, smooth, scented with lavender, she imagined. Embarrassed, she stirred in her seat. *The likeness were startling, sure*, she thought. Should this man ever walk down the streets of Marblehead she would know him, right enough.

Jedediah would be to sea a further two months yet. Mercy's eyes darkened to think of his feeling, should he hear some of what she must say. Though he knew well what she was about, so much the better that he be gone.

Movement stirred at the front of the courtroom, and Mercy worked her feet together, shifting her weight on the uncushioned bench. The current petitioner was led away, head hanging, wrists clamped together in irons, by two solemn constables. A frisson of activity around the bench and jury boxes signaled the beginning of the next case, and Mercy watched the clerk leaning in inaudible conference with the judge, who nodded and then cast his eyes upon her. Mercy's stomach rolled over and she swallowed, her tongue suddenly drained of moisture.

"Mehcy Dane Lamson versus the Town of Salem in the County of Essex!" called out the clerk, and a score of heads swiveled to look in her direction. The skin around Mercy's eyes tightened in momentary surprise, for she had been long gone from Salem Town and knew none of the faces now watching her as she rose from her seat. *How could this changed town have such a long memory?* she wondered, making her way to the bar. The judge, a great hillock of a man wrapped in black robes, with cheeks the sickly yellow of tallow wax, glared at her as she arrived in the empty rectangle at the center of the room. Idly, on the murmuring level below her conscious mind, Mercy assembled the list of herbs that he would need to tone his dying liver. He'd be a man who liked his drink.

"Have you no lawyer, then?" barked the judge.

Mercy opened her mouth to speak, but her dry tongue clung to the roof of her mouth, and a cough came out instead.

"*Well?*" the judge bellowed. Mercy straightened herself, smoothing her skirts with both hands, and then settling them on the polished bar before her.

"Indeed, sir, I have not," she said.

The judge harrumphed, and titters reached Mercy's ears from the corner of the room that held the jury box. She held her gaze steady on the warm eyes looking down from the portrait of the regal young man. The room settled into quiet. Mercy noticed a cloud pull away from the tall windows on the right side of the room, releasing a yellow square of sunlight onto the lawyers' tables. The windowpanes were just beginning to frost over with ice.

"Get on with it, woman!" roared the judge, and she felt the force of his impatience hit her like a hot wind.

"Youah to give yah deposition now," whispered the clerk, who had appeared at her elbow. He gave her an encouraging nod.

"Oh! Indeed," said Mercy, unsure. She unfolded a thick sheaf of papers that she had written out at home, periodically, over the past several weeks. They rattled in her hands, and she willed them to be still. She cleared her throat, and the room leaned forward, ears open, waiting for her to speak.

"I, Mercy Dane Lamson, late of Marblehead, do hereby petition the town of Salem in the County of Essex for the rightful restoration of the good name of my mother, Deliverance Dane, that all baseless charges heretofore held against her be cleared by the court, thus relieving us her family of shame and disgrace. Which infamy ha' resulted in difficulty in transacting business and affairs such that I ha' little means of sustaining myself and my family, leaving us well nigh in want and indigence, denied the favor and friendship of our fellow men."

How she hated saying these things. How wretched Jedediah should feel, as though she thought he did not do well enough by her. Mercy's cheeks flushed deep scarlet as the witnessing townsfolk murmured in response to her plea.

"Mr. Saltonstall for the town, if you please," said the judge, indicating a plush, elderly man seated at the lawyers' table to Mercy's left. With a grunt the gentleman rose, adjusting the flowing gray wig that sat, slightly askew, atop his head. His posture stooped somewhat, but he was lean, and his eyes glinted with the fervor of a much younger man. Mercy tried to read the intent in his face, finding as she did so a loose familiarity to his countenance, the context for which had years ago slipped away.

"Mrs. Lamson," he began, standing with both hands planted on the table before him. "Problems of reputation being famously difficult to quantify, you perhaps could provide the court with some further detail?"

"Sir?" she asked.

"You have a husband, then?" asked Mr. Saltonstall.

"I do," she answered, perplexed.

"With you today, is he?" asked the lawyer, making a show of craning his neck to look over the crowd.

"He is at sea," she replied, brows knitted.

"Ah!" said the lawyer, folding his hands behind his back and strolling into the space before the bar where Mercy stood. "A seaman. Difficult work, that. But it can provide." The gallery met this sarcastic pronouncement with mirth, and Mercy bristled.

"After my mother's imprisonment I was for some years neglected by young men of good fame who used to court me for marriage, 'til I was well and truly thought an old maid. Jedediah Lamson endeavored to gain my affection upon his arrival from England, in the thirty-fifth year of my age."

The women in the gallery whispered among themselves; Mercy felt stirring behind her an undercurrent of feminine anxiousness, as she stood before them embodying one of their many unspoken fears. She started to finger the hole in her cloak but then gripped the bar a little tighter instead.

"Indeed!" proclaimed the lawyer, pacing across the space before her again. "A most fortunate event. And before this inveigling of Mr. Lamson's, how did you gain a reputable living?"

"After my mother's trial my neighbors and friends had forsaken my company," Mercy said, her voice quiet. "I were made so odious in the eyes of all good subjects that they would refuse to employ me in my stated trade, nor entertain me in their houses, nor suffer to repast with me, nor barter with me, neither even to converse with me. I did forbear the practice of my trade, being the very offscouring of my society, and so made to make my home in a new town whereupon I resumed my healing work to a much diminished degree."

Still the whispers circulated in the mouths of the people seated behind her, occasionally spilling out whole words and fragments that Mercy could just overhear. *Disappeared*, she thought she heard, and *little child* and *neigh distracted*. Also one word, more often than all the others, the word she dreaded: *witch*.

"What is this healing work whereof you speak?" asked the lawyer, folding his arms and glaring at Mercy. She looked around her, worried, and then up again at the soft eyes in the portrait.

"I am able with plants and herbs, to assemble tinctures for the sick, or for women in the childbed, and to perceive what ails them to a true extent, to give counsel and to soothe their sufferings as well as can be done. For this work I receive goods in trade, or sometimes currency."

"What!" cried the lawyer, moving his face near to hers so that she cringed away from him slightly, "Are you a *cunning woman?*" The accusation washed over her face, and she began to see the folly of explaining herself to this man, him with his silver buttons and—she sniffed his breath—his snuff addiction.

"I prefer not to attach a name to my craft," Mercy said, steeling herself against the nausea that still circulated in her belly. Under all her many layers of wool and linen she felt a clammy sheen of sweat collect in her armpits. The air in her lungs grew more shallow.

"Ought not an ailing man be better served to consult with a *physician?* One properly trained in the movements of the humors and the machinations of the body?" asked the lawyer, aiming his question at the box of jurymen. One of them wore a satisfied smirk and was sitting with his boot propped against the polished box railing. *A doctor, surely*, Mercy thought. Educated down Cambridge way, at the college. As if all he need know could come from a book!

"There are those as prefer that," she conceded.

"Prefer!" the lawyer bellowed, and the judge smiled. "You are a charlatan, woman!" The gallery exploded in cries and commentary as Saltonstall pointed at her with one long finger, the lace of his cuff waving in its wake, and Mercy felt her patience slice in two.

"Whether I am a charlatan or no ought not concern us here!" asserted Mercy, her voice growing stronger. "I charge the court to clear the name of

Deliverance Dane, for her memory's own sake as well as my own, and for the sake of my infant daughter, as it did the names of all the other unfortunate souls condemned to death by the Court of Oyer and Terminer called by this town in 1692, which scurrilous evidence and vicious lies ha' been well established by Judge Sewall himself!"

As she spoke she brought her fist down on the bar before her, the strength of her will massing in her belly and crackling down her flying arm, her eyes faded to ice, and the force of the blow shot a crack through the wood, nearly severing the railing in half. The watching crowd gasped, silenced.

Richard Saltonstall, unfazed, strolled back over to where Mercy Lamson stood, her knuckles white with rage, her nostrils quivering.

"So true that the Court of Oyer and Terminer, in their haste to free our covenanted community from diabolical influence, did perhaps too hastily credit the evidence of specters and distracted little girls," he said, shaking his head sadly.

"And so true, too, that those unfortunate souls, now given over to the care of our almighty and merciful God, have since had their names restored by this court to the status duly accorded them for the benefit and improvement of their living progeny." He strolled back to stand before the jury box, where the twelve pairs of watching men's eyes sat fixated upon Mercy's quivering form.

"And so true that your circumstances have been rendered mean and insupportable following the condemnation of your mother, and yet . . ." Saltonstall paused, turning to survey the gallery. The gallery waited, holding its breath.

"And yet, Mrs. Lamson," he said again, and Mercy looked upward at the portrait with its warm, pink cheeks, and its luscious curls, all flat and made only of indifferent paint.

"And yet," he said a third time, now turning to meet her cool eyes.

"*Those* unfortunates were innocent."

CHAPTER ELEVEN

Boston, Massachusetts

July 3

1991

THE UPSTAIRS SPECIAL COLLECTIONS READING ROOM OF THE BOSTON Athenaeum was entirely empty, and Connie checked her watch for the fifth time in an hour, wondering if she should take the delay as a none-too-subtle hint. The research librarian had made no attempt to conceal his irritation when she asked for the book to be paged.

"All right, *fine*," he whispered. "But we close early today. Wait over there." He pointed at the chair positioned squarely in the patch of sun under the window, farthest away from the fan, and now Connie felt a blanket of warmth pressing into her back. A trickle of sweat snaked down from her eyebrow into the hollow on the side of her nose, and she wiped it away with irritation. *Fifteen more minutes*, she promised herself. *I can wait for fifteen more minutes.* Her pencil shaded in the leaves on the drawing of a dandelion that she had traced in the margins of her notebook. Presently her mind softened, pulling a transparent scrim of daydream up in front of the table where she sat, on which she saw projected a perfect film of Sam, brushing back his wet hair under the moonlight. She allowed herself to move further into the dream, her lips curving.

"You the one waiting for the Bartlett journal?" asked the young librarian, his face dour. Connie blinked, pulled back to her table, her notebook, the sun on her back, and the man standing bent over a cart bearing several stacked archival boxes.

"Yes," she said, pushing back in her chair to reach for the first box.

"Just a minute," said the young man, brushing her aside. "You're familiar with the rules, I hope. No pens. Use the foam blocks to prop the covers open so that the spines don't crack. No photocopying. Open only one box at a time. Handle the manuscripts as little as possible, wearing these." He deposited a pair of new white cotton gloves on the table next to her. "And frankly, you really shouldn't be sitting in the sun," he finished, casting a baleful look at Connie.

"I'm happy to move," she said, too tired even to argue.

Soon ensconced in the blessed shade at the end of a long table, Connie slid the first box toward her, gloved hands gripping the edges lightly. She opened the acid-free box, untied the fragile string that was looped around the book inside, and settled the first volume of the journal atop two green foam wedges. She eased the cover open and read the title page.

Diary of Prudence Bartlett, it read in faint, watery script. *January 1, 1741–December 31, 1746.*

Connie caught her breath, heady with anticipation. Prudence had not been mentioned by name in the fragmentary record of Mercy Lamson's 1715 lawsuit, but she had appeared as the sole heir on Mercy's probate record. Though New Englanders were a famously literate people, very few colonists had left anything so explicit as a diary—even fewer women. Connie was astonished when a cursory call to the Boston Athenaeum revealed that Prudence Lamson Bartlett kept a journal, which had found its way into their special collections. So far Connie knew that the recipe book had passed into

Prudence's hands at Mercy's death, or possibly before, but she had not been able to find Prudence's own will or probate. Records that old, Connie knew, were often incomplete or damaged, but the disappearance of Prudence's probate list had left her feeling crushed. There had been a dark afternoon last week when Connie telephoned Liz in a self-pitying panic, convinced that she would not be able to find Deliverance's book after all.

Now she sat at the reading table, poised to devour an unimaginably rare variety of primary source. Prudence's diary stretched over several volumes from 1741, the year after her marriage, when she was around twenty-six years old, to shortly before her death in 1798—over one hundred years after the Salem witch trials. Connie opened the book, her pale eyes shining in excitement, and began to read, pencil poised over her notebook.

Jan. 1, 1741. Very cold indeed. I have staid at home.

Jan. 2, 1741. Cold continues. I have stayd at home.

Jan. 3, 1741. Shawl nearlie done. Snow.

Jan. 4, 1741. Snow continues.

Jan. 5, 1741. Cold abates some. Dog stays in the bede.

Connie sank her head into her hands with a groan. Of course it was unrealistic to expect long, reflective passages about the nature of womanhood in the eighteenth century, but *really*. The tedium of an afternoon slog through the minutiae of Prudence's daily life stretched ahead of her, and Connie felt her excitement seep away, melting through her feet into the floor. She turned over a few thick leaves of the book, skipping ahead.

Mar. 25, 1747. Visit Hannah Glover. She is deliverd of a girl. Recid 3 lbs. Coffee.

Connie leaned closer, concentrating.

Mar. 30, 1747. Worked in the gardin.

Mar. 31, 1747. Gatherd herbs. Hung them to drye by the fire.

Apr. 1, 1747. Feel unwell. I have staid at home.

Apr. 2, 1747. Rain. Josiah to town. I have staid at home.

Apr. 3, 1747. Rain continues. Call'd to Lizabet Coffin in her labors.

Apr. 4, 1747. At Coffins. Lizabeth deliverd of a boy, born dead.

Apr. 5, 1747. At Coffins. Liza. In poor way.

Apr. 6, 1747. At Coffins. Lizabet improves. Rec'd 2 lbs. Pease.

Apr. 7, 1747. Home. Find Josiah returned.

Connie paged deeper into the journal, finding several entries of an almost identical content. She sifted through the stultifying repetition, trying to read between the lines to uncover details that Prudence would not have thought to state explicitly. Of course a woman who produced much of her own food would think that the weather was an important matter for her journal. She would have pored over almanacs for the same reason. Connie could feel frustrated that this distant daughter of taciturn Puritans would not have had the cultural knowledge necessary to reflect in print on her inner life, but that frustration would be misplaced. In some respects, Prudence's daily work *was* her inner life. Connie read further, working her way through day after day of weather reports, gardening projects, comings and goings of the inscrutable Josiah, repeated calls to aid suffering neighborhood women. All of a sudden Connie laughed when she realized the obvious answer.

"Of course!" Connie said aloud. "Prudence was a midwife!" The librarian glared at her from behind his desk.

"Oh, c'mon, there's no one else here!" she called across the room, annoyed.

"Shhhhhhhh!" he shushed, finger held to his lips.

Connie cackled to herself, enjoying her minor rebellion while jotting comments in her notebook. Maybe she gave in to her desire to defy the librarian in part to offset the taciturn restraint that bounded Prudence's experience. The more she read, the more she had to fight the urge to stand up on the table, turn a cartwheel in the aisle. She almost felt like she owed it to Prudence to misbehave.

Connie wrote down every fact that she could glean from the dates in the journal, trying to peer through the dull words on the page to see the living, breathing life that they portrayed. After four hours of concentrated work, she had read every entry from 1745 through 1763: nearly two decades of weather reports, domestic labor, and payment for delivering women's babies. Connie stretched, bringing her arms overhead, bending her shoulder blades over the back of the library chair. The blood drained down from her fingertips, and she flexed them, pencil held aloft. She pushed the open journal away, rubbing her eyelids, and then turned to her notes.

So far the journal mentioned nothing about Prudence's infamous grandmother. The contours of Prudence's life slowly emerged: she was a midwife and apparently a skilled one, as she had not yet lost a mother, and had lost only a handful of babies. She was married to a man named Josiah Bartlett, who appeared to make his living as a shoreman, loading and unloading ship cargo when it landed at the Marblehead docks. The Bartletts seem to have been long-standing friends of Prudence's family, though Connie could not quite pinpoint how she had gathered that impression. Prudence seemed well regarded by her neighbors, though perhaps lacking in what Connie would have called friends. She lived in Marblehead but attended church sporadically. She traveled only when called to see a patient, but those were scattered throughout Essex County: in Danvers, Manchester, Beverly, as far north as Newburyport and as far south as Lynn.

A few entries stood out enough to warrant copying verbatim, and Connie looked over them again.

Octo. 31, 1741. Growing cauld. Olde Pet. Petford dies. May God forgive him.

Connie was not sure what this entry could mean, but Prudence so rarely commented on anyone other than her own patients and her family that the note about Peter Petford—whoever he was—had leapt off of the page. Connie drew a dark asterisk next to the name in her notebook, a reminder to look for him elsewhere.

Novem. 6, 1747. Snow. Paines through much of the night. Safe deliver'd of a girl. Patience. I have staid at home.

Connie smiled. She had stared at this entry for all of five minutes before she deduced that it marked the day that Prudence herself gave birth to a daughter, whose name was as ponderous as Prudence's own.

Jul. 17, 1749. Rain and wind. Endives sav'd. Jeded. Lampson reported lost at sea.

Connie was not certain but felt reasonably sure that this entry marked the death of Prudence's father. She sat back in her chair, thinking. What restraint, Prudence writing such a sterile entry for a lost parent. She could not imagine responding so coolly if she had been aware when Leo went missing overseas. And though Grace rarely spoke of Lemuel Goodwin, her father, when she did so it was always with tenderness and regret. What was Mercy's response to the loss of Jedediah Lampson? The journal did not say. What had Granna done when she lost Lemuel? No historians that she knew of ever really talked about the mental world of women who outlived their men.

She frowned. Of course, most of the men that she had come across while looking into Deliverance's family had not just predeceased their wives; they had died in accidents. Violent, wretched accidents. She suspected that if she ever found more information about Nathaniel Dane, who predeceased Deliverance, he would fit the pattern as well. Dangerous work, living in the past.

No other evidence for the first name of Mercy Lamson's husband had manifested itself, but she could see no other reason for the event to be recorded as part of Prudence's day. Her suspicion was bolstered by an entry from the following month.

Augs. 20, 1749. Sun, quite hot. Mother arrives. Work'd in the gardin.

Prudence had made no previous mention of her mother, but following this entry Mercy appeared periodically, illustrated using the same language that Prudence employed for other members of her household. Mercy was described going to church, often taking baby Patience (called "Patty") with her, or working in the garden, or occasionally traveling with Prudence to visit an expectant mother. They seemed to settle in together, though no mention was made of Mercy's helping with the household expenses. She appeared to have been taken in by Prudence out of pity rather than preference.

Why Prudence had paid no visits to her mother in the preceding four years before they combined households, Connie could not fathom. Had they not gotten along? Of course mothers and daughters with strong personalities might see the world from very different points of view. She wrinkled her nose, uncomfortably aware of this echoing truth in her own relationship with Grace. Or Grace's relationship with Sophia, for that matter. Connie's hypothesis about their troubled relationship received modest support from an entry some years later.

Decem. 3, 1760. Very cauld. Patty unwell. Mother looks for her Almanack. Very vexed when told it given to the Sociall Libar. Makes her poultice. Patty improves.

Connie looked over this jotting, unsure. The journal writing was so brief and focused that reading tone or intent into the chosen words smacked to her of overinterpretation. Even so, this entry felt significant to her. Angry, almost. Connie rested her forehand in her hands, tapping at the top of her head with her fingertips, eyes fixed upon her notes.

Then, in 1763, Connie found the event that the church records and the probate office foreshadowed. She hazarded a look over her shoulder at the young librarian behind the desk and saw him absorbed with reshelving. Under the table Connie tugged on each gloved fingertip, slipped her left hand out of its warm cotton cover, and crept the naked hand across the desk to brush her skin over the handwriting on the page. Prudence's own hand had moved over that same page, pressed into the paper. The ink carried little ancient flecks of her skin where she had licked her quill tip, or had rubbed out a word. Connie tried to reach into the realm that Prudence and Mercy had occupied, tried to conjure the sensation that would illuminate Prudence's vanished self. Her fingers came to rest on a narrow block of passages written at the end of the page, words cramped together like little ants disassembling a beetle.

Febr. 17, 1763. Sleet and rain. Mother has ben unwell. Patty attends her. We have stayd at home.

Febr. 18, 1763. Rain continues. Called to Lawr. Slattery's wife. Patty goes to her. We have staid at home.

Febr. 19, 1763. Wet and caulder. Mother continues unwell. Josiah to town for doctor. Mother very vexed. Patty at the Slatterys.

Febr. 20, 1763. Cauld continues. Mother sleeps, though poorly. Asks after Patty. Asks for almanack. Josiah at Salem. Patty at the Slatterys.

Febr. 21, 1763. Cauld. I have staid at home. Patty returns. Mrs. Slattery safe deliver'd. Rec'd 6 sh. 3 p.

Febr. 22, 1763. Too cauld for snow. I have stayd at home. Mother very unwell. Rev'd Bates visits.

Febr. 23, 1763. Cold. Josiah returns with dr. Hastings. Mother will not see him. Asks for me. Seems much agrieved.

Febr. 24, 1763. Too cauld to write. Mother dies.

Connie lifted her head and gazed across the vaulted reading room. She thought back to Deliverance's probate list, a telescoping lens through which Connie could peer back in time and look into the living room of a distant woman. Here she held in her hands a daily log of the entire second half of another woman's life, and Connie felt like she knew her even less. Prudence's cold practicality, her obstinate refusal to reveal her feelings, no matter how culturally proscribed, created in Connie a whistling void of incomprehension. She wanted to throw the journal across the room, to bunch its fragile pages up in her hands and rip them into shreds, to shake Prudence out of her reserve. But Prudence sat removed from her frustration, insulated by a two-hundred-year-long wall.

A drop fell from somewhere, smudging the dandelion sketch in the margin of Connie's notes. She wiped her arm across her eyes and pushed the antique book away.

CHAPTER TWELVE

Marblehead, Massachusetts

July 4

1991

"FRANKLY, I AM A LITTLE SURPRISED THAT HE WOULD CALL YOU," said Grace. Her voice sounded mild, but Connie perceived a perturbed undercurrent in her choice of words.

"He was just really curious to find out what I learned from Prudence's journal," Connie assured her. "He knew that I had an appointment at the Athenaeum yesterday. And he knew that it was vital that I find a mention of the recipe book, or else I wouldn't know where to look next."

"How did he take it when you told him?" Grace asked, carefully. Grace always sounded careful when she crocheted. Connie wondered what form was emerging from Grace's rapidly moving crochet hook while they talked. She pictured her mother seated in her living room, phone receiver tucked into her shoulder, lap overlaid with a spreading, rainbow-colored confection of yarn, collecting in a heap around her feet.

Connie brushed her fingertip down the spiderwebbed surface of the entryway mirror and sighed. "To be honest, he sounded pretty upset."

In fact, *angry* might have been a more fitting word than *upset*. Manning Chilton telephoned her that morning as Connie sat, sipping coffee over her copy of the *Local Gazette and Mail* (headlines: "Fireworks Planned for Nine O'Clock"; "Model Sailboat Regatta Boasts Record Number of Participants"; "Rotary Club Meeting Postponed"). When Connie told Chilton that she found no explicit mention of the physick book in Prudence's journal, and had learned nothing apart from the fact that Prudence was a fairly grim woman who made her living as a midwife, he demanded to know what her next step would be. Connie, baffled enough by her advisor's telephoning her at home, on a holiday no less, had been caught unprepared for the question.

"Upset how?" asked Grace.

Connie hedged. "I think he's just excited, you know. It's such an intriguing source, and he really wants to see me do well. . . ." Which is a nicer way of putting what he really said, which was *What in God's name have you been doing wasting your and my time like this*, and *Frankly I had expected much more of you*. Connie shuddered, remembering the conversation.

"Upset *how*, Connie," Grace pressed.

Connie sighed again, cursing inwardly for having always wished for Grace to express interest in her work. "He sort of . . . screamed at me," she admitted, hastening to add "but it totally wasn't a big deal," at the same moment that Grace cried, "Oh, Connie!" and threw down her crochet hook in irritation.

"It wasn't, Mom," Connie insisted. *You had better put your mind to finding it*, Chilton had said. *Else I will seriously doubt your commitment to the study of history, and will not be able to guarantee your scholarship support in the coming year*. Her stomach contracted at the memory, but she told herself that he was only trying to keep her motivated—strong-arming though his techniques may have been. Grace only exhaled through her nostrils, blowing her hot breath over the telephone receiver and into Connie's ear.

"He just really wants me to find the book. But right now I have no way of knowing what Prudence Bartlett did with it, and so he's upset. I just should've been more prepared." Connie walked into the dining room, stretching the telephone cord out behind her until it stopped her just short of the crockery shelf. She had spent part of the previous week finally rinsing the heavy layer of dust off each of the dishes, and they now glowed in the dim corner of the room. Connie picked up a mug, examined it—British, nineteenth century, with a hairline crack—and replaced it on the shelf.

"He's got a point, anyway," she continued. "I've got no clue what to do next. Prudence didn't leave a probate record, and she didn't mention it in her journal. If I can't figure out where the book went next, I'll have to rethink the whole project."

"Hmmmm," said Grace, with barely perceptible disapproval. "Why do you think he's so invested?"

"All advisors are invested in their students' success," said Connie, conscious as she did so that she sounded unconvincing. Like a brochure.

"Things must have changed since I was in college." Grace sighed as Connie started to correct her by saying "graduate school," and Grace amended, "Of course, my darling, graduate school. Is it *really* that important?"

Connie inhaled sharply.

"I know," said Grace, before Connie's snap could finish taking shape. Connie squelched a sigh and decided to change tack.

"Are you doing anything for the Fourth?" she asked, toying with one of the dead plants still hanging in the dining room. Her mother released a peal of merry laughter.

"Not hot dogs and fireworks, if that's what you're asking. The co-op is running a bake sale and carnival to raise money. Any surplus will go to our subcommittee on the ozone layer. I'll be reading auras." Connie said nothing but thought, *And what color is my aura right this minute, Grace?* "You know, it might help if you think about this book in a different way," Grace said, filling Connie's silence.

"Oh?" Connie asked.

"Perhaps this woman—Prudence—didn't think of the book like a recipe book per se. She might've used different language to describe it. She's a hundred years after her grandmother, after all. Sometimes people see things differently from their mothers." Connie could hear the smile in her mother's voice and grinned in spite of herself. "And how are you celebrating the holiday?" Grace asked.

"Liz is coming up for the weekend. We'll make dinner and watch fireworks with Sa—with this guy I know. Go to the beach. Dodge my advisor's calls. The usual." Connie turned a blackened jar that stood atop one of the chests in the dining room, digging a dark circle into the layer of dust surrounding it.

"At last, the boy appears," Grace remarked. "I can't know his name yet?" She waited while Connie smiled into the silence.

"Oh, all right. Well, that sounds like fun," Grace said, brightly. "But I must run." She paused. "And, Connie," she said, sifting through her words, "I'm not sure what to tell you about your Chilton situation."

"What do you mean? All advisors get on their students' cases. I gave Thomas fits last semester. It's the same thing," said Connie, shrugging.

"I don't mean anything. Just tread lightly, my darling, that's all."

Connie threaded her fingers through the telephone cord and said, "I will, Mom. Don't worry." And just as she hung up she almost thought she heard Grace say *blue*.

CONNIE SAT AT GRANNA'S CHIPPENDALE DESK, ONE FOOT FOLDED UNDER her, paging yet again through her notes on Prudence's journal. She had read through the entire document and found no mention of Deliverance Dane, nor any indication of what might have happened to the book. Her frustration with Prudence deepened. Day after day after day of gardening, cooking, and delivering babies. Of course if it was frustrating to read, it must have been vastly more frustrating to live. Not that such a realization did anything to assuage Connie's aggravation. Prudence was a staid, practical, even harsh woman—a woman living up to her name.

As Connie worked, Arlo stretched out on his belly in the entryway, nose pressed against the crack under the front door, fur blending in with the color of the Ipswich pine boards. Presently his tail began to swish, and growls of excitement escaped from the corners of his mouth. His ears crawled up to the top of his head. Connie turned over another page in her notes, her molars stealing an unconscious gnaw on the inside of her cheek.

"Hey there, Captain Grody!" called a woman's sudden voice from the front door, and Connie, shaken out of her reverie, turned around from her desk to find Arlo, tail and hind legs a blur of pleasure, borne into the arms of Liz Dowers.

"Liz!" she exclaimed, rising from the desk in surprise. "I didn't even hear your car! Hi!"

"Today is a holiday, you know," Liz chided, hugging Connie with her unoccupied arm. "You're not supposed to be working."

"Tell that to Chilton," Connie groaned. "He even called this morning expressly to tell me what a total disappointment I am, and how I am completely wasting his time."

"Professor Chilton," Liz announced with solemnity, "is a bastard." Connie opened her mouth to respond, but Liz held up her hand to stave off disagreement. "I'm sorry, but it's true. He works you too hard. I've watched it for years. Now come on. There's groceries in the car."

Connie smiled at her friend. "Not too many groceries, I hope. Remember, there's no fridge."

"And that," said Liz, "is why I also brought ice."

"So," Liz began, placing forks alongside napkins on the dining table, "fill me in. How's everything coming?"

"I'm not sure where to start," Connie called from inside the kitchen.

"Do you want the story of the vanished book-slash-dissertation topic, complete with pissed-off advisor? Or do you want the details on the boy so that you can grill him properly when he gets here?"

"Um, both, I guess, but I was actually asking about selling the house."

Connie appeared holding a steaming colander between two oven mitts, and dumped pasta into a waiting bowl on the table. "Oh. *That.*"

"You haven't done anything, have you," said Liz, crossing her arms.

"Not true," Connie countered, pulling off the oven mitts. "I have put in a telephone."

Liz leaned over to adjust the oil lamp on the table, its orange flame flaring up and casting her narrow features in relief, then tamping down into a warmer glow. Outside, the sky was still the pale blue-gray of twilight, but the interior of the house was already cloaked in darkness. "If I have to find another roommate for the fall, you need to tell me," said Liz seriously.

"Liz!" exclaimed Connie. "Of course not! It's only July."

"I know, but I'm just saying," Liz muttered, not looking at Connie.

"Don't be silly. Anyway, now that I have no probate record for Prudence Bartlett to tell me where the book went, I will no longer be distracted by all this productive dissertation research. I can finally devote my days to cleaning and fixing and selling, dropping out of grad school, running off to join the Foreign Legion. . . ."

"And the guy?" asked Liz, ignoring Connie's sarcasm.

Connie tucked her lower lip under her front teeth, and then broke into a smile. "He said they set off the fireworks from the causeway. He's going to drop by later and walk us over to a spot he knows."

" 'A spot he knows,' " echoed Liz, waving her fingers on either side of her head as Connie, laughing, threw an oven mitt at her friend.

The two young women huddled at the end of the long dining table in the small pool of light cast by the oil lamp, swirling pasta on their forks. Liz supplied Connie with anecdotes from her summer Latin students ("One of them had this gigantic cellular phone that he kept on his desk! What kind of high schooler has a cellular phone anyway? Aren't those just for bankers?"), and embroidered her account with stories of her dilatory summertime life in Cambridge.

Connie watched Liz talk, enjoying the sound of a voice other than her own filling the house's dour rooms. When circulating in the Marblehead world—buying groceries, visiting archives, picking up a coffee—she engaged in brushes of conversation, her solitude briefly rubbing up against the presence of other people before retreating again to the isolated cavern of Granna's house. Sometimes she would look down to discover Arlo in her lap, his brown gaze reminding her that she had not spoken in several hours.

A soft rap sounded at the door, and Liz broke off her story of a particularly awful date from the previous week to look up, bright-eyed, and whisper, "Aren't you going to get it?"

Connie grinned and tossed her napkin onto the table. "Coming!" she called.

On the threshold of the door, the yard behind him a black tangle of shadows and vines, stood Sam, a six-pack of beer in one hand and a heavy-duty flashlight in the other. "Good evening, madam," he said, with mock solemnity, executing a stiff half-bow with the flashlight beam shining up under his chin. "Your local Sherpa has arrived."

Connie noticed that Sam was sporting an ANARCHY IN THE UK T-shirt, presumably in honor of Independence Day, and giggled in spite of herself. "Sam Hartley," she announced, gesturing into the dining room, "I would like you to meet Liz Dowers. Liz, this is Sam Hartley."

"A pleasure," said Sam, gesturing with his hand, as if doffing a tricorn hat.

Liz appeared behind Connie in the doorway with a blanket folded over her arm. "Mr. Hartley, I presume," she said, executing a delicate curtsy, holding the picnic blanket out to one side, as if sweeping up a heavy brocade train.

"Shouldn't we be going?" Connie asked. "The fireworks are at nine, right?" Connie noticed Liz cast her eye quickly over Sam, mouthing "nice" at Connie when Sam was distracted with the flashlight, and then assuming an angelic posture when Sam looked up again.

Their three silhouettes set off through the night, followed by Arlo's eyes glittering through the leaves in the sitting room window.

THE LAST SPARKLING TENDRILS RAINED DOWN ON THE INNERMOST CURVE of Marblehead harbor, and a few air horns blew their approval from sailboats moored on the water, their wails mingling with the echo of the explosions overhead and the collective sigh of townsfolk clustered on blankets in parks and on rooftops. The red flares ringing the harborside began to sputter, adding to the cloud of smoke drifting over the causeway after the last fireworks winked into nothingness. Connie heard claps and whistles from the park around her, and for the first time she felt a warm affection for the community where she was accustomed to loitering on the periphery. She enjoyed the anonymity of sitting hidden by the darkness, just one pair of eyes among many, dazzled by the lights overhead. She released a contented sigh and smiled over at her friends, both leaning back on their elbows, necks craned to face the sky.

"Amazing," Liz murmured, and Connie heard a soft plunk, the sound of Liz tweaking the pop tab on her empty beer can with one thumb.

The haze of smoke gradually pulled apart, dissolving by degrees until the night sky once again stretched out clear overhead. Around them families folded up blankets and collected children, beginning the slow trudge toward home. The three of them sat, enjoying the quiet, saying nothing.

Connie rolled onto her back and yawned, stretching her arms out overhead and feeling her knuckles and bare heels dip into the moist grass that surrounded their blanket.

As she watched, a bright meteor streaked by overhead, a tiny ball of fire flashing through the atmosphere. Connie smiled, deciding—selfishly—to keep it to herself. She thought she detected an instantaneous flash of blue light on the horizon where the meteor disappeared, but then it was gone.

"It's late," she ventured finally. "We should be getting back."

"So what are you guys doing tomorrow?" asked Sam, his voice emerging out of the dark. The park had emptied, and they could hear only the waves in the harbor lapping against the park's rocky face.

"Beach, right, Connie?" asked Liz, her voice sleepy.

"Beach," Connie confirmed, struggling into a seated position. "C'mon, Liz," she said, jostling her friend's leg. "Sam has to get home." Liz let out a protesting moan but rose, and they drew the blanket up off the grass and started the meandering walk back to Milk Street.

Sam's flashlight carved a neat round cone through the massed night, bringing focus to each pebble and leaf that had fallen in the road. "Anyway, Grace thinks I'm just being closed-minded," Connie was saying. "So I was thinking I should go over my notes again. She pointed out that maybe Prudence would have called it something else. . . ."

"Connie," said Liz with authority. "That's great and everything. But tomorrow, you're taking the day off. We are going to the beach, we're going to lie in the sun, we're going to float in the water, and then we're going to spend the rest of the night in the diviest bar we can find. Sam, are you with me on this?"

He laughed, sweeping the flashlight beam over the tips of their feet and then back into a long yellow oval in the road. "Hear, hear," he said.

"I knew I liked him," Liz said.

The flashlight brushed up against the tangled mass of overgrown hedge that marked Granna's house, and then spilled over the gate in the underbrush. Connie's arm reached into the light to withdraw the latch, and they jostled into the garden, picking their way through the tufts of herbs poking through the flagstone pathway.

"You do deserve a day off," Sam started to say as the bright oval slid up the flagstones onto the waiting front door.

In an instant all three froze. Liz let out a frightened scream.

"Oh, my God," Connie whispered, staring in horror at the door.

CONNIE PULLED HER SWEATER UP TO HER CHIN, SHIVERING. LIZ HUDDLED on the stoop next to her, knees pressed to hers, their eyes fixed on the silhou-

ette of Sam in quiet conference with two bulky men. Their hands were gesticulating, cast into sharp relief by the spinning flashes of red and blue light
from the police cruiser parked in the street, penetrating through the vine
overgrowth and splashing up against the impassive, silent face of the house.

"I'm sure they'll figure it out," Liz murmured, but Connie could tell that
Liz was trying to reassure herself as much as she was Connie.

"I know," Connie said, folding her arm around Liz's shoulders and
squeezing. But as she clutched her friend, she felt her heartbeat tripping
faster. She saw Sam point in her direction, and the two bulky forms moved
toward her through the night.

"You Connie Goodwin?" asked one of them. The other moved gingerly
through the yard to play his flashlight over the windows at the front of the
house. The officer looming over Connie had a head shaved nearly bald, and
his nose had the bruised-looking quality of the heavy drinker. The harsh,
spinning lights cast a diabolical sheen on his face that he probably did not
deserve. She got to her feet, Liz rising with her.

"Yes," she said.

"This yoah house?" he asked.

"Yes. Well, no, actually. It was my grandmother's. Sophia Goodwin.
She died." Connie crossed her arms over her chest, not looking at the front
door.

"Pretty hahd to find, yoah house. Even Officah Litchman and I had
trouble, and we live in Mahblehead," he said, unfolding a small notebook to
a fresh page.

"No sign of fawced entry, Len," called the other one—Officer Litchman, she supposed—from near the dining room window. He was peering
through the windowpanes with his flashlight.

"Okay," said the first one, jotting down notes. He turned back to Connie. "Anybody know yoah staying heah?"

"I don't think so," Connie said, frowning. "My mother, who asked me
to come for the summer. My friends, of course. I guess my advisor."

"Advisah?" the policeman asked.

"I'm in grad school. My advisor's the professor I work with," she explained.

"Gotcha," he said, making more notes. From behind them they heard a sudden torrent of fierce barking, followed by Officer Litchman crying out "Jesus Christ!" and then the thump of his flashlight tumbling to the ground.

"You got a dog?" the first police officer—Len?—asked Connie.

"Yeah. Arlo. He's inside. Sorry about that!" she called to Officer Litchman, who was cursing under his breath, hunting for his flashlight in the weeds.

"Pretty weahd he wouldn'ta scared 'em off," remarked the policeman, still jotting.

"Yeah," Connie said, perturbed. Sam had joined them by now, wrapping a protective arm around her waist.

"Officer . . . Cardullo," Liz began, reading the name plate on their interviewer's uniform. "Do you have any idea who could have done this? Why would anybody want to scare Connie? She doesn't even know anyone here!" Her voice rose, becoming almost shrill, and Connie placed a gentle hand on Liz's arm.

The group all turned to face the front door again, and they paused to stare at it.

On the door, about two feet in diameter, appeared a circle freshly burned into the wood. It held a smaller circle inside it, like a target, bisected along both axes by lines. In the top half sat the word *Alpha*, written in an uneven, almost archaic, hand, with two crosses or hatch marks above it. In the upper-left quadrant, on the outer rim, was the word *Meus* with crossed hatch marks on either end. In the same position on the upper-right quadrant of the circle appeared the word *Adjutor*, also framed by crossed hatch marks. Echoing the pattern, in the lower half of the circle, were the words *Omega* in the center, *Agla* in the lower-left quadrant, and *Dominus* in the lower right, each bracketed by crossed hatch marks.

"Hahd to say," said Officer Cardullo, resting a hand on his heavy equipment belt. "Sometimes ya get some weahdos up from Salem. Goth kids 'n' the like. Sometimes ya get stuff like this spray-painted on walls. Pentagrams 'n' whatnot. Usually not this complex, though."

"Could be they thought the house was abandoned, what with all the vines and everything, and no lights," Officer Litchman mused, joining them. "Just kids looking for trouble. Maybe yoah dog did scare 'em, else they woulda gone inside. You find anything missing in the house?"

"Nothing," said Connie, bringing a fingernail up to her mouth and ripping the tip of it off with her teeth, thoughtlessly. "There's nothing worth stealing in there, anyway." She felt her control starting to slip, her outward shell of calm becoming shot through with cracks.

"Any idea what the wuhds mean?" asked Cardullo, eyeing Connie.

"No," she whispered. The symbol sat there, inscrutable, the acrid smell of burned wood clinging to the nighttime air. The smoke still smelled fresh, as if the burn on the door had fizzled out only moments before they returned. Little heaps of ash were collected on the stoop. A hot tear squeezed out of the corner of one of her eyes and started to snake its way down her cheek.

"*Alpha* and *omega* are the first and last letters of the Greek alphabet," said Sam. Connie felt his grip around her tighten.

"*Dominus adjutor meus* is Latin," Liz added, her voice wavering. She took the flashlight from Sam and trained it more closely on the symbols on the front door. "Of course, the *j* in *adjutor* should probably be an *i*, if we are talking about ancient spelling. Roughly translated, it means 'God my helper,' or possibly 'the Lord my deputy.' Helper is the more likely use." She gazed at the inscription, frowning. "I don't know about 'Agla.' 'Aglaia' is a name for one of the Graces, but I don't think that's what they mean."

"Hey, that's pretty good," Officer Litchman said, elbowing Officer Cardullo. "I was an altah boy 'n' I couldn'ta told you that."

"But who is 'they'?" asked Sam.

They turned to face the two policemen, who exchanged a quick look.

"Listen," said Cardullo after an uncomfortable pause, sliding his notebook into his back pocket. "We've taken down yoah statement. I'll have a cruisah drive by a coupla times ovah the next week, but it looks like just a case of yah gahden-variety vandalism. Just kids makin' trouble."

"Garden-variety vandalism?" Sam echoed, incredulous. "Are you serious? Don't you think regular vandals would just use spray paint? Or markers?" Connie heard the anger in his voice and caught his blazing eyes with hers. She moved her head in a barely perceptible shake. Antagonizing the policemen would do nothing to get them to take this more seriously.

"Sorry, kids, I don't know what to tell yeh. It's a remote kinda house, no lights on. Yeh were off watchin' the fiahworks, so theh was plenty of noise and nobody watching. Looks to me like a case of bad kids and bad luck," said Cardullo, Litchman nodding his agreement. "Heah's my cahd. You have any moah trouble, you call us up, okay?"

"Well, thanks," Connie murmured, accepting the card, and the policemen withdrew into the night.

"Need some lights out heah!" one of them called out, and Connie smiled weakly. The rotating red and blue lights vanished, replaced by the blazing red of taillights.

Connie stood fixed in her place as a chill night wind circled around her rooted legs and blew the fine gray ashes away.

Interlude

Marblehead, Massachusetts

Late April

1760

loud crashing sound emanated from within the tavern, followed by riotous laughter and cheering. Above it all, Joseph Hubbard's voice bellowed out indistinct directions, and whoops and cries drew nearer the door until it exploded open, ejecting a young man in a tattered overcoat several sizes too large for him, with blurry face and bloodshot eyes.

"I war goin' to pay," he slurred, staggering onto his hands and knees. Prudence Bartlett's jaw clenched, the chill in her eyes growing a few perceptible degrees cooler as she stooped to hook one hand under the young man's arm. With some effort she helped him to his feet, her strong, wiry hands gripping his shoulders and holding him vertical until the worst of the swaying stopped. He was just a little thing, not much older than her Patty. His hair was clotted with sand, dirty hanks having pulled out of his pigtail and standing out in several directions. He had a faint down of whiskers scattered around his mouth, and nothing more. Prudence sighed.

"I war," the boy said again, his exhaled breath a corrosive cloud of Barbadoes rum, and Prudence closed her throat against the smell.

"Steeped in vice, you are," she said to him. The boy's nose flushed red, and his eyes and cheeks started to crumple in a sob.

She placed her hands on the boy's hot cheeks and looked him full in the face. Her eyes glowed white with concentration as she sent strict instructions through the palms of her hands, and she felt the boy's body absorb her intent, diffusing it into his suffering bloodstream. Under her fingertips the boy's skin flushed deep crimson, and he let out a tiny whimper. She whispered a short string of words under her breath, and then released him.

"Get you home," she said, "and with no need for strong drink neither."

The boy slowly reached up to touch his face where the bright red welts were already receding into nothingness, and he blinked, eyes clear. He swallowed, looking at Prudence with some alarm, and then without a word turned and fled along the alleyway toward the wharves. She snorted without mirth.

At the end of the alley, where the boy disappeared around a corner, an unseen voice called out, "Down buck-*et*!" as a wet pot of ordure rained down from one of the windows into the street.

"Up for air, you dirty bawd!" cried a passing shoreman, his breeches neatly splattered. A putrid smell began to suffuse the narrow thoroughfare, and Prudence wrinkled her nose in distaste.

She pulled open the tavern door and surveyed the scene inside, looking for the man whom she was appointed to meet. The room hung thick with smoke from tobacco pipes and the great stone hearth at the far end, veiling the clusters of men who lounged on low benches around rough wooden tables. It smelled not unpleasantly of woodsmoke and ale, boiling fish stew and wool coats crusted with seawater. Prudence shifted the heavy bundle she was carrying to her hip and passed a hand thoughtlessly over the stomacher that bound her waist. The pungent smell of the stew caused her mouth to flush with saliva, and she wondered if the man—this Robert Hooper— might be persuaded to treat her.

"Prue," greeted the graveled voice of the tavern keeper, who nodded at her from across the room.

"Joe," she said, nodding back. She waded toward him through the merry room, batting away the errant hands of a few drunken men with grubby fishermen's clothes. "Seen a Robert Hooper about today?" she asked, arriving finally at the keeper's table. He sat with a flagon at his elbow, flanked by a young laughing woman with lace spilling out of the bodice on her tight jacket and cheeks rather more rouged than nature had intended.

Joseph Hubbard reached up to scratch his whiskers, planting his other hand on his extended knee. His great belly lopped over the sagging waist of his breeches, and his coat was open. Under shaggy gray eyebrows his dark eyes gleamed. "That be that Robeht Hoopah of up the trainin' field hill? Great fine house he has. New built."

"The same," she said, scanning the room for a man who seemed to match such a description. The Goat and Anchor was hardly known to have been frequented by the gentlefolk of up the hill. Joe let out a robust laugh.

"Has some business with you, does he?" asked the man, taking a draught from his mug.

"Aye," said Prudence. "I'll just be waiting then." She located an empty bench by the wall and placed her parcel on the table. Settling in her seat, she reached up to adjust her mobcap, tucking loose strands of hair back into place, and tugged on the emerging sleeves of her shift to smooth out their wrinkles. Robert Hooper would be a man of fashion, after all.

"Not needin' you for his wife, I trow, poor wretch!" Joe bellowed as he waved over a serving girl. The woman seated with him laughed a high, irritating screech, covering her face with a fan. *She weren't as young as all that, then*, Prudence thought. "You'll fix her up, right enow." Joe chortled. "Set his gahl to rights, I hope."

Prudence scowled, resenting his implication. "How fares Mrs. Hubbard with little Mary?" she asked pointedly. The serving girl placed a flagon of ale before her and then waited, eyeing Joe Hubbard.

"Well enough, that one. Neahly two. Runs us ragged." He caught the serving girl's eye and shook his head once, and the girl withdrew without payment. Joe chuckled. "Yoah health, Prue," he said, raising his ale in Prudence's direction.

"And yours," she replied, raising hers in turn. *Brought out twelve of his,* she glowered, *and not all with Mrs. Hubbard neither.*

Prudence pulled a little ceramic pipe from within her pocket, together with the crumpled flyer that she had carried with her for the last several days. She smoothed it across the tabletop and contemplated it as she packed the pipe bowl with a pinch of tobacco, then lit it at the lamp on the table. OLD BOOKS WANTED, the printed flyer said. CURRENCY OFFER'D FOR THE RARE AND UNIQUE. INQUIRE WITH MR. HOOPER AT THE FOLLOWING ADDRESS. She inhaled, sallow cheeks growing hollow around the pipe, the harsh smoke filling her lungs and gradually seeping calm through her twitching nerves.

She supposed that she could still change her mind. He wasn't here, after all. Perhaps he didn't even want it.

Prudence hazarded a glance at the parcel and rested her hand on it for a moment, rubbing her thumb across the rough fabric wrapping. As she did so, she thought of the sum that he had mentioned in the note that had arrived in response to her inquiry. More than she would get in almost two years of midwifing. But the sum alone was not her main reason for selling the book. She had her reasons for wanting to be rid of it.

A circle of quiet rippled out in the vicinity of the door, and Prudence looked up to see the cause: a young man, dressed in a rich crimson jacket with shining buttons and long, elegant cuffs, stood sweeping his hair back with one hand where it had been ruffled by the removal of a new felted tricorne hat. He stamped his feet to loosen the mud from his butter-soft calfskin boots and surveyed the interior of the tavern, evidently looking for someone. She caught his eye and lifted her chin. He smiled and made his way toward her, hat under one arm, trailing silence in his wake.

"Mrs. Bartlett, I presume?" he said, half bowing.

"Just Prue'll do," she said as the man seated himself with a flourish. The room watched him join the midwife in the corner nearest the hearth, digested this incongruous piece of information, and then turned back to the business of merrymaking.

"Is this the volume?" the man asked eagerly, indicating the package between Prudence's elbows.

He started to reach for it but was stopped when she commented, as if for his own edification, "The Goat 'n' Anchor's known for its stew." She puffed on her pipe, blowing the smoke off to one side, and gazed at him evenly.

"Ah," said Robert Hooper, turning to the serving girl who had appeared by their table. "Of course. Two bowls of stew, if you please. And whatever punch is best."

The girl sniffed in reply, and Hooper turned back to the parcel. Prudence slid it across the table, and as he unknotted its dimity wrapping her eyes traveled over his countenance, gathering her impressions of him. The clothes were new, to be sure, but he wore them with the self-consciousness of a man not accustomed to them. He fussed with his lace sleeves, and kept shifting the hat about on the bench next to him, unsure how best to supervise it. His face was young and earnest, as yet unseamed by the wear of drink, or women, or soft living. It still carried the nut-brown hue of a man who had reason to be out of doors, or on the water. When the stew was brought to the table he gripped his pewter spoon in his fist, leaning over to bring his mouth nearer the bowl. Prudence half-smiled, and resituated the pipe between her lips. He pushed aside the bowl and reached for the book.

"Remarkable," he said, turning over the book's leaves one at a time. "Surely not all writ in one hand?" He glanced up at her.

"No, indeed," she said.

"What is this, Latin?" He turned another page, peering at the text.

"Most Latin, yes. Some English, too, near the end. And some in cipher. More 'n' that I couldn't say."

"And your note said this came from England?"

"So I'm told," she said. "A family almanac, like."

"How very curious," the man said, running his hands over the leather binding with a tenderness that surprised her. His fingers, she saw, were still thorny, rough, and callused. Perhaps his reverence for old books came from not having encountered any of his own. "And you've no idea the age? Which is the oldest entry?"

Prudence arched one eyebrow at him, and then delicately sipped at her stew, saying nothing. They sat for a moment in silence, Hooper squinting at a page covered over in symbols and hatch marks, Prudence wondering when the time would come to talk about money.

"I cannot read Latin," Hooper confessed, not looking at her. She gazed at him in an attentive attitude, hands clasped under her chin, but inwardly she heaved a little sigh. *Everyone has wounds as want healing*, she reflected. *Seems like they all find me.* She looked at this prosperous young man seated before her and perceived the areas within him where the damage lay. The whole idea made her tired. "But I mean that my son should learn," he added, glancing up.

She let her pale eyes linger on his face for a while, not speaking. "Why do you look for old books to buy, Mr. Hooper?" she asked finally, toying with the handle of her pewter spoon.

He chuckled, embarrassed. "My business interests have grown of late," he began, "much aided by a flourishing connection with some merchant houses in Salem." He took a long swallow of his punch and made to wipe his lips on his sleeve before checking himself. A fragile handkerchief appeared from within his sleeve, and he dabbed at the corners of his mouth before secreting it away again.

"I got . . . that is, I was invited by some gentlemen to join their Monday Evening Club. And now the Club, being comprised of sundry well-read gentlemen of sophistication and taste, decides to establish a private social library, that we may all benefit from our collective literary and scientific interests." He paused, turning his punch cup where it sat on the table. "We are all asked to donate volumes of our own collection, you see." He looked up at her.

"And you have none," she finished.

"I have acquired some fine specimens, and have hopes to secure still more. Though none so fine and rare as your own." He reached into his pocket and placed a small drawstring leather bag between them on the table. It looked heavy and fat. "I wonder how you can bear to part with it," said Hooper, watching her.

A sickening lurch gripped Prudence's stomach as she looked at the fat little bag sitting on the table next to her almanac—her mother's almanac, she should say, for her mother, though frail, yet still lived in her house. A vision of her mother's aged but beautiful face rose before her, framed by the whispers that had dogged her through her entire life. Mercy had more strength than she, carrying her head high every day as she did. She knew what great stock her mother placed in this tome, but Prudence herself felt only resentment for it. Her mother had passed her whole life on the fringes of her society. All the bitterness that Prudence might have held for the neighbors who shunned her mother, who sometimes whispered still when Prudence took Patty to the meetinghouse, she heaped upon the tattered leather binding of this wretched book.

She thought then of Josiah, and the shooting pains he complained of in his back, worsened by each day spent off-loading boats down the landing. Prudence imagined the frayed snap of a rope giving way, the rumbling of heavy wooden casks slipping their binds, bouncing down the gangplank toward the frightened form of her husband. She could not fathom a life with Josiah taken from her. She closed her eyes against the image. Her father had gone in an instant, washed away to sea, and her mother's father, too, felled with all the men who married into her line. If she could be rid of the book perhaps she could keep Josiah safe, preserve him from Providence's vengeful hand. He giveth, and He taketh away. Prudence wanted nothing more than to have the book out of her house, away from her, where it could sully her family no more.

Admittedly Prudence quavered to contemplate what Mercy would say if this betrayal were discovered. But Mercy was languid in her old age; she spent her afternoons puttering in the garden, needling Patty in the kitchen, napping under a tree with the dog. It was years since she had looked for the book, years more since anyone had sought her counsel. Mercy Lamson wended her way through her days, each one roughly like the next, until one day, soon enough, they would come to an end.

Prudence thought then of Patty, who had sprouted near three inches since Christmas. Her loping, warmhearted daughter, so deft with the garden and the chickens the family kept—every morning they presented her with eggs as ripe and round as little melons. What would Patty want with old shames and superstitions? The money in the fat little bag could be laid aside for a dowry, or could improve the Milk Street house. Patty, with her speckled cheeks from days in the sun, her blue eyes bright and warm, not cold and careworn like Prudence's own. Why, when Patty reached the age that Prudence was now, the nineteenth century would be upon them. She sometimes tried to imagine the world into which her daughter, all awkward limbs and knocked-over teacups, would vault, and as she did so she saw time flowing forward from the still point of the table in the kitchen of their house, unfathomably long and distant. Sometimes the magnitude of it overwhelmed and frightened her.

Prudence set her jaw and laid the spent pipe aside. She reached for the bag.

"I've no more use for it," she said simply.

Without another word Prudence rose, pocketed the little bag, and with a nod at the surprised Robert Hooper, strode across the riotous main room of the Goat and Anchor, through the weighty tavern door, and out into her future.

CHAPTER THIRTEEN

Cambridge, Massachusetts

Early July

1991

CONNIE TOOK A LONG SWALLOW OF HER COCKTAIL, AND WHEN SHE lowered the glass back to the bar, she noticed with irritation that her hand was trembling. Abner's had lately acquired an acoustic version of Led Zeppelin's greatest hits, which was playing for the entire hour that Connie had been leaning at the bar. Janine was running late, as was her wont. Connie reflected that if Janine did not walk through the front door within the next five minutes, the odds were better than even that she would stand up and break her barstool over the jukebox. In her mind she lifted the heavy stool and brought it down over the glass dome of the jukebox, feeling the crunch of the dome collapsing under the stool's weight, hearing the music drawl to a blessed stop. She smiled with satisfaction at the fantasy.

"Connie, hello, hello," breathed Janine Silva, settling her weight on the stool next to Connie and dropping her bag at her feet. "I'm so sorry I'm late. What are you drinking? Old-fashioned?" She held up two fingers to Abner behind the bar, who gave her a nod and turned away. Janine leaned on one elbow and applied a pair of bright purple reading glasses to the end of her nose.

"So," she said, and Connie, still sitting in profile, took another long swallow of her cocktail. Connie reached into her cutoff pocket, pulled out the key that she had found in Granna's house, and clapped it down on the table before turning to look at her professor.

"The very day I moved into my grandmother's house, I found a key that fits nothing," she said. Janine's face grew perplexed. "And inside the key I found a name. Deliverance Dane." She raised a fresh fingernail to her mouth and gnawed at it as Abner dropped two heavy tumblers of liquor, beaded with moisture, before the women and Janine wordlessly slid a few dollar bills across the bar.

"It turns out," Connie continued, pushing her empty tumbler away and reaching for the fresh one, "that Deliverance Dane is an undocumented Salem witch. Unlike all the other victims, she was a healer or cunning woman. And she left a record book of her work."

"But, Connie! That's wonderful!" Janine exclaimed, eyes widening. "What a coup for you. People can spend their whole lives and never find a source that unique! And what a rich area of inquiry for the history of women . . ." She trailed off as she saw Connie frown.

"I know!" Connie cried, her voice catching. "But now Chilton's threatening to get my funding yanked if I can't find it! And then these vandals came to my house." She took a deep hiccuping breath, suppressing the tears that were welling up in her eyes. "I don't know what to do."

Janine pressed her lips together in concern and placed a soft hand over Connie's with a reassuring pat. "Okay, okay, one thing at a time. First of all," she said, "I'll only say this to you because we are friends, and I'll expect this never to leave our confidence."

Connie nodded, wiping at her eyes. Her junior mentor leaned in closer and lowered her voice. "Manning Chilton . . . ," she began, then hesitated, taking a sip of her cocktail and gathering her thoughts. "Of course Manning is an eminent scholar, and of course his standing in the department is impeccable."

Connie's brows swept down over her pale eyes. If Professor Chilton's reputation had been blemished somehow, Connie's entire professional future could be compromised. Janine cleared her throat again, glancing around the dim bar interior before inching her barstool closer to Connie's knees. "It's just that his recent research . . . well, it's taken a turn for the *idiosyncratic.*"

"What do you mean?" Connie asked, confused. She knew that he was planning something significant for his keynote address at the Colonial Association meeting in the fall, but she did not know the substance of it.

"For a long while he was working on the use of alchemical symbolism in Jungian psychoanalysis," Janine said, voice barely audible over the music and the murmur of summer school students in the booths at the rear of the room. "He was interested in alchemy as a way of understanding a world that reasoned by similarity, rather than by the scientific method. He thought that the language of alchemy could provide a psychoanalytic interpretation of premodern magical thinking and ritual. But the last paper that he delivered at the Association of Historians of the American Colonies was a little more . . ." She seemed to rummage in her mind for just the word that she wanted. "Literal," she finished. "It was more literal."

"Literal? In what way?" Connie asked, leaning forward. Janine's soft breath brushed across her face, smelling faintly of peppermints.

"Have you ever heard of an alchemical concept called the philosopher's stone?" Janine asked.

"Sure," said Connie, her confusion deepening. "It was one of the major goals of medieval alchemy, wasn't it? Some mythical substance that could turn base metal to gold, but it was also the universal medicine, able to cure any illness. Right? But no one ever knew what it was exactly, or its true color, or what elements it consisted of. All descriptions of it and recipes for it were couched in riddles. It could only be revealed by God."

"Exactly," said Janine. "One of the riddles said that the philosopher's stone is a stone that is not a stone, a precious thing but without value, unknown but known to all. Well, the usual contemporary attitude toward alchemy is that it's just the historical ancestor of modern-day chemistry. And in a sense that's true, since alchemy was really the first time that scholars started to experiment with natural materials to see if they could be changed from one form to another. But many academics, Chilton among them, have emphasized the religious elements of medieval alchemy."

"Religious?" Connie asked.

"Sure," Janine replied. "The alchemists reasoned by analogy. According to them, the world around us contains meaning, and the patterns of the universe mirror the patterns of our selves. It's the same kind of thinking that underlies astrology: the movement of stars and planets both mirrors us and influences us, so that if we read them properly we can reveal truths about everyday life. So they started out by trying to sort the world into a set of categories based on similar qualities. You've got the sun on one hand, which rules heat, masculinity, progress, dryness, day. And then you've got the moon on the other, which is cold, femininity, regression, dampness, night. And every substance consisted of four basic elements: earth, fire, air, and water. And there are four qualities: heat, cold, humidity, and dryness. Everything on earth, they thought, could be described using these categories. Gold, for example, might be a combination of sun, earth, fire, heat, and dryness, which describes its color, texture, usefulness, what have you. I'm just guessing, but you see what I mean."

"I think so," Connie hazarded, unsure if she understood Janine's point. "It's just so weird to try to think in those terms. Gold is just an element, right?"

"Yes, but they didn't exactly know that in the Middle Ages," Janine said. "The world was a weird-looking place before we knew about atoms and DNA. They were trying to figure out what its component qualities were, not just to understand the world better but also so that they could try to *control* it. Alchemy says that these elements and qualities can be manipulated by gifted men, causing substances to change their form beyond what nature intended. They compared the crucible in which metals were melted to the human body, which transforms substances, too—food and water become bone and sinew. Sperm transforms in the body, like a seed in the earth, bringing something out of nothing. So the search for the philosopher's stone, or the Great Work, required the purest elements and the highest degree of talent. It was like the search for perfectibility, both in substance and in the soul."

"But this is all pseudoscience," Connie protested. "It hasn't been taken seriously in . . ." She paused, thinking. "Two hundred years! At least."

"Well, that's not what Chilton argued," Janine said. "I was there for the talk, and let me tell you, it was a real shocker. The paper dealt with the private journals of respected seventeenth- and eighteenth-century chemists—Isaac Newton among them—who also conducted serious research into what used to be called 'vegetation of metals' as the key step. That was a concept that connected the transformation of minerals under heat and pressure with the growth of plants and animals. Manning proposed that the base material in the riddle might be carbon, the basis of all life, which of course can be transformed under heat and pressure to anything from coal to diamond. He claimed that there was one further transmutation for carbon that was out of the reach of current science, but that might be accessible using alchemical techniques."

"Techniques?" Connie echoed.

Janine heaved a small sigh. "Connie, he was arguing that the philosopher's stone could be real. Essentially, he thought that alchemy shouldn't be considered as a *symbolic* way of looking at human thought and reason after all, but should be taken at *face value.*"

Connie's eyes widened, and she imagined her advisor standing at a raised podium, a bright light—the slide projector—splashing a dark red image of a stone across his face and into his eyes. He was pounding his fist on the lectern, and his mouth was moving, but the only sound that she heard was laughter. She blinked, and the image was gone. One hand rose to touch her temple, which had started to throb.

Janine laughed, continuing. "Gives me a headache, too. Well, of course the conference panel had a field day. Accused him of ahistoricism, at the very best, and of needing a long vacation at the worst." Janine exhaled through her teeth and dropped her voice even further. "The university president even had a conversation with him afterward. Asked if chairing the department was proving too taxing. That is strictly between you and me, by the way."

"That," said Connie, sitting back on her stool, "is surprising." It seemed incredible. What had Chilton said? *Wait until you have seen what I have to offer.* The threatened loss of his chair in the department would be devastating for him.

"Well," Janine continued, "you know Manning. You can imagine how he took their reaction. It was a real blow." She shook her head. "So if he's being even more strict with you than usual, now you'll have an idea why. I think he feels like he needs to come back from that to some extent. Rehabilitate his reputation. If he can point to an accomplished protégée who is doing serious, innovative work, then . . ." She trailed off, reaching her hand forward to finger the key.

"This is beautiful. Is it antique?" she asked, turning the key in the warm light of the bar.

Connie said nothing. As she brought the heavy tumbler to her lips, a tongue of liquor sloshed over the rim, and she reached up to clutch the trembling glass with her other hand, smothering its movement before Janine could see.

THE VOLVO CREAKED TO A HALT, A LARGE DROPLET OF RAINWATER splotching across the windshield. Connie paused, pressing her palm against her chest and feeling her heartbeat thrumming at an uneven pace, like a runner dashing and then stopping to rest, panting, up against a tree. She had told Janine Silva about the bizarre circle symbol burned into her front door, and Janine had responded with shock and concern. What did she mean, *burned*? Who would want to vandalize her grandmother's door? What had the police said? Well, so long as she had filed a complaint, she supposed there was nothing else to do. Though it must have been unnerving, especially as Connie was staying there alone. Did she feel safe?

Connie scowled, glaring out of the car window at the shop front across the street. Another few fat raindrops fell onto the hood and roof, plonking on the metal and rolling down the glass, leaving snail-like trails in their wake. Of course the circle, with its wisps of smoke drifting out of the black scars in the wood, asserted the problem of *why* much more acutely. Over their hours in the living room after the policemen left, Sam getting up at intervals to cast his flashlight nervously across the yard from the window, no answer was forthcoming. *The police are right, it's just weird kids from Salem,* Liz asserted. The explanation satisfied none of them.

When they could not figure out why the circle had appeared, they turned their attention to its possible meaning. " 'God my helper,' " Liz translated, together with the Greek letters *alpha* and *omega*, perhaps another indication of the godhead, the divine that is both the beginning and the end. But beyond that, the word *Agla*, the bizarre array of crosshatches—it clearly meant *something*, but they could not fathom what. Finally exhausted by tension and fear, she and Liz retired to the musty four-posters upstairs, not protesting when Sam insisted on staying, flashlight in hand, half-awake in the armchair by the fireplace as dawn started to creep across the sky. Connie shivered at the memory as a rumble of thunder lurked low in the sky, sounding like a beast or monster prowling three streets over.

The quiet gong rang out as Connie opened the door of Lilith's Garden: Herbs and Magickal Treasures to find the same earringed woman behind the counter, hair in a giant bun atop her head this time, sorting receipts on the glass-topped counter.

"Blessed . . . be," she said, recognizing Connie, and flipped closed the book that she had been reading, cover facedown.

"What does *Agla* mean?" Connie demanded without preamble, hands planted on her hips. How she resented this woman with her ridiculous earrings, the profits of her store built on the dead shoulders of a bunch of innocent people. Connie's eyes bored into hers, and she perceived that the woman felt herself to be a very kind and sensitive person, intuitive, but that most of her supposed intuition derived from her own soft view of the world. She was not a bad person, this earringed woman—her world was just very padded and small.

"What?" asked the woman, confused, tensing in her chair behind the cash register.

"*Agla*," Connie said, too loudly, stepping nearer to the counter. "I want you to tell me what it means. Especially when it appears in some crazy circle surrounded by a bunch of hatch marks." Her voice tightened, and the woman's discomfort radiated from her in nearly visible waves.

"I . . . I don't know!" she cried, eyes darting from Connie to the far corners of the little shop.

"Someone," Connie said, "*burned it* into the door of my grandmother's house. Trying to scare me." She pressed her palms on the counter as the woman's eyelids started to flutter. Connie wanted someone else to bear responsibility for the unrelenting fear that had gripped her since the circle appeared. Meanly, she willed this woman to argue with her, to give her an excuse to raise her voice, to vent some of the terror that she had to keep hidden in her everyday life. "*Burned it*. And I would at least like to know what all the words involved *mean*."

The woman swallowed and looked at Connie with a mixture of alarm and concern. "This circle," she began. "How . . . perfect was it?"

"What do you mean?" Connie asked.

"I mean, were there any stray burn marks? Variations in the depth of the scoring?" the woman pressed.

"No," Connie said, folding her arms.

The woman opened her mouth to speak, seemed to think better of it, and stood, gesturing to Connie to follow. "That's what I thought. Come with me," she said. "I don't know what it means, but I know where we should look."

Connie trailed behind her to the rear corner of the shop, the one with the racks of books on one side and the expired herbs on the other, and the woman plucked a dense tome down from one shelf.

"Look," she said, pages ruffling under her fingers. "I know a lot of people in the Wicca community here. And some of them are even level-three initiates, which is *really* hard to do." She looked to Connie for a sign of recognition and received none.

"And a lot of the covens have gotten very adept at conjuration, and make it a part of their sabbaths. But the thing of it is . . ." She ran her fingertip down the page that she wanted, then turned the book around to indicate an entry to Connie. "Nobody that I know of"—she paused—"*nobody* has ever been able to manifest a circle like the one you are describing. I know one group that tried once to manifest a circle by making a kind of brand, but it was very small. And even then the burned circle that resulted was incomplete. It pretty much didn't work."

The woman had pulled down a heavy encyclopedia of paganism and the occult, and Connie looked down at the entry under the woman's finger.

AGLA. A kabbalist notarikon that is thought to refer to *Atah Gibor Leolam Adonai*, an unspeakable name for God sometimes translated as "Lord God is eternally powerful." Ref. Appears 1615 in the alchemical treatise *Spiegel der Kunst und Natur* together with *Gott*, the German word for *God*, as well as the Greek letters *alpha* and *omega*.

"The mirror of art and nature," said Connie aloud, and the woman hovering over her asked, "What is that?"

"A book title," said Connie, eyebrows furrowed. "German. From 1615." She glanced up, meeting the woman's gaze, and read in her face a concern that felt genuine. Connie shifted the book's considerable weight back into the woman's hands and stood, arms crossed, thinking. "Do you think this is the kind of thing that a vandal might put on someone's door at random?" Connie asked finally, watching her out of the corners of her eyes.

The earringed woman took a breath, pursing her lips together. "I don't mean to alarm you," she said, "but no. A manifestation like that would take a lot of work. Nobody would do it just to do it."

The two women regarded each other, the store proprietor's eyes wide and sensitive, willing Connie to believe her. Connie's reason rebelled against what she was suggesting—manifestation! What did that even *mean*? She was implying that someone had simply willed the circle to appear. What a preposterous idea. Wasn't the world wondrous enough without a lot of make-believe?

"Look," the woman began, closing the book and pressing it to her chest, "I know that you don't believe in the Goddess religion. I can read it in your face." Connie frowned, not disagreeing with her. "But if you like, I can fix you up a really powerful protective charm."

"What?" Connie asked, incredulous.

"You know. A charm. To make your grandmother feel safer in the house." The woman's eyebrows rose, two little sincere quarter-moons over her eyes, and Connie thought, *It all comes back to money, doesn't it.*

"My grandmother has been dead for twenty years," Connie replied.

"Suit yourself," the woman replied, replacing the book on the shelf. "But remember. Just because you don't believe in something doesn't mean it isn't real."

Muttering a thank-you, Connie strode to the shop door and yanked it open just as the sky outside broke apart and the rain started to fall like drumsticks beating down on the earth.

HOURS LATER, AFTER THE RAIN PASSED, CONNIE SAT LISTENING TO THE silence in Granna's house, broken only by the click of Arlo's toenails on the wide pine floorboards and the breath of summer air stirring the leaves in the sitting room windows. The air in the house still felt close and heavy. Connie caught herself straining for a sound that seemed on the point of being audible, or glancing over her shoulder as she worked, expecting someone to be standing there. *The police said there's nothing to be afraid of,* she reminded herself, heart thudding in her ears. *There's no one. And if there were someone, Arlo would scare them away.* Though she found her logic utterly sound she nevertheless, after five more minutes of quiet, twitched her head up, ears open, listening.

Arlo appeared under her desk chair, tongue extended in a luxurious yawn. Connie reached down to scratch the spot between his shoulder blades as she flipped through her notebook.

"I really don't see why you're so relaxed," she remarked. "You weren't even freaked the night we got back from the fireworks and found the burn mark. Not until that cop shined his light in the window, anyway."

He rolled onto his side so that her scratching hand could reach under his jaw, his whiskered mouth drawn into a sleepy smile. Mentally Connie gathered her strands of thinking into thick handfuls, trying to braid them into a coherent whole. Deliverance's book had disappeared from Prudence's life records, but Grace thought it might have just undergone a transformation of name, or of description. Chilton was furious about her stalled research, but Janine thought his own work was the problem. The Wicca shop woman with all her amulets and sincerity did not know anything concrete about the circle on Connie's door. Her friends were worried about her staying alone in the house, while her usually nervous dog dozed, a bundle of contentment.

Connie propped her bare foot on the seat of the chair, pressing her shin against the Chippendale desk. Her notes lay scattered across the desk surface, occasional words leaping out from the blurred mass of her handwriting. *Home*, said one word. *Gardin*, said another. *Almanack. I have staid at home.*

"She tried to sell me a *charm*," Connie said to the dog. "Can you believe that?"

His breathing was slow and deep, a front paw twitching in sleep. She leaned over her notes again, fingers of one hand questing across her desk for something to handle. They settled on a sharp little metal object hidden under some papers in the far corner and picked it up, rolling it to and fro, pressing it for distraction while Connie's eyes roamed through all her notes on Prudence's journal. Day after day after day of gardening, weather, passing illnesses, strangers' babies born and paid for. Prudence's father dies. Mercy moves in. Josiah, Prudence's husband, comes and goes from town. Her daughter grows, assumes more responsibility in the house. Mercy dies. Patty moves away. Josiah dies—some kind of accident at the docks. And then, abruptly, in 1798, the journal stops. Her fingers walked the metal item from one digit to another and, squinting, Connie flipped backward in her notebook.

"'December 3, 1760.'" she read aloud. "'Very cold. Patty unwell. Mother looks for her Almanack. Very vexed when told it given to the Sociall Libar. Makes her poultice. Patty improves.' Huh," Connie wondered to the empty house. "Is 'Sociall Libar' an abbreviation for 'Social Library'? What do you think, Arlo?"

No response from underneath her chair. She looked down and found that the dog had disappeared. "Ingrate," she said. In her notebook she wrote down the words SOCIAL LIBRARY MARBLEHEAD OR SALEM? in block capital letters, and then drew little asterisks around it. She sat back in her chair, ruminating.

"An almanac," she said, trying the idea out to see if it sounded plausible. It did. A smile crept from her lips and started to spread across her face until it reached all the way up, casting a glint into her eyes. She looked down into her hand, suddenly aware of the item that she had been worrying while she worked.

It was a tiny, rusted nail, four sided and irregular. The nail looked small and tired, as if it had been at work for a very long time. It had been spat out by the rotting doorjamb when she first jimmied open the front door of Granna's house. Carrying the nail in her closed fist, she ventured out into the front yard.

Evening was starting to gather under the vine drapery overhead, and Connie stood on tiptoe, naked toes gripping the mossy flagstone stoop. Under the wet moss, the stone felt cool and hard to her feet. She pushed aside the tendrils of wisteria over the door, its flowers grown dull and papery in the heat, and found the horseshoe dangling at a sharp angle. Connie regarded the wide burned circle on her front door.

Dominus adjutor meus. Alpha. Omega. AGLA. She clenched her fist around the tiny nail, setting her jaw.

"Why not," Connie said aloud. Pushing the horseshoe into alignment with the rusted shadow in the house paint, she pressed the nail into the yielding wood with the ball of her thumb. Connie stepped back, folding her arms, and gazed up at the house, which stared back at her with something akin to approval.

"Blessed be," she said, wryly, to Arlo, who had appeared at her feet.

CHAPTER FOURTEEN

Marblehead, Massachusetts

Mid-July

1991

DESPITE HER BEST EFFORTS TO FEEL AT EASE IN GRANNA'S HOUSE, Connie often discovered herself to be confined—hiding, almost—in the kitchen. Her sharply circumscribed orbit could be blamed on the antique icebox, with its tempting, liftable lid, the only source of cool air in the dense heat of midsummer. She kept her notes restricted to Granna's desk in the sitting room, camped in the four-poster bed overhead late at night, and passed through the rest of the house quickly. In the kitchen, however, she lingered, running the water in the sink, chopping vegetables at the counter. In the kitchen she felt more on top of things; its small space presented a finite, achievable task in the rehabilitation of Granna's unsellable house, and its dated appliances at least gestured to a twentieth-century world outside, the world where Connie still felt herself to live. This morning she found herself leaning, one narrow arm propping the lid open, with her chin extended over the drifting mist rising out of the icebox's depths, letting the cool air creep up under the damp base of her hair, into the crevices behind her ears.

She felt calm this morning, focused. Her plans for the day were in place, and Connie liked nothing better than having her plans set firmly in place. Her tenuous sense of safety was bolstered when she stood in the little kitchen, with its cheap screen door into the backyard and its shelves of dead glass jars. She had developed the habit of each morning opening a few of the jars and scrubbing out their contents, black and desiccated, onto a compost heap in the far corner of the rear garden. She left the empty jars, rinsed and drying, lids open, in rows by the back stoop. She liked to peer at the rows from behind the screen door, admitting that the ever-growing compost pile and the ever-diminishing kitchen shelves formed her own private calendar system. The lowest kitchen shelf now stood empty, and Connie had even wiped away the last of the dust, washing it from a rag down the drain of the sink and feeling as she did so the release of a small chore finished.

Connie closed the icebox with some regret and turned back to the shelves, choosing the jars for that morning's purge. Three medium-size ones stood at eye level, their labels crisp with age, and Connie pulled them down one by one, slotting them into the curve of her arm around her belly. As she grasped the last one, her knuckles bumped against an unseen object, which she grabbed and pulled to the edge of the shelf. It was an undistinguished metal box, small, gray, with a lunch box clasp but no lock. Connie left it there while she carried the three jars to the compost heap, returning some moments later, wiping her wet hands on the seat of her cutoffs.

She took the little box between her hands and pried open the clasp. Inside Connie found a cache of note cards, the first one of which read *Key Lime Pie* in a cramped script that Connie remembered, just barely, as having belonged to her grandmother. She laughed quietly to herself. *Lard*, she read, extending her tongue in a *bleah* of disgust though no one was in the kitchen to witness it. She laid the box aside and shuffled through the note cards, sifting through Granna's penned recipes for almost defiantly 1950s cuisine: tomato aspic, pork tenderloin, bean and frankfurter casserole. Connie enjoyed a bloom of mischievous pleasure as she contemplated saving the cards for the now vegetarian Grace, mailing her a concrete reminder of her New England childhood. Checking her watch, Connie slid the recipe cards into the rear pocket of her cutoffs, grabbed her shoulder bag, and banged out the door on her way to the Salem Athenaeum.

AN AFTERNOON'S TELEPHONING TO THE VARIOUS RIVAL NORTH SHORE historical societies told Connie that there had, in fact, been something called the Social Library in Salem. Established at the end of the eighteenth century as an offshoot of a gentleman's social club, it had been maintained for some years by exorbitant membership fees and the donations of books acquired by wealthy Salem merchants' travels overseas. In 1810, however, the Social Library merged with a private membership library for science and technology, the Philosophical Library, to form the Salem Athenaeum. Connie was surprised, and deliciously pleased, to discover that the Salem Athenaeum had flourished through the nineteenth century, and while Salem's shipbuilding fortunes collapsed and its importance as a port was first eclipsed, then utterly surpassed, by Boston, Baltimore, and the Carolinas, the Athenaeum had trundled along blissfully unaware of its growing irrelevance to American letters. As the Volvo rolled to a labored stop across the street from the "new" Athenaeum building, erected in 1907, Connie felt—not for the first time—a private affection for the commitment to the status quo that undergirds the fierce Yankee impulse toward thrift.

Connie approached the desk on the left side of the sunny, well-appointed reading room, devoid of readers save for an elderly gentleman on the rear porch sipping lemonade, one long arm propped on a cane. At the desk a young matron was knotting thread on the underside of her needlepoint.

"Excuse me," Connie whispered, and the young woman looked up at her with a smile, laid aside her sewing, and stood to clasp Connie's hand.

"You must be Miss Goodwin!" said the librarian, and Connie was surprised that she spoke at a regular volume. She even had a cup of tea sitting on her desk; the crisp smell of lemon pierced through the familiar wood-and-books aroma of the library. "We spoke on the phone this morning! I am Laura Plummer."

"Hello," Connie said, smiling, enjoying the woman's warmth. Of course, in private libraries, one deals with little children and visiting oldsters more than neurotic graduate students. It must be easier to stay pleasant.

"You had inquired about seeing some of our original collection, is that right?" the woman said, ushering Connie toward the doorway into the stacks.

"Yes." Connie nodded. "I have been trying to track down this particular almanac—at least I'm pretty sure it's an almanac—that I have reason to believe was donated to the Social Library."

"We do have a number of almanacs," she said, snapping on overhead lights as she went. Connie felt the same sort of pleasure and safety in narrow book stacks that she had lately felt in Granna's kitchen. She shivered with excitement, reflecting that any one of these anonymous brown spines might be Deliverance's physick book. She might even be within an hour of finding it.

"Here we are," said Miss Plummer. She could not have been much older than Connie herself, but Connie had trouble conceiving of such a tidy woman, in her Peter Pan collar and pleated skirt, as a "Laura." She gestured to a short wall of books along the very rear of the stacks. "The Social Library only existed for fifteen or twenty years before the Athenaeum was formed. And the holdings, though impressive enough at the time, were modest by today's standards. Mostly printed sermons, a handful of novels, a few almanacs and navigational guides and suchlike. I'll be back at the front desk if you need any help." She withdrew with a smile, and Connie dropped her shoulder bag at her feet, weaving her fingers together and stretching them out before her with a preparatory crack.

Some hours passed, with Connie checking in the card catalogue first for Prudence Bartlett, Mercy Lamson, and Deliverance Dane as book donors, or perhaps authors, with no result. Next came several fruitless minutes thumbing through the cards for "almanac," though all examples seemed to belong to well-known mainstream publishing series, providing weather and planting guidelines for farmers. The library held one copy of Benjamin Franklin's satirical *Poor Richard's Almanack*, but none of the books were either particularly old or self-written. Finally, awash in frustration, she resorted to reading the spines and, eventually, the frontispieces of all the books in the almanac section of the collection, with no success.

Connie emerged despondent from within the archive, the weight of her shoulder bag with its bulging notebooks and pens digging into her shoulder more acutely than usual. She hooked her thumb under its strap and approached Miss Plummer's desk.

"I'm sorry to interrupt you," she said, and Miss Plummer looked up, smiling. The smile made the weight of Connie's book bag marginally less pressing, and she felt her shoulders unknot by a fraction.

"Yes?" asked the librarian. "Did you find it?"

Connie sighed. "I'm afraid not. Was there ever a point where some of the collection was de-accessioned, do you think? I know for sure that the book was donated here. And I can't imagine that anyone would have stolen it or anything. . . ."

"We de-accession things all the time," the librarian confirmed. "Usually bad novels and things after we have had them for a few years. There's very limited space in the stacks, as you can see. Let's check the files." She stood, turning to a large filing cabinet behind her desk. "I'm sure we'll find it," she assured Connie as she pulled open the cabinet drawer.

I hope so, Connie silently wished, wondering what she would tell Chilton if this lead failed.

"Here we go," said the librarian, paging through a discolored file. "Our first major de-accession occurred in 1877. It says here that books with no record of ever having been checked out were auctioned by Sackett"—she looked up and added, "That's like the Boston equivalent of Christie's or Sotheby's"—before continuing, "to raise money for collection maintenance and the building of the new library building." She closed the folder again and looked at Connie. "I'm afraid that there is no record of the titles of the books that were sold, but I feel certain that Sackett would still have the records on file. I'm sure you know how Boston institutions feel about record keeping."

Connie thought back to her experience at the Essex County probate department and chuckled through a gentle groan. "Thank you for your help," she said to the librarian, who was sliding the file folder back into place in the drawer behind her desk.

As Connie turned to leave, the young librarian, seating herself at her desk and reaching again for her needlepoint, brightly repeated, "I'm sure that you will find it." And for some reason, Connie believed her.

AS SHE MOVED THROUGH THE SUMMER AFTERNOON TOWARD THE SALEM Common, book bag knocking against her flank, Connie's thoughts roamed back to her conversation with Janine. As an undergraduate, Connie had read Manning Chilton's seminal book about the professionalization of medicine in eighteenth-century America, and had known that she wanted to study under him for her doctorate. Professor Chilton viewed science as an intellectual historian might—treating science not as a set of facts that are true no matter what the time period, but as a way of looking at the world that depended on historical context. And yet for all its breathless sweep, his work never overlooked the individuals who peopled his narratives. Doctors with their bleeding lancets, irritated midwives, mail-order laudanum salesmen, all stirred to life in Chilton's practiced words. The people in his history books felt as real to Connie as the students who passed her in the hallways of Saltonstall Court, or the panhandlers dotting the streets around her college. Chilton seemed to possess a special gift for peering from the present into the past, like the old glass-bottomed buckets that fishermen would plant in the water to view the secret depths below the boat.

Alchemy would naturally appeal to Chilton, with its search for transcendence through carefully honed technique. The alchemist sought to use the tools of chemistry and science to transcend reality—a spiritual quest, according to Janine, but with literal application. Alchemy sought to create value and beauty out of nothing. The dumb natural object hid fathomless realms of possibility, or so they had thought, which could be unlocked, given sufficient practice, patience, and study. For the adept with the correct formula, the philosopher's stone was within reach, with all that it promised: wealth, long life. Enlightenment.

Wealth. Connie frowned. Janine said that Chilton's paper argued that carbon could be the base substance for making the philosopher's stone, transformed in some heretofore unimagined way: it was a potentially precious thing but currently without value. Unknown, and yet known to all— the building block of life.

Connie stopped walking, lost in thought. Perhaps Chilton was not just risking his professional reputation, as Janine thought. Chilton was growing older, nearing the end of his career. He chaired the Harvard history department. He already had as much prestige as he could possibly need. Perhaps he was after something beyond prestige.

As she paused, Connie gazed through the latticed shadows lining the street that led to the church where, she knew, Sam was at that moment brushing thin gilding over the dome at the base of the steeple. Her head had been so sunk into her research that she was having trouble keeping track of her days. They had taken to speaking on the phone, five minutes at a time, late at night, but had not managed to see each other since the night the circle appeared on her door. Now she pictured him, one leg twined around the metal scaffold, ropes and harness fastened in place, droplets of liquid gold speckling the backs of his hands, dotting his forehead from the upward spatter of the stiff-haired paintbrush. Suddenly she saw how keenly she had missed him over the past several days, and she felt a pressing urge to detour to the church.

Connie lingered at the corner of the street for a full minute, shifting her weight from one sandal to the other. Finally she brokered an arrangement with herself in which Sam could work on in peace, provided that she call him that evening to make concrete plans. Satisfied, she continued her progress toward the Common, mind once again absorbed in thoughts of Chilton.

When Janine had said that Chilton claimed, in an academic conference no less, that alchemical work should be taken literally, surely he wasn't going around claiming that lead could be turned into gold, like Rumpelstiltskin at his spinning wheel, surrounded by magical ingots. Connie smiled at the image. No. He must mean something else. But what? Substance, or idea? When Manning Chilton said "the philosopher's stone," what did he mean?

The Salem Common stretched out before her, bald in spots, cracked and shimmering with the heat. Connie spotted a tree with a suitably dense pool of shade under its branches and stooped to pluck a dandelion. She brushed the soft white puff against her upper lip, closed her eyes, and thought *I wish that Sackett auction house could tell me exactly where Deliverance's book has gone* as she blew out a stream of hot breath. When she opened her eyes, the puff looked patchy, bedraggled, the flower stem still gripping its seed pods, giving away nothing. Connie tossed the dented stem aside and, reaching the tree, dropped her bag and then herself to the ground.

As she sat she felt a tight, uncomfortable lump occupying her rear cutoff pocket, and reached behind her to see what was pressing through the denim. She pulled out the offending object and discovered the packet of note cards found in Granna's kitchen that morning. Connie smiled, anticipating Grace's reaction when she opened an envelope in Santa Fe to find it full of Sophia's voice. She flipped the top card to the back of the pile, revealing another recipe. *Chicken Fricassee*, it said. *Pluck and scald fresh chicken thoroughly and boil with a carrot and celery stick. Season with salt and pepper. Serve with cream and a little stock. Allow six hours. Good with white rice.* Reading the card, Connie could see Granna in the kitchen of the Milk Street house, steel gray hair pulled back, left hand curled in, resting the outer wrist on her thickened waist, dipping a long wooden spoon into a bubbling pot. The aroma of cooking chicken drifted through the imagined memory, and in her mind Connie saw Granna turn to look over her shoulder toward where Connie was standing, smiling, saying *Just another hour or so.* Connie flipped the card to the back of the pile to reveal a new one.

Boiled Lobster, said the new card. *Wash live lobsters gently, then throw into pot of salted, boiling water with a tight lid. Add marjoram for the pain. Boil until bright red, quite awhile depending on how big. Serve with lemon wedge and melted butter. You'll need a nutcracker.* Connie pried each sandal off with her toes and rolled onto her stomach in the grass. As she held the note card, she imagined an older, bearded man with a bleached captain's hat and burned, creased eyes raising his hand to knock at the screen door of the kitchen, and Granna setting aside her broom in the corner where it still stood, holding the screen door open with one hip to accept a rough wooden box from the man, saying, *I always feel so sorry for them,* and the man saying, *I ha' liddle extrer in the catch this week, Sophier.*

"Granna," whispered Connie, wondering what other image of her barely remembered grandmother might emerge from the scant writing in her hands. *Works especially well for tomats,* said the next note card, and Connie heard Granna's voice in her ears saying "tomats" instead of "tomatoes," but the writing underneath that heading was difficult to make out, so Connie leaned in, bringing the card close to her nose, squinting in the shade to make out the hasty forms of the letters. She formed each letter in her mouth, gripping the card between her hands on the grassy ground, letting the words assemble one syllable at a time.

"*Pater in . . . caelo,*" she began, wondering how Granna could have a recipe written in Latin. "*Te oro et obsec . . . obsecro in ben . . . benignitate tua.*" She narrowed her eyes, gripping the card tighter because her palms started to feel prickly and hot, as if brushed against a stinging nettle.

"*Ut sinas hanc herbam, vel lignum.*" The heat and stinging grew more acute, edging nearer to pain, and she blinked her eyes rapidly as the note card seemed illuminated by a round bluish glow. She grimaced against the improbable pain, finishing, "*Vel plantam crescere et vigere catena temporis non vinctam.*"

The blue light condensed into a pulsing round orb between her hands, aiming crackling electric veins at a dry young dandelion seed on the ground. Connie's lips parted, her eyes wide in astonishment as the seed started to throb and heave and bubble, shooting a slender, fragile stalk up, up, up until its very tip exploded into a yellow flower. Before she could fully grasp what she was seeing, the yellow flower burst into a white seed puff.

Staring, transfixed, Connie dropped her hands, now suddenly freed from pain as instantly as it had appeared, just as the seed puff was caught up by a passing breeze, which lifted each tender white seed-cloud up and away until they all dissolved into nothing.

"Oh, my God," she whispered, frozen in place as the now-dead dandelion stalk abruptly withered back into the ground from whence it came.

Part II

THE

Sieve AND Scissors

In the beginning was the Word, and the Word was with God, and the Word was God. The same was in the beginning with God.

—John 1:1–2 (King James)

And I say also unto thee, That thou art Peter, and upon this rock I will build my church; and the gates of hell shall not prevail against it.

—Matthew 16:18 (King James)

CHAPTER FIFTEEN

Marblehead, Massachusetts

Mid-July

1991

THE CARDS SPREAD ON THE DINING TABLE LOOKED LIKE A GAME OF solitaire, set out in careful rows one after the other. Connie adjusted the wick of the oil lamp to brighten its orange glow, pulled out one of the shield-back chairs, and sat at the table, sliding her hands under her legs, shoulders pulled up by her ears. Most of the cards were just dull recipe cards: the boiled lobster, a few kinds of pie, casseroles, the chicken, all of them smudged with flour and thumbprints like any kitchen tool in constant use.

But then there were the others.

Connie pushed back from the table and stood again, pacing across the dining room. She had been shuttling like this for the past hour, first sitting at the table, then standing up again, unable to settle. Her energy was frayed, bringing her into uncomfortable awareness of the throb of blood in her veins, of the tingle of her nerves, and of the flush of adrenaline in her chest.

Three of the cards were not recipes at all. She cast a wary eye at those three, sitting aloof on the table.

The thing to do, of course, was to react rationally. After sprinting out of the Salem Common in a panic and roaring home in the Volvo, she had told herself in no uncertain terms that the dandelion was a coincidence; that she was tense and scared and spending too much time alone. She had spread the cards out on the dining table where they could be inspected safely, clinically.

Connie turned back to the table, picking up the card that was labeled *Works especially well for tomats*. Frowning, she carried the card out of the dining room into the tiny front entryway and squatted next to the dead plant-shell in the cracked China-export pot. Keenly aware of her ridiculousness, Connie raised one hand, aimed it at the corpse of the plant, and read the words on the card aloud again.

Nothing happened.

"See?" she said to Arlo, who had materialized on the steps. "It's fatigue, plain and simple." He gazed back at her, eyes questioning, fur mottled the color of the paint in the stairwell. She watched him for a moment, then got to her feet and returned to the dining room, the animal trotting after her.

This time Connie stood before one of the hanging planters that held the remnants of a spider plant. It had been dead for so long that a hand brushed against its leaves caused them to dissolve into dust. A few tattered spider-webs lingered in the hollows among the leaves, their occupants long since gone. The earth inside the pot had been sucked dry of all moisture, deep crevices yawning open between the tight knot of dead roots and the bowl's edges.

"Okay," said Connie, setting the card aside and turning her full attention on the dead plant. She raised her hands so that her spread fingers created a sort of spherical basket around it. She furrowed her brows, concentrating on the precise point at the center of the sphere, deep within the crumbling earth in the planter.

"*Pater in caelo*," she murmured, and a hot prickling sensation stretched across the palms of her hands. "*Te oro et obsecro in benignitate tua*," she continued, as a subtle bluish glow coalesced in a swirling bubble between her outstretched fingers. Her nerves jumped and snapped in pain. "*Ut sinas hanc herbam, vel lignum, vel plantam, crescere et vigere catena temporis non vinctam,*" she finished. The blue orb of light grew more solid, its electrical veins snapping in jagged lines from her fingertips and palms into the center of the ceramic planter. In that instant, the dried spider plant leaves flushed with water and health, the fresh, waxy green of life crawling down each black leaf, lifting and twisting as the color returned, and sending out fragile little shoots bursting with new baby leaves up and over the edge of the planter. By the time Connie dropped her hands to her sides, the smell of moist earth filled the dining room, and the spider plant hung thick and lush, swaying a little in the close evening air.

She staggered backward, groping for the support of the dining table, her breath coming in shallow gasps. Hot tears sprang into the rims of her eyes, and she realized that with each breath she was also letting out a high, panicked whimper. Her hand found the back of one of the shield-back chairs, pulling it toward her just in time to catch her falling weight. Horrified, Connie wrapped her arms around her middle and bent over, resting her forehead on her knees, her breath breaking into hiccuping sobs.

Within her mind great puzzle pieces shifted, each with a different woman's face, rotating and nudging together until a complete picture began to emerge. Across her mind's eye drifted an image of Granna's face, dark gray hair pulled tight, pale eyes shining as she held aloft a fat, glistening tomato from the plant outside. This image dissolved into a young, pink-cheeked woman, face framed with a perfect white linen coif, plain Puritan collar spread over her shoulders—Deliverance, or what Connie imagined Deliverance to have looked like, her mouth moving inaudibly as she read from a great open book. Then a careworn woman, tanned and mobcapped, tired—Prudence, sliding a package across a table into the hands of some unseen person. Last Connie saw Grace, straight hair falling over her shoulders, in the raftered kitchen of her Santa Fe house, her hands moving a few inches above a weeping woman's head.

All of them with pale, ice blue eyes.

Connie sat up, rubbing her palms over her flushed forehead. When she dropped her hands she saw first Arlo, his chin in her lap, worrying, and behind him, on the wall, the woman in the portrait, which Connie had never noticed bore a tiny engraved plaque that read TEMPERANCE HOBBS—with her sloping nineteenth-century shoulders and wasp waist—watching her over a tiny, knowing smile.

"It can't be true!" she whispered, clutching at herself and rocking to and fro in the dining chair. She thought first of Grace, that she must talk to her immediately. But Granna! Connie's eyes darted crazily around the house, taking in the few blackened jars in the dining room, the little corn husk doll with its dimity dress and yarn bow resting on the mantelpiece, Deliverance's name tucked deep into a family Bible.

The circle burned into her door.

Connie leapt to her feet, rushing to pick up the telephone.

At the instant that she arrived in the front hall, the telephone receiver clutched in her hand, the front door opened a crack. She froze.

"Connie?" asked Sam, peering into the entry hall. When she heard his voice, she dropped the receiver with a cry of relief, winding her arms around his neck and breathing in the salty smell of his skin, freshened by the chemical gloss of paint spatters still clinging to his ponytail. "Hey," he said, uneasy, holding his arms in a tentative shell around her trembling back before lowering them onto her waist. She tightened her grip around his shoulders, trying to wring the resistance out of his muscles, digging her chin into the spot where his shoulder met his neck until she felt him overcome his surprise and relax. They stood like that, him holding her, for a moment, the front door still open. Arlo wandered from the dining room, around their four feet grouped together, and out into the yard.

"Sam," she said, voice muffled. She had called him, she remembered now, as soon as she arrived back at the house, leaving a breathless, anxious message on his machine describing what had happened in the Salem Common and asking if she could see him later. Until his arrival, she had forgotten completely.

"Let's sit down," Sam suggested, leading her into the shadowed sitting room. He settled her into the armchair, hands balanced on her knees, and pulled up a low needlepoint footstool to seat himself at her feet. He propped his brown forearms on his knees and looked up at her, waiting.

"So," he began. "You were reading a note card out loud, and a dandelion blew away?" She read the concern in his face, but it was a concern that masked an underlying worry. Deep inside his eyes, behind the little glimmer in the retinas, she saw that Sam did not believe her. And why would he?

"It didn't just blow away, Sam," she said, impatient, unsure if she wanted him to be convinced of the truth of what had happened, or if she wanted him to convince her of the folly of what she now knew to be true. "I *made it* blow away. Just by reading some Latin from my grandmother's recipe card, I made it appear out of nowhere, bloom, and die! All at once!"

"Okay," he said. "But you can see why someone would assume that you just hadn't noticed it before until you accidentally exhaled or something and made it blow away. You admit that it would be the logical explanation here?" he prodded her, not unkindly. His face looked tired, Connie noticed. Her inner voice proposed that he would certainly think that she had lost her mind if she pursued this subject any further. Any reasonable person would respond by distancing himself. He would pull away, inventing reasons that did not have to do with her directly, and soon enough he would disappear from her life. She swallowed, eyes wide.

"I suppose," she said, drawing out the words.

Then she made a show of making up her mind. "Yes, I'm sure you're right. That would be the logical explanation." She did not meet his eyes, instead folding her arms tightly over her chest and looking at a spot on the threadbare carpet.

Sam leaned his head into his hands and massaged his temples with his fingertips, rubbing the skin over his forehead and jaw. It occurred to Connie that she had not even asked how his work was coming along. He had been suspended overhead in an abandoned church building all day, up by the ceiling where the heat collected, alone, daubing paint in the corners of the cupola.

"How did the gilding go?" she asked him, reaching a hand forward to brush an escaped lock of hair away from his forehead. His brow was sheened with sweat, and as her finger met his skin, she suddenly felt the great mass of his fatigue seep from his scalp into her hand and forearm, dragging them down with an almost physical weight.

"It was fine, just fine. Hot. But fine." He exhaled. Connie passed her thumb gently over the skin between his eyebrows; as an experiment, without even deciding to do so, she tried telegraphing intent along her neural networks, instructing his system to relax. With deepening surprise she felt the tissue under her thumb grow a little looser and heard Sam release an almost inaudible sigh. Connie pulled her hand away, gazing down at it with unconcealed wonder. A pale blue thumbprint glowed momentarily on his forehead, then vanished. She gaped, looking to Sam, who seemed unaware that anything unusual had just happened.

He moved from his seat on the footstool into one of the armchairs by the fireplace, pressing his palms to his eyes. "I'm just glad you're okay," he said from behind his hands. After a moment's hesitation Connie climbed into his lap, threading her arm behind his neck. Sam wrapped his arm around her waist, pulling her to him. "Your message sounded so freaked out! I was worried about you," he mumbled into her hair.

She smiled. "You were?"

"Yes," he admitted, tightening his grip. She felt the warmth of his hand pressing into the skin of her leg, secure and insistent.

Connie settled her head against his chest, hoping that she had deflected his curiosity for the time being. For the first time that day, her sense of confusion and anxiety began to ebb, subsumed in her delicious consciousness of Sam's proximity. They sat like that for a moment, tangled together in the armchair, not saying anything. His thumb stroked the skin of her thigh, testing its texture.

"Sam?" she asked presently, her voice muffled by his paint-stained work shirt.

"Yes?" he said, moving his hand down her back. His lips brushed against the spot where her neck met the back of her ear, his breath stirring the faint hairs at the nape of her neck, causing the skin there to tingle. He shifted beneath her, resettling his weight in the chair.

She cleared her throat. "If you want to stay over tonight, you know, that would be okay."

The invitation sounded pathetic in her ears, and Connie's memory spiraled backward to all the stilted conversations that she had suffered through in college, with boys who had all worn a seamless layer of arrogance that Connie never knew how to penetrate. She waited for his response, afraid that he would laugh at her.

He did laugh, but it was kind, and as he did so he tightened his grip around her waist. Through the soft flannel of his work shirt Connie felt the radiating warmth of his skin, and the sound of his laughter echoed deep within his chest. His chin grated a little against her forehead. She exhaled softly, only now aware that she had been holding her breath. "What a relief," he exclaimed, opening his eyes. "You just saved me from having to come up with some stupid line about protecting you from vandals."

She turned her face to him, and he kissed her, then again, more deeply, drawing his thumb gently along her jaw.

Before she knew what was happening Sam was standing up, hoisting her legs around his waist and carrying her toward the stairs. "Enough of this," he said, voice thick. Connie threw her head back with delighted laughter, ducking her head just in time to miss the joist as he started up the narrow staircase to the attic bedroom.

CHAPTER SIXTEEN

Cambridge, Massachusetts
Mid-July
1991

THE WOODEN BENCH IN THE VESTIBULE OUTSIDE OF MANNING CHIL-
ton's office in the Harvard history department was a hard, imitation
Windsor seat, painted black, with sharp pole-shaped slats designed expressly
to discourage sitting. Connie unfolded her left hand and gazed into the
palm, bending her fingers one after the other and touching each to her
thumb in turn. At Sam's insistence the previous night, she had finally pulled
out the Latin note card to show him, and he read it over several times. Once
he tried reading it aloud while holding his own hand next to one of the dead
plants in the sitting room, to no effect. *See?* he said. *It was just a coincidence.*

I know, Connie responded. *I've just been working too hard, I guess.*

Too many witches on the brain, Cornell, he teased her.

But that raised the question of why the recipe card had not worked for
Sam. Whenever she tried to grab hold of a possible explanation it pulled
apart like wet paper in her hands. For Sam's part, the confirmation that it

was just a note card appeared to bring the subject to a close. As for Connie, the further away the revival of the spider plant moved from her in time, the less possible it seemed. And yet, it had happened.

Rolling her wrist over, Connie glanced at her watch. It was uncharacteristic of Chilton to keep her waiting. Unlike Janine Silva, who was perpetually out of breath and behind schedule, Chilton maintained a rigid order to his days. His office hours remained consistent even across the blurry days of summer, when most academics fled the campus. She waved one flip-flop from the end of her outstretched foot, avoiding gazing at the disconcerting landscape painting with its matching sun and moon. Her shoulder blades shifted against the center splat of the bench back, which held a relief carving of the university seal with *Veritas*—truth—in deep scrollwork. The raised wood ground against her muscles, and she leaned her elbows onto her knees to escape its pressure. She wondered how much longer she should wait. It was unlike him, but perhaps Chilton had forgotten their appointment.

As she delved into her shoulder bag for something to read, the door to Chilton's office clicked open, and she saw two polished loafers appear side by side in the corner of her vision. She looked up and was met with the pinched face of Manning Chilton, pallid over his navy club bow tie.

"Connie, my girl," he said, voice sounding strained. "We do have an appointment, don't we? Why don't you come in." Without having a chance to respond, Connie gathered her shoulder bag together and followed him into his office. The sight of Chilton's preoccupied face pushed the strange events of the previous night into a deep corner of her mind as she concentrated on reading the situation with her advisor.

His desk, rather than being its usual wide expanse of naked, gleaming oak, was cluttered with untidy heaps of paper, drifting into dunes at its far corners. Half a dozen books stood stacked at his elbow, bookmark slips spilling out of them in several places. A yellow legal pad sat before him, covered from margin to margin in dense scrawled notes. An ashtray festered within arm's reach, and the mouthpiece of his pipe bore tooth marks. Chilton sat leaning back in his chair, fingers tucked into a temple before his mouth, and

Connie thought she even saw the ghost of a coffee ring staining one of the papers jutting out from under the green glass desk lamp. He rocked a little in his chair, not really looking at her, seeming only half aware that she had seated herself across from him.

"Professor Chilton?" she asked, leaning forward to meet his gaze.

He rocked for a moment more, then blinked and focused his eyes on Connie. Her advisor appeared even older than she remembered, his hair a fraction whiter, his skin a little more sallow. His work must be troubling him even more than Janine had implied. For the first time in her years as his student, Connie caught herself feeling almost protective toward Chilton, imagining the scorn that he must have faced at the conference that Janine mentioned. Perhaps his work had grown too esoteric, too philosophical for mainstream historians. She felt a glow of approbation toward him, of pride that she should be working with a man who had the power to change the way history was understood.

"Tell me, Connie, where do we stand with your colonial shadow book?" he barked, breaking into her thoughts, and she felt the warm glow dissipate, replaced in an instant with the quaking anxiety of the malingering student.

"Shadow book?" Connie asked. "My latest research suggests that the book is a kind of almanac." She quavered as she said this, hesitating to correct him.

"I have been doing some checking of my own, my girl," he said, leaning forward. "And a book of shadows is one contemporary term for a collection of recipes and spells that a given witch has found to be particularly effective, often handed down from master to initiate. You may call it an almanac if you wish, but I have satisfied myself that we are dealing with a book of shadows and little else. But if you do not know this, then I presume you have yet to locate it. So tell me, if you please, where we stand." He brought his hands to rest in a knot on the table and stared at her expectantly.

A book of shadows? Connie recoiled at the preposterous name. She wondered where exactly he had been doing this "checking," as he called it, and further, why he would have been following up on her research if his own work was in such a precarious position. A strange, territorial feeling gripped her, and she felt irrationally angry that he had been working on her research rather than on his own. Sorting through the details that she had collected, she chose ones that she felt willing to spare and hid the rest away in her mind, unwilling to give him access to the total scope of her thought. Was this new territoriality duplicitous? The desire to conceal her plans from her advisor suffused her. She would tell him her progress in locating the book but keep her suspicions about its contents for herself.

"I found that the book was de-accessioned from the Salem Athenaeum in the 1870s. My next step will be to visit the auction house archives, which I have been assured are quite complete."

"Sackett," Chilton interjected, sounding bored.

"Yes," Connie replied, raising her eyebrows in surprise. "How did you know?"

"My girl, all nineteenth-century Boston auctions of any consequence would have been handled by Sackett," he said, waving his hand in dismissal. He fixed her with a distant gaze that indicated the barest glimmer of surprise that she would not have known this fact already.

Connie continued, undaunted. "The librarian at the Salem Athenaeum seemed confident that the book would have been acquired by a collector of early Americana, and as such it would have left a traceable record, probably traveling through private hands. I just need a little more time."

Chilton sniffed, reaching for the gnawed pipe in the ashtray on his desk. "A little more time," he echoed, voice cold. He picked up the pipe and dug its bowl into a pouch of tobacco from the top drawer of his desk, his hands moving automatically through these preparations while his eyes stayed locked on Connie's face. The sweet, burnt smell of the cake box blend from the tobacconist's in Harvard Square reached Connie's nose. Idly, she wondered if the pipe was a habit left over from Chilton's undergraduate self, something adopted as a boy to buy himself a cheap sort of sophistication. She tried to imagine a teenaged Manning Chilton: hair slicked back, club bow tie sloppily knotted, lifting the glass lid of a wide jar of dried tobacco leaves. But the image jarred, impossible to resolve with the grim patrician man who sat staring at her with such disapproval.

"Connie," he began, after a long draw on his pipe. "I was going to wait to tell you about this until after you found the book, but I can see that you are in need of some more forceful motivation," he said, and Connie glowered in response. What could he possibly expect? Research takes as long as it takes. Surely Chilton must understand that.

"In the last week of September, as you know, I have been invited to present the keynote address to the Colonial Association on my recent research into alchemical technique and magical thinking in first-period America. My research, I think it's safe to tell you, has attracted some considerable interest. I would like to invite you to join me in this presentation."

He puffed on his pipe, bemused eyes seeming to expect an outpouring of gratitude in response to this invitation. Connie's initial feeling was one of pleasure and surprise. To be invited to present together with her advisor was a momentous development indeed. Still, a tiny cloud on the edge of her consciousness reminded her of Janine's characterization of Chilton's current research. She watched him, waiting.

When she failed to appear excited at this prospect, Chilton looked momentarily flustered but collected himself almost instantly. He cleared his throat. "As I am sure you know, this is a unique opportunity for a graduate student at this stage of your career. I would be very pleased to provide your research with such a worthy forum. And, it must be said, you would likely find some professional opportunities awaiting you from contacts made at this conference." He paused, lowering his voice. "*Considerable* professional opportunities. However, I will be unable to present you to my colleagues if the book remains unlocated. So you see, we have a bit of a problem."

Connie swallowed, preparing to tread lightly. "Professor Chilton," she began. "Perhaps if you gave me a sense of what the subject of your presentation will be, I would be in a better position to prepare."

He watched her, weighing his words before speaking. "A perfectly reasonable question," he said. "And one that I will be able to answer in some detail once you bring me the book."

"I see," she said.

He gazed at her, drawing on his pipe, and a haze of smoke poured from his nostrils, forming a sweet-smelling cloud around his head. "Do you?" he asked, leaning back in his chair.

"Yes," Connie said, unease radiating from her stomach. "And thank you. This is an incredible opportunity. I won't disappoint you."

The words left her mouth as if she were reciting them from a script. Connie got to her feet, gathering her shoulder bag to her chest, not meeting Chilton's steady gaze. She started to back toward the door, one foot behind the other, until her hand found the heavy brass doorknob and turned it. As she passed through the door she heard Chilton's voice follow her out into the hallway.

"Find the book, Connie," the voice said.

And then the door closed with a click.

CHAPTER SEVENTEEN

Boston, Massachusetts
Mid-July
1991

A CHIME SOUNDED, AND THE GREAT MASS OF HUMANITY IN THE TRAIN car bunched together near the doors, building up in a blockade of arms and legs and headphones and backpacks before pouring out, first in a trickle, and then in a slurry as the doors slid open. Connie felt herself carried along in the current of bodies roiling out onto the subway platform, closing her throat against the mixed smells of perfume, sweat, asphalt, melting tires. She gripped her bag more tightly under her arm, allowing the throng to float her along the platform, up a flight of stairs, over and around the man sleeping in a stained olive drab bedroll, and out the doors of the Arlington T station. The commuter mob dispersed in clusters of twos and threes once it reached the open expanse of the Public Garden.

Connie stopped beneath an elegant weeping willow, its branches drooping down to the ground. She rested against it in the shade, enjoying the sensation of sweat gathered up off of her brow and arms and carried away on the breeze. Though Boston as a general concept could be said to encompass the vast assemblage of tight, ordered towns all along the northeastern spread of Massachusetts, each little fiefdom did a much better job of retaining its own stubborn identity than most outsiders would expect. She had spent her childhood in the comfortable woods around Concord, and her present life strolling the brick streets of Cambridge, but during both blocks of time, she had found little reason to venture into Boston proper. Utterly disoriented, she now gazed down the lawn that swept from Boylston Street to the lily pond in the Public Garden. Tourists placidly drifted by in swan boats, disappearing under the footbridge. She reached into her bag and pulled out a crumpled paper, casting her eye over the directions that she had noted down over the telephone.

"Providence Street," she read, peering one way, then another. The address should only be a block or two away, but she always felt lost in downtown Boston, being accustomed to wandering past nearly identical town houses until she emerged on a street that sounded familiar. She eyed the Ritz-Carlton across the street, obscured behind a cluster of discreet Town Cars, and the facade of Shreve's behind her on the corner, where women laden with shopping bags grouped before the windows, admiring the sparkling wares inside. Connie squeezed her eyes shut, made a guess, and crossed the boulevard just ahead of the onward crush of afternoon traffic.

To her surprise, the guess proved more or less accurate, and after a few minutes' walk Connie pushed open the substantial doors of Sackett Auctioneers and Appraisers. She entered a cool vestibule that bore the proud, slightly worn elegance shared by many Boston institutions. The dark blue Oriental rug on the floor was threadbare in patches, its floral pattern eaten away by moths. A painting of a clipper ship under full sail, held in a gilt frame and stained brown with tobacco smoke, hung over a cracked leather couch. A few copies of *Yankee Home* magazine, decades old, were fanned across a demure coffee table. New York looks ahead, she mused, but Boston can't help but look back. She signed the guest register with a fountain pen and made her way up the stairs to the main gallery.

Preparations were under way for an auction of what looked like lesser American landscape paintings. Great canvases covered in dramatic clouds and blasted tree trunks were interspersed with undistinguished seascapes: still more clipper ships, and one scene of Gloucester harbor encased in ice, which nearly ran her over at the top of the stairway, art handlers' feet just visible beneath the frame. She passed a few moments being overlooked and in the way, finally tapping the shoulder of the workman who had just leaned the frozen harbor painting against a wall. With a jerk of his head he indicated an obscure door in the corner of the gallery, and Connie nodded her thanks.

She stepped through the door, finding herself in a long hallway lined with wooden doors bearing departmental placards. She passed MUSICAL INSTRUMENTS, FINE JEWELRY, PRINTS AND WORKS ON PAPER, finally stopping when she reached RARE MANUSCRIPTS AND BOOKS. Connie rapped softly on the door, but it yielded to the slight pressure of her knuckle, creaking open to reveal an office crowded with files and papers, a rotund, genial man with jeweler's magnifying glasses clipped to his spectacles seated in the middle.

"Ah!" he said, rising to a quarter-crouch, the gesture of a proper gentleman who is nevertheless always in a hurry. He made no move to introduce himself but instead seemed to be expecting her. "Sit, sit." He waved one hand at a pile of papers across from him, which proved to be hiding a stiff armchair. Gingerly Connie lifted the pile—auction catalogues, most of them—and settled them on the floor.

"I'm sorry," she began. "But are you Mr. . . . ?"

"Beeton, yes," he said, continuing to thumb through the catalogue open before him on the top layer of his desk. "I must say it's been some time since anyone asked me something *worth* researching." He exhaled a disapproving puff through his nose. "No real collecting strategies anymore, these people." He flipped another page. "But then I was given your message. Whom did you speak to?"

Connie started to answer, but Mr. Beeton cut her off. "Never mind. These useless girls at the front that they have. Only want to get married! Go to New York if that's what you want, I tell them. Do they listen?" He flipped a page again. "No real intellectualism to them, poor slight little things. Come pouring out of Mount Holyoke and Wellesley thinking, ooh, with my little *art history* degree I shall find someone with real *means*! As if collecting were mere *acquisition*!" He spat out the word, reaching one gray hand up to adjust his jeweler's lenses.

Connie pressed her lips together to suppress the smile that was fighting to get out. "As a matter of fact," she ventured, "I went to Mount—"

"Tell me, Miss Goodwin," the redoubtable Mr. Beeton interrupted. "What do you think is the hallmark of a truly fine collecting sensibility? Hmmm?" He set aside the catalogue that he had been perusing, marking one spot with a long slice of paper, and pulled out a thick file folder. "Is it just buying whatever one can afford, willy-nilly?"

"No?" Connie guessed.

"Is it merely gathering together those various symbols of taste and affluence that one's decorator tells one to acquire?" He shuffled through the file folder as he spoke, licking his thumb with each turn of a leaf.

"Ah," Connie demurred.

"Or is it rather the refinement of a given taste through study and contemplation, developing the understanding of what differentiates the merely expensive from the truly rare through *discipline* and *self-education*?" He looked at her expectantly, gazing over his complex lenses. Her mouth opened, but nothing came out at first. Mr. Beeton waited, tapping his fingertips together.

"Discipline," she said, finally.

"Precisely!" he exclaimed, pushing the catalogue and the open file together across his desk. "Junius *Lawrence*," he said, shifting himself in the seat, elbow swerving dangerously near a pile of papers stacked on the end of the desk.

"I beg your pardon?" asked Connie, scanning the files that he had passed to her.

"The fellow who bought the entirety of the Salem Athenaeum collection in 1877. Conducted through an intermediary, of course, as the man didn't care to broadcast how utterly *indiscriminate* his taste was. And rightfully so." Mr. Beeton settled back in his chair.

Connie looked more closely at the catalogue that advertised the sale when it was conducted, complete with estimates for some of the rarer volumes (of which the almanac appeared not to be one). Then she turned to the open file folder, which listed the buyer's premium for the bulk of the Athenaeum collection, charged to an anonymous holding company. Behind this list in the folder Connie found a series of receipts and signatures tracing the holding company through various signatories to one Junius Lawrence of the Back Bay, Boston, Massachusetts.

"But who was he?" Connie asked, looking up. Mr. Beeton emitted an ill-concealed smirk.

"Industrialist. New money. Made a mint in something wretched—granite mining, I believe—and like many *gentlemen* of his ilk set about promptly purchasing the social credibility that he otherwise *lacked*."

"But why would he buy books?" Connie asked, confused.

"Well, he didn't *just* buy books," said Mr. Beeton. "He also bought furniture—Belter mostly, and other high Victorian claptrap. And quite a few examples of American landscape painting. Got good advice in that department, apparently. One or two of his pieces wound up at the Museum of Fine Arts. Tried to spread his money around, that one. One of his paintings, a lesser one, should be installed upstairs right about now. Meant to be a Fitz Hugh *Lane*. Luminism. Probably fake. But the books, Miss Goodwin. Why do you think he would want them?"

The man watched her, and Connie felt the dust of his overcrowded office beginning to sneak into her nasal passages and down the back of her throat. Her eyes were starting to itch. Why would someone back then buy old books, anyway? Expensive ones?

"Why, to fill his new *library*, of course," spat Mr. Beeton, as if responding to her unspoken thought. "I did a bit of research before you arrived. In 1874, he began building a great new town house on the water side of Beacon

Street—I've a copy of the architectural sketches here somewhere—and his architect naturally included a *library*. Well"—Beeton sniffed—"the man was a *miner*. He had never collected a book in his life. Needed to get his hands on some, but quick. In December of 1877, his wife—she was a distant cousin of the Cabots, penniless branch, of course—threw a party." He thrust a yellowed newspaper clipping into her hands, entitled "Seen Around Town," with an engraving of the facade of the Lawrences' town house.

"Smartest party of the year, it was. Really burst Lawrence onto the scene. Good thing he had some nice old books to scatter around the house. Much easier to be accepted if one manages to *look* the part. When the time came, both his daughters did quite well." Beeton smiled a tidy, evil little smile and pushed his complicated lenses up his forehead. The man was able to expound about hundred-year-gone social machinations with such enthusiasm that they could have been happening to people he himself knew; his mind held maps of Brahmin interrelationship, intermarriage, bank account, and scandal, all throbbing with life. She sometimes forgot that to be a good historian one must also have an ear for gossip. She passed the newspaper clipping back to him.

"This is fascinating," Connie said, wondering what all this meant for her quest for Deliverance's book. "I had never heard of the Lawrences."

"Endowed a small wing in the Boston Public Library in 1891," Beeton said. "Married off the two daughters, who went on to a healthy *obscurity*. Family lost the last of the money in the crash of '29. Sold the town house to a small local college." He made a *pshaw*ing sound.

"Do you think the almanac that I am looking for would have ended up in the Public Library wing? Or would one of the daughters have kept it?" Connie asked.

"Oh, I think *not*," said Beeton. "Here in Rare Manuscripts and Books, we like to keep *tabs* on some of the more major collections that pass through our hands." He spoke with authority.

"Naturally we hoped that the family would think of us if they wished to pass on the Athenaeum collection. But my understanding"—Mr. Beeton paged through another several papers in the file—"is that one or two of the volumes went to the daughters—not great *readers*, those two—and that on Junius Lawrence's death in"—he hunted for a moment through another of the papers—"1925"—he passed Connie a clipped obituary from the *Boston Herald*, entitled "Junius Lawrence, Philanthropist, Granite Magnate, Dead at 74"—"the collection was donated to . . . yes, here it is . . . Harvard." A slip of paper was thrust into Connie's hands, which proved to be a copy of Junius Lawrence's will, itemizing his charitable donations. *Four years later his daughters must have regretted* that *generosity*, Connie reflected as Beeton's last comment sank into her mind.

She paused for a beat. "Wait—Harvard?" she asked, in a small, unbelieving voice.

"Why yes!" cried Beeton. "They pretend to care how old one's money is, but of course they don't *really*." He waggled a thin, gray eyebrow at Connie.

Gears ground together in Connie's mind, and she felt the muscles in her hands contract, wanting to dig into the copy of Junius Lawrence's will that was clutched between her fingers. "Do you think that Junius Lawrence ever read any of the books that he bought from the Salem Athenaeum?" she asked, her voice sounding very far away in her ears.

Mr. Beeton pursed his lips together, seeming to think for a moment. "Unlikely," he finished. "Rather too busy enjoying his *money*, I should think."

The book was at Harvard. It had been there this entire time! She looked down again at the will, and up again at Beeton, dwarfed by his precious catalogues and papers. He smiled a watery smile at her.

"This has been very helpful," Connie said, struggling to keep her voice even. "May I keep a copy of this list?"

"It's yours," said Beeton, waving his hand in a shooing motion. Then he sighed. "If only *today's* collectors were as interested as you are, Miss Goodwin." Beeton shook his head. "Hell in a *handbasket*, I am afraid."

"Indeed," said Connie, rising. Her mind leaped ahead, shooting through the dim marble halls of Widener Library at Harvard, where Deliverance's book was waiting. She could find it tomorrow! Then she could figure out what Chilton wanted with it. The book was hovering, just out of her grasp, but she finally knew exactly where to look. "Thank you so much."

"Good luck," she thought she heard Mr. Beeton say as she made her way back down the hall, the photocopy of Junius Lawrence's will grasped to her chest.

"IT'S AT HARVARD, MOM!" CONNIE BURST JUST AS THE RECEIVER WAS picked up in the Santa Fe desert.

"What is?" asked Grace Goodwin.

Connie exhaled. "Deliverance's physick book. I met the funniest little man today. He'd done half my research for me already." She pulled the long phone cord behind her as she made her usual rounds through Granna's dining room, running her hands over sundry objects in the dark.

"How fortunate," said Grace, her voice tinged with irony. "I don't suppose you thanked him?"

"*Mom*," Connie warned.

"Yes, my darling, I know." She sniffed. "Well, what do you do next? Look under 'Exact Book I'm Looking For' in the card catalogue?" Grace chuckled, a surprisingly girlish sound, high and in the back of her throat.

"I wish," said Connie. She was not at all clear how the book would have been catalogued. In a sense its proximity, while tantalizing, was also frustrating. Widener, the main central library at Harvard, was on par with the New York Public Library for vastness and complexity. Though Connie, like most graduate students, had call numbers in the library for which she felt a proprietary sort of affection, the whole of the Harvard University library stacks loomed before her, stretching under the Yard walkways in multiple moleish directions, a vastness barely navigable even with a specific book title in mind. Connie did not relish the task that lay before her.

"Of course nothing says that you have to find it," Grace ventured.

Connie clenched her jaw, draping her fingertips over a chubby earthenware teapot on Granna's end table. "Chilton wants to include me in his big presentation to the Colonial Association in the fall. If I'm going to do that, I have got to find the book."

"And *are* you going to do that? You don't sound very excited about it." Grace kept her voice mild, but Connie could hear the faintest hint of reproach. The phone receiver slipped for a moment, then was replaced on Grace's shoulder, and Connie knew that she was working away at something with her hands.

"It's an amazing opportunity," Connie said, aware that she sounded as if she were trying to persuade not only her mother but also herself. Connie hooked her free thumb into her cutoff belt loop and leaned against Granna's sideboard.

"So you've said," Grace commented. Then, "Dammit!" she said under her breath.

"What are you doing?" Connie asked. "You're not cooking, are you?"

"No," Grace said through gritted teeth. "I'm trying to repot some of my succulents. This weather is just killing them. I keep stabbing myself on the spines." Connie heard her mother put a bleeding palm to her mouth and soothe it with her lips.

"They're cactus," Connie said. "Aren't they supposed to like hot weather?"

"Yes, but not like this. We're in a warming cycle," Grace said, distracted, and from the sound of her voice, Connie could tell that she was inspecting her wound. "It's a natural shift, but it's being hastened beyond belief by the hole in the ozone layer. My poor aloes just can't take it."

"Ozone layer?" Connie echoed.

Grace sighed. "You should pick up a newspaper, my darling."

Connie glanced at her dangling spider plant. "I've . . ." She paused, wanting to ask Grace about the Latin note card but unsure where to begin. "I've had some funny things happen with the plants since I've been here."

"Oh, I'm not surprised at all," Grace said. "You had such a wonderful green thumb as a girl, before you got so involved in research."

"It's a bit more pronounced than that," Connie said, voice low. "Mom, I found a bunch of Granna's old recipe cards in the kitchen, and . . . something happened that I haven't been able to explain."

Her mother laughed softly. "You know," she said, "it's hubris to assume that we always ought to be able to explain everything. Take the connection between people and their environment, for example. I moved out here in part because this region of the earth has different things to teach me than New England does. The air is different, the light is different, the plants, the soil. Our bodies are living, breathing organisms, you know—it's easy to forget that. We are profoundly influenced by the rhythms of the world around us. Most people don't understand that the earth moves in cycles, not just over the seasons, but on a bigger level, too. They think that the natural world just carries on in a constant state of stasis. It's silly, really."

"Mom," Connie tried to interject.

"Take this ozone layer business. It's not the warming *per se* that is the problem," Grace continued. "It's the *pace*. It's too accelerated. It's happening before its time. These planetary rhythms, why, they affect everything around them. The weather will change, plants will shift, animals will lose their habitats." She grunted with the effort of hoisting a large cactus out of a planter, and Connie heard crumbled dirt spill across the faraway patio. "Most people don't understand this yet." Grace paused. "All kinds of things about us are inextricably bound up with the nature of the earth. Our auras, our bodies, the way they work. The impact we have on other people. Some things—traits, inclinations, what have you—may grow more . . . pronounced."

"*Mom*," Connie pressed, "listen!"

"For instance," Grace continued, undaunted, "did you know that this kind of disproportionate rhythm change has happened before, but in reverse? North America was in a miniature ice age when the colonists first arrived. It's true!" Grace's breath blew across the mouthpiece, and Connie held the receiver a little away from her ear. As she did so, Arlo walked out from under the dining table, wagged twice, and made his way into the kitchen. ". . . was one of the reasons that so many people died those first few winters," Grace was saying when Connie brought the telephone back to her ear. "Have you ever read any descriptions of how people dressed through the eighteenth century?"

Connie smiled a mirthless smile. "I am a colonial historian, Mom," she said, patiently.

"Well, then you know what I'm talking about. All those layers and wool, they wouldn't be practical in New England with the weather like it is today, would they?" She grunted again, apparently heaving another pot over the patio edge. "And those Yankees were nothing if not practical."

Connie inhaled in preparation for breaking into her mother's non sequitur, but Grace cut her off yet again.

"Of course, the little ice age reached its peak in the early 1690s," Grace said, offhand. "It's a shame, really. One can never predict exactly how these things will play out." She sighed, a little sorrowful.

1692. Connie paused, the telephone receiver gripped in her hand. Unaware of what she was doing, Connie reached to the sideboard to steady herself. "Mom," she said, her voice detached. "Why are you telling me this?"

Grace chuckled again. "Just thinking out loud, my darling. Reminding you to experience your body for what it is—a collection of wondrous coincidences assembled by an intelligent Goddess, engaging with the world on its own terms. But tell me—how is Arlo? You're not forgetting to feed him, are you?"

"No, I . . ." Connie paused. Grace always talked in these oblique New Agey ways. She could sense that Grace had told her something important, but she was using her own language to do it. Connie glanced at her reflection in the spiderwebbed gilt mirror of the front hall, seeing the image of her face distorted by the layers of time built up over the glass. *We can understand the world only through the language that is at our disposal. Every period has its own linguistic—and perceptive—lens.* As this realization solidified, Connie saw the front door crack open in the reflection behind her, and Sam appeared, carrying a bag of groceries with a wine bottle poking out of the top. Her face split into a happy smile.

"I'll have to call you back, Mom," she said, fingertip hovering over the telephone connection.

"Connie, wait—" Grace began to say, voice urgent. "Is that him?"

"I can't talk now, Mom, I've got to go. Love you."

Grace started to protest, but Connie's finger fell, and the receiver emitted a click and drone of the empty dial tone.

CHAPTER EIGHTEEN

Marblehead, Massachusetts

Early August

1991

THE BACKS OF CONNIE'S EYELIDS GLOWED RED, AND SHE BECAME aware of gentle cheeping in the ivy over the bedroom window. She squinted, eyes still shut, and felt a slim sunbeam thrown across her face, its warmth brushing against her nose and cheeks. She could tell that the summer was nearing its end; this sunbeam used to fall across her waist when she awoke in Granna's four-poster bed, but it had been making its way upward over the passing weeks, crossing the threshold of her chin around the end of July. Connie smiled, stretching her arms overhead under the pillows and knocking the backs of her wrists against the headboard.

Next to her someone groaned a little in sleep, and she rolled onto her side, opening one eye to peer through the mesh of her scattered hair. Half submerged in a puff of white pillow rested a tanned plane of stubbly cheek and one closed, sleeping eye. On the inside hollow of the eye, just under the brow, glinted a tiny, dried droplet of gold paint. He moved slightly, the gold paint fleck twinkling in the morning sun. Then his mouth opened, releasing a deep, rattling snore. Connie's face broke into a grin, and she pressed her mouth into the pillow, muffling the sound of her delighted laughter.

"You're shaking the bed," said Sam, eyes still closed.

Connie gulped down her snickers long enough to gasp, "What?"

"Your laughing. It's shaking the bed," he said, the half of his mouth that she could see curving up into a smile.

"You were snoring," she explained.

"Impossible," said Sam, eye still closed. "I never snore."

"Oh, but you do," she said, grinning.

"Arlo?" asked Sam. "Back me up on this one." The dog, who lay camouflaged on the comforter between Connie's and Sam's feet, responded by rolling onto his back, paws splayed in indifference.

"He says yes," Connie said, inching closer to Sam.

"I didn't hear that at all. I heard him say 'Who's shaking the bed while people are trying to sleep?'" Sam replied, smile widening, green eye now open and watching her.

"Yeah? Maybe he was saying 'It's time to get up for everyone who has a cupola to paint.'" She snaked her hand over to him.

"That can't be it," Sam began, ending in a yelp of protest as Connie's questing fingers reached his armpit. A scuffle ensued. Arlo leapt leisurely off the bed, wandered into the second attic bedroom, and settled on the other, older four-poster bed. Flopping down with a sigh, the creature dozed, feet twitching, as the sunlight lengthened through the window of the second bedroom. Once the light reached the headboard the dog vanished, leaving a dust billow on the quilt in his wake, reappearing a few minutes later at the doorway into the kitchen, where Connie stood, in her bathrobe, holding a mug of coffee and still laughing.

"So how will you be spending your day today?" Sam was saying through a mouthful of toothpaste.

"If I were a good grad student, I would go into Cambridge and start looking for Deliverance's book in the Widener stacks," Connie said. "But if

I were a good daughter, I would stay here and actually try to make some progress on this house."

"And which are you? Since apparently it's impossible to be both," Sam said, rinsing his toothbrush under the faucet in the kitchen sink.

"Fortunately being a good daughter is also conducive to being sort of lazy," Connie remarked. "I think I could use a break from dead witches and shadow books. I think," she said, holding up her coffee mug in tribute, "that today I shall clean."

"Excellent," said Sam, tucking his toothbrush into the front pocket of his coveralls. Connie had noticed the toothbrush that morning, and a part of her wondered if she should feel flattered or dubious. She reached forward, sliding it out of Sam's pocket and fixing him with a wicked, arched eyebrow.

"What?" he asked, widening his eyes, innocent.

"Call me later," Connie said, dropping the brush back into his pocket. He kissed her quickly, and she had just enough time to register the feeling of his warm stubble chafing against her chin before he was gone.

"I DON'T THINK YOU SHOULD OVER-READ THE TOOTHBRUSH," LIZ WAS saying. Connie had finished with her breakfast dishes, scrubbed out another few sealed glass jars in the kitchen, and stumbled over the drying mandrake root that she had stashed away her first night in Granna's house. It did look sort of like a gnarled homunculus—a shriveled baby doll with long, coiling cilia for fingers and toes. Connie turned it over in her hands, brushing away the dried dirt and wondering if the lethal vegetable was safe to bury in the compost pile.

"You don't think?" Connie asked, chewing on a thumbnail. Remembering that first night at the house made Connie conscious of how much she missed Liz. Soon enough, the autumn would be upon them, and Connie would be able to return to their quiet rooms in Saltonstall Court. The thought of her life in Cambridge, her predictable days shuttling between research in the library, meetings with the anxiety-wracked Thomas, conferences with Janine Silva or Manning Chilton, produced an odd tug within her. That life now seemed at once wonderful and unfamiliar, as if it had carried on about its business despite her not being there to live it.

"No way," Liz insisted. "Maybe he takes it to work so he can brush after lunch. Lots of people do."

The sound of her roommate's voice pushed away the loneliness that Connie often felt in Granna's house. To Connie, Liz sounded like real life. With relief she had dispensed the new developments on the location of the almanac, before diving directly into an analysis of the previous night with Sam.

"I guess," Connie demurred.

"Don't ask him about it, though," Liz cautioned through a mouthful of cereal. Connie had caught her in the hour between her classes, and she imagined Liz waving her spoon for emphasis. "You'll sound insecure."

"I *am* insecure," countered Connie.

"Well, don't be," Liz instructed. "Listen, I have to go in a minute. We're learning the Latin words for gladiatorial contests today, and for the first time all summer the kids are actually excited." She sighed. "But I was thinking about those markings on your door."

"It's still there," Connie said, her voice dropping. "I was thinking of painting over it this weekend, but I don't like to touch it." She paused. "At least I haven't heard anyone sneaking around outside. But every time I look at it, I get scared all over again."

"Well, anyone would," soothed Liz. "At least you haven't felt too weird staying in the house. But to tell you the truth, the more I think about it, the more I think we're misinterpreting the circle."

"What do you mean?" Connie asked, perplexed.

"We assumed that it was meant to scare you, right?" Liz said.

Connie held the telephone receiver to her cheek with one raised shoulder and opened the front door. Leaning against the jamb, she surveyed the circle that stood before her. The wisteria blooms clinging to the façade of the house had all nearly died away, and their remnants smelled papery and sweet. The symbol with its Latin inscription and multiple crosshatchings stared back at her, impenetrable.

"It certainly looks scary," said Connie, brushing a fingertip across the shallow scorch marks. A little of the scoring lifted off in the grooves of her fingerprint.

"Only because we've never seen anything like it before," Liz said. "Think about it. The circle contains different forms of the name for 'God,' right? The *alpha* and the *omega*, referring to the idea that God is the beginning and the end. *Agla*, which you told me was a Hebraic acronym for God's unspoken name. And *Dominus adjutor meus*: Lord God my helper, or possibly, God help me. Names of God in Latin, Hebrew, and Greek, all written around a request for God's help. And what surrounds the writing?"

"Crosshatchings and *X*s," said Connie.

"Or *crosses*," Liz said, a note of triumph in her voice. "Greek Orthodox crosses, remember, don't have the rectangular proportions that modern crosses have. They fit inside a square."

Connie's eyes widened. As she looked at the symbol, it seemed to shed its dark, clinging drapery of malice. Under her steady gaze, the circles appeared to realign themselves, to shift and glisten with an entirely different intent.

"Shoot," said Liz, breaking into Connie's thoughts. "I've got to go, or I'm going to be late. You have a copy of Lionel Chandler's *The Material Culture of Superstition*, don't you?"

"I think so," Connie said. "It was on my orals list, anyway."

"Well, check my hypothesis in there. Because the more I think about it, the more it seems like the circle's meant to be *protective*, rather than hostile. Not that it will tell you any more about who put it there, but at least you'll have a working theory about what it means."

Connie stared at the circle for a moment. "Liz," she said finally, "you are a genius."

Her friend sighed. "Tell that to my summer school students. I'm thinking of giving them a pop quiz just to watch them suffer."

Connie replaced the receiver in the cradle, front door still standing open to the afternoon. Outside Arlo was digging under a thorny herb bush, tail trembling with effort. Connie folded her arms and looked out across the yard, enjoying the sensation of her unease falling away. She inhaled deeply, drawing air into the spaces between her ribs. The telephone rang as she stood there, and Connie picked it up on the first ring, thinking that Liz had called to add a final thought.

"Didn't you say you were going to be late?" Connie said without pre-amble. The person on the other end of the line paused, not speaking, and then cleared her throat.

"Is this Connie Goodwin?" the voice, a woman's, asked, and from its tone Connie could tell that something was wrong.

"Yes," she said. Her thoughts raced first to Grace, but with a rush of la-serlike precision she knew that at that instant Grace was in an adobe house, kneeling, lowering her hands onto the ailing knee of one of her aura work clients. Safe. "Who is this?"

The woman paused, and a dull announcement played over a public address system in the undefined space behind her. Connie could not tell what the announcement was, but the woman seemed to be listening to it before she continued.

"This is Linda Hartley, Connie," the woman said. "I'm Sam's mother."

Connie heard a man walk up behind Linda and address her. She must have placed her hand over the receiver because Connie could only hear Linda's muffled murmur *He is?* And then *Okay*. The hand was pulled away again. "He asked me to call you. He's . . ." She swallowed.

"Where is he?" Connie asked, already grabbing her bag and feeling in-side for her car keys.

CONNIE REMEMBERED ALMOST NOTHING OF THE DRIVE TO NORTH SHORE Veterans' Memorial Hospital. The next moment that she was able to take stock of her surroundings found her striding through a sliding glass door, unsure even where she had parked her car. She was stuffing her keys into a jeans pocket and reading the signs for directions to the emergency room, and her feet were carrying her along the arrows weaving through the drab taupe hospital corridors. She was propelled around corners, into an elevator, where one of her hands selected a button. Then she left the elevator and traveled down yet another taupe hallway, this one lined with crumpled old women in loose paper hospital shifts, parked in wheelchairs along the corridor. None of them looked up as she hurried by. A public address system issued some kind of announcement, and a young doctor, her eyes ringed in fatigue, jogged by with a stethoscope draped over her shoulder. Connie blinked, looking around, and followed her feet around yet another corner.

Three doors down, her feet stopped her across from a row of scratched brown fiberglass chairs, where a kind-looking woman in a droopy cardigan and sensible shoes was sitting, a large handbag balanced on her lap. The woman was looking down, gazing through the linoleum squares on the floor at worlds visible only to herself. Connie waited, hovering on the outer edge of the woman's field of vision, before the woman looked up at Connie and smiled a smile of worry and, possibly, sadness, too.

"Linda?"

"You must be Connie," the woman said, extending her hand. Connie took it, and it sat in her palm like a limp fish. "You're as pretty as Sam said," the woman told her, smiling weakly.

Connie lowered herself onto the fiberglass seat next to Sam's mother. "My husband is using the pay phone," Linda said, glancing down the hall. "I know he'll be glad you're here."

Connie was not sure if Linda was referring to Sam or to her husband but decided not to ask. The fluorescent lights in the ceiling beat down on Linda's head, turning her hair a dull shade of gray. Connie's hands clutched and unclutched her shoulder bag; she could tell that Linda Hartley was the sort of woman whom she would like, with whom she could imagine sharing tea over a kitchen counter. As Connie watched her, noticing the pattern of smile lines in the corners of her eyes, which were identical to Sam's, Linda continued.

"Well, the good news is that it was only his leg that was hurt. That high up, he could have hit his head." She cupped her hands over her elbows. "He could have been killed."

"What happened, exactly?" Connie finally asked. As she spoke a small, serious man in a sweater vest approached from the opposite end of the hallway, his hands thrust into the pockets of a weathered pair of corduroys. He claimed the seat on Linda's other side and put his hand on Linda's knee.

"They say he'll be out in about ten minutes," said the man. "He'll be groggy, but we can go in and see him."

"Oh, that's wonderful," Linda said, shoulders sagging. "Mike, this is Connie. Sam's friend." Linda motioned toward Connie, and the man nodded an acknowledgment. She smiled a tight smile back at him. Connie had just enough time to wonder how much Sam had told his parents about her when Linda spoke again.

"He was working on the scaffolding this morning. Painting." Linda took a breath. "And for whatever reason, he didn't have the safety harness on."

"He fell," Mike interjected. "Two stories at least. They're in there now, pinning his leg."

Connie felt her stomach lurch, her mind traveling back to the morning, seeing Sam, his mouth frothed with toothpaste, grinning at her over the kitchen sink. She wanted to reach forward, to grasp his arm, and a dark curtain of self-recrimination dropped over her, cursing her own inability to perceive that he would walk into danger when he left the house. *Don't be ridiculous*, she told herself. *How could you possibly know that he would forget to put the safety harness on?*

"No damn reason for him to have that job," Sam's father glowered, jaw muscles bunching.

"Michael," Linda quelled him, placing her hand over his.

The three of them sat, Connie's legs crossed at the knee and one foot hooked around her ankle, waiting in the hospital hallway. Time proceeded around them in bright, empty snapshots: two nurses, carrying lunch trays, talking; a stooped janitor in coveralls, catching a mop bucket before it tipped; a tiny, withered man with a liver-spotted scalp, in striped pajamas, his wheelchair being pushed by a bitter-looking middle-aged woman. The lack of windows and constant blare of the fluorescent lights locked the hallway in a void where time felt difficult to gauge. Connie was not completely sure how long they sat waiting, but finally an earnest young doctor approached and said, "Mr. and Mrs. Hartley? Would you come with me, please?" Sam's parents rose, Connie trailing after them as they followed the doctor into a room a few doors away.

She waited outside while his parents entered, knitting and unknitting her fingers. Now that she had had time to think about it, Connie could be pleasantly surprised that Sam had asked his parents to call her. Usually her reserve kept people—men especially—at a distance, but Sam was different. She felt at ease with him, comfortable. More herself. How was it possible to be more yourself when you were with another person? Connie always assumed that she was most purely herself when she was alone. She thought of Sam, grinning at her surprise when he dropped down from the roof of the church, thrusting a box of doughnuts into her hands. Her throat tightened. The door opened a crack, and half of Linda's face appeared.

"Connie?" she asked. "You can come in, you know."

Connie swallowed and pushed open the door.

Inside Mike and Linda stood grouped around a hospital bed, with the young doctor standing at the foot, examining a clipboard. In the bed, propped on several pillows, Sam lay, face wan, leg hoisted up by pulleys and straps. Several bars or pins extended from his shin, which was a mottled black and purple. Connie moved to the opposite side of the bed and smiled down at him. "Hello," she whispered.

"Hey, Cornell," he said, voice hoarse from fatigue. He attempted a smile, but it was unconvincing, and halfway through turned into a grimace. She reached down and took his hand between both of hers. To her surprise, she felt the disorder and confusion in his cells that is the result of extreme and sudden pain. It was as if his body were still undergoing shocks that continued to ricochet through its closed system, unable to escape or quiet. Like ocean waves in a swimming pool.

She pressed his hand, weaving her fingers together around his palm, her awareness groping forward under his skin. She was stunned to find that her hands were gathering information about Sam, information that she did not know fully how to process. Since her experiment with the plants, Connie had found that she was more attuned, as if a heavy filter between herself and the world had been suddenly lifted away. The shift was daunting, incomprehensible. But now she received the incontrovertible impression that the disorder that was gripping his body extended somewhere beyond the catastrophe of the broken bones in his leg. Connie frowned, and she glanced over at the doctor.

"Well," the doctor began, flipping through what must be Sam's intake forms. "The good news is that the leg should heal nicely. He's strong, and soon enough we'll be able to have him in a cast and back home. There is one major caveat, however." The doctor tucked the clipboard under one arm and clasped his hands together before his mouth, looking at Sam and at his parents in turn. They waited for him to continue, Sam's grip tightening around Connie's hand.

"I'm afraid that we also have to consider what may have caused the fall in the first place," the doctor said.

"Should have been wearing his goddamn safety harness, is what," Mike Hartley growled as Linda murmured, "Michael, please."

"That's not it at all, Mr. Hartley," the doctor replied, unflappable. "Sam, how much do you remember from immediately before the accident?"

Sam licked his lips, and Connie watched him frown as he tried to push through the haze of receding anesthesia that was clogging his thoughts.

Sam cleared his throat.

"Not that much, actually," he began, looking up at his parents. "I was finishing up the last of the gilding in the church cupola." He paused, swallowing.

"I was kind of tired, 'cause I didn't"—he glanced up at Connie—"didn't sleep so well. So I climbed down to take a break. I had some water from the cooler that's there, but it was . . ." He worked his mouth a little, his body recalling the taste. "It was . . . bad. Metallic. But I didn't care. I sat in a pew for a minute, resting."

He took a breath, lines of tension contracting around his eyes. "I climbed back up and went back to work." He stopped, confusion sweeping across his face. "That's all. That's all I remember." He looked up at Connie, per-turbed.

"You don't remember falling? Or the ambulance ride?" the doctor pressed.

"No," Sam said, realizing the gravity of his situation. "I don't even know who found me." He looked back to his parents. "Who *did* find me?" They looked at each other but said nothing.

"Interesting," said the doctor, making a note. He paused, looking gravely down at his patient. "Sam," he began, "I believe that your fall was caused by a grand mal seizure."

"What?" Sam asked as his mother said, "Oh, my God." Mike put his hands on Linda's shoulders, and Connie looked down at Sam. His face con-torted in dismay. She swallowed and pressed his hand harder.

"In a generalized seizure of this type, occasionally a patient will experi-ence what we call an 'aura,' which is often marked by drastic alterations in sensory perception or emotional state. Changes in the brain can sometimes cause the patient to experience strange tastes or smells. The metallic taste of the water and your unexplained fatigue, for example. In the second stage of a seizure like this, the limbs go stiff and the patient will fall, his limbs then launching into convulsions. The patient emerging from a seizure of this type will have no recollection of the event."

The doctor continued to make notes, casting a critical eye on Sam. "I'm afraid that that is not all. Though we had you under sedation at the time, you underwent another seizure while we were operating on your leg, together with serious vomiting. Unfortunately you didn't seem to respond to the anticonvulsant that was administered to you. Is there any family history of epilepsy or other seizure disorders?"

"No," said Linda, appalled. She glanced over at her husband, who looked as though he had just caught a boulder hurled at his chest: crumpled over, out of breath, strained.

"Not that I know of," Mike said, voice subdued. Sam, for his part, was growing more alert, edging up farther in his pillows and shifting his weight in the bed. Connie laid a hand on his arm.

"Does this mean that I could have another one?" Sam asked, looking levelly at the doctor.

"Unfortunately there is a strong possibility of that, yes." As the doctor said this, Linda gasped, putting her hand to her mouth. "It's a bit unusual," the doctor commented. "We still have to determine if there's a genetic component to it, or if there are any external factors in play. The vomiting, obviously, raises some serious questions, so I'd like to run some more tests. But it goes without saying that Samuel will have to stay here until we have been able to stabilize his condition. He is at risk of severely jostling the broken leg when his body is convulsing, to say nothing of the neurological implications. And there's a risk of dehydration if the vomiting should return with the same degree of severity. I can't let you leave until we've brought the situation under control."

Sam's parents looked from the doctor, to Sam, to each other. Connie gripped his hand tightly, one tear escaping out of the corner of her eye. She rubbed it away with her shoulder, unwilling to let Sam see that she was afraid.

"It is unusual for epilepsy to appear for the first time in adulthood," the doctor continued. "Usually this syndrome first manifests itself late in childhood or during adolescence. Further, I do not yet have an explanation for the vomiting, which seems to occur independently of the neurological events. However"—here the doctor smiled, but Connie could read the anxiety that underpinned the doctor's sheen of confidence—"my sincere hope is that we will have a more concrete treatment plan in place by this time tomorrow."

The doctor shook hands with everyone in the room, brisk and business-like. As Connie watched the doctor's white coat disappear out the door of the room, the fear in her belly calcified into a cold, hard lump.

For she perceived, as clearly as if she were looking at a bright color photograph, that the doctor had no idea what to do.

Interlude

Salem Town, Massachusetts

Late February

1692

*T*he belly of the egg split open with one swift crack, spilling its slippery contents into a waiting hand. The hand's fingers parted just a bit, allowing the viscous white to drip into a thick glass of water below, but retaining the round orb of the yolk. Mercy Dane sniffed at the yolk cupped in her hand, rolling it under her thumb. Its membranes gave a bit but held together, smooth and warm, and its color was a deep healthy orange. It smelled clean and earthy, nourished by wheat chaff and dried maize kernels. She slipped the yolk from her hand into a little earthenware bowl, where four or five others already sat, glistening in the dim light of the hall. Mercy's mouth watered a little as she contemplated the custard that she would make later with the surplus yolks. A little milk, rye meal, some currants—she had squirreled some away a week previous—and molasses. She ran her tongue over her front teeth, behind her lips, imagining the smell of cooking pudding that was to come as she wiped the egg residue from her hands.

Meanwhile, the egg white had collected in a hazy cloud in the water glass, and her mother's tired hand reached forward to grasp the glass, holding it aloft and turning it this way and that. She heard her mother murmur a phrase under her breath and replace the glass on the scarred board on trestles that served as the hall table.

"Well?" asked an anxious young woman's voice. Mercy busied herself at the hearth, using a long iron hook to swivel a small, simmering cauldron a smidgen off of the hottest part of the fire. She was permitted to assist with her mother's work, provided she keep her opinions to herself and not interrupt. The iron hook clattered against the hearth bricks as Mercy stoked the fire, sending a smattering of impatient sparks up and around the base of the cauldron. Though her back was turned to the two women seated at the table, Mercy felt her mother glower in her direction. A glance over her shoulder confirmed this guess, as her eyes met Deliverance's silent glare. Mercy returned the look with a sulk and turned back to the greens boiling over the fire. She could not fathom that Mary Sibley. *Why would Mother attend to her? She's just a meddling gossip, is all*, Mercy brooded. When she took up the craft herself, why, she'd sure forbear to meet with that Mary. Too right she should.

Deliverance Dane sighed, saying, "I cannot say, Mary. 'Tis a poor scrying glass withal."

The young goodwife seated at the hall table twisted her handkerchief between grasping hands. "But, Livvy! You *must* see! 'Tis on three weeks now the girls are afflicted. Let us break another." The matron reached for another egg from within the basket at her elbow, proffering a smooth, speckled orb. Deliverance raised one hand, fending off the egg that Mary Sibley thrust at her.

"And you are certain these hail from the Parris barn?" Deliverance asked, looking steadily at Goody Sibley.

"I was told so," said Mary, her eyes slipping a fraction down from where Deliverance had held them.

"How came you to have them?" Deliverance asked, her voice weary.

"I cannot think the Reverend Parris would wish his eggs be used for divination."

"You'll ha' not seen his Betty, then," Mary whispered, eyes shifting left and right. "She is gripped with insensible speeches and fits most violent, and theah servant Abigail Williams, too. The reverend having no time to attend his bahn passes all his days in prayerful meditation."

"Then with God's blessing these girls shall recover their senses soon," Deliverance said, rising to her feet. "How fare those greens, Mercy?" she said, moving nearer the hearth. She took up a rag and used it to lift the iron lid of the cauldron, sniffing at its bubbling contents. As she did so a cold gust of wind burst down the chimney, billowing ashes around the women's feet. Mercy and Deliverance fell to shaking out their skirts, brushing away the grime lest a live ember should catch their clothes.

"Livvy!" Mary Sibley cried through the passing commotion, rising to her feet, her hands planted on the hall table. "He ha' called in William Griggs!"

"Oh?" said Deliverance with indifference. "A goodly physician is Mister Griggs, I'm told."

Mary hurried around the table, planting her hands on her hips as she came. She thrust her face near to Deliverance, so that even Mercy could feel her hot breath. "And Mister Griggs ha' saith he sees the *evil hand* in this," Mary said, teeth clenched. "Now cannow we look again?" She held out the egg, but Deliverance turned away. Mercy glanced from her mother to Mary and back again. It was unlike her mother to dissemble so.

"I cannot see, Goody Sibley. Perhaps the Devil clouds my sight," Deliverance said. She looked back over at Mary, whose jaw was tight, and whose eyes were shining with anger. "We must place our trust in God," Deliverance finished, folding her arms. "May His miraculous providences restore those girls to health. I feel sure 'twil be altogether over soon enough."

Mary stamped her foot in frustration, and Mercy edged away from her, pressing her back to the wall as the young matron shouldered her way past her to the door. Deliverance watched her go, impassive. When she reached the door Mary Sibley turned, fumbling with her heavy woolen cloak as she spoke.

"Them gahls are bewitched shah as I'm standing heah," she said. "If you cannow see fit to help them, why, I'll make a cake myself. Theh's no talent to this!"

With a significant sniff she tied the cloak under her chin, flung open the front door, and stepped into the wall of cold out of doors, shutting the door with a slam behind her. A small flurry of snowflakes blew in after her, collecting in a drift over the floorboards of the entryway. When she was gone, Deliverance moved to the three-legged chair at the end of the table and settled herself in it, resting her head in her hands. Her fingertips drummed on the back of her coif.

Mercy pretended to tend the greens on the fire, and to check the progress of the bread loaf baking in the brick hollow oven in the hearth, but her attention was on her mother. She waited.

Deliverance sighed, bringing her fingertips to her temples, elbows resting on the tabletop. Mercy stole a glance at her and observed that Deliverance's eyes were closed. "As if her cake will do a lick of good," Deliverance said, mostly to herself, eyes still closed. Mercy took this comment as an opening, hanging the iron hook back amongst the other cooking implements near the fire and sitting at the table. She pulled over the bowl of yolks to start mixing the custard. As she sat, her feet under the table met a warm lump, which murmured at the touch of her toe. Most winters found Dog sleeping under the hall table, almost invisible in the darkness.

They sat for a few moments in silence, Mercy breaking the yolks with a wooden spoon and stirring in a spoonful of molasses. Presently she ventured to speak. "Why should you tell Goody Sibley you couldn't see, Mother?" she asked. "You always see in the egg-in-water."

Deliverance opened her eyes and looked at her daughter. When she gazed on her thus Mercy always felt like Deliverance could see directly through her, as if she herself were just an egg white suspended in a water glass. She averted her gaze, but her mother's eyes lingered.

"How long since that shift was washed?" Deliverance asked, reaching out to finger the linen shirt at Mercy's throat. "I've an old one in the trunk. We'll air it out on the morrow."

Mercy laid aside her wooden spoon and turned to face Deliverance. In the past year she had grown taller than her mother, and a little thicker, too. But still she was given no authority in this house, though she nearly ran it now. "*Why*, Mother?" Mercy demanded, growing impatient. "I'll have you answer me!"

"Oh, you shall?" Deliverance said, with a mirthless laugh. "And what, pray tell, would you have me say, Mercy Dane?" She rose and moved to the window, rubbing aside some of the frost. The air by the window was colder, and Deliverance's breath escaped in a visible film of vapor, collecting anew on the glass. "Shall I say the girls are dissembling?" she asked, coldly. "That they invoke diabolical influence to bring mere sport and variation to their sorry days? Then I shall be impugning the pastor's daughter. I shall be calling her a liar, and so be open to the charge of slander, too, if I be proven wrong.

"Or"—she turned to face Mercy again, her arms folded over her chest— "shall I say that Mary Sibley be in the right, the girls are sure bewitched? What then?" She moved across the room, nearer to where Mercy sat by the fire. Deliverance reached forward and took a lock of Mercy's hair where it hung folded over her shoulder, and rubbed the flaxen strands between her fingers.

"Whom do you think the townsfolk will look to?" she asked, voice soft. "How soon before all their healed calves and found pewter and well-timed plantings and soothed ailings vanish in their haste to find someone to blame?"

"But, Mother," Mercy whispered, blue eyes wide and catching the flicker from the fire. "Lying is a mortal sin."

Deliverance smiled down at the youthful girl seated at her hall table, long of leg and spotty-faced. "My immortal soul belongs to Jesus Christ," she said, smoothing the lock of Mercy's hair back into place. "To do with as

He will. If I am saved, it is by the mercy of His grace alone. And if I am damned"—she paused, still smiling, and Mercy felt a blackness gather in her chest—"then I shall spare my daughter in this life the torments that I must suffer in the next."

THE FOLLOWING FEW DAYS PASSED AS MOST WINTER DAYS DID IN THE Dane household. The two women lingered within a few feet of the hearth fire, baking bread, boiling cornmeal, squinting to mend clothes by candle-light, Dog snoring under the table. In the afternoons, Deliverance would pull out her book for Mercy to study by, draping first one dried herb, then another before the girl at the table, asking her to recite its name, properties, and uses in the same precise tone as she recited her catechism. Outside, the snow heaped up against their two-room house in a sloping white drift, pressing in against the hall windows, blowing down the chimney, and creep-ing in at the gap under the front door. They had few visitors, only neighbors running short of supplies and looking to make a bargain. Mercy bridled at the monotony, her fingers growing itchier with each passing day, yearning for some gossip from the village.

"I'll go down to the wharves," she announced the afternoon that March began, the cold still unabated. The world outside was one undifferentiated cloud of white. Mercy started pulling on her heavy cloak and rooting for one of Nathaniel's old felt hats in the trunk at the foot of the bedstead in the keeping room. She had preserved most of Nathaniel's clothes when he died the previous year—all but those he had been wearing in the accident. Some-times in her mind's eye she still saw the bright splash of red in the road, still heard the crunch of the splitting wagon wheel. She rubbed her eyes, pushing the unwelcome memory away. Mercy found herself resurrecting his old hats and blouses to wear when she was feeling most disagreeable and low. She felt that way more and more, it seemed.

"Whatever for?" Deliverance demanded from the doorway.

Mercy drew herself up to her full height, hoping to attain some semblance of nobility in spite of the blue tinge of her lips. "I wish for news from the Farms," she said, using the old-fashioned name for Salem Village.

The town of Salem, where they lived in their little house, a close walk to the waterfront, had grown at a steady pace over the past decades, and sometime previously had established an outlying region called Salem Farms to funnel food into the swelling city. By and by the Farms region obtained a degree of autonomy, changing its name to Salem Village. Even the area's culture was different: the Villagers were country people, clannish and suspicious. Not ship people. Despite her growing stature, Mercy still felt rather small on the inside, overwhelmed by the pressing in of new faces around her. They streamed into town from "out the eastward," the Maine frontier, where settlement had been pushed back by Indian attacks, and poured off of ships arriving from England. Each day fresh waves of strangers spilled over the streets of Salem Town, washing up into every corner of Mercy's experience: at the market, at Sunday meeting, sometimes even into their shabby hall, seeking Deliverance's various services. In a feeble effort to lay claim to her presence, Mercy had lately fallen into the habit of clinging to dated terms for the areas and squares around her. It peeved her whenever she caught herself doing it. She crossed her arms over her chest.

"You've no reason to wish for news from the Farms," Deliverance said. "But as you've donned your cloak already, the cow could stand a feeding." Deliverance turned back to the warmth of the hall as Mercy's face contorted with anger at her thwarted plans.

"I've a mind to know what's happened!" she cried, face red.

Deliverance turned back to face her, eyes cold. "We'll be needing more wood for the kitchen fire as well," she said, in the tone of voice that always signaled ultimate finality to Mercy, and which had begun to fray at Mercy's nerves. Scolding and muttering, she gathered her cloak around her and groused out into the frigid afternoon.

The New England winter pressed against her as she stepped into the yard, chapping her cheeks and blowing her skirts out at an angle against her legs. As she plodded toward the cowshed behind the house, feet sinking several inches through the crust of fallen snow, she felt with irritation a creeping sense of relief that her mother had forbade her to travel down to the wharves. Had Deliverance not forbidden her, she must needs have gone, for pride's sake. And already her toes were fallen numb in her boots.

Within an hour or two, her chores were done, and she drew the rear door open with one mittened thumb, wrestling the split logs into a less cumbersome attitude in her arms as she edged her way through the doorway. She stamped her feet to loosen the worst of the ice and entered the hall, grunting with effort. Mercy dumped the logs in a heap near the fire and turned her face to the hearth, beating her mittens together to bring the blood and feeling back into her hands. As she turned back to the table and pulled off Nathaniel's tattered hat, she started to find Sarah Bartlett's great bulk seated at the table with her mother. Goody Bartlett's face was grave, and her hands were clasped over Deliverance's own as they whispered together. Deliverance looked up quickly, swallowed, and then said, "Here is Goody Bartlett with your news, Mercy."

The girl lowered herself onto the hard bench drawn up to the table and watched the two older women. "Good noon, Goody Bartlett," she said, and folded her hands in her lap.

"And to you, Mahcy," said Sarah Bartlett, her usually ruddy face turned gray by cold or worry, Mercy could not tell which.

"Go on, Sarah," Deliverance said. "Mercy ought to hear as well."

Sarah Bartlett looked from Deliverance to the girl and back again. "I suppose," she said, unsure. She heaved a heavy sigh, shaking her head, wrapping her hands around the mug of hot cider that Deliverance had set before her. Mercy reflected that she had never known Sarah to cast a pall over any events. She was unaccustomed to seeing their neighbor so grave. "Things grow ugly, Livvy. I can make no sense of it. Of the morn I war tarryin' in the Village," she began. "They are altogethah distracted, the lot of 'em. Some gahls just younger than Mahcy heah, 'tis on a month they are in their fits, and the reverend's daughter among 'em. Reverend Pahris, he is shah there be some diabolical mischief done in the Village. He ha' spake against it in the pulpit, and urged the entire congregation to fast, and pray for God's forgiveness. Then it passed that that Mary Sibley bade Tituba, she being the Indian woman in Pahris's house, to make her a witch cake."

Deliverance groaned a little and shook her head. "And what receipt did she use, I wonder?" she asked dryly.

Sarah smiled. "She took water of the afflicted gahls and mixed it with some rye meal and fed it to a dog, thinking the bewitchment should pass into the beast and the gahls would be delivered of their torments. Dogs being the known familiars of witches, she ha' saith."

Deliverance sniffed with disapproval and took a swallow of her own cider mug. Mercy stifled a giggle, and her mother shot her an icy glare. Mercy pressed her lips together and arranged her face into a semblance of seriousness. *Dull as a box of rocks*, she thought to herself.

"Reverend Lawson being called in to assist some days hence, he denounced this witch cake as diabolical means. No amount of theah sufferings must allow us to use the Devil's tools, he saith, and from the pulpit, too!" Sarah exclaimed. "In that same meeting that Abby Williams bade him to name his text, and the Reverend Lawson doing so, she saith 'It is a long text.' Never in my life ha' I heard such utterances, and to a dignified personage at that."

"Indeed," said Deliverance, taking another sip of her cider. "Not the physick I would choose," she remarked aside to Mercy, who nodded.

"Why, Livvy, theh be more," Sarah said. "They bade the gahls name theah tormentors, declare whose forms the Devil did take. This very week they called out against Sarah Good, Sarah Osborne, and that Tituba herself!"

Deliverance and Mercy exchanged glances. Sarah Good and Sarah Osborne were two notorious beggars in the Village, forever roving from house to house demanding food or lodging. Grasping, suffering women, they both struck fear into the hearts of the sturdy Villagers; they were avoided, as if their crushing misfortune might be catching. Tituba was an Indian servant in the Parris house, brought up with them from the Barbadoes islands. "Mary Sibley must walk with God, then," Deliverance murmured. "How fortunate for her." She rose, moving back to stare out the window.

"Livvy, attend to me! Just today them three was brought to be examined in the meetinghouse!" Sarah cried.

"What?" Deliverance asked, turning to face Sarah, who was still seated at the table.

"Today, Livvy! And that Tituba, she ha' confessed!" On the last word Sarah brought the flat of her hand down in a smack on the tabletop. Mercy's eyes widened.

"Merciful Jesus," Deliverance whispered, bringing a hand to her temple. "But surely 'tis a lie. There be no diabolical workers here."

"Reverend Pahris saith she must come to Jesus and confess, and name what others walk with her." Sarah swallowed, eyes burning with urgency. "Livvy, I come direct to tell you. That Peter Petfehd war at the meeting. He asked if Tituba evah walked with *you*."

Silence descended on the hall, and the blood drained out of Deliverance's face until she began to sway, gently, where she stood. Mercy leapt to her feet and wrapped an arm around Deliverance's waist.

"Let us sit, Mama," she said, easing her mother into the three-legged chair at the head of the table.

"I . . . ," Deliverance said. "Mercy, I . . ." She gasped, appearing unable to draw her breath. Mercy fumbled at the laces that bound up the front of Deliverance's dress, pulling at them with her fingers until she felt the stays loosen and her mother inhale deeply.

"A compress, Goody Bartlett, please," Mercy said without looking around, her voice carrying a new note of authority. Sarah Bartlett bustled about behind her, finding a clean rag and dipping it in the bucket where Mercy had collected snow to melt for washing. Sarah pressed the compress into the girl's hand, and Mercy smoothed the cold cloth across Deliverance's brow, pushing back her coif until the first gray-brown strands of hair drifted down over her mother's face. "Gather your breath, Mother," she whispered, working the compress behind Deliverance's ears and onto the base of her neck. She felt her mother's breathing grow more deep and steady, and she held her gaze until Deliverance's vision grew focused once again. For the first time Mercy observed the quality of her mother's skin—somehow it had grown more papery and thin, spreading a fine mesh of lines around her eyes and mouth. She had never considered Deliverance to be anything other than powerful, competent. She remembered, in the most hazy terms, the year in her childhood when her mother had been distant and difficult to reach, and now she read in her mother's face the same worry and fear that she had not been fully able to understand then.

"That Peter Petford, he is sorry and distracted," Mercy said, looking into her mother's face. "Is he not, Goody Bartlett?"

"That he is," Sarah affirmed, crouching next to where Deliverance was seated. "Nowt could countenance his railings. I saith so in meeting myself." She reached a plump hand forward to pat Deliverance on the knee.

Deliverance swallowed, reaching forward to rub Mercy's dress sleeve reassuringly. "So I well know," she said. "But I'll know what ha' been said." She looked into Sarah's face and waited.

"That Tituba saith she knew not one way or t'other. Then the reverend asked what made Petfahd wonder so, and that Petfahd claimed that you presided o'er the death of his little Mahther, lo these years ago."

Deliverance heard this news in silence, though her face grew stricken. She clutched at Mercy's sleeve. In the distance Mercy thought she heard the thrum of hoofbeats approaching their lane, but she said nothing. Out of the deepening darkness in the house the form of Dog coalesced in Deliverance's lap. Sarah gasped, rocking back on her heels.

"Oh!" she cried. Deliverance and Mercy both looked at her, saying nothing. "He be a quiet one, is that little cur." She laughed, a weak sound in the silent room. The hoofbeats grew louder, muffled by the snow but unmistakable.

"And what did the assembly decide?" Deliverance asked quietly.

Sarah swallowed again. "Reverend Pahris saith . . . ," she began as the hoofbeats galloped to a halt outside the front of the Dane house. Someone dismounted, someone large, and proceeded to wade through the snowdrift to their door. The three women heard the hushing sound of woolen trousers dragged through dense, wet snow. "That they perhaps needs ha' words with you, Livvy." She choked, clasping her hands together. Deliverance gazed at Sarah, her face growing calm and resolved.

"Well," Deliverance said, rising to her feet. She smoothed her skirts with both hands, and set to tightening the laces at her breast, retying them in a tidy bow. She reached up to adjust her head covering, tucking a loose strand of hair back into place. She inhaled, and exhaled with authority. A knock sounded at the door. "They are fast withal," she remarked. "You'll get the door, Mercy."

Mercy, meanwhile, had grown more panicked with each moment as her mother grew more calm. "Mother!" she whispered, voice urgent. "We could hide! I can conjure up a slowing receipt, and you can run into the cowshed, and I—" She stopped as Deliverance shot her a solemn look.

"'Tis only the mournful wailings of a bewildered man," she said, touching Mercy's cheek. "I've needs only explain so to the gentlemen of the Village, and all will be well." The knock sounded again at the door, loud and businesslike. "Now, you'll get the door, daughter."

Sarah stood frozen in her place, and so the girl gathered her wits together and moved toward the door. "Mercy!" Her mother stopped her with a whisper. "While I am gone you shall say nothing of the book. To anyone." Mercy nodded wordlessly, and when Deliverance gestured to the door she turned, opening it to find the great lurking form of Jonas Oliver, from Marblehead one town over. He wore the formal cloak of a county magistrate on an official errand. His broad-brimmed hat was thickly covered over in frost, and snow had gathered on his high shoulders. Behind him his flea-bitten horse stamped its foot, making a dull thud on the frozen ground. "Good evening, Mahcy Dane," he said.

"Goodman Oliver," she said, without warmth. She observed him slowly scanning the interior of the hall, taking in her mother standing, white-lipped, at the head of the table, and Sarah, hands clutched together, rooted in place off to one side. The dog was nowhere to be seen.

"S'pose you'll know why I'm heah," he said. Mercy reflected that this was probably the longest sentence she had ever heard Jonas Oliver utter.

"I'll just ready myself," Deliverance said, pulling on her heavy cloak and taking up the mittens that Mercy had left to dry by the fire. Sarah had roused herself from her reverie long enough to pack some hard corn bread into a parcel together with a small bladder of cider. All the while Jonas Oliver waited at the doorway, unmoving, face impassive, a gale blowing into the house around him, bringing wafts of dirty snow and ice into the hallway. Mercy watched these preparations, feeling the frigid night air washing over her and pulling out with it any semblance of safety or security that she might feel in that house. Panic rose in her chest, coursing through her body like a great red and black wave, and she ransacked her brain for an idea, for something that she could do to keep this horrid man from taking her mother away with him. She tried to recall a receipt for time reversal that she had been practicing, something that shrank fruits back into seeds, that might work on a situation or on a man, and as she shuffled through the drawers in her mind looking for the words that she needed, her mother took up the parcel that Sarah had assembled and made her way to the door.

Deliverance laid a hand on Mercy's shoulder and looked into her eyes. "Remember what I told you," she whispered. Mercy nodded, feeling as if she were on the brink of explosion.

"While I'm away, I leave the house to you. Do not shirk your labors." Mercy nodded again, and as she saw Jonas Oliver step out of the doorway with a gesture for Deliverance to come with him, Mercy's control dissolved completely, and she cried out, "Mama!" She flung herself around her mother's neck, a rush of tears and mucus flowing forth from her face into her mother's cloak and hair.

"Shhh, shhhh," Deliverance soothed, stroking her back just the way her father used to, and Mercy shuddered, sobbing harder at the thought of him. "This'll be settled soon enow. We must pray for God to give us strength."

Gently she disengaged Mercy's clinging arms, breaking their embrace by degrees until Mercy stood, head down, roiling in fury and sadness.

"You've been a good friend to us, Sarah," Deliverance said to her friend, who responded, "Go with God, Livvy Dane."

With that Deliverance placed a kiss on Mercy's forehead, looked around the house one last time, and followed Jonas Oliver out into the night.

Mercy watched her go, hating the man, the Village, Reverend Parris, the ridiculous squealing girls, her dead father, Sarah Bartlett, even—she hated to admit it—God Himself for letting this happen. As the horse galloped off with its heavy burden and a mist of snow closed behind their retreating form, Mercy watched them go, waiting in the doorway until the hoofbeats drained away to nothingness and there was only the dead sound of the snowbound night, encased in silence, even down to the small dog who had appeared at her feet.

CHAPTER NINETEEN

Marblehead, Massachusetts

Mid-August

1991

Night came under the tight canopy of vines over Granna's yard before it arrived outside, but Connie had no trouble making out the burned circle that still sat on her front door. She dropped her shoulder bag at her feet where she stood, placed her hands on her hips, and felt fatigue seep into her limbs. The afternoon at the hospital had left her feeling empty and unmoored. Sam's leg was improving, slowly, but his seizures were growing worse. They ripped through his body with a frenzy that clearly frightened even the jaded nurses on his ward. The muscular convulsions gripped his arms, legs, back, and neck, stiffening and bending him into terrifying shapes, robbing him of consciousness, lolling his tongue, and were often followed by vomiting that was wrenching and extreme.

Exhaustion was beginning to show in his face: deep purple circles spread under his eyes like a growing stain, and he could sleep only in abbreviated snatches. The doctors had given him three or four different anticonvulsants, all with no effect. She had overheard them bandy about a number of different theories, none of which seemed to account for all of his symptoms. Not cholera. Not epilepsy. Not a tumor. They had even ordered something called a Reinsch test, which Connie had had to look up—it was designed to test for poisoning, possibly from chemicals in the paint. But the results were inconclusive. Though the doctors affected an attitude of confidence in front of Sam and his parents, Connie could see the crawling doubt under the surface of their taut faces. When she arrived that afternoon, she had interrupted a group of seven or eight medical students watching Sam's body convulse, pens poised over note pads but not moving. They all looked up when she entered, not yet trained enough to hide their gaping.

Now she stood, casting her eyes over the burn mark on the front door, turning over Liz's hypothesis in her mind. Liz claimed that the circle might have been meant to protect, rather than frighten. Her theory still did nothing to explain where the circle had come from—or more importantly, who had caused it. Connie pressed her fingertips over her eyebrows in frustration, and a white flash of hate for her own powerlessness burst behind her eyes.

Connie detested feeling out of control of her own life, hated that she could do nothing to help Sam, and her ire extended outward to encompass the unseen hands who had marked her house, and to the doctors with their incompetence and their useless white coats. That very afternoon, she had overheard Linda whispering into the pay phone in the hallway, "He's dying, Michael. My only boy . . . If they don't find out what's wrong soon . . ." Linda had spotted Connie listening and abruptly changed the subject, but the pallor of her face revealed the depth of her despair. Connie grabbed up her bag, wiping an arm across her face, and pushed through the door into the waiting house.

Night awaited her in the sitting room, so Connie groped her way past the two armchairs by the fireplace until her hands found Granna's Chippendale desk. "Arlo?" she called, but the house was silent. She listened, straining her ears for the sound of paws or snoring, but heard nothing. From within her cutoff pocket she produced a cheap cardboard matchbook, striking fire into her cupped hands. She lit the small oil lamp that rested on the desk, adjusting the flame inside the glass chimney until the sitting room filled with a warm, round orange glow.

Granna's desk was covered with thick layers of Connie's research notes, and the books that she had brought up from Cambridge sat heaped in disordered piles on the floor. Connie knelt, running her hands over the spines of the books until she found Lionel Chandler's *The Material Culture of Superstition*. Connie could barely remember the book's central argument from studying for her oral exams in the spring. Settling into the desk chair, bare feet folded under her, Connie cracked open the book and cast her eyes down the contents, looking for a chapter that might talk about crosses, or circles together with crosses. She paged past the frontispiece, past the publication details, past the acknowledgments. After all the front matter of the book, but before the first chapter, "Superstition and the Vernacular Tradition," her gaze fell upon a rough woodcut illustration showing a young woman in simple peasant garb holding out a thick book on one outstretched hand. Connie's eyebrows knit together. The caption read: *Young woman practicing the key and Bible, Anonymous woodcarver, East Anglia, 1587. Reproduced in* Maleficia Totalis, *British Museum Special Collections. See p. 43.*

"*What?*" Connie said aloud, and as she did she felt a soft dog tongue lick her knee. "Oh, hi, Arlo," she said to the animal, who appeared sitting at the feet of the heavy desk. He whimpered. She flipped to page 43, dragging her fingertip down the page.

". . . often had to resort to artifacts commonly found around the house," she read, starting at the top of the page. "A widespread vernacular divination technique mentioned in several sources, and found to occur as late as the first decade of the nineteenth century, was the so-called 'key and Bible.' In this simple process a key would be placed inside a large, heavy book, usually a Bible, and the supplicant would ask a question aloud while holding the book. If the book turned over and spilled out the key, then the supplicant could assume the answer to the question was 'yes.'"

As Connie read, she felt the house closing in around her shoulders, squeezing her into a tiny little box. She read further: "A variation on this technique allowed the supplicant to write a name or a question on a slip of paper, which would then be slid back inside the key and direct the nature of the inquiry more precisely."

Connie snapped her head up, pulled the book off the desk and into her lap, and rooted through the papers until her fingers found the key that she had carried in her pocket for most of the summer. Slowly she withdrew it from beneath her notes, raising it before her eyes and turning it in the warm glow of the oil lamp. A shine glinted down its long shank. She used a thumbnail to catch the protruding end of the minuscule scroll that had first brought Deliverance Dane's name to her, withdrawing it from its hiding place and rolling it between her finger and thumb.

Connie's mind traveled back to the first night that she had spent in Granna's house, fearful, unable to sleep, Liz sacked out in a sleeping bag on the damp quilts upstairs, oil lamp burning. What had she been doing that night? She had been anxious, looking for something to read. Connie rose, taking the lamp with her over to the bookcase, retracing her steps. *I found the crumbling copy of* Uncle Tom's Cabin, she remembered, placing her hand atop the small novel. She walked her fingertips along the brown spines of the books. *Then I looked down at the big books on the bottom shelf,* she thought, getting to her knees and holding the lamp near to their spines. *And I pulled out the Bible.* She rested her hand on the dense book. Connie frowned.

"But I don't remember saying anything out loud, much less asking a question," Connie said to Arlo, who had followed her to the bookcase. He looked up at her, impassive. She brought her thumbnail to her teeth and nibbled at it for a moment. "But I was *thinking,*" she continued. "I'm always thinking." Connie paused. "What was I thinking about?"

She conjured the image of herself in her pajamas that first night, looking down at the specter of herself paging through the first chapters of the Bible. She saw herself reading, and then she narrowed her eyes, trying to peer into the remembered version of herself who was kneeling on the floor. Connie stared at the imaginary scene, watching until she saw herself recoil from the sizzling pain that had shot into her hand, this time observing a bluish puff or haze drifting out from her fingertips, which she did not remember noticing that night. The specter of herself dropped the antique book, rubbing her hand and flexing the fingers to free them from the pain. "What are you thinking about?" she asked the image. The image turned its face to Connie, smiled, slid the key out of the Bible where it had fallen on the floor, held it aloft for the real-world Connie to see, and then faded into the dark.

At that moment a curtain was pulled aside in Connie's mind. "I was wondering whose story I would find here," she said to the void where her imaginary self had been. "The key and Bible answered my question, even though I didn't know I was asking it!" Connie wrapped her arms around herself, quelling the leaps and jumps that were gripping her heart. "It's something in the words," she whispered to herself.

She hurried with the oil lamp back to Granna's desk, Arlo galloping behind, as if equally engrossed. "But it's not just in the words. Sam tried out the Latin note card, and it didn't work." She sat, turning over these details in her mind. She took up the book on superstitious practices again, scanning the page where she had left off to see if it could tell her more. Her eyes skimmed over the various examples of the key and Bible in the late medieval and early modern period, coming to a stop three pages deeper into the chapter.

Another widespread vernacular divination technique, similarly crude but available to all regardless of social class, was the so-called "sieve and scissors." This process consists of balancing a sieve atop an open set of shears and asking a yes or no question. Like the key and Bible, the toppling over of the sieve was thought to signify an answer in the affirmative to the supplicant's question. It has been argued that the genesis of this technique can be tied to the relative expense of scissors; a common household tool, they nevertheless were comparatively costly and difficult to manufacture. They were of particular value in the New World, which only acquired the means to manufacture local scissors and shears

rather late. Some evidence suggests that this method was favored to reveal the location of lost property, and in particular the identity of thieves
in an age when official channels for the enforcement and redress of petty
crime apart from community pressure and observation were almost non-
existent.

Connie sat back in her chair, pulling her knees up to her chest. She let
out a slow breath. Her mind traveled to Sam, vulnerable and alone. A freak-
ish accident, and now he was trapped in a hospital bed. She wondered how
Grace had managed, pressing on with her life after Leo disappeared. How
could she have faced her days without knowing what had happened? Of
course, there had been a war. People disappeared. A tide of grief rose in Connie's chest as she thought about her mother, twenty-one, at the end of college, waiting. Connie wondered how long Grace had spent waiting, clinging
to hope, before she understood that she should stop.

All at once, Connie came to a decision.

"C'mon," she said to the dog, who trotted after her as she strode with
the oil lamp toward the kitchen.

AFTER SOME RUMMAGING, CONNIE HAD MANAGED TO LOCATE THE 1970s
vintage colander, covered with chipped lime green ceramic plating, and a
rusted pair of pruning shears, which a few drops of cooking oil rendered
loose and functional once again. "Do you think a colander counts as a
sieve?" she asked the empty kitchen. Arlo loitered at her feet, watching her,
but she had not really addressed her inquiry to him. Perhaps she was hoping
to perceive some sense of what Granna would have thought. Granna had
clearly not been much for cooking. Other than the bottles and jars ranged
across the shelving, the kitchen was surprisingly spare. Two cooking spoons.
One chopping knife, dull. One iron skillet. Connie smiled to herself. Grace
once complained that Granna gave her nothing to eat growing up but
Velveeta, crackers, canned beets, and deviled ham. One does not especially

need cooking implements for that. She worked the two blades of the shears back and forth, feeling the rough grind of the joint begin to give.

"Okay," she said aloud. She looked around, thinking vaguely that this experiment might require a more dramatic backdrop than the narrow kitchen, with its leaning broom clotted with wax and its cheap screen door. But she felt more at ease in the kitchen, more in command of things. The glow from the oil lamp filled the little room completely, throwing the thin space behind the remaining jars into dark shadow, but leaving Connie with the reassuring feeling that her world was bounded, controllable.

"All right," she said. She opened the scissors at a right angle and balanced the colander, round side down, between the outstretched blades. Slowly she removed her hand from the colander, grasping only one of the scissors handles and letting the other wobble free. Now, she had only to ask. Yes or no questions only, the book said. Connie set her jaw, straightening her spine a fraction. She thought about what she had overheard Linda fearfully whispering into the pay phone.

"If he doesn't get help soon," Connie began, "will Sam die?"

A now-familiar tingling, stinging sensation collected in the palm of the hand that was holding the scissors handle, shooting vibrating, nearly painful energy through her fingers, up her forearm, and down the blades of the scissors. A bluish glow crackled in the empty center of the colander, shooting forth miniature jolts of electricity, one or two of which spewed outward, touching first the counter by the sink, then the antique icebox, then the ceiling, then the floor. Suddenly the free blade of the scissors shot outward, and the colander fell with such force that it seemed to have been slapped away by an unseen hand. The instant that the colander smacked and bounced against the floor, the bluish energy vanished.

Connie stood rooted in place, gripped with astonishment. *It had worked*. It had worked! How was such a thing possible? Maybe she could rationalize away the appearance of the dandelion in the Common or the spider plant in the living room as a coincidence, an accident. But here and now, in this kitchen, the pain still rocketing through her nerves insisted that what she was experiencing was true, it had just happened. *Just because you don't believe it*, the earringed Wiccan's voice echoed in her mind, *doesn't mean that it's not true.*

But what had the Chandler book said? Toppling of the sieve signified an answer in the affirmative. That meant yes.

If something was not done soon, Sam would die.

Connie swallowed thickly, bending to retrieve the sieve. Arlo watched from the corner of the kitchen, half-hidden behind the icebox.

"Okay, okay, okay," she whispered to herself, balancing the sieve once again on the outstretched open scissors blades. Grace had said that it was a kind of hubris to expect to be able to explain everything. Connie tried to shove aside her wonder at the mechanism underlying what was happening and concentrate on the effect. She extended her arm, focusing her vision on the colander, and bringing her free hand down to her side. She cleared her throat, packing her fear into a small, lockable chest in her mind.

"Will the doctors be able to help him?" she asked, her voice filling the small room. Again the tingling spread through the nerves in her hand and lower arm, again the blue sparks gathered in the colander and shot forth, zapping against the nearby surfaces in the kitchen. But this time the colander did not move. The sparks started to simmer down, their trails growing shorter, and the glow began to recede back into the belly of the vegetable strainer. Connie's eyebrows shot up.

"No, no, no!" she muttered, and she jostled the scissors, rattling and shaking them, willing the answer to be different. The sieve stayed on the blade, unbudged. It felt thoroughly a part of the scissors blade, as if it had been glued there.

Hot tears welled in the red rims of Connie's eyes, and she rubbed at her tired face with one arm. "What . . . what . . . what do I do?" she whispered, on the edge of panic, panting, mind rushing through possible yes or no questions that she could ask to clarify Sam's situation. She swallowed again, breath coming shallow in her lungs. "Okay," she assured herself, "it's okay, it's okay, I've got it." She took a deep breath, straightening again, and wiped the clammy palm of her free hand on her cutoffs.

"Can *anyone* help him?" she asked.

The tingling was stronger now, more painful, and Connie clenched her teeth against the unpleasant, crawling, sizzling sensation that spread far enough up her arm to reach her shoulder. The blue jolts shot out farther from the colander, rocketing off several of the glass bottles, the ceiling, and Connie's sweating forehead. As she squinted against the blue shock so near her eyes, the colander spun off the end of the open shears, smashing against one of the unlabeled glass jars, which rained broken shards and rotted fruit in a great splatter across the kitchen shelf, ricocheting to the edge of the kitchen counter, and pitching to the floor. *Yes!* Connie exulted. *That means yes! And I'm getting better at it. It's just like the plants. The result becomes more unambiguous the more I practice.*

"But it won't tell me *who* can help him," she reasoned aloud, picking up the colander again. It had a fresh chip where the paint had been smacked off by the sharp edge of the counter, and Connie rubbed the naked metal with her thumb. "Because it only answers yes or no." She ruminated for a moment, sorting through her options. She extended the scissors again, placing the sieve gingerly in place and withdrawing her hand. With each trial the pain grew appreciably worse. She had better choose her questions carefully. Soon enough the pain might be too much for her to continue.

Suddenly, the question that she must ask appeared fully formed from deep within her, and she knew.

"Am *I* the one who can help him?" she asked, summoning extra reserves of strength to fill the room with her voice. She squinched her face tight, eyes open only a slit, holding her head back, away from her outstretched arm as a fresh rain of blue sparks began to cascade forth from the inside of the bowl. The hurting, snapping feeling reached all the way up her arm to shoot tendrils of pain through the muscles in her chest and around her upper back. She became aware that she was emitting a high-pitched whining sound through her molars and nose as the colander flew off of the scissors blade, hurling itself against the uppermost kitchen shelf and plummeting straight to the floor, where it clapped without a bounce.

The instant it reached the floor the pain vanished, and Connie panted, puffing air out through her pursed lips. She transferred the scissors to her free hand, shaking out the pain and knots from the hand that had been holding the shears, bending and flexing the finger joints. Connie guessed that she could handle one more question before the pain grew excruciating. She had to be strategic. After a moment's reflection, she knew precisely what she must ask.

With a hand only just trembling, she extended the open pruning shears until they were stretched out level with her shoulder. She brought the colander down, placing it softly between the sharp blades of the scissors, and bringing her free hand back so that it was clenched behind her back. She dug her nails into her palm, hoping that the sharp digging sensation would distract her from the coming pain. She heard a small whimper from well behind the icebox. "Almost done, Arlo," she whispered. "We can take it, right?" She took a breath, let it out, and then said, "Right."

Connie straightened again, and in a voice summoned from the deepest part of her lungs, she spoke.

"Does the solution lie in Deliverance Dane's shadow book?" she said, and as the words escaped her lips blue sparks immediately began to spew forth from within the colander. The cool glow mushroomed out of the center of the metal sieve, boiling over like bread left too long to rise, and sparks showered down on all sides of Connie, drumming and cracking against every surface of the kitchen, beating on her face and chest and arms and legs. Her arm felt shot all through with molten metal, flowing from her fingertips all the way up her neck, down her left side, into her leg and ankle and toes. She pressed her lips together, breathing quickly through her nose, digging the fingernails of her free hand into the flesh of her palm so hard that she felt blood begin to pool in her knuckles.

The colander began to rattle in place, and the scissors swung open with such force that they went spinning out of her grip, cartwheeling across the tiny room and hitting the wooden jamb of the screen door with a dull thwack, the blade sinking two inches into the wood. The colander hovered in place for an instant before hurtling against the corner of the overhead cabinet, a great dent sinking into the metal from where it struck, then ricocheted across the room to strike the opposite wall, where it rebounded against another of the preserves on the shelf, shattering them, before it flung itself to the floor, sinking half an inch into the linoleum.

Connie leaned over, placing her hands on her knees, face drenched with sweat, gasping as the last of the blue sparks withdrew into the broken belly of the colander on the floor, surrounded by a spray of paint chips and broken glass. The flame in the oil lamp flickered, and the shadows in the kitchen jumped and slanted, dancing behind the objects that cast them. Connie squeezed her eyes closed, then opened them, slowly pulling herself back into a standing position. A brown eye appeared from the impossibly small space behind the icebox, and blinked once.

"It's okay, Arlo," she said to his emerging face. "Now I know what I have to do."

CHAPTER TWENTY

Cambridge, Massachusetts

Late August

1991

T HE GUARD BARELY LOOKED UP AS CONNIE FLASHED HER LAMINATED
identification card. His feet were propped on the counter by the metal
turnstiles, and the ornate marble cavern of the entrance to Widener Library
was filled with the somnolent hush of late summer. He nodded, buzzing her
through the turnstile with disinterest, never lifting his eyes from the cross-
word puzzle in his lap. Connie strode toward the reference room, stuffing
her identification back into her cutoff pocket. The sound of her flip-flops
smacking against her heels echoed, making her feel small and self-conscious
as she headed for the computer terminals.

A row of dismal green computer screens waited for her, yellow cursors
blinking at the ready. Connie did a few quick keyword searches, looking for
"almanac," for "Deliverance Dane," for "recipes for physick." All digital
catalogue results stopped at 1972. She frowned, turning to the imposing oak
edifice that contained the reference librarians.

Connie drummed her fingertips on the scarred top of the desk, waiting for the spectacled young man seated behind it to notice her. He was bent over an open workbook, clutching a pencil, and held up one long index finger to signal that he would be with her in a moment. She blew an impatient breath out of her nose, and he slapped the pencil down as he stood. The workbook was filled with Chinese characters.

"Sorry," he said. "Translating. Can I help you?" he asked, voice brusque but not unhelpful.

"Yes, I was just using the Unix system to look up a rare book, but all of the catalogue entries seem to stop in 1972?" she asked, leaning her elbows on the top of the reference desk.

He rolled his eyes with barely concealed exasperation. "Well, yes. The database is only complete back to 1972, because those are the records that have been scanned. The library started with current materials and is working its way backward. If you want complete records of books that were published earlier, you'll have to use the card catalogue." He pointed with his pencil eraser at the wall of small wooden drawers.

Connie sighed. Another day in a card catalogue.

"What year was your book published?" he asked, turning to his terminal.

"I'm not entirely sure," she said, "but certainly before the 1680s." She craned her neck a little to see what he was typing.

The librarian emitted a low whistle through his teeth, fingers tacking over the keyboard. He hit the return key with a final, authoritative peck. "Yeah, those call numbers are all stored in the special collections library," he said. "I'll need to give you a special pass. ID?"

She passed him her identification and watched as he scribbled her name on a small green card. Judging from the typeface the same form must have been in use since at least the 1920s.

As he wrote down a complex series of codes, the young man said, "They pretty much only let faculty in there, but you're advanced to candidacy, so it shouldn't be a problem." He slid the form across the desk to her, indicating with his pencil eraser a line for her to sign. "Show this when you get to the entrance, along with a list of the call numbers you plan to look up. They might make you sign the register, but as it's summer, you'll probably be okay."

"Great," Connie said, voice devoid of any enthusiasm. "Thanks." The young man mock-saluted her with his pencil and sat down to his translations again as Connie dragged her feet to the card catalogue. When she reached it she paused, enumerating to herself the sum total of details that she had gathered about the book.

Junius Lawrence had left Deliverance's shadow book, together with the rest of the Salem Athenaeum collection, to Harvard when he died in 1925, that much she knew. Connie stood, arms crossed over her chest, confronting the wall of tiny wooden drawers. Mystery number one: how would the author be listed? It seemed unlikely that Deliverance would appear as the author, particularly on the off chance that the book was older than about the 1650s. It probably had been authored by several people, perhaps dozens, depending on how long the book had been in use. Even authorship of known occult texts was often obscured through layers of translation and myth; the few extant European examples were variously attributed to biblical figures or prophets, many of them apocryphal.

Mystery number two: the book's title. So far it had been described, at different points in time and from different points of view, as a receipt book, a book of recipes for physick, an almanac, and—Manning Chilton's term— a shadow book or grimoire. The very parameters of the book seemed to shift, changing contour depending on who was describing it. None of the sources had referenced a concrete title of any kind. It seemed likely that the book had none.

So she had no title, no specific publication year, and no author's name by which to search. What she did have was the book's approximate age, and the exact year in which it was donated to Harvard. But libraries, unlike museums, do not often keep track of the acquisition date for a given volume. Do they? As a test, Connie looked under the listing for *Uncle Tom's Cabin*, just to observe how the different editions were catalogued. As she had suspected: the entries offered no acquisition information. Publication dates and edition details only. Connie swore under her breath. For completeness's sake, she looked to see if there was a subject or keyword heading for "Salem Athenaeum collection," but there was not.

She passed a few minutes rifling through different drawers under different subject headings, noting down the locations of a few tentative candidates, frustrated and aware that her method was scattershot at best. A privately published almanac, listed as dating from the 1670s, in the special collections library, with no author listed. A book on medicinal herbs and vegetables, also with no author, with an estimated date at about 1660. An early medical textbook, published in England in the 1680s, authored by an Oxford professor. She contemplated looking under alchemical guides and textbooks but rejected the idea: if Chilton had not found it in all his years stomping through that intellectual turf, it would not be shelved there. Connie found a few other possibilities, but as she jotted down the call numbers, she reflected that she was about as likely to find the book this way as she was to trip over a gold ingot lying in the middle of the Yard.

Her mood blackening, Connie made her way through a series of vaulted marble hallways until she reached the special collections desk. She submitted her list of call numbers, her special pass, and her university identification card to the bored librarian, who didn't even bother to hide his computer solitaire game before waving her through the door that led to the stacks.

Though she was accustomed to the unique physical sensations of archival work, of dust coating the inside of her nose, or the neck crick that results from reading book spines sideways, Connie was not fully prepared for the feeling she got when she walked in the special collections stacks. Most older books have a distinctive smell of silverfish, mildew, and dissolving leather. Even Harvard, with its vast wells of funding and its reasonably consistent climate control, could not insulate these books from the pressure of time on their fragile bindings. The library had begun a campaign to place the most delicate volumes on microfilm, locking the original objects away from the oily fingers of prying students, but the task was Sisyphean. Now she padded through stacks that were disturbed barely half a dozen times a year, and the books around her seemed to fill the air with a tangible aura, as if they had each absorbed some fraction of the essence of the vanished generations who had handled them. Connie pushed through the close atmosphere, nudging aside shreds of personality—readers, writers, possessors, annotators—that drifted in invisible tendrils from each spine. Connie suppressed the urge to shiver.

She reached the first aisle on her list, and peered down its shadowy depths with not a little trepidation.

"Ridiculous," she said aloud, trying to dispel the distinct feeling that she was not alone among the books. She twisted the timer at the end of the shelving, flooding the aisle with electric light and inaugurating a loud ticking, which counted down fifteen minutes. She hurried down the aisle, running her fingertip over the passing spines, reading the call numbers aloud in a whisper. The first possibility on her list emerged under her fingers, and she gingerly withdrew the book. It was a text on medicinal herbs, written in about 1660, and a pasted frontispiece on the inside of the cover mentioned in thin, watery script that it had been given to the library by one Richard Saltonstall in 1705. If the textbook had been in the Harvard library since 1705, it could not be part of the Athenaeum collection. Connie sighed, replacing the book on the shelf. She drew a line through its call number on her list and moved deeper into the stacks, wiping the red leather residue on the seat of her cutoffs.

Her next candidate was shelved three aisles down, and the ticking behind her receded under the muffling influence of shelf upon shelf of books, retreating to a faint *tack-tack-tack* just under the level of her awareness. She twisted the timer on the next aisle, this time finding her quarry on the bottom shelf. Connie dropped her shoulder bag and settled herself on the floor, sliding the book into her lap. It was covered in a thick patina of grime, and she sneezed into the hollow under her arm. The cover had been nibbled into a latticework by decades of worms, and Connie reflected that she must be doubly careful or the book might fall apart in her hands. Using a fingernail, she smoothed the book open, paging through the blank front leaves. As she did so, her ears pricked up—she thought she heard a rustling.

Connie sat, listening, breath stoppered in the top of her lungs. Under the timer of her aisle she heard a faint ticking, followed by one loud click. She let her breath out. It was just the timer shutting itself off in the first aisle. No one else could possibly want to come into this archive, especially not in the middle of the summer. She nosed past the remaining front matter of the book to find herself faced with an engraving of a dead body, sliced open in front, with different organs removed and labeled in Latin. *This must be the British medical textbook*, she thought, disappointed. She ran her fingertips over the raised etching, slightly appalled at the flayed, dead face of the cadaver in the illustration, his lips pulled back in a silent grimace. Dissection was hardly a mainstream practice in the 1680s, when the book was written. She shuddered, paging further into the book. It was entirely in Latin, and without Liz to translate she had no way of really understanding what she was reading, but it certainly did not seem to be a vernacular book. Also, she could not detect more than one hand at work; the text was all printed, and seemed to be organized in a scholarly way.

As this thought passed through her mind she heard another click, louder, and in the same instant that she registered the sound, the aisle was plunged into total darkness.

"Dammit," she muttered. The timer must have run out. She closed the book, groping in the blackness for the gap on the shelf that signaled the book's proper location, and struggled to her feet. She felt along the shelves until her hand plunged into blank space, indicating that she was back in the main central walkway. Her next possibility, the anonymous almanac, was only one aisle over, and Connie pawed through the darkness until her fingers landed on the timer for the next aisle. She twisted the little knob, and when the ticking timer burst into light she started to find the smiling figure of Manning Chilton.

"Oh!" Connie gasped, bringing an involuntary hand to her chest.

"Connie, my girl," he said, folding his arms and leaning, jovial, against one of the shelves. "What a pleasant surprise. Researching, are we?"

He arched a wiry eyebrow at her, and Connie reflected that only her advisor would wear a silk club bow tie and loafers to do research in an archive as filthy as this one. He was standing near enough to her that she could see that the tie was covered in tiny snarling boars' heads: the Porcellian, one of Harvard's more select men's societies. The club was known to serve as a clearinghouse for Brahmin Boston men, to ensure that those not already connected by blood or marriage would nevertheless be assured the right professional and political contacts. It was a world in which wealth was assumed, class prerogatives unapologetically reinforced, and women . . . well, there were rumors about how the men of the "Porc" regarded women.

Connie swallowed and blinked. "I didn't realize anyone else was here," she said.

He smiled, bloodless and taut, in response.

"I've only just arrived," Chilton said. "Come to work on a few more sources for that conference presentation that we discussed," he said after a moment. She tried to smile back at him, but it came out looking more like a cringe. "Which reminds me," he said, edging nearer to her, "where do we stand on that research that you were going to show me? I am most eager to see that book."

Connie suddenly saw that she was trapped. Perhaps it was a coincidence, his appearing when she was so near to finding Deliverance's book, but she realized that there was the possibility, however slim, that it was not. As she gazed at her advisor's patrician face, his eyes a watery blue and bloodshot, his teeth yellowed by pipe tobacco, she suspected her fear was true. He must have searched for the book himself and been unable to find it—that was what he had meant when he said he was doing some checking of his own. Now he had followed her here so that she could not conceal her discovery from him. But there was no escape. She had reached the last possibility on the list, and he was here, waiting.

Connie still had not explained to herself why she wished to protect her research from him; she knew that he was relying on the success of her work to bolster his own reputation. And she had overheard him promise results— results for what, she did not know—at the Colonial Association conference. At their last meeting, Chilton had even dangled prestige before her, as a carrot to make her work faster. But if he was here, poised to swoop down upon her primary source, then his desperation must be even more acute than Janine had implied.

"As a matter of fact," she wavered, "I think there's a good chance I am about to find it. Today." She swallowed again, willing the saliva back into her mouth. A smile broke across his face, like a crack wending its way through a stained china plate.

"What excellent news," he said. "I knew that you could do it. By all means, carry on." He waved a knotty hand at her in a beneficent gesture.

Under his hungry gaze she pulled the slip of scrap paper out of her pocket and turned her attention to the tattered book spines, scanning for the proper call number.

"My girl," he began as she hunted through the books. "Do you know why I have devoted so much of my work to the history of alchemy?"

She continued working, not looking at him. "As a matter of fact," she said, "I don't believe we have ever discussed it."

He laughed a dry, acerbic little laugh. "Rather unusually so for a man of my background," he began, and Connie was distracted as usual by his accent. *Rathah*. "I believe in hard work above innate talent. Technique, Connie. You know," he continued, warming to his topic, "on some level I don't believe that innate talent exists. No. I have always been a bit of a meritocrat in that regard. Take sufficient study, technique, and attention to detail, and one can transcend whatever one's former circumstances. Such are the ingredients necessary for intellectual triumph."

She sensed him eyeing her, waiting for her to express her approval. In his voice resonated the timbre of a man who thinks he has convinced himself of an idea, but masks his own doubt by laboring to persuade others. Connie said nothing, making a show of concentrating on her task. She suspected that the narrative that he told himself about his interest in alchemical research differed rather drastically from the narrative that others might deduce from his actions. When she did not respond, he continued.

"On this score, the ancient alchemists and I see the world in strikingly similar terms. These men—straddling the Dark Ages and the Enlightenment! Standing on the very cusp between rank superstition and the scientific method! They believed in the power of science to unmask the divine. Through manipulation of the physical world, they intended to touch the very nature of truth." His eyes gleamed, and she slowed her pace along the book spines, walking along them one finger at a time, saying nothing.

"Truth," he repeated, pausing with significance. "In this age of relativism and shoddy humanitarian nonsense. The hermeneutics of this, the gendering of that, discourses of the other thing." He emitted a derisive snigger, edging nearer to her. "What price would you pay to be able to stand before your colleagues and say, Within my very hand I hold the key to the deeper structures of reality and perception?" He breathed, and she smelled the pipe tobacco on his breath.

"I would think that particle physics has the lock on the true nature of reality," Connie hazarded, peering at him out of the corner of her eye. She saw Chilton's eyebrows sweep together in a storm cloud over his face.

"Ah, but that is where you are wrong," Chilton said, voice slightly too loud for the narrow confines of the stacks. "Science still knows how to doubt, but it has lost the ability to believe. Faith is what distinguishes the alchemical mind from the purely scientific one. And this is where the real value of alchemical knowledge lies."

"But I don't understand," Connie said. "What sort of value?" She had found the call number that she was looking for but hesitated to rest her hand on the telltale spine. Her nerves vibrated with tension and anxiety. In the back of her mind hung the specter of Sam, and the torments that were wracking his body. *Every couple of hours*, she repeated to herself, hating that her advisor was still loitering over her, grasping, demanding, waiting.

"But don't you know yet?" he asked, bemused.

"No!" Connie exclaimed. "Colonial almanacs. Shadow books. What does that have to do with anything?" she demanded, emboldened by the sight of the exact book that she wanted. If she could distract him, perhaps she could come up with a way to get him to leave. But then, if he had followed her here, he would already know what call numbers had attracted her attention. She could not merely lie. Connie sorted through different strategies for diverting Chilton's attention from the book but rejected each one as impossible.

"Why, Connie," he said, in a bantering tone that caused her to flinch, "I am no *sexist*." He snickered, and she cast a confused look in his direction. He observed her bafflement and smiled wider. "Countless men—some of the greatest scientific minds in human history—turned their considerable powers to the quest for the philosopher's stone. Like the Puritan elect, those people singled out by God for a higher purpose, the alchemical adepts were men of the highest order, worthy of practicing the Great Work. This wondrous substance could transform base materials into pure ones at a touch, and at the same time could effect profound changes in the human body," he added. "Though its color, content, and structure have long been subject to debate, there is no doubt that it was real. The philosopher's stone is the single most rare and spectacular product of human intellect and effort: a conduit for God's power, acting on the stuff of life on earth."

As Chilton spoke, a tremble traveled up Connie's spine. She saw that her hand, ever so slightly, was shaking.

"All of them," Chilton continued, "despite their prodigious learning and scholarship, despite being the greatest minds of their time, in the end, stopped short of success. And why do you think that was?"

Connie glanced at him from under her lashes and saw that he actually expected her to answer. "Because it is a myth," she whispered. "The philosopher's stone is just an allegory. It represents everything that man wants and can never have."

Chilton threw back his head and laughed.

"Ah! How spirited you are," he exclaimed. "Of course you would think that. But consider this. None of them"—he paused significantly, one long finger raised in emphasis—"*none* of them bothered to consider the textual insights that might be offered by practitioners of vernacular magic. The alchemists had the materials, and they had the knowledge, but they were missing a crucial element of technique. And they did not know to look for it! Because most of the practitioners of vernacular magic were women, of course. Learned men in the early modern period would never have consulted with a cunning woman, no matter how well regarded, because her social rank and knowledge level would have been so drastically inferior to theirs. The alchemists were brilliant but shortsighted in that regard. I, however, as a man of my own time, have no such prejudiced illusions. Now—have we found what we were looking for?"

Surprise and fear gripped Connie, tightening the muscles around her neck. Her mind was reeling, astonished that Chilton actually believed that what he was saying was true. *I would like you to see what I have to offer*, he had said on the telephone. He was looking for the formula for the philosopher's stone—and he thought he was on the point of finding it. The idea struck her as preposterous, and yet Chilton's fevered smile told her that it must be true.

Further delay was futile. Kneeling, she placed a hand on the waiting book, edging it out of its hiding place on the shelf and supporting it with one protective arm. She glanced up at her advisor to see if he expected her to give him the book directly, but he was looking down, eyes eager, and she read in his face the real passion and curiosity underlying his prodigious self-aggrandizement. Deep within himself, Manning Chilton was still at heart a scholar. Whatever wealth and influence he may be clutching for, Chilton hungered even more for the discovery. Flexing her fingers, she caught the corner of the unmarked cover and edged it open. One page flipped by, then another, and another, and Connie felt a little smile of triumph pull at the corners of her mouth.

"Do you want to see?" she said, looking up at Chilton. He nodded, gesturing for her to hand him the volume, so she stood and passed the book to him. He grabbed it eagerly, a thin strip of fragile leather binding ripping off the spine and falling to the floor in his haste. He licked a thumb and then turned over the frontispiece. Connie recoiled to contemplate the damage that this would cause but let the feeling go as she watched his reaction.

"But what . . . ," he began, voice trailing off as the excitement melted off his face in great tallow sheets. "This is just a tide table!" he exclaimed, turning a leaf over. " 'Weather predictions for January of 1672,' " he read aloud, then flipped another page. " 'Hints for the Cultivation of Maize.' " He looked up at her, face contorted in a tense mask of anger. "What is this!" he demanded.

"It's an almanac," she replied, simply. Peeking at the notes she had made on her scratch paper, she clarified. "Privately published in Boston in the 1670s, no author listed."

"This isn't the shadow book?" he said, voice boiling.

"I guess not." She shrugged. "I thought it might be. But it looks like it's just a regular old farmers' guide."

An oily sheen washed over his eyes as he thrust the book back into her arms, scattering more figments of binding across the archive floor. "This is most disappointing, Connie," he hissed through a tightening jaw. He turned away from her, striding briskly back to the central passage in the stacks. When he reached it, he turned to face her again.

"I must warn you," he said, one index finger extended. "You have every reason to want to find that book. I am sure you know what I mean."

She stared at him, saying nothing. "And," he continued, pointing to the ticking light switch, "you are almost out of time."

As he said this the timer emitted a loud click, and Connie was swallowed up in darkness.

OVERHEAD, THE ELM TREES DOTTING HARVARD YARD BRUSHED THEIR leafy branches together, filling the air with a shushing murmur that announced an evening rainstorm in the offing. Connie walked, arms folded, head down, shoulder bag thumping against her hip. A chill breeze circulated around the trunks of the trees, swirling up her bare legs, sprinkling them with goose bumps. The change of seasons always took her by surprise, even after a lifetime in New England. She rubbed her hands briskly over her upper arms, bringing warmth to them. Soon enough the campus would be crawling with students again, tossing Frisbees, heads nodding to headphones, leaves rustling around their feet. When the seasons started to change Connie always felt that time was slipping away from her, like earth crumbling through her fingers. She disliked the sensation, for it filled her with a vague sense of fear. The onward crush of time reinforced how small she was, how powerless.

Connie glanced over her shoulder; no one was following her. She assumed that Chilton had gone back to the history building but could not be sure. The threat that he had uttered when he left her in the library now hovered in her mind, ominous yet imprecise. The Colonial Association conference clearly posed some sort of deadline for Chilton's research. But the darkness in his eyes alluded to still more menacing threats. After he left her sitting in the dark in the special collections archive, a few minutes passed as she tried to ascertain what further steps to take. As he rambled on about alchemy, the philosopher's stone, and the promises that its discovery seemed to hold, an idea had begun to glimmer in the back of Connie's mind.

I'm no sexist, he had said, with some sarcasm. Now as she strode across Harvard Yard, shoulders hunched, the idea took root and grew, branching into her consciousness. She walked past the oldest edifices on campus, squat brick buildings covered in webbed clinging vines, and paused before the dense traffic careening through Harvard Square.

Striding in fits and spurts across the car-clogged breadth of Massachusetts Avenue, Connie again turned her thoughts to Sam. Since her experiment with the sieve and scissors her all-encompassing worry had folded back on itself, creating a screaming feedback loop that followed her everywhere she went, for she knew that only Deliverance's book could free Sam from the new horror in which he found himself. Her understanding of the book had shifted yet again; it had gone from being an exquisite primary source to being the only thing that could restore Sam's life. The text still held its intellectual value, of course, but she had stopped caring about it in that way. Connie glanced up as she passed the old Cambridge Burying Ground, its headstones leaning at dangerous angles, its rusted gate chained shut against the incursions of the morbidly curious and the vandalism prone, and thought only about Sam.

Connie felt her jaw tighten. The research didn't matter. Chilton didn't matter either.

The idea that had formed in the solitary darkness of the Widener stacks was beating against the backs of Connie's eyes, and she knew with an aching certainty that she was finally correct. A book considered a mere women's text by Harvard in 1925 would have been banished to the humble library of Harvard's underfunded sister college, Radcliffe, now an all-but-defunct collection of ill-maintained buildings housing only forgotten relics and visiting feminist scholars on grants. She turned left at the corner of the Cambridge Common, breaking into a trot as she headed through the humming streets toward the Radcliffe Quadrangle.

THE VOLVO ROCKED TO A STOP AT THE WEEDY END OF MILK STREET, struts groaning in protest, and Connie tumbled out of the car. Pushing through the creaking iron gate into Granna's yard, she nearly stumbled over Arlo, who was lying in wait under a dense rosemary hedge along the flagstone path. He galloped after her as she sprinted into the house, hardly noticing the glimmering sheen that washed over the burned circle on the front door, and on the horseshoe nailed overhead. She banged through the door and grabbed immediately at the telephone, fingertip hurrying through the progression of numbers that would connect her with Grace Goodwin in Santa Fe.

"I can't talk long," her mother said without preamble as the receiver clattered to life. "I've got Bill Hopkins here, and he needs an aura cleansing.

You should see it—jagged lines every which way. He's been terribly depressed—"

"Mom," Connie interrupted, gasping. "*I have it.*"

"Have what, my darling?" her mother said, followed with a whispered *I'll be just a minute, Bill—it's my daughter* spoken over the bottom of the receiver.

"Deliverance Dane's shadow book!" Connie burst, heart thrumming.

"But of course you do, my darling. Though I still say you don't need it." Grace sighed softly. "Well, I suppose it can't hurt. You've been so worried about him. It can be nice to have some concrete guidelines when you're just starting out." *Tea,* Connie heard Grace mouth to the waiting Bill, whoever he was, waving a hand in the direction of the kitchen in her low desert house.

Connie frowned, confused. "What do you mean?" she asked.

"Why, helping Sam, of course," Grace replied, and Connie envisioned her mother's fragile eyebrows rise into two sincere arcs over her eyes. "Frankly, I'm a little surprised he's come to harm so early. There must be a terribly strong bond between the two of you."

"*What?*" Connie said, incredulous.

"Usually they go quite a while before the accident happens. But it always does," Grace said, her voice quiet. "Never have had a good explanation for why. The Lord giveth, and He taketh away, was how Mother always put it, like it was a price exacted in exchange for seeing clearly into others. We have the gift, but it brings pain to us at first—headaches, usually—and finally sorrow on the ones we hold most dear. And like all things, it goes in cycles; the intensity varies, tied to the state of the earth. As we near the end of this century, the rhythms have only gotten more acute. I had just eighteen months with poor Leo, while Mother and Dad had twenty-odd years. And now here's your Sam, after only eight weeks." She sighed, sorrowful. "My poor darling."

"How do you know about Sam? How do you even know his name?" Connie demanded. She was willing to admit a certain degree of intuition between herself and Grace, but she had been circumspect with her mother about her relationship with Sam. Was this why Grace had been asking about him so assiduously?

Grace blew an impatient sigh through her nose, mouthing *I'm sorry, Bill,* while waving him into a seat on the sofa in her raftered living room. "Listen, Connie, whatever you decide to do, make sure that it all happens *inside* the house," she said, voice firm. "You can't be safer than at home, on your own turf, as it were, can you?"

"But, Mom, I . . ." Connie started to speak, then trailed off. "Wait. Are you saying that you *knew* something was going to happen to Sam?"

Grace sniffed with impatience, her customary signal when she thought that Connie was willfully overlooking some point that to her was clear and unambiguous. "Really, Constance. Sometimes it's like you simply refuse to see what is right in front of you."

Connie froze, the telephone receiver gripped in a hand that now seemed somehow detached from the rest of her body, floating next to her face like a moth. What had Grace said?

Constance.

Her full name.

Like a lot of people who are known only by nicknames, Connie tended to forget that she had any connection with that word. She and Liz had talked about it once. How had Liz put it? Whenever someone calls her "Elizabeth," she always thinks that they are talking to someone standing behind her.

Constance. A prissy, patent-leather-shoes-and-ruffled-socks sort of name. She loathed her name as a little girl, and her mother's loose counter-culture friends drifting in and out of the Concord commune were never ones for full names, anyway. Those who had babies when Connie was growing up gave them all overwrought hippie names—Branch Water Alpert, who was now an undergraduate at Brandeis, and Samadhi Marcus, a priggish, right-leaning young man who was now living in Asheville and going by "John." As if anyone could blame him.

So Connie had let the name drift away from her, putting it away with the same finality that she put away her shoes as they were outgrown year after year. It was so thoroughly discarded that she now rediscovered, with a dawning sense of wonder, that the word had a meaning beyond its function as a name. Constance. Abidingness. Fealty. The act of remaining steadfast. A state of being, or a condition to which one might aspire. Like grace.

Like deliverance.

"Oh, my God," she whispered, eyes widening with sudden certainty. *But of course.* And Sophia—Greek for wisdom, Liz had said. Mercy. Prudence. Patience. Temperance, whose placid mid-nineteenth-century face watched her from the portrait in Granna's dining room, a silent link connecting the line of women in her present life with the line of women she was chasing in the past. Their last names morphed over marriages and time, but the first names traced a genealogy that was undeniable.

Connie stared with wonder down into her palm, into the little fleshy hollow where her will had somehow manifested itself in painful, prickling blue-white light as she consulted the sieve and scissors, or placed her fingertip on Sam's forehead to soothe his suffering body. She reviewed the details of her mother's life, clearing away the opaque clutter of New Age terminology, watching the truth change its contours under the shifting parameters of language. Just as all these women—each locked in her own moment in history, and yet somehow also a variation on Connie herself—described the craft in terms specific to their time. She swallowed, bringing the telephone nearer to her mouth and dropping her voice to a whisper.

"Mother," she said, "do you know who put that burned symbol on my door?"

Connie heard her mother chuckling softly, in a tone that stopped just short of being smug. "I'll tell you this much," Grace said. "No one—and I mean *no one*—wants to keep you safe more than I do."

Silence fell between them as Connie suddenly understood.

"But how——" Connie started to say, only to have Grace cut her off.

"I am so sorry, my darling, but I really must be going. Can't keep Bill waiting. His aura's just a disaster."

"Mom!" Connie exclaimed, protesting, but Grace shushed her.

"Now listen—it's all going to be just fine. Remember what I told you about these natural cycles in the earth? Other people feel it just as changes in the weather? I'm not worried in the slightest. Trust your instincts and you'll know just what to do. It's like"—she paused, rolling her eyes heavenward, groping for words—"it's like making music. There is the instrument. There is the ear. And there is the practice. Bring all those disparate elements together, and you can play. There is also the sheet music, of course. It can guide you, give you hints. But by itself? By itself, it's just marks on paper."

Uncertainty and fear descended over Connie, as if she were standing in a shallow stream, hunting through murky water for something bright and precious that has been dropped. "But there is so much that I don't understand," she whispered, pressing the telephone receiver so hard against her ear that it began to flush an angry red.

"You see a mystery," Grace said, voice confident, "but I see a gift." Before Connie had a chance to respond, her mother called out *Be right there, Bill!* and then turned back to the telephone, saying, "I love you, darling. Be careful."

The receiver clicked and Grace was gone.

"But it hurts," Connie said into the dead receiver, flexing her free hand and feeling a faint electrical tingle coalescing, just under her skin.

Interlude

Boston, Massachusetts
June 28
1692

*T*he rat had spent the better part of the last quarter hour washing his face, scrubbing with his fists behind his ears and over his bristly cheeks. He was a fat and leisurely beast, and now that his ears were sleeked down and sparkling, he turned his attention to the pink-brown tail coiled around his haunches, clever fingers working their way from base to tip, combing away any fleas or muck, bringing the end of the tail up under quivering whiskers to meet his tongue. The narrow square of sunlight in which he crouched, leaking from the barred opening overhead where feet and hooves could be seen passing by, drew an intelligent glitter out of his hard button eyes. As he worked away at the tail a soft moan rose from within the darkest corner of the cell, and the filthy straw on which the rat was sitting stirred under a stretching foot. Startled, he loped out of the square of sun to complete his toilet elsewhere.

His place in the sunlit patch was now occupied by the quivering foot, two dirty toes extending forth from the unraveling snarl in a dingy, stained woolen stocking. Clamped around the outside of the stocking was a heavy iron cuff, attached with a short length of nautical-grade chain. The foot and its ankle were so small that the cuff had about half an inch of space remaining inside it, though it was on its smallest setting; the stocking underneath the cuff was blackened with rust stains.

The foot's owner, one Dorcas Good, lay on her side in a trembling ball in the dim far corner of the cell, knees and arms pulled up to her chest, face overlaid with a webbing of matted hair. Her eyes were open wide, but vacant, and her mouth suckled on one of her tiny thumbs. In the last few weeks, her language had forsaken her; though she was four years old, and by all accounts had been a lively and engaging child, she now appeared thin and wasted, and her only utterances were the moans and wailings of a babe.

A hand reached over to smooth away the hair, which a layer of sweat had glued to the girl's forehead. The air inside the cell was heavy with the heat of beginning summer, and thick with the stench of molding straw and overfull ordure buckets with which the occupants were supplied. Deliverance Dane held her hand, a prickling warmth radiating from her palm, over the little girl's staring eyes, and whispered an incantation under her breath, the one that seemed to work best as the days had worn on. Dorcas's eyelids lowered, raised, and lowered again, shuttering away what remained of her mind from the horror in which her body lay. The girl's breathing deepened, and she fell into a dreamless sleep.

"She sleeps ag'n, eh?" croaked a broken voice from another corner of the cell.

"She does," Deliverance assented, withdrawing her hand back into her lap. She shifted her shoulder blades against the rough stone wall. She had grown thinner in the past few months, and her bones could no longer find a way to settle. Flesh had fallen away, it seemed, a few pounds at a time, and gaps now appeared between the fingers of her hand; she held it up to the tiny square of sunlight and could see the opposite side of the cell through the spaces between her fingers.

"I've nevah saw one as could sleep thus," the voice continued, knowing. "'Taint natural."

Deliverance sighed, closing her eyes. She had had this conversation with Goody Osborne enough times already. "God shields the souls of the innocent as best He can from the Devil's torments," she murmured.

The voice laughed, a derisive cackle that dissolved into a fit of hacking coughs. When the hacks subsided Sarah Osborne's indistinct shape heaved in the shadows at the opposite corner of the cell, crawling forward until a pockmarked face, topped by a coif the color of dishwater, appeared a few feet from where Deliverance was sitting. The parched lips pulled back from gums dotted with teeth, and Deliverance closed her throat against the foul odor coming from the woman's mouth. "I *know* you, Livvy Dane," the woman hissed. "And Dahcas's mother do, too, though she be in some othah hellish hole. I've a mind to tell 'em what you done. We all knowed it."

Deliverance's eyes traveled slowly to the side, where they paused to take in Goody Osborne's face. The skin between the older woman's eyes was creased and rubbery; the crone had always had a distemper about her. Her mind jumped from one path to another, with scolds and rails in between, and because of this distraction she had lived only by the beneficence of the Village. She would appear scratching at a door, demanding coin or a heel of bread, or a night in the cowshed out of the elements, and the Villagers would comply, outwardly avowing the Christian virtues of charity and goodwill, while silently willing her to be gone. Sarah Good, Dorcas's mother, who was held several cells away, though younger than Goody Osborne, was just as wretched and labored under similar constraints. Goody Good's eyes were forever vacant and unfocused, yellowed with misery and drink. It was whispered in the Village that Dorcas's father was unknown, and that Goody Good had passed her confinement in prison because of it, convicted and fined for fornication.

Deliverance pressed her lips together, looking upon Goody Osborne's ravaged face with an uncharitable mixture of pity and disgust. Pity for the life that she had been entreated to live, and disgust for the certainty that

Goody Osborne would embellish her meager ministrations to the cringing, suffering Dorcas until the suspicions building against her in the town would harden into acknowledged fact. Over the months that they had sat imprisoned, ankles chained to the wall in clamps, waiting for Governor Phips to arrive in the colonies bearing a new charter, and with it a legal mandate for a trial, Goody Osborne had passed her few moments of lucidity keeping a weather eye on Deliverance, lying in wait like a spider.

The governor had arrived from England in May, at once decreeing that a grand Court of Oyer and Terminer, or a court "to listen and determine," be established in Salem Town for the prosecution and containment of the spreading diabolical menace. For months the possessed little girls, Reverend Parris's daughter Betty among them, had cast pointing fingers at every imaginable personage. And some unimaginable: a rumor reached the prison that they had even cried out against one of their former ministers. The Village grew jumpier and anxious, inflammable, and the band of frightened little girls, gripped in the clutches of violent fits, spread their accusations to farther reaching towns, even up to Andover and Topsfield, seeking in vain to push the Village's accusing eyes away from themselves. The court had met for the first time at the very beginning of June, condemning Bridget Bishop to be hanged by the neck; and so she was, barely a week later, strung up and dangling before a great, cheering assembly on the desolate hilltop on the western side of town. There were those who held that justice done to Bridget Bishop might draw the matter to a close. Yet still the accused women sat in prison, waiting.

In spite of the heat in the cell, Deliverance wrapped her arms around herself, shivering. She folded her bony fingers together. "Come, Goody Osborne," she said, her fatigue seeping through her voice. "Let us pray together."

The beggar woman snorted, a great rattling "Pah!", and retreated back into the shadows of the cell. She fell to muttering and incoherence, but then out of the patter of her meaningless utterings, Deliverance discerned her whisper, "Shah no prayah can help us now."

For some hours Deliverance sat, her hands folded under her chin, mouth moving in silent prayer. Little Dorcas slept on, limbs shuddering in her sleep, the chain on her ankle sometimes scraping on the floor, and Goody Osborne lurked in her corner, rearranging the straw over her lap. Deliverance had not lost her wonder about how time in the prison could move so slowly. The tiny square of sunlight crept across the moldering floor, folded itself up the far wall, and presently stretched into a long, distended rectangle. Deliverance watched its progress, waiting.

Down the narrow hall on the other side of the heavy cell door she heard what she thought might be the sound of keys jangling together, punctuated with murmuring women's voices. The sounds grew nearer, and her suspicions were confirmed when a creak and clank in the darkness announced the unlocking of the cell door, which swung open to reveal the warden holding a tallow candle aloft over a grouping of three or four modestly attired women of middling years.

One of the women stepped forward, and Deliverance recognized her as a respected midwife from down by Rumney Marsh, though she could not produce the woman's name. Was it Mary? Deliverance looked up at her, moving her head a fraction. It could have been. 'Twas hard to tell in such dimness. The woman approached her, keeping her face a careful mask of neutrality, though her quivering nostrils betrayed an unhappy awareness of the smell permeating the cell.

"Come now, Livvy Dane," she said evenly, holding out her hand. "Mister Stoughton would have us examine you afore the morrow."

While the woman spoke, the warden was stooping to unlock the iron cuff around Deliverance's ankle, and she stiffened as his fingers brushed familiarly over the stocking covering her lower leg. She withdrew her foot under her skirts as soon as the ankle was free, and the man's grimy face leered up at her where he knelt with the keys. One of his eyebrows raised perceptibly. *I kin help yehs,* he had said some weeks ago. *Look 'pon me softly like, 'n' we kin see, eh?* She focused her eyes on his and sent a pristine image into the center of his brain. The image said *spiders*, and immediately the man dropped his key ring with a strangled cry and started scratching at his arms and hair.

Deliverance took the woman's hand—Mary Josephs, it was, she remembered now—and rose to her feet. She swayed, unsteady, as her stagnant blood moved down into her legs. Goody Josephs wrapped an arm around Deliverance's waist and led her to the group of women waiting at the door. "We'll away to Goody Hubbard's house," the midwife said, and the group ushered her down the prison hallway, leaving the scratching warden to re-lock the cell door, his oaths echoing after them in the hallway.

Though the streets of Boston were well into the evening, the gloaming light hit Deliverance's face with the brilliance of full noon, and she realized how long she had been locked away. "So the trial's for tomorrow, is it?" she asked Goody Josephs, as if they were two women pausing over their labors to review the gossip of the day.

"'Tis," Goody Josephs nodded.

"The girls are still in their fits, then," Deliverance remarked. The women said nothing.

They arrived on the stoop of a simple frame house, like Deliverance's own in Salem Town but more tightly arrayed between its neighbors. The women led her into the front hall, where a girl, about Mercy's age, was tending to the fire in the hearth. When the little band appeared she tossed another two split logs onto the fire and mounted the ladder into the loft overhead without so much as a word. *She's been warned away*, Deliverance thought. *Or she is afraid of me.* She surveyed the room and felt a rising tide of sadness creep throughout her body. It had been months since she laid eyes on her daughter. She wondered how the girl was able to pay the prison for her keep.

"Goody Hubbard, we will have a candle, if you please," said Goody Josephs, rolling her blouse sleeves up her sturdy forearms. She turned to Deliverance. "I'll have you unlace your dress, Livvy. And quick now. Soon enough the night will be upon us."

Deliverance's gaze roved among the women's impassive faces. Goody Josephs was the only one she recognized, though she knew the others must be midwives as well. She imagined they had placed themselves at the disposal of the court in part to ensure no inquiring eyes would be laid upon themselves. *'Tis forever women leaping to condemn each other*, she reflected. She wondered why that was. Women posed dangers to one another that they somehow did not pose to men. She reached for the laces at her breast and worked to unknot them, loosening the bindings that held her dress together. It was odd to disrobe as a roomful of people watched, arms folded, one holding a smoking candle behind her cupped hand. Presently she stood in her coif, shift, and stockings, aware that the cuffs, collar, and hem of the shift were blackened where they had been exposed from beneath the dress. She rubbed the top of one foot with her stockinged toes.

"Shift and coif, too," Goody Josephs prodded, and Deliverance's eyes widened in momentary panic. She could not remember the last time she had appeared before another without a shift. Even in the most trying hours of her confinement with Mercy, she had kept her shift on, stained with blood and sweat though it was. In their youth, Nathaniel had once entreated her to shed it, and she had demurred for weeks into their marriage. Now as she struggled out of the stained cotton underclothes the image of that night rose before her, the night when she had given in to his pleadings. She had stood, in stockings only, hair unbraided and running over her shoulders, arms wrapped around her nakedness as the warmth from the fire lapped at her bare haunches. *Oh, Livvy, how beautiful you are*, he had said.

Deliverance cast the crumpled cotton garment to the floor, and looked down at her naked body with a kind of wonder. Deep shadows ran through her ribs, under her tired breasts, and her hip bones jutted at an eerie angle where the poor prison victuals had sloughed away her heft. She reached up to unpin the head covering that she always wore, dropping it atop the pile of clothes at her feet, and then bent to roll her knitted stockings down, stepping out of them one foot at a time. *Merciful Jesus, Nathaniel, how I yearn to see you again*, she thought as she stood, head bowed, graying hair draping across her face to hide the flushed trembling that had seized her.

One of the women whom she did not recognize gestured for her to climb atop the long hall table, and on shaking legs Deliverance did so, spreading her limbs out under the grasping hands of the midwives. She squinted her eyes closed, body gripped with shame, as the women's knowing fingers hunted over her skin for the telltale mark. She felt them poking through the tufts of hair in her armpits, running down her flanks, moving the little puddle of candle warmth so that it shone first behind her knees, then into the secret depths between her legs. Another set of hands combed through the hair on her scalp, moving methodically from her brow to the crevices behind her ears.

Deliverance felt the candle loiter between her spread thighs, its flame hideously hot next to the tender skin of her most secret folds, and she heard the women whispering in discussion. *Preternatural excrescence of flesh* she heard one of them mutter, jotting notes, and murmurs of assent sounded at the end of the table as rough fingers poked and spread her apart. Hot, miserable tears filled Deliverance's eyes, overflowing the corners of her lids and trickling down into her ears. Then the candle was removed. When she opened her eyes she looked up to see the ring of faces staring down at her, all of them closed off in damning judgment.

"You have the witches' teat, Livvy Dane, and at the very cusp of your accursed womanhood, too," one of them pronounced as another chimed in, "I trow you ha' given suck to diabolical imps or familiars! Confess it!"

Deliverance propped herself on her elbows, face contorted in anxious fury. *Salacious myth, that, is all,* she thought, *for familiars be not diabolical at all.* But of course she could not say that to the women.

"I ha' done nowt of the sort!" she spat, and the women pulled away from her, intimidated by her forcefulness. Deliverance clambered off the table, throwing on her shift in white anger. "You are a foolish wretch, Mary Josephs!" she exclaimed. "How many babes ha' you caught, yet you know not the God-made body of your women! I am made in God's image, and so are you! Hand me a candle and I shall find this witches teat on the lot of you!"

The women crowded angrily around her, mouths open in scolds and recriminations, but Deliverance had closed her ears to them. As she threw her garments on with haste and was borne back to the prison amongst the chattering, finger-waving women, she turned her mind to the trial that was to come tomorrow, but more than anything, she thought about her daughter.

CHAPTER TWENTY-ONE

Marblehead, Massachusetts
Early September
1991

THE SURFACE OF THE DINING TABLE WAS SPREAD OUT WITH NOTES and papers, and in the middle sat Constance Goodwin, her head bent over a thick, open manuscript that was bound in dark oiled leather sewn with heavy twine, its pages brown-yellow with age and bearing the dry silverfish smell of the Radcliffe special collections library. The book was about the size of an antique bible, with a few pressed, shriveled herbs jutting out from between its leaves. She was reading, and had been reading for several days now. At her elbow sat another book, the title of which seemed to be *Guide to Herbs and Indigenous Plants of New England*. It, too, was open, to a page with an ink drawing of a feverfew plant. Three small note cards were arrayed across the table above the manuscript: one, with a title that alluded to tomatoes, written all in Latin, and two others. *Sure cure for Fever and the Chills* was written across the second; the third had no title, but instead bore some sort of word puzzle. A pen tapped in a regular rhythm against her temple, but the notepad sitting at her other elbow was still empty, forgotten as she grew more absorbed in the text. As she read, her lips moved without making a sound.

Her other hand supported a heavy brass-handled magnifying glass, located some days previously in a drawer in Granna's desk, and under it the scratchy words swelled and stretched, gliding across the glass surface as Connie tried to sound them out. The book seemed to have no real progression or order, and certainly no table of contents. She had already counted six or eight different handwritings, and not a few different styles of print, with many of the entries jumbled together, interleaved indiscriminately. Some of the entries appeared to be in Latin; from her longtime friendship with Liz, Connie was able to sift snatches of meaning from these passages, but only snatches. But most were in forms of English of various archaism, complicated further by their nonstandard spellings and dated terminology for plants, substances, and processes. She had already read through a section enumerating recipes for poultices to cure festering wounds, infections, black lung, apoplexy, and "the ague."

Several pages were devoted to what looked like prayers, but which were more likely charms—all of them invoking assistance from the Almighty. Connie was surprised at the explicit religiosity of the text so far, of a type that alluded to Christian practices from well before the Reformation. The text reflected a world in which Christianity was utterly bound to the conception of reality. No wonder Puritan theologians had found witchcraft—if that is what this was—so threatening. In a system of thought in which salvation, and therefore all goodness, could come by grace alone, in which one's actions were believed to have no effect on the state of the soul, and in which illness or misfortune were often read as signs of God's disfavor, a method that counteracted illness and misfortune by direct personal appeal to God, together with arcane proto-scientific practice, would have gone against everything that the Puritan power structure wanted to maintain. Puritan theologians would have seen such work as sacrilegious.

Even diabolical.

As far as Connie could tell, the recipes outlined in the shadow book relied on a combination of prayer, attentive mixing of herbs and other natural substances, and something else—something ineffable. Will? It was not that, quite, but almost. Intention. In the book it was called variously "technick," "crafte," and "authoritie." But Connie still had trouble articulating, in modern terms, what such a concept might be. Thinking back to the spider plants when she first found Granna's recipe cards, she recalled that Sam had tried the same spell—she allowed herself to use the term, though she felt self-conscious doing so—yet he had been unable to render any change in the dead plants. She frowned, concentrating, and turned another page.

Sam. He was growing worse. She planned to visit him again that afternoon, to relieve his parents from what had started as regular visits but had evolved into a kind of vigil. His exhaustion was extreme, and though his leg was healing, it was only because he passed most of the day in tight restraints so that the convulsions ripping through his body every few hours would not jostle his shattered bones. The periodic violent vomiting made it difficult for him to stay hydrated, and so his skin was starting to appear sallow and tired. Even his humor was starting to ebb. The doctors still expressed confidence that a solution would be found, but Connie read in their faces the draining away of their certainty. When she peered into Sam's eyes, she saw that he, too, could read their confusion; his faith in their ability to help him was starting to flicker and fade. And behind that vanishing faith, Connie saw in Sam the first inklings of real fear.

She turned another page of the manuscript, refocusing her gaze through the magnifying glass as the words bled together. Her head was starting to ache, and she laid aside the glass and squeezed her eyes closed for a moment, rubbing her fingertips over her eyelids. Then she forced herself to take up the brass handle again.

The word *Fitts* swam into view across the convex plane of the magnifying glass, and Connie bent lower to the page, bringing the glass nearer to the difficult text.

"Method for the Redress of Fitts" read the heading, and Connie caught her breath. Historians had never been fully able to describe precisely what colonial chroniclers meant by "fits," whether they more closely resembled fainting spells, or perhaps episodes of religious ecstasy, with shaking and speaking in tongues. Arguments had been made for both. Connie thought about Sam's shaking, trembling body when it was gripped by muscle convulsions during one of his seizures. His eyes rolled into the back of his head, revealing their whites, and his tongue extended.

If that was not a "fit," then what was?

"To determine if a Man's mortall Suffering be caused by bewitchment," the instructions began, "catch his Water in a witch-bottel and throw in some pins or nayles and boil it upon a very hott fire."

Connie raised her head, thinking. What was a "witch-bottel"? Bottel. A phonetic spelling of "bottle." A witch bottle. She pushed aside the manuscript and riffled through her notebooks, bringing up her transcription of Deliverance's probate record, running her finger down the page. There it was: 30 shillings' worth of "glass bottels." Connie recalled wondering at the time why the probate would have made special mention of the bottles, and had never come up with an answer.

She lifted her head, scanning the crowded shelves of the dining room. Connie had spent considerable time scrubbing the earthenware dishes and glassware stacked in the alcove next to the large hearth fireplace, and had peeked into the dark cabinet under the alcove but been repulsed by the dense layers of grime that awaited her inside. The cabinet contained a number of antique bottles, among other things, though they seemed uninteresting at the time. Just junk, ready for a curio shop. And the kitchen was full of sealed jars, of course, but those were all of recent vintage—the remnants of Granna's work, however she might have conceived of it.

Now Connie turned, looking over her shoulder and gazing at the wooden alcove with its small cabinet underneath. She narrowed her eyes, focusing her attention on the corner of the dining room, picturing the flowered back of her grandmother, a thin cotton apron tied behind her waist, getting to her knees with a tired grunt and swinging open the door. The imaginary Granna brushed aside a loose strand of hair before seeming to reach inside the cabinet, and Connie thought that she heard a rummaging and tinkling from behind the wood.

Not junk.

Connie unfolded herself from the chair and knelt by the cabinet door. Awkward storage spaces were built into all sorts of areas of the house; the tiny attic bedrooms each had a built-in window seat, in which Connie had discovered extra quilts, a game of Scrabble with most of the vowels missing, and the unpleasant evidence of several generations of mice. She unhooked the tiny latch and swung open the door.

Inside, clad in thick layers of dust and festooned with a few tender spiderwebs, lay an untidy heap of crockery of all shapes: small iron cauldrons and skillets, what looked like a rusted waffle iron, a long-handled grill for roasting fish over an open fire, a few copper bed warmers, green with age, designed to be filled with glowing coals. And thick glass bottles. Dozens of them, perhaps a hundred, of a wavery blue-green hue that spoke of molten sand and age. The lips at the tops of their necks were uneven, their bases as dense as slabs of rock. They were of varying size, but all appeared to hail from before the dawn of the industrial age, when glass was blown by mouth and not by machine.

The bottles were unstoppered and empty for the most part, and Connie reached in to free one from the crust of grime in which it was resting. She held the bottle aloft, catching the dim light of the dining room in the bottle's thick, bubbled walls, and saw that inside it were two or three deeply rusted nails. She carried the bottle back to the dining table, turning her attention again to the thick manuscript.

"Throw the bottel into the fyre whilst reciting the Lord's Prayer follow'd by this most effective Incantation: Agla Pater Dominus Tetragrammaton Adonai Heavenly Father I beseech thee bring the Evildoer unto Me."

Connie straightened in her chair, perturbed. She pressed her hands to either side of her head, willing the spreading throb in her brain to recede. *Agla*, like on the burn mark on her door. A long list of names of God. And

Tetragrammaton—where had she seen that before? She moved the heels of her hands until they rested over her closed eyes, exhaling in the darkness behind her eyelids. Connie sorted through the different drawers in her mind, rooting through the file labeled MISCELLANEOUS. For some reason the word made her think of Sam.

Then her eyes opened wide, and she remembered: "Tetragrammaton" was carved on the charmed boundary marker that Sam had shown her, on the first night that they met. She sorted through her notes again, finding the definition that she had jotted down from the book on the material culture of vernacular magic. It was a word describing the four Hebrew letters that signify "Yahweh," yet another name for God.

Connie looked at her watch. It was getting late. She would finish reading this passage, and then she would go.

"When his Water is well Boilt so shall the Sorcerer be drawn unto the fyre," the manuscript continued. "And so with the pins and crafte may he be entreated to free his Victim from Diabolicall machinations. Refer to receipts for Death-philtres to ascertain other means." The remainder of the page contained a long list of Latinate names for plants and herbs, headed up by the words "Fuel for sure Withdrawal."

Leaning back in her chair, Connie paused for a few quiet minutes, tapping the pen against her teeth. Then she took up the small bottle with its contents of rusted nails, slipped it into her shoulder bag, and hurried out of the house.

Interlude

Salem Town, Massachusetts

June 29

1692

*T*he sound roiling inside the meetinghouse had already reached deafening proportions by the time Mercy Dane arrived. She paused outside the entrance to the building, knocking her boots against its stone steps to loosen the hunks of mud picked up on her long trek across town. Mercy had tarried too long at the house, she knew; pacing to and fro across the hall and promising herself that she would leave, yes, she would be ready to go in only another minute or so. She did not fully grasp the reason behind her delay. Certainly she missed her mother and yearned to see her again. Perhaps she was afraid.

If she could have pressed her hands to her ears and willed the world to disappear, she would have. She would linger in the house, clutching Dog in her arms, sitting perfectly still in a bargain with God that if she refused to move, not even an *inch*, then time itself would cease to progress, and at least that way nothing could get any worse. In her pausing she recognized her childish obstinacy, as if without her presence, the Court of Oyer and Termi-ner would not proceed. After a few more turns around the hall, Mercy over-came her silly illusions, finally running most of the way through the damp streets of Salem all the way to the meetinghouse steps. The day was thick and gray, and Mercy felt her clothes plastering themselves to her sides, and her cheeks flushed an uncomfortable red.

To her chagrin, the trial seemed well under way by the time she slipped through the door. At the front of the room, behind a long library table, sat a row of distinguished gentlemen in sparse black coats and curled hair, each more dour than the last. The one in the middle, a sallow man with a wide lace collar, long nose, and wobbly double chin, must be William Stoughton, the lieutenant governor. Mercy had never seen him before, but he presented a very fine personage. He and the other judges seemed to be talking amongst themselves, but she was too far back in the room to hear what was being said. She rose on tiptoe, craning her neck to see if there was any space nearer the front.

Over the shoulders and heads of the townsfolk she could just see the row of accused women, their hands clasped together in chains, heads bowed, standing immobile before the raised platform of judges, with the railed box of jurymen off to one side. Deliverance was the second from the left; Mercy recognized the dress that her mother had been wearing when Jonas Oliver took her away, though it was now browned, splotched with filth, and torn in places. Mercy edged around the back corner of the room, keeping her eyes locked on her mother's back. As she climbed over the legs crowding the aisle, she saw Deliverance glance quickly over her shoulder, meeting Mer-cy's gaze with a tired face showing blurred relief and dismay.

"Watch yahself, gahl!" growled a grizzled man, his clothes reeking of fish. He rubbed his shin and stared at her accusingly. She murmured an apol-ogy and continued to creep through the crowded pews, wishing to reach the far front corner of the room, where she might see her mother's face. All around her swirled snippets of gossip and conversation, none seemingly tied to a particular person, but all arising as a whole from the observing crowd.

". . . ne'er ha' thought Rebecca *Nurse* would do . . ."

". . . came to hah in the night, the very image o' her, ridden on a broomstick, with a candle in the straws . . ."

". . . an' her eight children gone, born then withered in her arms . . ."

". . . for suckling devils and imps, they said . . ."

". . . vengeful scold, and I seen it too . . ."

Mercy's eyes darted from face to face in the crowd, and all of them—wrinkled, toothless men, fresh young matrons, lace-collared gentlefolk, ruddy-cheeked children—all were contorted with biliousness, mouths opening and shutting like angry fish snapping at shreds of flesh in the water.

Mercy reached the far corner of the meetinghouse, pressing her shoulder against the wall and balling her fists together in her apron. Behind the row of the accused, in the front pew, at the very center of the whole room's breathless attention, sat a passel of girls about her own age, some a little older, quite a few even younger, wringing their hands and writhing about, squealing and carrying on. Mercy scowled. She knew one or two of them. That Ann Putnam, she knew her, and Lord forgive her, but how she loathed that girl. Proud and flighty, never first with a new thought, but always embraced others' notions with the loudest voice. Mercy's nostrils flared. Ann was a mite older than the other girls; oughtn't she to be in better straits?

Of the accused women, apart from her mother Mercy recognized only two: Sarah Good, a common enough sight in both Salem Town and Salem Village, roaming the streets with her little girl, raving and distracted. Even now she stood, eyes rolling, mouth slack, one hand twitching. Mercy had always been a little afraid of Sarah Good, and her wild infant was known to squall and bite. She wondered where little Dorcas was. A scan of the assembly did not reveal her. Then, on her mother's other side, Mercy recognized with some surprise the wizened stoop of Rebecca Nurse—and she a full church member! A godly woman, known to all, and not for a witch neither.

She being accused, why, the judges must forbear to carry forth this madness, Mercy thought in her father's voice. How she wished that her father were here. His word had carried weight in the Village. He would know what must be done. He would never loiter in the house 'til past time for the trial to begin.

As these thoughts traveled through Mercy's mind the conference among the judges drew to a close, and one of them—"John Hathorne, him who was a magistrate afore," according to a whisper a few rows behind where Mercy stood—spoke to someone seated in the pew just opposite the wailing girls with a few curt words, too quietly spoken to reach the farthest gallery.

Mercy squinted—her eyes did not always focus on the same point all at once—and saw a bony, aged man, his bald head speckled with liver spots, get to his feet. Judge Hathorne spread his hands in a gesture of calm and quietude, and a wave of shushing traveled from the front rows of the meetinghouse, washing over the assembled populace and then breaking in a coil up against the farthest walls. As quiet overlaid the assembly, the man started to speak. Mercy strained to hear what he said.

". . . long suspected Goody Dane of sorcery," he was saying when the whispers finally died enough for Mercy to hear him. "My fears were most horribly confirmed on a night these ten years ago, in which my poor daughter Martha died at the hands of some diabolical mischief whilst Goody Dane was ministering to her."

At this the pewful of girls broke out squealing and wailing, and Ann Putnam rose to her feet with a scream, pointing at Deliverance and crying, "I ha' seen it! Her very image is come to me in the night, and she saith 'I killed Martha Petford, and if you call out on me I shall kill you, too!' "

The crowd gasped, and a few of the other girls burst forth with their own revelation of Deliverance's threats and recriminations. "She came in at my window, brandishing her fiery broom!" one screamed, as another cried, "And at mine! She bade me come to her wicked sabbaths and sign my name in the Devil's book!"

Lieutenant Governor Stoughton, his wattles quivering in rage, pounded on the library table with a gavel as one of the girls fell over fainting, and

Ann Putnam, her voice rising, added, "Aye! And she bade me take off my clothes, and showed me a specter of my father all dressed in winding sheets, and saith I must go with her, lest my father be kilt as well!"

Hands reached forth to restrain the flailing Ann, who seemed to be tearing at the collar of her dress, as someone lifted up the fainting girl and smacked her gently on the cheeks until her eyelids started to flutter. Governor Stoughton rose from his seat, smashing down the gavel and bellowing, "Abominable! Abominable! I shall hear what the accused has to say for herself!"

And at this the crowd quieted, loath to miss what Deliverance might say. As a body they leaned forward, holding their breath. Mercy knotted her fists more tightly together under her apron, lest her rage and indignation result in an unwanted and uncontrollable effect. "She lies," Mercy hissed under her breath. "She never had nowt to do with us! She lies!"

Down in the space before the bench, Deliverance seemed to be surveying the faces of the judges and of the crowd at either side of her. Next to her Mercy saw Rebecca Nurse reach a gentle, wrinkled hand up to stroke Deliverance along her arm. Deliverance drew herself up marginally taller, lifting her chin, and even from as far away as she stood, Mercy could see how her mother had grown thin over the past months, and older looking, too. Beneath her eyes were deep purplish circles, and her hair looked more watery and gray. The color drained a little from Deliverance's eyes, leaving them a cold pale blue, and she began to speak.

"Lo these ten years ago I were called to the side of Goodman Petford's daughter, Martha, who was in her fits and much aggrieved," Deliverance began. The crowd grew silent, listening. "I made to attend to her, thinking she were ill, and so I gave her some physick which I had brought with me, and I prayed o'er her into the night."

"But 'tis readily acknowledged that a witch cannot complete her prayers!" cried an unseen person in the gallery.

"I pray every day," Deliverance said quietly, and Mercy observed a flutter of doubt passing through the belly of the crowd. She brought her hands out from beneath her apron and clasped them together under her chin, eyes wide, waiting.

Deliverance paused, looking down at her chained hands, and up again at the waiting bench of judges. Mercy wondered what she was thinking and tried to focus her attention squarely on her mother's face, listening. She could not perceive it. Her mother swallowed, licked her lips, and then said, "Goodman Petford, he ha' lost his wife barely some months afore his daughter's fits, and I ha' long believed that"—she cast a sidelong glance at Peter Petford, who was seated, staring at her with unconcealed malice—"that his grief like to ha' colored his thinking of the facts."

"And did the child die that night?" asked another of the judges, identified by the whisperer behind Mercy as "Jonathan Corwin, him who ha' taken the place of Nathaniel Saltonstall, that war so distraught with the hanging of the Bishop woman."

"Alas, so she did," Deliverance said. "Whilst I held her in my arms."

Peter Petford's jaw was quivering, color creeping up his face.

The same judge, Corwin, leaned forward on his elbows and leveled his gaze at Deliverance. "And was the gahl ill? Or war she bewitched withal?"

Deliverance's eyes shifted left and right, her nostrils quivering, and Mercy felt a sinking dread grip her entrails. "She were bewitched, of a sort," Deliverance allowed. "I have testified so in court, when I sued to clear my sullied name, and I will not go against it now."

"And how came you to know that she war bewitched? Who might the culprit be, if it is not you?" the judge pressed, one wiry eyebrow rising wickedly.

"That I cannot say, sir," Deliverance whispered. "I know not the machinations of it. But God in His wisdom and goodness sometimes reveals things to me, if I beseech Him thus, that I may better serve Him."

"God?" said Judge Corwin. "You speak to God, Goody Dane?"

"I believe that all God's children may speak to Him," Deliverance said, shifting her eyes to the cluster of ministers who sat observing the proceedings. One or two of them were nodding, but a few sat with their arms folded, glowering.

"Now, Goodwife Dane," broke in another of the judges, but the whispering voice did not tell its companion the name of this one, at least not loudly enough for Mercy to overhear. "How can you be sure it is the Almighty God who reveals these things to you?"

"Sir?" Deliverance asked, voice confused.

"Him whose machinations you yourself claim not to know. How came you to believe that this is the work of our Savior?" he asked, drawing his hand along his chin, as if stroking an imaginary beard, and gazing at her with the smug face of a man who thinks he is about to win an argument against a child. "Could you not in fact be serving the Devil, who deludes you with promises of wealth or fame, and tells you to *pretend* that you do the work of God?" The crowd responded with impressed murmurs, heads grouping together, nodding.

Deliverance appeared to think for a moment, and then raising her voice so that all could hear her clearly, said, "For He created all the Heavens and the Earth. I believe that there is nothing in this world or the next that is not the work of God."

The crowd hissed and muttered, casting dubious glances at her, and Mercy heard a bitter whisper behind her say *Sacrilege!*

Governor Stoughton, eyebrows raised in surprise, said, "Why, Goodwife Dane, surely you believe in the Devil? And that he has been working his vile sorceries on the innocents in Salem Village, through his loyal servants here on earth?"

The room paused, waiting. She said nothing. Governor Stoughton continued. "You would not say that this court is *deluded* in its object, would you, Goodwife Dane?"

"I am afraid that I would, sir, or else that the Devil achieves his object through the condemnation of the innocent, and not the railings of these wicked, distracted girls," said Deliverance, closing her eyes as the crowd bellowed and the girls screamed out in rage, surging toward the chained women before the bench, held back only by the crush of several men and ministers who had been seated near the front of the room.

"I see him!" screamed Ann Putnam, pointing, her face empurpled and bursting with fury. "There! A black demon whispers in Goody Dane's ear! Cannot you see him? There! He stands just there!"

The hubbub in the meetinghouse rose to a furious level, and for a time Mercy, huddled against the support of the church wall, could not hear what was being said. She saw her mother standing quiet and still, with Rebecca Nurse whispering something into her ear, as the other accused women crowded up against them, cringing away from the rushing, screaming, grasping bodies all around them. The judges had bent their heads together, hands gesticulating, fingers jabbing into one another's chests. There seemed to be some sort of disagreement amongst them, but within a few moments the discord had passed, and they regained their seats. Governor Stoughton banged his gavel to signal that the crowd must get ahold of itself long enough for him to pronounce judgment.

"Susannah Martin," he intoned as the crowd simmered, "Sarah Wildes, Rebecca Nurse, Sarah Good, Elizabeth Howe, and Deliverance Dane. Pursuant to the evidence presented here against you, that your specters have come to these girls in the dead of night, besieging them and demanding that they serve the Devil, that diverse ones of you are found by trustworthy examination to have unnatural teats whereby to give suck to hideous imps, that several of you have been seen to quarrel with your neighbors and then cause damage to their persons or their property through invisible means, and that you have been observed here in congress with devils and yet deny the truth of that statement, we hereby find you guilty of the crime of witchcraft and so sentence you to be hanged by the neck until dead."

Mercy screamed out in horror. Governor Stoughton banged the gavel down on the library table as the meetinghouse exploded in cries of relief and dismay, several onlookers wailing, "God be praised! We shall be delivered!" as the afflicted girls trembled and shook.

"See how she comes!" cried Ann Putnam. "Goody Dane sends her spirit out to strike me! It is not I, Goody Dane, who condemns you! It is not I!" She huddled down, hands held over her head as if to fend off a blow.

Mercy threw her gaze at the cowering girl, and without thought hurled a ball of pure intention in the direction of the sniveling wretch, whose head rocked back as if she had been slapped. A bright scarlet welt rose across her face, and Ann Putnam started to cry.

Mercy looked up from the hysterical girl and met her mother's cool eyes. To her surprise Deliverance did not look angry or afraid. As the warden led the chained and weeping women to the waiting cart outside, Mercy reflected that if anything, her mother seemed only sad.

CHAPTER TWENTY-TWO

Salem, Massachusetts
Early September
1991

CONNIE EASED THE HANDLE OF THE HOSPITAL ROOM DOOR DOWN-ward, feeling the click of the bolt withdrawing through the metal, and slipped silently into the room. The bed nearest the door was empty, its mattress folded back on itself, naked pillows stacked at the foot. She crept toward the farther bed, careful not to disturb the sleeping occupant within. He had so little opportunity to sleep.

In the bed lay a muscular young man, one leg still encased in plaster from the knee down. He lay on his back, mouth just open, breath moving over his lips with a gentle whisper. His hair was swept back from his brow, and even in sleep his eyes were bracketed by lines etched by years of smiling. Connie rolled up the doctor's examining chair so that it was positioned by the bed. She rested her chin in her hands, watching him. His eyelids twitched in a dream, and his mouth fell open with a quiet snore. The doctors had taken out his nose ring, and without it he looked younger, less dangerous.

She allowed her eyes to travel down his body, tracing the pattern of a stark black Celtic tattoo that ringed his upper arm—a college indiscretion, he had called it—and roving to his chest, down his muscled arms, until they took in the soft straps that bound his wrists to the metal frame of the bed.

Oh, Sam, she thought.

"Connie, I want you to know that we would understand," his mother had said over coffee the previous week.

"Understand?" Connie had asked, confused. "Understand what?"

Linda Hartley turned her coffee mug between her hands, not meeting Connie's eyes. "Sam's father and I—we would understand if this was all a little . . . much for you," she said.

She's giving me permission to break up with him, Connie realized. Not that she had any intention of doing so.

"It's not," Connie responded, meeting Linda's gaze.

Now she listened to the silence in the hospital room, broken only by the occasional muffled announcement of the loudspeaker system in the hallway. Sam's chest rose with a sigh, shifting the thin sheet, and Connie reached forward with two fingers to ease it back into place. He did not stir.

Though she longed to talk to him, it was probably fortuitous that he was asleep, at least for now. Connie opened her shoulder bag, sliding out the small glass bottle that she had carried up with her from the Milk Street house, together with one of the note cards from Granna's recipe collection. The one with no title.

If anyone catches me at this, they will think I've lost my mind, Connie reflected, her mouth flattening into a grim line. *And that goes for Sam, too.*

She looked back to his sleeping face. He was scowling now. A bad dream. Flurries of tension moved across his eyelids, and Connie told herself that she should act quickly.

She pushed the long sleeves of her T-shirt up over her elbows and rolled a length of paper towel out of the dispenser on the wall. Spreading the paper out on the windowsill behind her, Connie set the dusty bottle on the paper and removed its stopper. She padded back to the door of the hospital room, easing it open and looking up and down the corridor, checking for nurses, doctors, Sam's parents—anyone who might happen upon her. A knot of teenage candy stripers giggled together at the far end of the hallway, but otherwise it was deserted, fluorescent lights reflecting on the scrubbed linoleum floor. Connie clicked the door closed.

She sneaked back to the bed where Sam slept, his arms straining momentarily against the restraints. In the back of her mind Connie wondered when Sam's rest would break apart; at any moment his body could seize up, rocking into muscle spasms and dragging him up out of his sleep. Her heartbeat tripped a little faster, sending adrenaline tingling down her arms and legs as she got to her knees under the metal bed.

There it was—a hanging plastic bag, fed by a catheter that snaked up under the covers. Working quickly, she unfastened the bag from its tubing, lip curled in faint distaste. *If it were anyone else*, she thought, balancing it in her hands as she clambered to her feet, looking down at his face. Nothing. Good.

She turned to the windowsill, tipping the container on an incline until its meager contents trickled in slow waves down the inside of the bottle. She emptied it about halfway, filling the bottle two-thirds full, its blue glass shimmering green around the liquid from Sam's body. In an instant she was done, and Connie got back to her knees, fastening it back in place under the bed.

As she crouched on the floor on her hands and knees, there was a shifting in the bed over her head and she heard a hoarse voice say, "That you, Cornell?"

Quickly she sat up on her heels, looking into Sam's face. His lids had eased open halfway, soft green eyes underneath growing more awake. "What are you doing on the floor?" he whispered, half-smiling.

"Nothing," she said soothingly, easing herself into the chair. "I dropped an earring. No big deal."

His grin widened, one eyebrow traveling up his forehead. "Nice try. You don't wear earrings," he remarked.

She smiled back. "Says you. I'm sorry I woke you up."

"Nah," he said, shifting his weight in the bed. "You didn't. Doctors say I need to sleep whenever I can, but it comes and goes."

"Do you want some water?" she asked, mind skipping ahead to consider ways to distract him from noticing the bottle on the windowsill. He licked his lips, seeming to find them dry, and settled his head into the pillow.

"Sure," he said, straining a little against the straps. "You might take these off, too. Frickin' irritating."

Connie rose, turning to the small sink that was under the paper towel dispenser and scrubbing her hands briskly under hot water. "Have you had any of them today?" she asked quietly, reaching for a glass and filling it with water from the tap.

"What time is it?" he asked, voice thick.

Connie glanced up at the institutional clock overhead. "Four thirty-three," she said.

"Then it's been about two hours since the last one," he said. He sounded weary. She brought the water to him, placing it on the nightstand and bending to loosen the straps at his wrists. When they were free, he stretched his arms overhead, rolling his hands at the wrists and exhaling with a great, shuddering sigh. She watched him, enjoying the revealed tautness of his body, at the same time appalled at herself for thinking of him that way in such a context. He eyed her, drinking down the water.

"What?" he asked, bringing the glass down from his lips.

"Nothing," she replied, feeling a flush creep down from her hairline, wrapping around her ears.

"*What?*" he teased, setting the glass down again on the table and folding his arms.

"*Nothing,*" she said, a smile twisting her mouth. He reached forward, sliding his hand behind the nape of her neck and pulling her to his mouth. When their kiss ended, some moments later, he rested his forehead against hers, their noses touching.

"I didn't expect this to happen," he said, hand still resting on the back of her neck. Connie felt the warmth of his fingers pressing there and reached up to drape one hand over his bent arm.

"Which part?" she asked. Through the tight skin of his forehead she could sense his anxiety, knowing that as the minutes passed they drew closer to his next seizure, and that there was nothing either of them could do about it.

"Any of it," he admitted, "but I was really referring to the part where I met you."

She smiled, but her smile was strained and sad. She reached up to pull on his earlobe, saying nothing.

"Listen," he started to say. "I want you to know something,"

"Don't worry about it," she said.

"You don't know what I was going to say," he objected.

"Yes, I do," she whispered, pressing her forehead more firmly against his. They sat like that for a while in silence, both eyes closed, communicating without speaking.

Presently Sam sighed, saying, "You should probably put on the bands again," and she heard fear coiled under his matter-of-fact tone. She nodded, stooping to kiss the back of his hand before easing it into the padded Velcro strap hanging from the railing of the bed. "Make it tight," he told her.

"Sam," Connie said, working on the strap for his other hand, "I don't want you to worry, but you might not see me for a couple of days."

"Why?" he asked. "Something up?"

"You could say that," she said, finishing with his left hand. "I have something pretty important that I have to do."

"Is this for that conference that you mentioned? The one Chilton wants to take you to?" He tried to brighten as he said this. He always asked about her work, always made an effort to carry on as if they were just talking over coffee. Connie's heart contracted with guilt when he did so, though he swore that he preferred the normalcy of discussing work and ideas to nonstop reflection on his worsening condition. She tried to believe him.

"Yes and no," Connie said, stroking his hair. "Maybe. But I want you to know that I'll be thinking about you the whole time." She leaned in to whisper in his ear. "I have the book."

Sam's eyes sparked with excitement, and he sat up against the pillows. "No way!" he gasped. "And you didn't bring it? You've got to bring it! I can't believe you came to see me and you didn't bring it." He looked genuinely thrilled. A burst of softness and warmth stretched out under Connie's rib cage, causing her to deepen her breath. She grinned at him.

"You'll see it. Soon. I just have to do this one thing first." She placed one palm on his forehead, easing him back into the pillows. She tried to telegraph a feeling of lightness, comfort, and sleepiness from her hand into his skin, filtering it deep into his brain, attempting to prepare his body for the tremors that were—she looked up at the clock, and wished as she did so that she had done it more subtly—probably only moments away. "Don't worry," she murmured. "This is all going to sort itself out. Very soon."

As she spoke, his eyelids grew heavier, draping over his eyes like a thick velvet curtain. A tiny smile played about his lips, and his body loosened, hands falling slack in the restraints. *Maybe he'll sleep through this one*, she hoped as she felt his consciousness drift away under her pressing hand. When his eyes were completely closed, she slowly removed her hand, watching his chest rise and fall.

Satisfied, she turned back to the bottle standing unnoticed on the windowsill, pushed the stopper back into its neck, and slid it into her shoulder bag. Then she folded up the paper towel, easing it silently into the garbage can by the sink.

She returned to the bed, pulling the small note card with no title out of its hiding place in her pocket. It had been secreted away in the same packet as the Latin charm for growing tomatoes, interleaved with unremarkable midcentury recipes for aspic and casserole. Rereading its contents, Connie shook her head, smiling and incredulous.

The card held a seemingly nonsensical sequence of letters, arranged in a triangle, and though Connie could still not entirely believe it, she knew that even a little child would recognize it for what it was. The charm looked like this:

```
A  B  R  A  C  A  D  A  B  R  A
A  B  R  A  C  A  D  A  B  R
A  B  R  A  C  A  D  A  B
A  B  R  A  C  A  D  A
A  B  R  A  C  A  D
A  B  R  A  C  A
A  B  R  A  C
A  B  R  A
A  B  R
A  B
A
```

Underneath the strange triangle was written only one instruction. "To draw out the sickness, apply as a charm to the body," Connie read aloud in a whisper. She folded the card into a tiny square and leaned forward, brushing Sam's forehead with her lips as she slid the charm into the pillowcase under his head. He snored gently in his sleep, and Connie gazed down at him, her face softening. "This has got to work," she said to herself, but perhaps to the universe as well.

Then she crossed the room on silent feet and slipped out the door.

Interlude

Boston, Massachusetts

July 18

1692

A flurry of voices traveled down the grim hallway, a young woman's in rapid and emphatic discourse with a sullen male. The prisoners in the narrow, grimy cells lining the passageway raised their heads, listening. The volume rose, then dropped, and the sound of clattering keys signaled the opening of the door at the far end of the hallway. Dirty faces pressed against the small openings at the top of the heavy cell doors: here George Burroughs, a deposed minister in the Village, his hair grown weedy and long; there Wilmott Redd, a plump fishwife from up Marblehead, her usually merry face now thin and drawn.

Mercy Dane looked on the faces with sorrow, slipping a thick, hard biscuit through each cell slot. She had not known how much to bring; Sarah Bartlett told her it was best to bring too much. Hands extended from the cell door openings, grasping at the meager sustenance, most of them too exhausted even to utter thanks. Mercy made her way slowly down the passage, distributing her bread, finally stopping at the last cell at the end. She peered through the slot in the cell door and could just make out two figures huddled in the darkness: what looked like a little girl balled up in the far corner, clad in only a stained undershirt, and a woman sitting up, her head leaning against the stone wall, her back to the door. The floor was scattered with a thin layer of straw, and the stench of mold was almost overpowering. The cell was barely lit by a small, barred rectangular window high overhead, all available sunlight blocked by the boot heels of a loiterer standing in the street.

"Mama?" Mercy whispered through the cell door. The leaning figure inside the cell did not move. Glancing around her to ensure that she went unobserved, Mercy raised her hand to the lock on the cell door and whispered a long string of Latin words. A blue glow swelled from the inner depths of her palm, warm and crackling, and it pressed outward from the surface of her skin to envelop the rusted metal of the lock. When the glow subsided, Mercy pressed her fingertips against the heavy wood of the door and felt it yield to her pressure. She edged through the open crack, shutting it silently behind her.

"Mama?" she whispered again, creeping nearer the huddled figure on the floor. When she reached the fragile woman in the cell, she dropped to her knees and placed a gentle hand on her mother's shoulder. Slowly Deliverance turned her head to face Mercy, the light of recognition flickering in her eyes.

"Mercy?" she asked, blinking. "But how did you . . ." She trailed off, clutching her trembling daughter to her chest. Mercy buried her face in Deliverance's neck, winding her arms around her waist and breathing in the soothing feeling of her mother's skin.

"I told them I ha' come to settle the bill they sent," she said, her voice muffled in the folds of Deliverance's collar. "Then with some technique, I made them let me pass."

Deliverance stroked the long hair that tumbled down Mercy's back, rocking her a little. She smiled. "And where did you find the coin for such a feat?" she asked. In her voice, Mercy heard that Deliverance was proud of her.

"Goody Bartlett helped me," Mercy said. "Lent me the money and her bay mare, too. I brought biscuits." She produced a few hard lumps of bread from the sack that she was carrying. "Shall I give one to Dorcas?" Mercy looked worriedly over at the tiny girl lying immobile in the darkness on the opposite side of the cell, eyes closed, thumb between her lips. "And where is Goody Osborne?"

"I'll feed her when you've gone," Deliverance said. "None too settled when others approach, is that little one." Her voice was sad, resigned. "And Goody Osborne, she has no more worries in this world. God took her to Him some three weeks ago."

"When I've gone?" Mercy echoed, meeting her mother's tired eyes. "But, Mama. 'Tis all arranged. You're to come with me."

Deliverance looked on her earnest daughter's face and laughed weakly. She reached a hand forward to cup Mercy's flushed cheek, and at her touch, Mercy could feel the depths of Deliverance's resignation.

"Oh, my daughter," Deliverance said, the corners of her mouth just turning up. "You know I cannot go."

"But you can!" Mercy cried, grasping her mother's wrists. "The warden sleeps from the physick I gave him, and I ha' learned the charm for managing the locks! We've only to go, Mama!"

"And leave the others? Them being innocent of a crime which, you must see, I ha' committed?" Deliverance asked, searching her daughter's face for understanding.

"Committed?" Mercy asked, sitting back on her heels. *But sure she is distracted*, Mercy thought. *In these many months in prison her mind must ha' gone as well.*

Deliverance shifted, adjusting the position of her back against the stone wall of the cell with a soft grunt.

"Then you *did* kill Martha Petford?" Mercy asked, face growing stricken and confused.

"Ah! No," Deliverance said, shaking her head. "Not I, though 'tis no surprise I am not believed. For she *were* bewitched, you see. Of a sort. And the physick that I chose spoke to the wrong ailment."

"But why?" Mercy asked, baffled. "Who would seek to kill a child?"

"None but the most wretched and hideous of devils. But think on it, Mercy. How come you to call something by bewitchment?" She watched her daughter, eyebrows drawn down over her pale eyes. "The suffering needs be caused by some certain malefactor, and not by mere happenstance or divine Providence. And yet the malefactor mightn't know wherefore he does what he does, nor even the means by which it is enacted. The error lies in looking for the ill *intent*, and not contenting oneself with treating the effects." Deliverance closed her eyes, resting for a moment and swallowing. "A man need not be a sorcerer to bring bewitchment upon a suffering soul."

"Mother," Mercy said, "I don't attend. Who was the malefactor, then, for little Martha?"

Deliverance opened her eyes again, and Mercy thought that they looked marginally duller, as if their glitter were being gradually tarnished by fatigue and undernourishment. "Why, Peter Petford, of course," she said, voice thick.

Mercy gasped. "Goodman Petford!" She sat balanced on the balls of her feet, her lips parted in shock.

"Through no knowledge of his own," Deliverance added. "Poor, long-suffering man."

"But how?" Mercy demanded.

"When I first arrived at his daughter's sickbed, I thought her to be suffering from common fits. Or maybe she were malingering, a sad little thing entreated to maintain the household at too tender an age. And her with no mother neither." Deliverance brought a fragile hand to her forehead, seeming to massage away the unpleasant memory. "I fed her a mild tincture for the nerves and prayed o'er her, thinking some warm tonic and soft words should bring her round." She heaved a sigh, her thin chest rising and falling with the effort. "Rarely ha' I been so wrong. It were saturnism withal. Brought about by too much lead, like to ha' leached from poor pots into her victuals. Her fits worsened whilst I were with her, and though I spoke some better charms to combat metals and poisonings, it were altogether too late. And the poor child died."

"Saturnism," Marcy breathed, eyes widening with comprehension.

"Aye, for Saturn be the planet of lead, as Mercury be the planet of quicksilver. I see you've kept up your studies, clever girl." Deliverance smiled at her daughter.

"You saw which pots then?" Mercy asked.

"A few—some crockery with chipped leaden glaze, though naught to be sure. It accounts for his great distraction, as well. What kills a child in great fits and torments drives a grown man's senses well away. And perhaps it undid Sarah Petford, too, she being dead some months afore the girl fell ill." A great swath of sadness wiped across Deliverance's face. "So Martha were bewitched, of a sort, but there were naught to do withal. Shall I ruin the aggrieved father with the truth? Move him from distraction to utter destruction, and with none like to pay me heed?"

"But then you are innocent, Mama. You tried to minister to Martha, not to harm her," Mercy insisted. "We must tell Governor Stoughton! He is a learned man. He must hear reason when it is spoken to him."

"None on the Court be well disposed to the hearing of reason, I'm afraid," Deliverance said. "They are gripped with fear for their own reputations. So long as those wild girls cry witchcraft, 'tis impolitic for the court to do otherwise. And while the girls taste power through their fancy and their petty manias, the trials will continue."

Deliverance shut her eyes again, resting a hand on Mercy's knee. "May Christ in His infinite mercy forgive them."

"But you *must* come with me, Mama," Mercy cried, her voice growing shrill. "It were a grave injustice otherwise."

Deliverance laughed, her face grim. "Injustice?" she repeated. "By that wall the very picture of injustice lies." She gestured to the ruined,

broken little girl lying chained to the opposite wall. "There be no diabolism to witchery—to say that alone approaches sacrilege—but a witch I
be nonetheless. How can I vanish and leave innocents to die in my place?"
She stroked Mercy's cheek, bringing her daughter's chin up so that their
eyes met. "What would such an action indicate about my immortal soul?"

Deliverance's eyes bored into Mercy's, and for the first time, Mercy realized that she could not carry out her plan. How could she have thought otherwise? To ask her mother to cast aside eternal life and the hope of divine
salvation, that they might have a few paltry years together in this one? The
realization caused Mercy to confront her own selfishness, and her temples
flushed with shame. *I am a wretched girl*, Mercy thought, detesting herself,
for though she knew what needs must happen, she nevertheless yearned for
her mother to come with her still.

As these unpleasant thoughts battled together in Mercy's mind, crum-
pling her face, she felt her mother toying gently with her hair. "Now, listen
to me, my daughter," Deliverance said, her face grave. "I'll have you leave
from Salem Town. I'll brook no argument." She held up a hand, staving off
Mercy's sputtering objections. "You'll see from poor Dorcas that the Court
enjoins to look for malefaction within families. You're to go."

A vision of her life as it was soon to come unfolded before Mercy: a long
stark corridor, empty and void. Everything that she knew was in Salem
Town: her friends, her mother's friends, her meetinghouse. Her father was
buried there. Soon enough, her mother would be, too. At this thought her
lip started to tremble, and the beginning tremors of panic began in her belly
and sent malevolent shoots up behind her ribs, down her legs, into the hands
that were clutching and unclutching at her apron.

"Daughter," said her mother, once again gripping Mercy's chin and
forcing her to meet her gaze. "We've a plan. Our house I sold to Goodman
Bartlett these many months ago, after Mary Sibley come to us, remember? I
saw some of this in the egg-in-water, but knew not precisely when 'twas
coming. The proceeds I used to order a little house built up Marblehead way,

that's nearly done. 'Tis on Milk Street, the end of a long lane alone, well hidden in the woods."

While Deliverance spoke, confusion, surprise, and fear warred across Mercy's face as she struggled to keep up with what her mother was telling her. The house? It was sold? Sold these six-odd months ago? But she knew no one in Marblehead!

"I'll have you take the receipt book, and the Bible, and be gone," Deliverance continued. "You can take Goody Bartlett her bay mare. Goodman Bartlett, he being informed of our plans, can help to remove the furniture when Providence allows."

Mercy stared into her mother's face and in it read the absolute immobility of her will. She wished, not for the first time, that she could be as forthright as her mother was. So she was to be on her own—after tomorrow, she would be well and truly alone. Mercy wrapped her arms around herself, trying to force her fear and panic into submission.

"Mercy," Deliverance said softly, reaching out to trace her fingertips over her daughter's dampening, trembling face, "it is written in the New Testament, in Matthew, that God came down and spoke to Peter, saying that upon this rock shall his church be built." She smoothed Mercy's eyebrow with her thumb, and smiled.

"It is you who are Peter, my daughter. You who are the stone on which the church is built. For through you may His power in all its infinite goodness be felt upon the earth. And so you must not pass your days in fear and recrimination. You must endeavor to secure your safety, and then you must not forbear to resume your craft, for it is God's work that you do."

"But, Mama," Mercy said, voice breaking, overcome with how small, weak, and powerless she was in the face of all that was to come.

Deliverance shushed her, placing a finger on Mercy's lips with a firm shake of her head. "Enough. I'll have you go tonight. I'll not have you come to the western hill tomorrow."

At this Mercy buried her head in her mother's lap and began, silently, to keen. They sat that way for several hours, as the tiny window overhead grew dim, and then dark, and then a thin, watery gray.

THE CROWD ON THE WESTERN HILL OF SALEM TOWN HAD BEGUN TO assemble hours earlier. Somberly clad men and women milled about with a false seriousness arranged on their faces to mask their overweening excitement. Voices mixed together, each speaking in a register slightly higher than usual, blending into a grating, screeching miasma of self-righteousness and anticipation. Clusters of women dug into pockets tied at their waists, swapping tough bread and cheese. A band of children scampered around the legs of the adults, chasing one another, emitting happy screams. Under the heat of the afternoon the mud that had been churned up by boots and horse hoofs since well before dawn hardened into deep, riveted crusts, crumbling under ever more feet until beaten into a powdery dust that rose through the crowd, staining dresses, streaking faces, and casting a gray pall over the sun. In the distance, rising from within the haze of dust and the buzzing populace, stood a narrow wooden structure, consisting of a slender platform topped with a high wooden plank, from which hung six snaking lines of heavy rope.

At the bottom of the western hill, where the crowd thinned, a tallish girl in an overlarge, badly pinned coif stood, one hand holding the bridle of a skinny, antsy little horse weighted down with several bundles tied together with rope. At her feet sat a small dog, who seemed the exact same color as the cloud of dust; several onlookers who passed en route to the front of the crowd looked once and then again, unsure if the animal were really there. The girl's pallid face was devoid of expression, betraying none of the pleasure and excitement, or subdued smugness, that animated the faces around her.

As the day wore onward toward noon, the energy thrumming through the crowd grew in almost palpable layers. Thick masses of dread and anticipation built up in the chest of each onlooker; it was the same heavy, expectant mood that falls over a tavern just before a fistfight breaks out, a heady blend of fear and dismay, touched with excitement. The chattering became more lively, and when someone finally spotted the prison cart lumbering toward them in the distance, screams and bellows began to thread through the throng, punctuated by scraps of audible prayer and remonstration.

Mercy placed her hands on the Bartletts' bay mare's flank, balancing on her toes and peering over the horse's knobby back. The cart drew closer, led by a warden, with six women of varying heights and ages standing, their hands gripping the bars of the cart for balance, swaying and knocking over the ruts in the road.

As the cart reached the outer edges of the crowd, the first head of rotten cabbage went flying, striking old Susannah Martin squarely on the chest with a wet splat so loud that even Mercy, from her distant vantage point, could hear it. The stricken woman in the cart turned her face away, mouth pulled into a miserable frown as the rancid leaves clung to her already filthy dress. Rebecca Nurse, eyes still wizened and kind, incredibly, after her months of imprisonment, reached a bony finger up to pluck one of the leaves off of Susannah's collar, whispering a few words in her ear as she did so. Susannah nodded, mouth still frowning, and closed her eyes, seeming to pull deep within herself as the next cabbage exploded across the wooden side of the cart.

Mercy observed the condemned women huddling together, Sarah Good's mouth open, screeching at the mob now roiling around the wheels of the cart, arms reaching up to claw at the hems of the women's dresses, spoiled vegetables soaring ineffectually overhead or, sometimes, glancing off a cowering shoulder. Sarah Wildes held her arms up over her face, hands clutching her soiled coif, shoulders trembling, and Elizabeth Howe was seen to spit square upon the face of a bellowing matron in the crowd. In the middle of the group, half a head taller than the rest, Deliverance Dane stood, brow soft, gazing off into the far distance. Mercy squinted and saw that her mother's mouth was moving imperceptibly, but she could not tell what charm or prayer she might be saying. A maize cob sailed by, just missing Deliverance's cheek, but she did not flinch. Mercy straightened her shoulders, willing herself to feel the strength that she saw in her mother's face.

The cart slowed, weighed down by the throng lapping up against its sides but drawing ever nearer to the scaffold on the hilltop. The sound rising and bubbling from the crowd was so intense that Mercy thought she could almost see it, hovering, yellowish black, pouring forth from the gaping mouths and angry eyes of the villagers. The cart drew to a rickety halt a few feet from the base of the scaffold, and as the six women were led down from their perch, the mob surged to overtake them, held back only by the linked arms and entreaties of a small band of ministers from the surrounding towns. Chained together at the wrists, they were escorted up the steps to the wooden platform, and Mercy's grip tightened unconsciously around the thick leather bridle, causing the bay mare to jerk her chin and nicker.

Each woman was led by her wrists to stand directly behind the six hanging ropes, their loops lying in wait like six fat snakes. A magistrate mounted the scaffold steps, hooking his thumbs importantly into his overcoat and surveying the wild crowd. A rotten squash tumbled onto the platform at his feet, and he glowered, clapping his hands together sharply to indicate that the crowd must collect itself. Silencing began in the shadows of the scaffold, gradually working its way in fits and spurts across the surface of the crowd, and Mercy perceived the boiling noise lower to simmering.

"Susannah Martin," the magistrate began, voice shaking in the timbres of self-imagined gravitas, "Sarah Wildes, Rebecca Nurse, Sarah Good, Elizabeth Howe, and Deliverance Dane! You have been tried by the esteemed Court of Oyer and Terminer gathered together at Salem Town and found guilty of the heinous and diabolical crime of witchcraft, which being a crime against the very nature of God Himself, is punishable by death. Do any of you wish to confess, and name those agents of your very undoing? Will you do your duty to purge your community, struggling and alone in a wilderness fraught with sin, of the evils that lie in our midst?"

The six women stood, saying nothing, some with their heads bowed and others with their eyes closed, cheeks twitching. One of the ministers, a nervous man just down from Beverly Farms, stepped forward from where he had been hovering behind the magistrate, a small Bible clutched between his hands. Mercy's eyes narrowed, and she strained to hear what the minister was saying.

His voice did not carry with the weight of the magistrate's, but he seemed to be entreating each woman in turn to confess her witchcraft, and that if each would confess and submit herself to Jesus then she should be spared, if only she would name those others in the town who were her confederates in diabolism. Mercy's conclusions were confirmed when the man reached Sarah Good, her eyes manic, her distraction made more pronounced by her palpable fury.

"I, a witch!" she screamed, and the crowd gasped. She cast a black look at Deliverance, then thrust her chin at the crowd and bellowed, "*I* am no more a witch than you are a wizard, and if you take away my life, God will give you blood to drink!"

Upon this outburst the crowd exploded in a rage, more spoiled vegetables raining down upon the women on the scaffold, hurling oaths and condemnations upon them. Mercy's hands were clutched underneath her chin, her lips drawn back in a grimace, and two hot tears squeezed out of the corners of her eyes. She tried to collect herself, knowing that she must concentrate in order to accomplish the duty she had set for herself. She fastened her eyes on her mother, whose mouth was still moving silently, and whose eyes were traveling across the faces of the women standing at her side.

"Very well!" cried the magistrate. "If you women shall not give yourselves into the hands of your willing Savior and confess your sins here before God and your fellow man, then you are to be hanged by your necks until dead. Have you anything further to say for yourselves?"

Rebecca Nurse, straightening her thin and withered frame, folded her hands into a manner of prayer. The mob hushed, waiting to hear what this widely respected woman, this full church member no less, would say in the instant of her death. "May the most gracious Almighty God forgive them," she said, and the crowd was silent enough that Mercy had no trouble hearing her, though Goody Nurse's voice was reedy and weak. "For they know not what they do."

Murmurs burbled in the mouths of the watching populace as a man clad in black fitted a noose around Susannah Martin's neck. Susannah's face was a mottled shade of purple and red, weeping, mucus bubbling at her nose. The noose tightened down at the base of her skull, and Susannah started to emit a high gasping whimper, her breath coming faster in her chest as she gulped for air. The man moved to kick Susannah off the platform, and as his heavy boot made contact with her cowering back, a frisson of excitement ran through the crowd. At that moment, time seemed to slow imperceptibly, and Mercy saw Susannah's feet rise from the wooden platform, her eyes cast upward, her face contorted with fear and anguish, the rope trailing loose behind her as she traveled through the air. Then in an instant a great crack sounded over the heads of the crowd, and Susannah Martin's body swayed at the end of the taut rope, lifeless, left foot twitching. The crowd erupted, and Mercy heard an unseen woman cry out, "God be praised!"

The man in black moved to Sarah Wildes, who fell to bawling, begging, and pleading to be spared, that she was no witch, that she could never confess to a lie for that be a mortal sin, that she loved Jesus and craved His grace and forgiveness. The crowd hooted as the weeping woman clutched at her face, and the thin, nervous minister approached her to hold her by her hands and pray with her as the man fitted the noose around her neck. Her screams rose in pitch as the minister stepped aside, the man kicked her, then stopped suddenly as a great cracking sound tore across the empty hillside.

Throughout the preparations under way about her neck, Rebecca Nurse had held her hands folded under her chin, her eyes closed and her face serene. Her lips moved as she repeated the Lord's Prayer, and she did not interrupt her communion with God for even an instant as the noose was tightened and the foot went flying, sending her frail body cartwheeling into space. When the rope stayed her fall with a brutal snap the crowd gasped, as if they had not fully understood until that moment that this gentle, well-regarded woman would really be put to death.

An unbroken stream of curses and oaths had been pouring from the mouths of Sarah Good and Elizabeth Howe, each spitting and kicking out at the grasping hands below them amid the rising cheers of the mob. "Damn you all! God damn you all!" Sarah Good was screaming when the man's rough foot connected with her side, and she fell twisting and flailing over the side of the scaffold, her body stopped with a bounce by the choking grip of the rope.

Mercy tore her gaze away from the horror on the scaffold, pulling a handful of herbs from the pocket beneath her apron. She glanced down at the familiar animal seated at her feet, who looked up at her sadly. Steeling herself against the coming pain, Mercy began shredding the herbs in her hands, scattering them in a precise circle at her feet and muttering a long string of Latin words quietly enough to be unobserved.

Five women now dangled at the end of the long ropes, the kicking having drained from their feet, all their faces unaccountably smooth and white, loosened hair hanging around their faces, a vengeful smile even lingering around Sarah Good's lips, though her head now flopped at an impossible angle. The man in black clothes approached Deliverance Dane, and she held her head stiffly, folding her hands in prayer. Mercy fastened her gaze upon her mother, channeling all the love and fear and terror in her heart into a torrent of pure will, which coalesced into a barely visible glowing blue-white ball held in her outstretched hands. The man tightened the rope around the base of Deliverance's neck, and she gripped her hands together more tightly, bracing for the impact of the man's foot but still jerking in surprise when it came.

For a split second time halted, the crowd frozen immobile, Deliverance hovering suspended in the air before falling as the blue-white intention ripped forth from between Mercy's trembling fingers, cracking like a lightning bolt over the heads of the slavering populace, landing on Deliverance's forehead and bursting outward with a glittering of invisible sparks. In that instant Mercy felt the connection of her will with her mother's own, watched the unfolding flashes of her mother's life rush across her own eyes, glimpsing now the great ship pulling away from the coast of East Anglia, the smallness of her mother's feet running through a garden forty years ago, the bursting in the chest at the face of a young Nathaniel, the overwhelming love mixed with terror at the great squalling mouth of the infant Mercy, the sadness that it all must end, and the unshaken faith of something, something ineffable but beautiful, yet to come. All this passed into the palms of Mercy's hands as she filled her mother's body with the will and possibility to be released from pain, her brows knitted in effort. Then all at once she perceived the release as it happened, sensed her mother's soul freed from the constraints of her mortal envelope, feeling time resume and her mother's body grow limp, her face bright and serene, and Mercy's hands dropped to her sides, faint whiffs of smoke trailing up from her fingertips. Mercy's nerves and muscles quivered with the blinding pain that she had siphoned away, and she stumbled, nearly faint. She climbed with the last of her strength onto the sagging back of the bay mare, and by the time the sound of Deliverance's neck breaking echoed over the heads of the howling crowd, Mercy was gone.

CHAPTER TWENTY-THREE

Marblehead, Massachusetts

Autumnal Equinox

1991

T HE LONG DINING TABLE STOOD CLEARED OF ITS USUAL FLOTSAM, and its surface evinced a deep golden polish, as if someone had finally taken the time to get after it with lemon oil soap and a clean rag. The interior shutters had all been pinned back, welcoming what little late afternoon sunlight could penetrate the overgrown garden outside. As summer had broken down into the brittleness of autumn, the dense ivy on the windows of the Milk Street house had faded from a rich dark green to angry, vibrant red. Then, one day, a meddlesome wind dashed through the garden, lifting away the top scrim of leaves, sloughing them off like dead skin. Connie fastened back the last shutter and surveyed the orange and yellow garden with pleasure; as the garden layers fell away ahead of the advancing winter, she felt the house shaking off its vegetal shadows, filling with life as the world around it changed. As she watched, a fresh gust blew by, rolling along another armful of leaves. She inhaled, enjoying the crisp smell of the earth as it underwent its preparations.

She had preparations under way herself, she recalled, turning away from the window. On the table she had laid the thick Dane manuscript, open to the page marked *Method for the Redress of Fitts*, together with her own scribbled notes, diverse dried herbs collected from the garden and kitchen jars, including the mandrake root, and the bottle that she had smuggled out of the hospital. Next to these implements stood the antique oil lamp, lit and at the ready in the event that the daylight drained away too soon. She moved back to the hearth, where after some effort—the chimney was hesitant to draw, full with decades of undisturbed soot—she had kindled a low, steady fire. Stooping, Connie prodded the embers with a long poker, sending a glittering of sparks up along the brick sides of the fireplace. An iron cauldron hung, ridiculously, suspended on a hook to the side of the fire. She leaned the poker against the wall and looked down to where Arlo was sitting, primly, his paws together, under the table.

"All I need is a pointy hat," she remarked. He blinked.

The plan was simple. She had placed the charm under Sam's pillow already. Now the recipe prescribed a short ritual that would draw the "malefactor"—she took that to mean whatever agent was making him sick, but the manuscript was ambiguous on that score—out of a person suffering from fits. She would conduct the ritual, and it should pull the illness out of Sam; the charm under his pillow would keep it from coming back in. She was prepared for the practice to hurt somewhat; with each successive experiment that she had conducted, either with the plants or the divination tools, she had felt a higher degree of pain the harder she worked. Connie placed her fingertips on the table and closed her eyes. Did Grace feel pain when she cleared the auras of her Santa Fe friends? Connie would have to ask her. A tiny smile pulled at her lips. The rational voice that dwelt in Connie's most private core still balked at what she was about to do, but that voice had grown smaller in the past few weeks. Instead she focused her thoughts on Grace's warm face, beaming her unshaken confidence in what Connie could do. And she thought about Sam.

She opened her eyes. "Okay then," Connie announced to the empty room, and she pushed the sleeves of her turtleneck sweater up over her elbows. Running a finger down the manuscript page, she found her place in the text and began.

"To determine if a man's mortal suffering be caused by bewitchment," she read aloud, "catch his water in a witch-bottle and throw in some pins or nails and boil it upon a very hot fire."

For the past few days Connie had been ruminating on the nature of this word *bewitchment*. The language of this strange work seemed slippery across the ages, with meanings shifting over time in the same way that the description of the book had changed according to who was doing the describing. Modernity took "bewitchment" to mean something caused by magical intervention. But early modern people lived in a world that largely predated science, operating without sophisticated understanding of the difference between correlation and causation. Connie had a suspicion that "bewitchment" might imply not magical causes per se, but only nonorganic ones. Poisoning, say, rather than common illness. Something attributable to an outside source, rather than to the mysterious workings of Providence. Just because a situation had a magical solution might not necessarily mean that it had a magical cause.

She took hold of the antique bottle, half full with Sam's stolen urine, and released the stopper. Two or three pitted old pins were still inside, rusted in place, but she dropped in three brand-new silver eight-penny nails that she had purchased that week at the Marblehead hardware store. She added an open safety pin, a plastic-pearl-topped sewing pin that pricked her foot one morning in the bathroom, the still-threaded needle from within the grinning little corn husk doll on the mantel, a few new staples retrieved from the stapler in the Widener Library reference room, and an upholstery tack pried from the underside of a pew in the church where Sam was working on the day that he fell from the scaffold. Each addition tinked against the glass bottleneck, falling into the water with a hiss and releasing a faint but perceptible curl of smoke. Connie replaced the stopper, pausing to watch the water inside begin to simmer and boil, though the bottle was still standing on the table, away from any source of heat.

She then turned her attention to the fire, bending to stoke it again with the long poker. Connie added a few pinecones, which snapped and hissed, bursting immediately into flame and jostling the fire to burn hotter. The manuscript listed a long array of herbs and plants to be burned for "sure withdrawal." In the past few days Connie had gathered as great a variety as she could from the garden and woods immediately surrounding the house, hanging them in the kitchen to dry. First she tossed in a dried bunch of thyme, rosemary, feverfew, sage, and mint, the aromatic herbs disintegrating in a fragrant blue puff of smoke, most of which tumbled upward to the chimney, but some of which spilled over the top lip of the hearth, drifting to the ceiling of the dining room. Her nose twitched, enjoying the sharp sensation of the oils in the herbs popping in the fire. Next Connie threw in a fragile bunch of flowering angelica, its lacy flowers desiccated and crumbling. The fire leapt to consume the dried flowers, and Connie's shadow ducked and shimmied across the floor behind her as she worked, her face shining orange in the firelight.

Last, she reached for the Plymouth gentian, a tender pink blossom that was almost impossible to find, which she had discovered struggling for life along the slurried bank of the little water hole called Joe Brown's pond, a few minutes' walk from Milk Street. The flowers had wilted without really drying, and as she took them up they drooped in her hands. She pitched them into the fire, and to her surprise the fire spat forth a bright white orb that seemed to explode with an audible poof. Connie swallowed, nerves clawing at her belly, and forced herself to turn back to the manuscript.

"Throw the bottle into the fire whilst reciting the Lord's Prayer followed by this most effective incantation," she read, hands planted on her hips. "Okay," she said, wondering if saying so aloud would push her fear away.

It didn't.

"Okay," she said again, grasping the bottle with a shaking hand and holding it up into the fading sunlight. The fluid inside was churning and bubbling, the sharp pins and nails swirling in a great angry froth. "Our Father," she began, "Who art in Heaven. Hallowed be thy name."

As she spoke, Connie turned, bringing the bottle nearer the fire. "Thy Kingdom come, Thy will be done, on Earth as it is in Heaven." The flames in the fire jumped, lapping higher against the hearth bricks, and Connie could feel the hot miasma rising out of the embers and pressing into the room. "Give us this day our daily bread," she continued, squinting her eyes against the heat. "And forgive us our debts"—she chose the old, straightforward, Congregational wording—"as we forgive our debtors. And lead us not into temptation!" Her voice rose; she had never really listened to the words closely, but now the fire was growing fierce, its flames whitening, and she felt bizarrely as if she must be heard over the noise of its crackling. She held the bottle suspended over it with two singeing fingers, and blisters began to bubble forth. "But deliver us from evil! For Thine is the Kingdom! And the power!" At this a tongue of flame licked hungrily up toward the glass, meeting the bottom of the bottle. "And the glory! For ever and ever! Amen!"

She dropped the bottle. It spiraled, slowly, from her fingers down, down, down until it landed with an explosion of sparks, and the fire closed over it with a ferocious roar. Now she had the incantation to recite. Unsure what to do with her hands, Connie folded them at her chest in a prayerful attitude and bowed her head. The new blisters on the hand that had been holding the bottle felt tender and soft under the pressure of her fingers.

"Agla!" she said, and the fire spat in response, a thick column of white smoke beginning to billow out from the center of the burning logs. "Pater! Dominus!" With each word, the white smoke grew thicker until the chimney could not swallow it all and it began to spill forth from the hearth to the ceiling, crawling in waves across the rafters overhead before pouring through the open windows. "Tetragrammaton! Adonai! Heavenly Father I beseech thee, bring the evildoer unto me!"

As the last words escaped her lips, the white smoke seemed to condense into a tangible substance, or long-tailed creature, hurrying up out of the fire and skittering across the ceiling to escape through the windows. In that instant, with a rushing, gulping sound the fire tamped itself down. Connie opened her eyes to find the room suddenly calm, the smoke entirely vanished, the fire crackling and friendly.

She surveyed the room, hands still folded under her chin. There was the fire, burning politely. There was the bottle, blackened with smoke, nestled in the embers. There was the dining table, still holding the manuscript and an unused assortment of herbs and plants. Her eyes traveled over every surface in the room, wondering if she had just imagined it all—the smoke, the noise, the leaping flames.

"Is that it?" she asked the empty room. Arlo was nowhere to be seen. She looked under the table and found him there, huddled in a little ball the color of night, watching her with worried eyes. "I think you can come out," she whispered, beckoning to him. "It's over." He refused to move. Connie stood back up, frowning. Something was not right. The house felt suspended, alert. She waited, unsure what to do next.

As she stood by the table, fingertips resting on the tabletop, eyes wide, she heard a rumbling in the distance, like a heavy truck rolling over a wooden bridge, only the sound seemed to be drawing nearer. In the time it took for her to begin to move around the table and make her way to the nearest window, the sound built and grew, sending tremors through the ground under her feet, bending and rocking the wide pine floorboards. Connie fell to her knees, the shaking moving into the walls of the house, clattering the crockery in the dining room alcove and swaying the hanging spider plants in wide, jerky arcs. She crawled under the table, floor thumping and vibrating under her hands and knees. From the kitchen she heard the sound of a jar exploding across the linoleum floor. She reached Arlo, wrapping her arms around his small body just as the rumbling stopped with a single great *whump*, the sound of the front door flying open. Connie extended her head out from under the table, mouth flopping open in surprise.

There, adjusting his club tie, stood Manning Chilton. She backed away on her knees under the table, getting to her feet as she heard him start to chortle.

"Gracious, my girl," he boomed from the front door, stepping into the house. "And I thought you were exaggerating. This is a wretched hovel, indeed."

Her stomach contracted in fear, but a little voice in the back of her mind reminded her about the burned symbol on the door. *Better to be on your own turf,* she heard Grace say, voice knowing. *Nobody wants to keep you safe more than I do.* Connie straightened, face contorted in confusion.

"What," she stammered, confused. "What are you doing here?" She cast one eye back down to the recipe, double-checking the words. "Bring the evildoer unto me" the incantation said. And then she saw that she had overlooked a last line. *When his Water is well Boilt so shall the Sorcerer be drawn unto the fyre,* the manuscript promised. *And so with pins and crafte may he be entreated to free his Victim from his Diabolicall machinations. Refer to receipts for Death-philtres to ascertain other means.* Then the page supplied the long list of herbs for sure withdrawal. At the very bottom of the page, in faded script such that she had not noticed it before, was written *Cont'd.*

Connie glanced quickly up at her advisor, who was approaching with a thin smile attached to his face. "I've been meaning to drop by for some time," he remarked, voice jovial. "I believe that you have something for me, do you not?" He looked bemused, as if a theory he had long held had just been proven correct.

"How," she began, swallowing when she found her throat sticky and dry. "How did you get here?"

He chuckled, drawing nearer. "Why, in a car, of course."

Connie had read several historical accounts of the witch-bottle technique, all of which were ambiguous in their depictions of what would happen. She had thought that it would draw the illness—the malefactor—out of Sam, perhaps into the bottle in the fire. But now she saw that the instructions could be read another way. It could be seen to draw the *agent responsible for the illness* to the fire. Chilton might have thought he was stopping by of his own volition, but the realization began to dawn on Connie that, in fact, his appearance was the result of the work she had just done. Her mouth fell open, horrified.

He bent to inspect one of the shield-back chairs that Connie had pushed to the side of the room. "Eighteenth-century. Marvelous," he said to no one in particular. Reaching a long finger forward, he brushed a fingernail against the patterned splat. "Inlaid," he confirmed to himself. He straightened, looking again at her. "Yes. Well, in truth I was spending the afternoon working away on some compounds in my office. And then, rather abruptly, it occurred to me that I might come see you." He smiled again, his mouth devoid of humor. "I hope that the quicksilver doesn't boil over. Imagine how I shall explain an office chemical fire at the next history department meeting."

"I was . . ." Connie began, her mind attempting to skip ahead of her tongue. But why would the witch-bottle spell have summoned *him*?

She watched her advisor poking through her grandmother's dining room with detached interest, saying, "So this is the old bird's house that you've been so bothered with," and rejected the obvious conclusion as impossible. Chilton was a distinguished, ambitious old academic. He wrote books, he delivered lectures, he smoked a pipe, for God's sake. He was concerned with truth, he said, with reputation. He was ambitious, yes, and single-minded in his desire. But he was no poisoner.

The logical voice that Connie had pushed away now screamed at her in her mind. *Alchemy! Compounds!* Chilton was desperate to get ahold of the physick book to further his own alchemical research. He had tried to prod her using praise and the promise of professional success. Then he had tried dogging her as she hunted for the book in the Harvard library.

Connie stared at her advisor, her eyes growing wider as the logical chain began to form in her mind. Chilton wanted the book for himself. He had to force her to find it for him. And if he knew what the book was used for, then what better motivation could he supply?

Connie's hand flew to the manuscript, horror dawning across her face. "It was you," she said, voice hollow as she realized that Chilton had been willing to risk Sam's very life in service to his ambition. "You're the one."

"Hmmm," Chilton said, inspecting the portrait hanging on the far wall of the dining room, of the broad-foreheaded, wasp-waisted young woman, a small dog just now visible in the shadow under her arm. "Did you know, Miss Goodwin, that ancient Arabian alchemists believed in the doctrine of the two principles? Would you happen to know what those two principles were?"

He looked over his shoulder at her, expectantly. She stared at him, uncomprehending, sick with revulsion.

"No? All metals, they thought, consisted of different proportions of mercury, to correspond to the moon, and sulfur, for the sun. Mercury bears the essential metallic property—or quicksilver, I should say, as Mercury is actually its planetary name—while sulfur provides the combustibility. They weren't referring quite literally to quicksilver and common sulfur, of course, but to the metaphorical qualities of each. The aesthetics of substance." He cocked an eyebrow. "Great ones for metaphor, the alchemists," he added, circling around the dining table, past the portrait. Connie moved around the opposite side of the table, gathering the manuscript to her chest, balled fists clutching handfuls of herbs that had been lying on the table.

"To these two fundamental elements that make up all metals, a distinguished man named Paracelsus added a third: salt, which he thought accounted for . . ." Chilton seemed to grope for the correct word.

"Earthiness," he finished. "Fixity. Groundedness. So, metal, fire, and earth. The three fundamental elements which, in pure form, are the building blocks of all reality. The original alchemical recipe for gold brought together the very purest forms of mercury and sulfur: the liquid—metallic, the difficult to contain—together with the explosive—the yellowish, the stuff of demons. And salt, for stability. For tangibility, even wholesomeness. One might also think of these three elemental forms as representative of the spirit"—he ticked off each on a finger—"the soul, and the body. Like many folkloric, magical, even"——here he arched an eyebrow meaningfully at Connie——"*religious* systems, the alchemists put great stock in multiples of three. Naturally, the central problem facing the alchemists was one of purity. How to refine a substance into its purest——its *best*——most elemental form."

A wicked smile spread across his face as he continued. "Of course, when added in the correct proportion to a supply of drinking water, say, the effects of these basic elements on all three aspects of a man's person can be quite . . . pronounced. Even lethal. Particularly antimony. Its alchemical symbol is an orb with a cross on top of it——the same symbol used to denote royalty. The circle at the center of the glyph for the philosopher's stone. And"——he chuckled——"a rather close relative of arsenic."

Connie thought back to Sam's description of the water in his cooler at the church, how it had had a metallic taste. She remembered that no one seemed to know who had called the ambulance that day. And then she saw Sam falling, his leg shattering against the hard back of the wooden pew, heard the wet crunch of his body crushed by gravity, and her vision clouded with red.

"Why?" she demanded, her voice growing stronger. "Why would you harm *him*? I nearly had the book. I was going to give it to you."

"Ah," Chilton said, his hand roaming over an earthenware teapot. He lifted it up to the thin light in the window, flared his nostrils with disapproval, and set it down again. Then he gestured to the book that she was grasping to herself. "As a matter of fact, you apparently *have* the book. And I don't recall being informed."

He watched her, but she said nothing. Chilton turned to gaze out the window over the garden, his hands folded behind his back. When his eyes were averted she quickly began to shred the herbs she held in her hands, ripping the stems and leaves apart.

"I did try to encourage you," he said, his back still to her. "I told you what an important find it would be for your own work. I even"——his voice took on a wounded cast, as if he could not bear the disappointment that she had brought upon him—"invited you to let me present you to my colleagues at the Colonial Association. To share in my triumph. I have been grooming you, my girl. At great sacrifice to my own busy schedule, it must be said. Preparing you to rise to the very top of your field, under my tutelage." He heaved a woeful sigh. "The conference, alas, is at the end of the month. And you have brought me nothing."

While he spoke, Connie closed her eyes, recalling the instructions that had been written on the page in the manuscript. The text read:

When the Sorcerer appeareth, hee may be implor'd to reverse the malefaction by divers means. 1. Ref. death-philtres, pages 119–137,

I can't do that. Connie thought. I can't kill him! Her hands scrabbled through the herbs that were scattered across the tabletop, sifting the dead leaves through her fingers. *I don't know what to do!* her inner voice whimpered, but she locked it away in a disused corner of her mind and concentrated on the work. A growl rumbled from under the table.

2. Simple reversal, whereby the bottel its contents be placed in a pot upon the fyre within not more than three feet of said Malefactor combined with stinging Nettle and ground roots of Mandrake altogether to bring his bewitchment back unto him, and 3. if lessen'd effect be desired withal do the same adding Goldenseal and mint whilst reciting the Most effective Incantation.

Connie opened her eyes and saw that Chilton was still gazing out of the dining room window, shaking his head and tsking.

"A shame," he was saying. "I had had such high hopes. As you have probably gathered, I am on the point of achieving the one true recipe for the philosopher's stone. A discovery that mankind has been awaiting for thousands of years." His hand rested again on the earthenware teapot, tightening its grip. "In point of fact, I have already promised to sell the rights to the formula, and for not a small sum, either. The philosopher's stone is not only real, but likely an ancient name for an arcane arrangement of carbon atoms, able to bring purity to any disordered molecular system in everything from physics to biochemistry. All the metaphors and riddles in the alchemical texts suggested it. Valueless, and all around us! Unknown, and yet known to all. Carbon is the basis of all life on earth, after all. In varying degrees of purity and arrangement, it assembles into coal, diamond, even the human body. It is like God's Tinkertoy." The hand wrapped around the teapot squeezed, and a crack suddenly shot through the pot's side with a snap.

His laughter stopped abruptly as an image assembled itself before Connie's eyes, of Chilton sitting at his desk in the Harvard history department, his ear pressed to a telephone receiver, his face purpling as a male voice said, *Well, of course I was interested, but you didn't really expect me to take it to the board, did you?* The voice broke into gasps of laughter as Chilton's upper lip quavered, and a pencil clutched in his fist snapped in two as he uttered, *I just need a little more time, dammit!* Through the telephone the laughing voice said, *Face it, Manny. You've got nothing for me,* just as the image pulled apart like oiled tissue and Connie found herself back in her grandmother's hall.

Chilton continued steadily. "I plan to reveal the formula at the Colonial Association, bringing history and science together at last. And then I can finally stop being little more than a glorified schoolteacher." He spat out this last word with surprising venom. "But unfortunately, a crucial element is missing. One that I am unable to define. A process, I am reasonably sure. A final step." His eyes met hers, and she saw in his face the dark, dull throb of desperation.

"Let us say that I, too, needed to broaden my source base," Chilton continued, voice growing cold. "Of course I knew you were a top-notch researcher; that's why I admitted you to the program in the first place. But when you told me of this extant shadow book, well . . ." His lips drew back, bloodless and frigid. "You do surprise me, my girl. References to an original colonial-era shadow book, used by an actual witch, and the first clue found in your blessed old grandmother's house, no less! I knew then that you would be of even greater use to me than I had anticipated." He started to approach the table. The growling grew louder.

Connie held his gaze, her fingers surreptitiously tearing a corner off of the mandrake root and ripping it to shreds. She did not speak. A flicker of tension twitched in her cheek. She watched him approach, her hands moving automatically through their preparations, as if they had always known what to do, leaving her consciousness free to contemplate how loathsome her advisor had become to her, how his ego and hunger for prestige had made him twisted and debased, how behind his eyes she saw a soul whose very humanity had been squashed under the impossible weight of his ambition.

"As you know, I place no faith in innate talent, Miss Goodwin," Chilton said, his voice morphing into a snarl as he drew even closer, his hand tracing the shield back of one of the chairs tucked under the dining table.

"One cannot go skipping about, expecting one's romantic inclinations to lead the way. No. The cornerstone of the best practice of history is effort. It is work! I had to devise a way to hasten your research, as my own meager encouragements were proving insufficient." He paused. "At the same time, I could also ascertain if the shadow book was as powerful as I believed. A little alchemical compound in the body can confound modern medicine, but it should be no match for a true premodern physick book, particularly in the hands of a *motivated* querent." His eyes began to gleam. "After I observed you one afternoon in the, ah, shall we say *affectionate* company of a young man, why, the idea naturally presented itself.

"And I was right," he exclaimed, surging toward Connie. He lunged for the book that she held in her arms, grabbing ahold of her shoulders. "Give it to me," he growled, fingers digging painfully into her flesh, his sour breath hot on her face. She screamed, twisting herself in his grip, struggling to free herself, but his weight crushed down on her, one gnarled hand prying for the book.

All at once a blurred form leapt out from under the table, enfolding Chilton's arm in a snarling flurry. Chilton cried out in pain, dropping to his knees in an attempt to disengage his forearm from the tearing, jerking grip of the dog, who held fast to the flesh, as if killing a rat. As Chilton fell, Connie lunged forward, plunging her hand straight into the crackling fire to grasp the antique bottle. Its glass was so fearsomely hot it almost felt soft to the touch, her fingertips sinking into the searing gel as she lifted it from within the flames and dropped it into the waiting cauldron. It carried away a charred layer of skin from Connie's fingers, coils of smoke drifting up from her hands as she squinted her eyes against the overweening consciousness of pain.

She lurched back to the end of the table, grasping the shredded heap of mandrake root in one raw and bleeding hand, skin sizzling at the touch of the deadly root, and flinging it toward the cauldron, where it fell with a sinister hiss, releasing a puff of oily black smoke. Meanwhile Chilton hoisted himself up with a grunt, leaning on the table. His foot shot out and connected with the dog, who let out an angry yelp as he went skidding across the floor before vanishing in the instant before he would have struck the opposite wall.

"I want it," Chilton commanded through gritted teeth. "Give it to me. I must have it!" The sleeve of his tweed jacket and oxford shirt hung in red ribbons from the elbow, and he staggered to his feet, wrapping the trailing rags of clothing around the ripped, oozing gashes that crisscrossed his arm. He crept nearer, loops of blood falling from the shredded arm that he now held clutched to his chest.

With a quick movement, Connie pushed through the crumbled leaves and herbs on the table, her grasp moving automatically to a few stalks of stringy white flowers with broad, rough-textured leaves holding hard, waxy berries—the goldenseal. She took it up together with the nettles and crushed the stalks and flowers in her palms, naked skin screaming against the pain, and dropped them into the pot. Beneath the cauldron, the fire dodged and shimmied, flinging her and Chilton's shadows crazily about the room.

"It won't work for you!" Connie screamed, clutching the manuscript to herself and stepping back.

"It will! I will make it work!" he bellowed, and he reached out again with a stagger, clawing at her forearm. "It has to work! The philosopher's stone is the conduit! It is the medium for God's power here on earth! The rock on which God's church is built!"

She wrenched away from his grip, edging nearer the hearth.

"No," she said, her voice grave. "It's not for you. I won't let you have it."

And then she turned, her heart contracting, and opened her arms, casting the manuscript into the fire.

Surprise broke across Chilton's face, dissolving quickly into dismay and then anger as a cry worked its way through all the layers of restraint that he had acquired in his sixty-odd years—layers applied first in the echoing hallways of the Back Bay town house where he idly loitered, book in hand, overlooked; then in his Gold Coast dormitory at Harvard, as he pulled a silver-backed hairbrush through locks that simply refused to lie along his scalp; next at his club, as he tried to master his grip on his pipe; layers waxed in the secret hallways of the Faculty Club and buffed in the faculty meetings as he watched anxiously for the inevitable discovery that his work, his life's work, would fail. Layers that now peeled away, revealing in Chilton's eyes the naked certainty that his deepest fear was true, that all the prestige that had been laid at his feet and burnished, carefully, over the years of his life could never suffice, could never mask the fact that he was a weak man, Manning Chilton was, a trembling and grasping little man, and that no alchemical transformation could be wrought on his soul to make him into the great scholar—into the great person—that he yearned to be.

Chilton fell to his knees in anguish, scrabbling at the glaring embers of the fire, reaching and darting his fingers in to retrieve the manuscript leaves that were already starting to curl and blacken at their edges.

Connie watched him fall, kneeling by the cauldron, which had started to bubble and steam, and she began to recite the Lord's Prayer in a whisper. Her heart filled with pity; she hated to see this man, her once-esteemed mentor, reduced to a cowering, clutching, horrid animal. In his own desire for truth, for the wealth, prestige, and promise that the philosopher's stone offered, he had traded away his humanity, leaving little more than a shattered void. The stone was everything that he wanted, and could never have.

She reached down to the floor, picking up the sprig of dried mint that, when added to the brew in the pot, would finally pull the sickness out of Sam. She dropped it into the cauldron, and as she did so, the fire burst forth with a smattering of bluish sparks, and Chilton pulled his burned hands away with a wail. For another moment Connie gazed on him, and then, steeling herself, she completed the incantation.

"Agla," she said softly, and the thick white smoke began to congeal in a column in the center of the fire. "Pater, Dominus," she continued, as the dense smoke wrapped its arms around the steaming cauldron. "Tetragrammaton, Adonai. Heavenly Father I beseech thee, bring the evildoer unto *he*," she finished in a whisper. The white smoke bent in a sinuous arc from around the cauldron, reaching into Chilton's mouth, eyes, and ears, and seeming to flow into his body. His eyes became obscured by smoke, and he stayed kneeling, immobile for an instant before the smoke pulled back out of his body, emptying from his mouth and billowing in reverse back into the belly of the fire. He bent forward, hacking and coughing, his arms clutching at his midsection, a long shuddering cry wrenching forth from a dark, secret part of himself.

All at once Connie felt the strength drain out of her legs, and she slid to the floor. Leaning her head against the leg of the table she rested, cradling her badly singed hands in her lap. The burns felt scraped and raw, and as she flexed her fingers, the nerves in her skin tore and spat. Out of the corner of her eye, she saw the thin yellow mandrake venom bubble up out of the burns in her hands and lift in invisible droplets into the air, vanishing, pushed up out of her skin.

For a while she leaned there, watching the now tame fire crackling as Chilton wept silently into the hands pressed over his face. Then, after a few minutes, a gurgling tremor gripped his midsection and throat, and his limbs suddenly stiffened as the first seizure tore through his body, rolling his eyes backward in his head and knotting his muscles in contortions that were horrifying to behold.

"I'm sorry," she whispered, one tear trickling down her cheek as Arlo materialized by her side.

POSTLUDE

Cambridge, Massachusetts
Late October
1991

A FIRE BURNED MERRILY IN THE BRICK HEARTH AT THE REAR OF Abner's Pub, and as Connie arrived in the doorway, she smiled. As usual, someone—maybe even Abner himself—had gone overboard with baby pumpkins, heaping little pyramids of them at the center of every table, together with paper cups full of markers and paint pens for the addition of wicked, toothy faces. At the bar, a woozy undergraduate sat wearing a cocktail dress and clip-on mouse ears, jabbing her finger into the chest of a young man in formal dress, his bow tie and cummerbund speckled with snarling pigs. "No, *you* lissen," the girl was slurring, and Connie laughed.

"Halloween is the same here every year," she tossed over her shoulder at Sam, who had appeared behind her.

"Isn't that what you like about it?" he replied, edging past her, carrying a duffel bag. She grinned.

Connie spotted a hand thrust above the heads in the bar, flapping at her, and she and Sam picked their way through the throng to the booth near the back. It proved to belong to Liz, who rose from her seat to enfold Connie in an enthusiastic hug. "There she is!" cried Liz, squeezing her briefly before turning to hug Sam.

"Thank God you're back," said Thomas, shaking his head. "I am totally not prepared to answer these essay questions. Do you realize that grad school applications ask you to write an *intellectual biography*? What does that even mean?" Liz prodded a sharp elbow into his ribs. "Ow!" he cried. "What?"

Connie dropped her shoulder bag, still stuffed with books and dirty clothing, on the floor and settled into a vacant chair with a sigh.

"So. How was the conference?" Janine Silva asked, nodding greetings at Sam.

Connie smiled out of the corner of her mouth. "Pretty good, I guess," she said as Sam broke in. "C'mon! Tell them what happened."

"It's not a big deal," she demurred, gratefully accepting the old-fashioned that a waitress had deposited on a coaster in front of her.

"What isn't?" asked Liz through Sam's insisting "It is *so*!"

Everyone at the table watched with expectant eyes as Connie delicately sipped at the brimming cocktail glass, her eyes closed. When she opened them, everyone was still waiting.

"Cambridge University Press said they want to see a copy of my dissertation when it's done," she admitted, and the table vibrated with appreciative whoops.

"I knew it," Janine Silva said, shaking her head. "Do you have a title yet?"

Connie nodded, reaching for her notes. " 'Rehabilitating the Cunning Woman in Colonial North America: The Case of Deliverance Dane,' " she recited from the page. Liz and Thomas chinked their glasses together. Janine smiled with approval.

"A little wordy," her new advisor cautioned, "but there's still time to revise it."

"So the paper went over well, is what you're saying," Liz said. "I wasn't sure the Colonial Association was ready for a feminist reconception of vernacular magic."

"I wasn't sure either," Connie said, "but apparently they are."

"How are you liking chairing the department, Professor Silva?" Liz asked, with a pointed look at Thomas, indicating that he had put her up to asking the question. He blushed, and Connie felt a wave of protective affection for him. Being in proximity to professors always made his hands clammy.

Janine shrugged. "Well, I'll tell you," she said, sipping at her beer, "it's a lot of work. It was a real shock, having to step in right at the beginning of the semester like that." She paused, looking down with a shake of her head. "What a shame, what happened to Manning."

"What did happen?" asked Sam, accepting his own drink from the waitress.

"He fell ill," she said, eyebrows rising. "Nobody really knew what it was at first, but then when they opened his office to get me the departmental files, they found all kinds of crazy heating elements and compounds in there. Heavy metals. Toxic stuff." She sighed, looking down into her glass. "It looks like he started out by dabbling in some of those old alchemy textbooks that he had kicking around, you know, just to see what would happen. But now they think that he must have poisoned himself. Gradually, over several months or years. Frankly," she said, voice growing serious, "it would account for some of his odd behavior over the past year. He was always an eccentric guy, of course, but lately . . ." She sighed again. "Such a pity. He used to do such good work."

"He can't teach anymore?" asked Thomas, looking crushed. Connie knew that Thomas had counted on working with Chilton in the coming year.

"He's on indefinite leave," Janine said. "Apparently, he has some extensive neurological damage from the exposure. Causes him to have grand mal seizures, almost two a week!" She took a sip of her beer, shaking her head. "Can you imagine? At his age." Sam glanced over at Connie, who avoided his gaze.

"At any rate," Janine continued, "the university didn't think he could maintain a steady teaching schedule, much less chair the department. There's talk of giving him emeritus status if his health should stabilize. But they're not certain that it will. Speaking of which, how are you doing, Sam? Connie told me that you had kind of a rough summer."

"I did, just for a little while," Sam said, looking down at his hands. "Fell from a scaffolding at a restoration job. Really messed up my leg. They think I may have clocked myself on the head, too, and that's what really worried everyone. Especially my parents. But one day last month it all just sorted itself out." He eyed Connie. She smiled at him.

"Really?" asked Thomas.

"Yeah." Sam laughed. "I've been getting regular checkups and scans, but they tell me everything looks fine. You should have heard my father. 'This wouldn't have happened if you'd gone to law school,' he kept saying." Everyone at the table groaned.

"See—it's not too late, Thomas," Connie said, nudging her student under the table.

"But now you're back to restoration work? What do you call it?" Janine asked.

"Steeplejacking," Sam said, smiling crookedly. "Yeah. I'm just a lot more careful now with the safety harness." He turned to Liz. "You've got to come up and see what I've done with the house. It looks incredible."

"Does it have electricity yet?" Liz asked, dubious.

"Not quite," he said. "Grace insists she likes it better this way. Brings her closer to the changing rhythms of the earth, or whatever." He rolled his eyes.

"When do I get to meet your mom, Connie?" asked Janine. "You mentioned that she'd moved back, but do you ever get to see her?"

Connie smiled, twisting the coaster under her cocktail glass. "Grace kind of keeps to her own schedule," she said.

The truth was that even though Grace announced at the end of September that she had reconsidered selling the Milk Street house, preferring instead to return from Santa Fe to her "root soil," she found reasons not to go to Cambridge. Too much to do in the garden, or too many aura clearings to attend to. Connie suspected that she just preferred to have Connie come to her. She had taken to spending weekends puttering with her mother in the house, which had been freed of its tax abatement by the considerable profit from selling Grace's place in New Mexico. Together they cleared room for the herbs in the garden, trimmed the overgrowth of ivy on the windows. They did not talk about it, preferring instead to work in silence. But one afternoon, while she was poring over some scribbled notes at Granna's paw-footed desk, Connie looked up to see a rag drag an empty dust-free stripe through the window above the desk, and through the empty stripe appeared her mother standing outside in the garden, rag in hand, smiling, long hair swinging. And Connie smiled back.

LATER THAT NIGHT, CONNIE AND SAM WALKED ALONG THE BRICK-cobbled streets of Cambridge, supporting Liz's sagging weight between them as they headed home to Saltonstall Court.

"I still can't believe you *burned it*," Liz moaned, head lolling. "All that gorgeous Latin! Stuff that no one has seen in hundreds of years! Oh!" She leaned more heavily on Connie, resting her head on her friend's shoulder with mock drama. "So selfish! There was a whole classics dissertation to be had in there, you know."

Connie renewed her grip on Liz's waist, hoisting her friend up a curb.

"I hated to do it," Connie said. "But Chilton was right there. It was the only thing I could think of. He thought the missing element of the philosopher's stone was in the book. Said something about it being the conduit for God's power on earth." She shuddered. "I was terrified!"

"Peter," Liz slurred. "Thass the philosopher's stone."

"What?" asked Connie and Sam together, eyes meeting over Liz's drooping head.

"I thay to you that thou art Peter, and on this rock I shall build my church! Or whatever." Liz waved her hand like a Roman orator and then giggled. "*Peter* is Greek for *rock*. Issa tautology. Bible's full of riddles like that." She hiccuped. "You'd think he woulda known that. Should of done classics, is what."

Connie whistled through her teeth. "Incredible. So it's not a substance. Peter is the rock—on Peter shall I build my church." She paused. "So Chilton was sort of half-right. The philosopher's stone *was* real. But it wasn't a rock, and it wasn't something that could be made from elements and experiments. It was a person—an idea. Someone who could spread God's healing power on earth."

"Wow," said Sam.

Connie cast her gaze up to the night sky overhead. The orange lights of the city washed away some of the stars that could be seen in Marblehead, but that night she thought she could just see them, glittering through the haze. For a moment she closed her eyes, enjoying her secret knowledge.

Finally, she could not resist. "I'll just say this, and you had better not say a word. Promise?" She looked into Liz's eyes, which already were shining through their mist of alcohol.

"What?" Liz whispered.

Connie leaned in, bringing her mouth close to Liz's waiting ear. "Radcliffe had made more progress microfilming their special collections than Harvard had."

There was a moment of silence as Connie's statement penetrated Liz's brain.

"Oh, my God," Liz said, looking into the middle distance. She blinked, and then stopped walking, turning to Connie. "Oh, my *God*. Radcliffe? I thought you said that Mr. Whatsisname Industrialist gave all the Salem Athenaeum books to Harvard," she said, voice a fraction louder.

"Yeah," Connie replied, mouth cracking open into a grin. "Remember how I could never get a handle on how the book should be described? How here it was an almanac, there it was a shadow book, there it was a recipe book. . . ."

"Holy mackerel," Liz said, understanding sparkling in her eyes.

"Exactly," said Connie.

"You can't be serious," Liz exclaimed, bringing one hand to her forehead.

"Radcliffe," Connie continued, resuming her stroll toward their dormitory, "as we all know, has one of the most renowned collections of cookbooks in the world."

"Incredible," Liz breathed. "No wonder Chilton never found it."

"Yeah," Connie said, flushing a little. Sam reached a hand back behind Liz to stroke Connie's arm.

"So it's still in there somewhere?" Liz asked, regaining her pace toward home.

"Yes. I changed up some of the details on the catalogue card," Connie confessed. "I probably shouldn't have. But at least that way I'll know the text survives, hidden in their archives. Though"—she paused, looking up at Sam—"I think Grace was right."

"How's that?" Sam asked, smoothing a strand of hair back from Connie's forehead. As he did so, a group of costumed undergraduates tripped across the street, hollering jovial insults at one another. One of the girls swanned by in a long, billowy black dress, a tall, wide-brimmed pointed hat on her head, trailing a broom in her wake. In her arms she carried a stuffed toy cat.

"I don't think we need it," Connie said, her pale eyes gleaming in the night.

ABOUT THAT TIME, TWENTY-ODD MILES AWAY FROM CAMBRIDGE, ALONG the roadway by the sea, dusk was creeping across Marblehead. In the distance a cannon fired, followed shortly by another, and then another, their blasts echoing off of the craggy granite face of the cliffs as the yacht clubs ringing the harbor announced the sunset. On the northern side of Old Town, past Milk Street, past a boatyard full of empty wooden hulls overturned like elephant ribs in the darkness, an older couple strolled in silhouette along the highest ridge of Old Burial Hill. They were moving toward a bench that stood on the site of the first meetinghouse in town, long since gone; it was the spot that afforded the best view of the harbor as the surface of the water turned a lavender orange-gray in the setting sun. The couple eased themselves onto the bench, settling their backs with relief. For a while they sat, enjoying the salt air as it washed up the sides of the hill, carrying with it the faint sound of rigging clanking against the masts of sailboats moored on the water, and a few distant cries and thumping feet of children at play.

"Hey," said the man, shaken out of his reverie. "Thah's no dogs allowed up heah! Shoo!" He clapped his hands at a smallish dog, barely visible in the grass on the hill, who had been napping, curled up, against one of the headstones. The animal raised his head leisurely, looking at the man.

"Go on, now!" the man said. "You go on home! Get!"

The woman clucked with disapproval. "It's all them new people," she murmured to the man, reaching a hand up to pat his sleeve. "None of 'em can be bothered."

"They should have a little respect," the man groused, wrapping his arm protectively around his wife.

"They should," she agreed, settling herself nearer to him. The orange tinge on the rippling harbor surface had started to recede before an advancing inky blue, seeping up from the hollows of the waves and spreading over the surface of the water.

The dog, meanwhile, had taken his time getting to his feet. He reached his front paws forward in a luxurious stretch, yawning. Then he moved away from the headstone where he had been sleeping, and when the man glanced back to scold him again, the creature seemed to have disappeared.

The headstone itself, now receding behind the coming night, was slate, chipped at the edges and leaning, and all of the carving on it had melted away, carried by rain and the passage of time. Though if one looked closely, the first letter of the name on the headstone might have been a *D*.

POSTSCRIPT

Real Witches, Real Life

The Salem witch trials of 1692 are hardly new territory, either for a historian or for a novelist. However, when the trials appear in literature or in history, it is generally assumed that they are acting as a proxy for something else. Either the trials exploded out of social rivalries in Salem and present-day Danvers (the former Salem Village), or else they articulated tensions around the changing role of women in colonial culture, or else the afflicted little girls had all eaten moldy bread, which caused them to hallucinate. What is usually overlooked in these accounts is that, to the people who experienced the Salem panic, the trials were *really about witchcraft*. Everyone involved—judges, jury, clergymen, accusers, and defendants—lived in a religious system that held no doubt whatsoever that witches existed, and that the Devil could make mischief on earth through human interlocutors. When I started thinking about the story in *The Physick Book of Deliverance Dane*, I decided to take the Salem villagers at their word for once: what if witchcraft was real?

And to some extent, witchcraft *was* real, though not in the ways that we think of it today. Medieval and early modern England held a long tradition of so-called cunning folk, local wise people who sold occult services ranging from basic divination, to the location of lost property, to the healing of assorted illnesses. Specifically, the cunning person specialized in unbewitchment; if you suspected that a witch had cast a spell on you, the cunning person was your best hope for redress. They were usually canny businesspeople, and their reputations were always rather suspect; after all, anyone with the power to remove spells could be assumed to have the ability to cast them, too.

Most cunning folk came from the artisan, rather than the laboring, class, in part because tradespeople had more flexible time for seeing clients, but also because they were more likely to be literate. The charms on offer derived both from published grimoires, or spell books translated from Latin into English, and from practices dating from pre-Reformation Christianity. It is thought that the cunning folk tradition did not travel to New England with the colonists, both because of the extreme form of Protestantism that they practiced, in which even Christmas was considered too pagan, and because of the newness of the physical space of the New World. The tangible qualities of magic, derived from special objects, special prayers, and special places, were rooted inextricably in the haunted realms of the Old World.

Or were they? When the Salem panic first broke out, villager Mary Sibley suggested that the culprit might be revealed through a witch cake, a biscuit made of rye meal and urine from the afflicted girls that was baked and then fed to a dog. Though her personality in the story is the product of my imagination, her actions are not. The real Mary Sibley was chastised for resorting to diabolical means to ascertain diabolical actions, but she nevertheless was confident that this popular magic technique held real power to address Salem's witchcraft problem. Similarly, the mysterious charmed boundary marker in the story is based on a real charmed boundary stone, located in Newbury, Massachusetts. Magic still lurked in the daily lives of colonial New Englanders, though its face was hidden.

I have endeavored to be as accurate as possible in my rendition of the historical world of Deliverance and her family, paying special attention to details of dress and room interior. In addition, numerous real people pepper the narrative, though I hasten to add that they are used fictitiously and that some details of their lives have been embellished or changed. The judge and jurymen during Deliverance's 1682 slander trial are all real, as is Robert "King" Hooper, the wealthy Marblehead merchant. My description of Lieutenant Governor William Stoughton, who presided over the Salem witch trial, derives from an extant portrait of him.

The nature of the evidence entered against the accused witches is also accurate, including the so-called witches teat for suckling imps and familiars. This phenomenon provided the only reliable form of physical evidence against an accused witch; almost all other evidence was "spectral," or claims by witnesses that they had seen the accused's specter doing malefic work. Historians differ on what the witches teat might have really been, arguing variously for anomalous third nipples, for skin tags, for moles, and most notoriously, for the clitoris. In a world lacking in artificial light, hand mirrors, private bedrooms, or bathrooms, the suggestion that women might have been somewhat alienated from their own bodies seems less incredible.

Most important, Deliverance's codefendants in the witchcraft trial— Sarah Wildes, Rebecca Nurse, Susannah Martin, Sarah Good, and Elizabeth Howe—together with the dates on which they were tried and executed, are all correct. I have attempted to be true to these women's personalities insofar as they are known, though I took some liberties with Sarah Good. Other real accused witches make passing appearances: Wilmott Redd of Marblehead; Sarah Osborne, who died in prison; and deposed minister George Burroughs. Sarah Good really did threaten from the gallows that "*I am no more a witch than you are a wizard, and if you take away my life, God will give you blood to drink.*" Interestingly, local tradition holds that the man on the receiving end of this threat, Nicholas Noyes, died years later of a hemorrhage, so in a sense Sarah's prediction came true.

Sarah Good's daughter Dorcas, meanwhile, inspired my illustration of how the effects of the trial echoed years later for the families involved. The real Dorcas, at about four or five years old, spent eight months imprisoned in Boston, and her mother was hanged. As a result of these twin horrors, little Dorcas lost her mind. In 1710, her father, William Good, sued the town for help with her support and maintenance, claiming that Dorcas "being chain'd in the dungeon was so hardly used and terrifyed that she hath ever since been very chargeable having little or no reason to govern herself." Association with the trials, even for those who were ultimately acquitted, caused entire families to suffer economic and social aftershocks until well into the eighteenth century, a harsh reality that informed the reduced circumstances of Mercy and Prudence in the story.

The representation of Prudence Bartlett as an eighteenth-century Marblehead midwife who keeps a daily log I owe directly to the scholarship of Laurel Thatcher Ulrich on Martha Ballard, an eighteenth-century Maine midwife (though not a witch, it must be said) who kept a diary of her quotidian activities.

The assorted magical elements woven throughout the story are based on research into grimoires held at the British Museum, in particular a text of disputed age and authorship called the *Key of Solomon*. (No North American colonial-era grimoires have been found—at least, not yet.) The magical circle conjured on the door of the Milk Street house is based on a circle drawn in a manuscript in the Bibliothèque de L'Arsenal in Paris, reproduced in a contemporary book of occult history. Similarly, the "Abracadabra" healing charm derives from a Roman talisman, the triangular shape of which was thought to draw illness out of the body, and discussed in a different modern source on vernacular magic. Urine and witch bottles were a common tool of cunning folk, following the widespread logic that a small part of the body can be made to stand in for the whole. And finally, the "key and Bible" and "sieve and scissors" were both widespread, mainstream divination techniques in use as late as the nineteenth century. Anyone who has flipped a coin or shaken a magic eight ball in the course of making a decision has touched the modern descendants of these techniques.

And what of Deliverance Dane herself? The real Deliverance Dane was accused near the end of the Salem panic, when the accusations were spreading deeper into the Essex County countryside. She lived with her husband,

Nathaniel, in Andover, Massachusetts, and she was imprisoned on suspicion of witchcraft for thirteen weeks in 1692. Little is known about her, apart from the fact that she survived the trials, and unlike some of her contemporaries, there is no evidence that she was actually a cunning woman. The only record that I have been able to find is an account listing how much Nathaniel owed for her maintenance while she was in jail. This document, along with transcripts and digital images of the actual court documents, can be viewed in the Salem witchcraft papers digital archive maintained by the University of Virginia.

And then there is me. Family genealogical research by successive generations of Howe women indicates our connection both to condemned witch Elizabeth Howe, who appears briefly here, and to accused witch Elizabeth Proctor. The latter connection is thought to be more direct, as she survived the trials, while Elizabeth Howe, as you know, did not.

For a long while this knowledge was just one of those weird, amusing details about me that not many people knew. Then after a few years working and living in Cambridge, I arrived in Essex County, Massachusetts. As we settled into life on the North Shore, I was moved both by how fully the past in New England still haunts the present, especially in its small, long-memoried towns, and also by how the idiosyncratic personhood of the early colonists seems to have been lost in nationalist myth. In the bedroom of our little antique rental house my husband and I even found a tiny horseshoe, caked in paint, nailed over the rear door for luck, or to ward off evil, we were not sure which.

I began telling myself this story while studying for my own PhD qualifying exams, in American and New England studies at Boston University, taking my own dog on rambles through the woods between Salem and Marblehead. I honed it further while teaching an introductory research and writing seminar on New England witchcraft to two groups of BU freshmen. (They especially liked the extra-credit assignment, which was to look up two different methods of un-bewitching a cow and explain the pros and cons of each.)

The narrative offered a unique opportunity to restore individuality, albeit fictional, to some of these distant people. I was also drawn to Deliverance's story by my sympathy with the New England legacy of difficult, and sometimes overly bookish, women. Did the knowledge of my distant ancestors' unconventional pasts help steer me toward graduate work in American culture? I feel certain that it did. But even lacking that knowledge, I suspect that their witchiness, however we understand it, contributed to my being the kind of person I am. I am grateful to those vanished people for whatever fragments of them may persist within myself.

—Katherine Howe
    Marblehead, Massachusetts

ACKNOWLEDGMENTS

That this story was able to travel from an idle thought experiment to a finished manuscript is due entirely to the involvement of the following people: my literary agent, Suzanne Gluck, whose brilliance, friendship, and insight has informed every aspect of this project from its inception; Ellen Archer at Hyperion, whose vision, kindness, and confidence in the book encouraged me at every turn; my editor, Leslie Wells, who ushered the manuscript from rough draft to completion with marvelous attentiveness, precision, and care; Pamela Dorman, whose belief in the book helped to make it a reality; and Matthew Pearl, my sensei, without whose guidance, cheerleading, and mentorship this book would never have come into being.

I have been fortunate to work with some amazing people in the publishing world whose support and advice eased every stage of this project. At William Morris, I would like to thank Sarah Ceglarski, Bill Clegg, Rob Clyne, Georgia Cool, Raffaella De Angelis, Michelle Feehan, Tracy Fisher, Erin Malone, Cathryn Summerhayes, Elizabeth Tingue, and Eric Zohn. At Hyperion and Voice, my appreciation and thanks go to Anna Bromley Campbell, Marie Coolman, Barbara Jones, Kristin Kiser, Sarah Landis, Allison McGeehon, Claire McKean, Linda Prather, Shubhani Sarkar, Nina

Shield, Betsy Spigelman, Mindy Stockfield, Katherine Tasheff, and Jessica Wiener. My thanks also go to Mari Evans at Penguin UK for her splendid feedback, enthusiasm, and warmth.

A book this grounded in history would be nothing without its source base, and I am grateful to the many historians whose work has guided me through this project. In particular, Anthony Aveni, whose *Behind the Crystal Ball* provided the "abracadabra" charm; Paul Boyer and Stephen Nissenbaum, for their definitive books *Salem Possessed* and *Salem-Village Witchcraft*; Owen Davies, for *Popular Magic: Cunning-folk in English History*; John Demos, for *Entertaining Satan*; Cornelia Hughes Dayton's history of the early colonial legal system, *Women Before the Bar*; Grillot de Givry, for *Witchcraft, Magic, and Alchemy*, the source of the magic circle symbol in the story; Carol Karlsen, for the feminist history *Devil in the Shape of a Woman*; Mary Beth Norton, for *In the Devil's Snare;* Keith Thomas's *Religion and the Decline of Magic*; Laurel Thatcher Ulrich's *A Midwife's Tale*, which directly inspired the journal-keeping midwife in my narrative; and the Museum of Fine Arts, Boston's exhibition catalogue *New England Begins: The Seventeenth Century*. The University of Virginia online archive of Salem witchcraft papers held in special collections all over New England enables an ease of research that an earlier generation of scholars could only dream about; see http://etext.virginia.edu/salem/witchcraft/.

In addition, many friends and colleagues have offered reading notes, brainstorming, and encouragement when it was most needed, especially Mike Godwin, Greg Howard, Eric Idsvoog, Emily Kennedy, Kelley Kreitz, Brian Pellinen, Shannon Shaper, Weston Smith, Raphaelle Steinzig, Michelle Syba, and Tobey Wiggins. I am indebted to the students and faculty of the American and New England Studies Program and the Writing Program at Boston University, with special thanks to Roy Grundmann, Virginia Myhaver, Michael Prince, Bruce Schulman, and especially my students in WR 150 "New England Witchcraft." Justin Lake at Texas A&M lent me his considerable Latin expertise and taught me how to gamble. Alice Jardine in the Committee on Degrees in Women's, Gender, and Sexuality Studies at

Harvard gave me that rarest of things in graduate school: a steady teaching job. Will Heinrich helped me to imagine what was possible, in writing as well as life, and forbade me from letting fear stand in the way. I am also deeply grateful to my advisor, Patricia Hills, whose scholarship in art history and American studies brought me to graduate school in the first place, and whose friendship and support kept me there.

Finally, as this is a book essentially about families changing over time, I would like to thank my own, both extended and immediate: especially Grandmother and Grandfather, Mere and Charles, all of whom haunt this story in their own secret ways; Julia Bates, poet, musician, New Englander, great-aunt, and dear friend; Greg and Patty Kuzbida; and Rachel Hyman. Most important, thanks to my parents, George and Katherine S. Howe, whose influence and significance in my life are difficult to summarize in such a narrow space. And lastly, Louis Hyman, partner in all things, both life and crime, inspiration, muse, chef, counselor, and nag, who every day makes me realize that I somehow managed to win a contest that I didn't know I had entered.

Reading Group Guide

1. The story follows several sets of mothers and daughters: Connie and Grace, Grace and Sophia, Deliverance and Mercy, Mercy and Prudence. How are these mother/daughter relationships different? How are they the same? Did you identify with one set more than the others?

2. Many of the characters in the book, like Manning Chilton and Prudence Bartlett, are heavily constrained by their social class. How are characters in the novel constrained or defined by their social position? Do the twentieth-century characters have more freedom than the seventeenth- and eighteenth-century characters, or less?

3. Most of the main characters in *Physick Book* are women. How have women's roles changed from the seventeenth century to the twentieth century? What about their obligations? Their opportunities?

4. Connie is a historian who likes to interpret the past in light of the present. Sam, however, is a preservationist: He likes to keep the past intact, at the expense of the present. Are you more of a historian or a preservationist? Do you see a difference between Connie's and Sam's feelings about the past?

5. How do some of the buildings, like Saltonstall Court, the Harvard Faculty Club, and the Milk Street house, function as de facto characters in the story?

6. Discuss the role of Arlo in the novel. Do you think Arlo exists? Can he exist without Connie? What does Arlo imply about relationships in general?

7. What role does religion play in *Physick Book*? Is Christianity contradictory or complementary to magic in this story? Is Wicca more like magic, more like Christianity, or is it something else entirely?

8. Do you think magic, as represented in this book, exists in the real world? If so, how do you think it manifests itself?

9. Some characters in *Physick Book*, like Connie, have their ambition rewarded, but others, like Manning Chilton, are thwarted. Is ambition a virtue or a vice?

10. Deliverance has a chance to escape with her daughter the night before she is set to be put to death. Why does she make the choice that she makes?

11. Near the end of the story, we learn that having the talent for witchcraft comes at a pretty steep price. Would you like to be a witch, as represented in *Physick Book*? Why or why not?

12. *Physick Book* is the latest entry in a long bibliography of writing about witchcraft at Salem. Why do you think we are still so enthralled by this moment in history? What does Salem have to teach us about our culture today?

13. Historians differ on what, precisely, caused the Salem witch panic to grow so disproportionately, relative to other colonial-era witch trials. Some blame infighting between a rural town and its bustling seaport; some point to the violence of the Indian wars along the Maine frontier; some even blame the hallucinatory effects of moldy rye. What do you think was the ultimate cause of the Salem panic?

An Interview with Katherine Howe

Q: *If you could meet any of your characters in real life, who would you choose?*
This may sound strange, but I would most like to meet Connie. Lots of people assume that Connie and I are pretty much interchangeable; we have similar jobs, and we both have long brown hair. But Connie and I are actually very different: She is more serious and focused in her work, she has fewer friends, and our upbringings could not be more dissimilar. She doesn't always do what I would do, and I don't always like her. In fact, I often wonder how she would feel about me, since I suspect I'm a lot sillier than she is. Maybe we wouldn't get along?

It would be tempting to meet Mercy as well, given the opportunity; of all the characters in the story, we see the most stages of Mercy's life, following her from childhood through adolescence, and even into old age. Maybe that's why, even though the historical passages are shortest, I feel like I know Mercy best.

Q: *What's your writing routine?*
Since I write historical fiction, a lot of my writing routine is really a reading routine. Before I am ready to start writing, I spend a lot of time reading source material about whatever time period I will be visiting. For *Physick Book*, I read all the major histories of Salem witchcraft, along with histories of folk magic in England, of material culture, furniture, and food in colonial New England, of the evolution of the English language, and so forth. For my next project I have been reading early-twentieth-century gossip newspapers, histories of the spiritualist movement, and accounts of the opium trade. Then I spend a lot of time walking around in circles and banging my head against the wall. Well, not literally, but it feels that way sometimes. I find that I have to write every day. If I miss a day of work, then I waste another day getting back into the rhythm of what I was doing. I will usually get up, make coffee, and head straight to work, either in my attic office at home or in a local café, if I'm desperate for a change of scene. My one office window looks out over our neighbor's roof, and in some ways I find it useful to have nothing interesting to look at; all the better to spend time building worlds in my head.

Q: *How did the idea for this book originate?*

To relax while studying for my Ph.D. qualifying exams, I would take my dog on rambles in the woods along the old railroad tracks between Marblehead and Salem. We were living in Old Town Marblehead, a concentrated historic district of antique seventeenth- and eighteenth-century houses. Many of them had horseshoes nailed in various secret places, including one tiny one over the door in the bedroom of our little rental house. Further, Salem, one town over, has built its tourist industry on the Salem witch trials, and I often found myself thinking how vastly the popular account of the witch trials differs from the historical understanding of them. The book began as a thought experiment on my rambles in the woods: What if magic were real, but not in the fairy-tale way that we now imagine it? In the seventeenth and eighteenth centuries, magic was very small, very personal, very tied to individual belongings, and to health. I tried to imagine what magic would have looked like, had it been real the way that the colonists understood it.

Of course I knew the general outlines of what had happened during the Salem witchcraft panic, but now, having settled only one town over, I started to think more specifically about how life must have felt for those women. Genealogy serves a paradoxical purpose: On the one hand, it provides extreme specificity, with concrete people living in a concrete moment in the past. It is a powerful way to feel personally connected to a time period that might otherwise seem hopelessly remote. But on the other hand, by the time we start looking at ten generations back, what we mean when we say "family" is actually several thousand people. At that point, the connection becomes less about "family," I think, and more about humankind. Everyone has a right to feel connected to the women (and men) caught up in the Salem panic, for the story touches deep reservoirs of feeling about community, religion, relationships, and spirituality still at work in American culture today.